DOMINIQUE DAVIS

Catching the Con

Copyright © 2024 by Dominique Davis

All rights reserved. No part of this publication may be reproduced, stored or transmitted in any form or by any means, electronic, mechanical, photocopying, recording, scanning, or otherwise without written permission from the publisher. It is illegal to copy this book, post it to a website, or distribute it by any other means without permission.

This novel is entirely a work of fiction. The names, characters and incidents portrayed in it are the work of the author's imagination. Any resemblance to actual persons, living or dead, events or localities is entirely coincidental.

First edition

Cover art by Bia Shuja

This book was professionally typeset on Reedsy. Find out more at reedsy.com

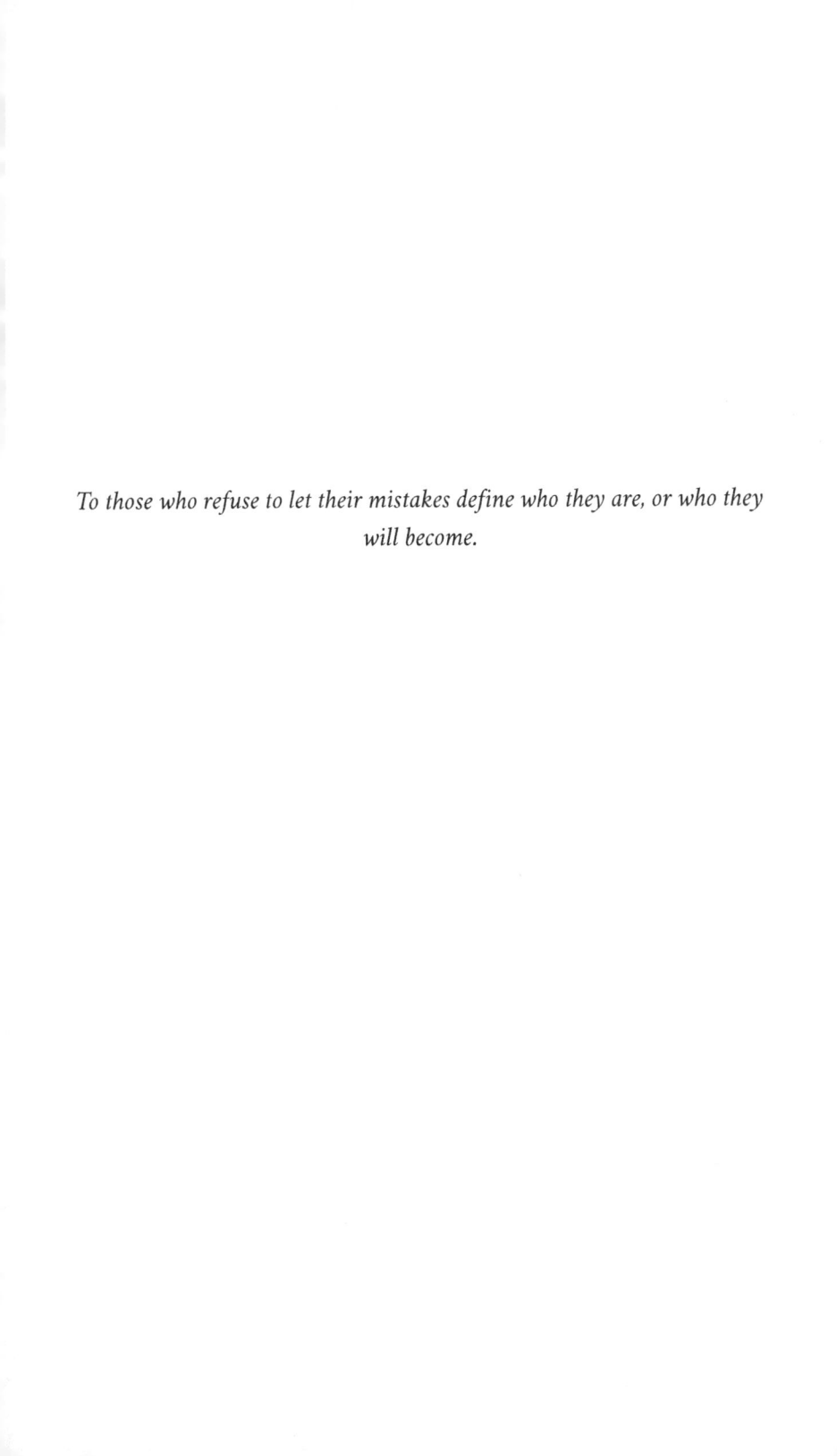

*To those who refuse to let their mistakes define who they are, or who they will become.*

# Contents

*Content Advisory*   iii
*Get the Free eBook Version*   iv
*5 Years Ago*   vi
1 Hard Eight to Break Even   1
2 The Changed Ms. Taylor   6
3 The Investigator Job   13
4 Once More For Old Times' Sake   20
5 A Storybook Start   26
6 The Color of Her Money   33
7 House of Games, House of Lies   39
8 A Hustler At Heart   46
9 Love's The Trap   56
10 In the Shade of Her Past   69
11 Con Meets Her Match   77
12 Where The Trouble Always Starts   84
13 The Ordinary Family   91
14 Sweet Revenge of His   99
15 Shattered Facade   105
16 Navigating Tricky Waters   121
17 No Man of His Own   134
18 Losing the Mask   140
19 The Truth Narrated by a Liar   152
20 Breaking Old Patterns   162
21 Maverick Gone Rogue   172

| 22 | The Art of Stealing Hearts | 178 |
| 23 | Then the Fireworks Ignite | 185 |
| 24 | Night with The Red-Blooded Woman | 204 |
| 25 | All That Money Can't Buy | 222 |
| 26 | There's No Going Back | 227 |
| 27 | Light in the Aftermath | 247 |
| 28 | Making Preparations | 255 |
| 29 | At the End Lies the Truth | 261 |
| 30 | The Ultimate Gambit | 271 |
| 31 | Forgive Me Tonight | 282 |
| 32 | Foolish Love | 291 |

*Epilogue - One Year Later* — 303
*A Bonus Chapter Awaits You* — 312
*About the Author* — 313
*Also by Dominique Davis* — 315

# Content Advisory

To check out the list of potentially sensitive subject matters contained within this story, please scan the QR code below or visit my website.

# Get the Free eBook Version

As a special thank you for purchasing this physical copy of Catching the Con, readers receive its digital version for free. Simply scan the following QR code or visit my website to access the proof-of-purchase form and upload your receipt or the book's cover to claim your complimentary eBook.

# 5 Years Ago

Outside, the sky promised a storm. But inside, only Nicole Wright could command the mayhem brewing. As she gazed into the foyer mirror, the final stages of her plan fell into place. With a few strokes of crimson lipstick and a careful brush of powder, Nicole created a mask of innocence to deceive her prey. Adjusting the pearls around her neck, she became the flawless ingénue of her self-authored play. The mirror reflected not a woman, but a work of art — her finest con brought to life.

Four agonizing months had passed since her husband William's last taste of intimacy. Not once since their honeymoon in Bora Bora had Nicole given in to his desires. Her excuses of exhaustion, wet manicures, and headaches kept her new husband at arm's length. The man was a tech millionaire. After hitting it big with his electronics company, Wison, he was getting sex on the regular.

Sex had become a fact of life for him. With Nicole holding out, more focused on spending his money than giving him what he needed, William was in a bad way. Right where Nicole and her daughter Maya needed him.

William's heavy footsteps stopped behind her. "Going somewhere?" The hiss of a beer opening followed his question.

"Yes. To the car dealership."

He let out a mirthless chuckle. "The dealership? In that dress and heels? In this weather?"

Her black, shapewear dress was his favorite. He loved how it accentuated Nicole's curves and ass from every angle. It was the wearing it out in public part he hated. "A little rain won't hurt me."

"Are you sure? I thought water was supposed to melt witches."

"You're hilarious."

"No. I'm wondering why my wife is going out dressed like that."

"A woman likes to look her best when she goes out. She never knows who she might run into or meet."

"On the prowl for husband number three?"

Ignoring he would actually be husband number five, she caught William's eye in the mirror. "That's not funny."

"It was a joke. Why are you even going to the dealership? What's wrong with the Porsche?"

"A girl can't window shop? You should know by now I like to admire the finest things your money can buy."

His grip on the neck of the bottle tightened until his knuckles blanched. Perfect. "And how much will this latest purchase drain from our accounts?"

"Don't pretend you'll notice the money missing, darling. You make more in a week than I could spend in a year."

"Your lifestyle is unsustainable, Nicole. Something has to change."

Leaning against the counter, she turned to meet his gaze. "Are you threatening me, William? Telling your wife how to spend the money you provide?"

She set the bait. Now for him to take it. "Threatening you? God forbid I should have a say in the life we're supposed to share."

"A life where I'm supposed to do what? Stay at home and keep your bed warm until you need me to look pretty on your arm? That's no life."

"At least then you would serve some purpose around here, other than bleeding me dry!"

She jumped off from the counter and jabbed her forefinger into his chest. "How dare you? After all I've done for you — the charity galas I've planned, the dinner parties I've hosted. I'm not a leech or a gold-digger whoring myself out for your money."

"Aren't you though?"

Bait taken. "What did you say to me?"

"You heard me. I tried to deny it because we had it so good for those first few months. Back when you didn't know I had money and we would talk about life in that diner where you worked. I fell in love with you there. I thought you did too, but nothing has felt right since I told you who I really was."

"So because things aren't quite the way they were in the beginning, I've become nothing but a gold-digger in your eyes?"

William ran a trembling hand through his hair. "What am I supposed to think when the affection stopped as soon as the wedding rings were on?"

"I fell in love with the kind, generous man I met. Not some dollar figure. I thought I proved that to you when I signed our prenup."

"Then why am I more your ATM than I am your husband?"

"Is that how you see our marriage? As me taking from you endlessly? If that's the case, and you don't see me as a partner, then why are we doing this?"

The thunderhead finally broke. William deflated, no comeback ready to fire back at her. A tear, as strategic as Nicole, slid down her cheek. She pushed all the right buttons for an optimal explosion. "I'm going to stay at a hotel for the night," she said, wiping away her tear. "Give you time to decide what you want."

William gave a silent nod. Her lamb was leading itself to the slaughter, and soon, she and Maya would feast. With one last shuddering sigh, Nicole grabbed the umbrella by the door and headed out. Her tears were as false as her vows, but William was none the wiser.

As she parked her Porsche up the street, Nicole fumbled for her phone. She was on edge, hating they chose this particular day to finish the con. The rain may have been appropriate for what they were doing, but the grey weather wasn't in her corner. Rather mocking her from the heavens above.

On her phone was an app showing footage from cameras William had installed before she moved in. She waited in her car as the rain pelted on her windshield, watching the screen. An hour passed before Maya walked down the stairs and into the living room. There, on the couch, William nursed a beer, transfixed by a football game.

Nicole refused to listen in. Even in character, hearing Maya and William bond while they disparaged her would be too much. She watched them, waiting for the point of no return. It took some time, but as always, Maya worked her magic.

Her words coaxed William into doing the unthinkable. He resisted until temptation broke his will. One forbidden kiss eased his restraint, and with it, Maya led him upstairs. An hour was all it took for the trap to spring shut.

In truth, the seduction stretched over four calculated months. During which Maya held William's gaze longer than necessary. Swimming in their pool in a tight bikini designed to get his heart pumping as he watched. Accidental touches igniting flames of desire. All building to this premeditated betrayal.

When Maya planted a kiss on him, William lost out to a hunger too strong to resist. Another five minutes later and Nicole pulled back into their gate. She put in the code. The alarm sent to his phone wouldn't matter. Not with it left unattended on the coffee table.

Pausing at the door, she braced herself for what lay ahead. This was the third man they'd done this to, and this part never got easier. Seeing her daughter entangled with a man twice her age made Nicole's stomach turn.

The money comforted her, but nothing could erase the iniquity of using her daughter as bait. As the guilt ate away at Nicole, she told herself she hadn't forced Maya into this scheme. Yet it didn't change the fact her method of providing for her family was morally bankrupt.

She was no longer a common thief trying to make ends meet as a single mom. Nicole was a con artist, using her daughter's youth and beauty to swindle rich men. What kind of mother would let these sorts of men near her daughter, let alone touch her? She was a step above the parents who pimp their children out to the highest paying john. But she wasn't far behind them either.

The marble floors gleamed under the soft glow of the chandelier as Nicole returned. Her rain-tracked heels clicked on the polished finish. The grandeur of the six-square-foot Sacramento mansion was in stark contrast to the storm brewing outside and upstairs. Nicole dropped her keys and purse on their once tidy coffee table.

Half drank beer bottles and empty mugs sat on the surface, no coasters in sight. Rings carved where their moisture had seeped into the wood. Nicole smirked at the mess. It resembled the mess of her crumbling marriage. Its once pristine surface now bearing the marks of their discord. A testament to the chaos she had brought into William's life.

She kicked off her pumps, leaving them and her umbrella by the mink Lawson sofa. The key to going about this was to act as if she suspected nothing. Lawyers and judges would review the footage and see William as the guilty party. And Nicole as the woman wronged. She would have the best divorce lawyer money could buy by the time the sun rose.

"William?" Her voice called out, breaking on the last syllable of his name. "I'm sorry for the way we left things. I didn't mean the things I said."

She moved through the quiet floor, avoiding a look at the camera.

x

"William, are you here?" she asked, feigning confusion as she entered the kitchen and didn't find him.

Nicole took her time on the stairs, knowing her husband was too busy with Maya to be listening out for her. She checked his office and found it empty. Their bedroom held no signs of him either.

She stood in the doorway, her back to the hallway, and listened. There was faint moaning coming from Maya's bedroom across the hall. No mother in her right mind would dare interrupt her adult child when those sounds were coming from their bedroom. For Nicole, it was all part of the plan.

"Maya, have you seen—oh my God! William!"

Maya and William froze. His body was on top of hers, his cock twitching against her panties. Wrapped around his waist were Maya's legs, her nails leaving indentations on his back. Seeing her mother's face, Maya pushed William away, causing him to stumble off the bed. The color drained from his face, his eyes bulging as he gaped at his wife.

Nicole rushed into the room, snatching a blanket from the bed to cover her daughter. She helped her out of the bed and pulled her toward her, using her body as a barrier. She held Maya close to her chest, letting the blanket fall to the floor.

The move was deliberate. The camera in the hallway sure to capture Maya in all her glory. Her small breasts, tiny brown nipples, and flat stomach were on full display. She may have been nineteen, but she wasn't the ideal sexual fantasy. She was a young, innocent thing, and her stepfather still fell victim to her trap.

Maya clung to her mom. "Did he hurt you? Did you hurt her?!"

Sweat beaded on his brow as his head shook. "You think I forced this on her? Nicole, that couldn't be further from the truth. This was all consensual. She seduced me!"

"You expect me to believe my nineteen-year-old daughter came on to you? Is that seriously the story you want to sell me? Maya is not some promiscuous girl you can take advantage of and then dump as soon as you're satisfied."

"Maya, tell her! Tell her the truth. Tell her how you came on to me and how we wanted to sleep together. Please tell her the truth."

Maya looked up at her mother with her glassy eyes and quivering lips. It was the most innocent and frightened Maya ever looked, but the mischief in her eyes was evident to Nicole. The way she bit the inside of her cheek, barely suppressing her laughter.

"Mom, it's true. I came on to him," her voice broke. "He didn't force this on me. I wanted him. I wanted this."

William sighed, breathing again. Nicole pretended to be on the verge of suffocating. Her arms dropped from Maya's shoulders, looking between the two. "How long? How long have you been having an affair with my daughter?!"

She whirled around to Maya's bedside table, her fingers latching onto the lamp. Her eyes blazed as she chucked it at William's head. He ducked down in time to avoid the blow of the metal.

"Mom! Don't!"

Ignoring her daughter's pleas, she continued. "I brought her into this house because I thought you wanted us to be a family. And you had the audacity to sleep with her the second I turned my back? How could you do this? How could you have sex with a girl young enough to be your daughter? What kind of sick bastard are you?!"

"I didn't plan it. Nicole, I love you. I didn't plan on leaving you for her. I love you. Only you."

"Love me? What better way to show you love me than to sleep with my daughter?!"

She graduated from the lamp to the next closest thing, one of Maya's shoes. This time, it hit its mark. William grabbed the side of his head. He was going to have a nasty bump at their preliminary divorce hearing.

"I do love you! This was a mistake."

"Damn right it was. The biggest mistake of your life. I will make sure you pay for this."

"Mom, please." Maya rushed to her, her hands gripping onto her mom's wrists. "He's right. This was a mistake. Let's forget this ever happened."

"Forget? I won't be able to burn the image of him on top of you out of my mind. I don't know what possessed you to do this, but you and him are dead to me."

"Mom, you don't mean that."

Nicole pulled away from Maya and gave her a firm shove. It was hard enough to make her fall back onto her peach plush carpet. Nicole glared at her. This was the easy part because she didn't have to act or remember her lines. Nicole simply recited from memory what her last foster parents ever told her.

"You disgust me. You allowed him to enter your bed and let him deprave you. How can you expect me to look at you in the same way again? You don't deserve the title of being my daughter. No daughter of mine would ever be so foolish and unbecoming. Get out of my house and don't come back."

William moved toward his wife. Nicole stepped back and held up her hand, halting him. Her eyes were still on Maya, and her expression was murderous.

Tears streamed down Maya's face, just as they once did Nicole's. She grabbed her clothes and shoes from the floor before running out. The sound of the front door slamming downstairs told them she'd listened to her mother's threat.

"Don't do this. Don't throw away your relationship with your daughter because of an indiscretion."

"Make no mistake, William, I hate you more than I could ever hate her. She's a stupid child. You're the adult who couldn't resist getting sucked off by a kid. You make me sick, but the best medicine I'm going to get is to strip you of everything you own."

"Nicole, you're angry, but let's not get ahead of ourselves. We've both had a hand in this marriage falling short of its full potential. Let's put our mistakes aside and try again. We can make this work."

"You took away the most important thing in my life. Believe me when I say I will do the same to you. I will take your millions, your possessions, your dignity, and your pride. I will take so much from you. It will take years for you to recover. I'll walk away from this with a fat check and you'll have to live with the knowledge you threw it all away for nothing. I hope that memory keeps you warm at night when you have nothing to show for your life but regret."

William swallowed. Hard. His eyes held her gaze, but no words came. Nicole's crooked smile met his blank stare. "You will regret ever meeting me, William Harrison. You have my word."

Her promise hung between them in her daughter's bedroom. Between them again, in the boardroom when William handed her half of his savings. It followed him everywhere he went and in everything he did for the next five years.

Until one Facebook message changed everything William thought he knew. Following the truth coming to light, William made a promise of his own. He would take everything from Nicole and Maya until they had nothing left. Just as they had left him.

# 1

# Hard Eight to Break Even

The sunlight filtering through his curtains wasn't what caught Spencer's attention upon waking. It was the curious weight next to him. He could have sworn he'd gone to bed alone last night. The barely contained chorus of giggles gave him a clue to who the body belonged to.

A smirk tugged at the corners of his mouth, but he bit it back and resisted the urge to open his eyes. He wanted to let her savor this moment. Anytime he could coax a laugh out of her, even at his own expense, was a good thing.

"Finished with your artwork yet, Picasso?"

The giggling ceased. "How did you know?"

He rolled onto his back, confirming his suspicion. Nessa had decorated his arm with an assortment of colored markers. "Your artistic talents are hard to miss," he said, grinning as he admired her handiwork.

"Do you like it?"

"The colors are amazing, but it's a little abstract for my taste."

"I've seen your real tattoos. Your taste is questionable." Her brunette braided space buns rocked back and forth as she laughed again.

"Touché." He winced, looking at the ocean waves. He'd gotten the shoulder tattoo to cover the name of an ex-fling he'd gotten on a dare. "If you don't want to make stupid mistakes like your uncle, stay in school."

"I will. As long as you start getting me there on time."

Spencer looked at the alarm clock and jumped. It was a quarter to nine. She needed to be on the bus by eight thirty at the latest. "Looks like I'll be taking you today."

"Oh, lucky me," she muttered.

"Brush your teeth, you smart aleck."

She followed his instructions as he hopped out of bed and began rifling through his drawers. He had to be at the office by ten and it would take a half an hour to get there from her school. Spencer had left behind his days and nights of living like a frat boy, but the early mornings still got to him. If only he could figure out how to set his alarm and actually hear it.

Nessa was waiting by the car when he came down, her purple backpack slung over her shoulders. As they got in, his eyes met hers in the rearview mirror. "Put your seat belt on and remember, never drive like this when you're older."

Her seat belt clicked into place as she promised, "I won't."

Spencer sped out of the driveway, praying they would not pass a police car. Luckily, they didn't, and they arrived at the elementary school with minutes to spare. "Alright, get out of here before you make us both late. Love you."

"Love you too."

Spencer watched her run inside, his chest full of affection for the kid. The last year of her life had been anything but normal. Yet through it all, she hadn't lost her smile. He didn't know if she kept it for him or for herself, but it relieved Spencer every time he saw it. Making her happy was what kept him going on days when all he wanted to do was crawl back into bed.

The office was quiet when he finally got in, something he'd grown accustomed to. Scuffed wooden floors, a couch whose black leather was beginning to peel off, and sunlit dust particles were the sight of his lobby. It was a small space, with only two more doors. One to his office and the other to the bathroom. A makeshift break room fit into the corner of the lobby. It featured a dorm room-sized fridge, an unplugged microwave, and a beat-up coffee maker.

In the middle of the room sat his secretary, Yara, at the front desk. She sported a grey buttoned up blouse, matching jean skirt, and a sad smile she tried to make resemble a happy one. "You don't have to tell me. I can tell by your face we've gotten no calls."

"I'm sorry. I thought I was getting better at not showing it."

"Yara, I don't care if you let your emotions slip from time to time. It's not like we have clients coming in to see them." He went into his office and closed the door behind him. He and Yara were alike in that they didn't do well at masking their emotions. The difference was, Spencer wouldn't let anyone in on that secret.

They were the only employees in today. His paralegal, Rachel, had come in early, but only for a few hours before she left. Part of him felt bad for having her work for nothing, but her job was secure. If the agency went under tomorrow, she would have no trouble finding another job. Spencer didn't have that luxury anymore.

Growing up, success got handed to him on a silver platter. Spencer never had to lift a finger to make things happen for him. He breezed through school without ever having to study. Scholarships fell into his lap, even when he took a gap year. He spent his weeknights at parties, but his name was always found on the Dean's List.

But as they say, all good things must come to an end. Three years out of graduate school, Spencer's world changed overnight when his dad died of a sudden heart attack. The stress of running his own father's private detective agency and dealing with his daughter, Melanie's drama, had caught up with him.

As if dealing with his grief wasn't enough, the biggest thing left to Spencer in his father's will was the agency. Left behind for him to run. Spencer's interest in it was zero. He made plans to sell it, but his mom shot it down. She cited it as his long overdue time for responsibility.

So here he was, two years later, struggling to keep the failing agency afloat. It didn't help the agency was already past its prime when his father was still around. Then you add in it shutting down for a year while Spencer got his necessary qualifications. Not to mention his sister left him with another massive responsibility to manage.

Despite not wanting the job, Spencer planned to do whatever it took to make the agency work. It was his father and grandfather's legacy, and he refused to let it crumble under his watch. But old clients weren't returning his calls. They doubted his ability to fill his father's shoes, and new clients were scarce.

It was as if the world knew what a mistake it would be to have him at the helm. He wasn't qualified for this. He couldn't help but feel like the universe was playing a cruel joke on him. Revenge for all those years of him skating through life with ease.

He was so lost in his thoughts the ringing of his cell phone startled him. More than the sound, it was the name of the caller that sent a shiver down his spine.

His sister, Melanie, was on the screen.

He let it ring, just as she had done for the last year of their lives. After a moment, her name disappeared, but returned to tell Spencer she left a message. He was about to delete it without listening to it, but something inside him stopped him.

A year and three months. That was how long they'd gone without talking. Not something Spencer ever expected, considering how close they were. Melanie was four years older than him, so Spencer relied on her a lot when they were kids.

With her, he was never without a maternal presence. His mother filled the role as best she could, but she, like his father, was career-oriented. They made sure their children never lacked for anything. Spencer knew how privileged he was to have that. But there were times he wished there was someone around who cared about things other than money.

Melanie was the one who was there. Then one day she wasn't. Leaving only Nessa behind. At Spencer's door.

"I understand why you don't answer, but I hope you'll listen to this. You must be thinking the worst of me right now, but I'm telling you I'm doing so much better."

Spencer stifled an eye roll. Melanie's sobriety had been in a state of flux since her teenage years. It renewed itself in the wake of their father's death. He wanted to believe the best in his sister, but the woman speaking on his voicemail wasn't her. The sister he knew would never abandon her child.

"I can't ask for your forgiveness. Not when I haven't forgiven myself, but I want to be a part of Nessa's life again. I want to see her. And I want you to see me, Spencer. See how well I'm doing. Let's meet—"

He cut the message off, knowing there was no chance of reconciliation between them. Spencer could have forgiven Melanie for leaving if she had only left him. But she hadn't. She deserted Nessa too. He refused to entertain the possibility of a reunion between them.

Nessa was too young to understand what it meant to be abandoned by a parent, but the pain of it was still felt. Spencer wasn't about to let his sister waltz back into her life and have the chance to cause that pain all over again. He hoped she got the message loud and clear: she was no longer welcome in their lives.

## 2

## The Changed Ms. Taylor

"You must be bursting with pride," one of Eric's nameless friends beamed at Nicole. She forced herself not to cringe as the guest chattered on. The woman's cheery voice grated on her nerves like nails on a chalkboard.

Nicole hovered on the outskirts of the Hayes's massive living room. A hodgepodge of people had gathered there to celebrate Maya's performance. Eric's pretentious coworkers mingled around the fireplace, sipping from their champagne flutes. Crew members stood by the bottom of the stairs, swapping inside jokes. Maya's co-stars ate around the dining table, their faces stripped of makeup and hair pulled into buns.

Nicole, herself, was immediately placed at the after party. Not into a group, but as being someone special. In her sapphire silk blouse and black cigarette pants, she stood out from the crowd in the only way a supportive mother could.

"Maya was nothing short of amazing," the woman continued. Nicole listened half-heartedly. "And I heard she had a hand in writing it, too? Next, you'll tell me she's releasing a song."

"Only if she gets Mariah Carey's voice overnight."

The woman laughed. "Well, even without the ability to sing, she's a star. Both on stage and off. I mean, I've never seen anything like The Hustler's Heir before. Where did she get the idea to write a story about a con artist?"

Nicole was in no mood to give a history lesson. Instead, she recited her rehearsed answer. The one she'd been giving ever since Maya told her she was adapting their lives for the stage. "Maya always loved those crime movies. I let her watch Ocean's Eleven too many times. Her imagination took off from there."

"She's talented at making up stories. From the cons to Jade's backstory. Going in, I thought it would be hard to root for her. With her being a thief and all. But after seeing where she came from, it was hard not to root for her. When you grow up with a mom like Gwendolyn as a role model, well, it adds up. Being raised by a woman like that would screw anyone up."

Similar comments had been pouring in all night, praising Maya and the play. They should have made Nicole proud, but instead, they left a bitter taste in her mouth. How could she be proud when these compliments came at her expense?

Their image of Maya hunched over her laptop, researching heists for her script, was fake. Maya's script was akin to a diary. Memories from her past strung together into a coherent narrative. The truth disguised by creative license and name changes. Only four souls in the room knew. And to keep it that way, Nicole would have to get used to the insults.

She needed a break, so she excused herself under the guise of getting more champagne. As she made her way through the party, Nicole greeted guests, feeling like an impostor. A feeling she was used to, but not like this. It was in the kitchen where she could finally breathe a sigh of relief.

The caterers swarmed around her like ants, but Nicole ignored them. She was busy smoothing the tension from her face. A slight smile found its way to her lips. Followed by a relaxed posture and a melodious laugh at the absurdity of it all. She had long since mastered the art of putting on the perfect front.

A front she had shed for good a year ago when she gave up her life as a con artist for the mundane life of a civilian. But donning it again for one night wouldn't hurt Nicole. And if it made Maya happy, it was a small sacrifice.

Nicole poured herself a glass of champagne before striding out of the kitchen. Her eyes scanned the crowded room for Maya, not finding her. She was likely off with Kennedy, as she always was these days. It was almost disgusting how inseparable they were. Looking at them, no one would have guessed Maya came into Kennedy's life with impure motives. And certainly not with the intention of seducing her father, Eric, and stealing his money.

It wasn't the typical love story you recounted to the grandkids. And yet, Maya and Kennedy were a love story. With new chapters written every day. The latest being how supportive Kennedy was as she watched Maya bask in the glory of her play's success. She showered Maya with flowers, praising her for all to hear, and hosted an after party in her honor.

Against all odds, Maya and Kennedy were still together. Defying all logic, they were still happy. Much to Nicole's chagrin. She played it cool, but she did not like Kennedy. She thought Maya could do better than to be with the woman who plotted against them after she found out about their scheme.

The disdain Nicole shared for her daughter's choice in partner was not one-sided. Kennedy never said it, but her eyes often followed Nicole, always suspicious of what she did next. As if she were waiting for her to slip up and pull another con.

And who could blame her? Nicole had not exactly proven herself trustworthy. But she didn't need to prove it to Kennedy. She needed to convince Maya.

To avoid any more painful conversations, Nicole retreated to the empty patio. With a light push on the door, she slipped through unnoticed. The sound of her heels clicking on the concrete made a voice nearby speak lower. She paused, recognizing Kennedy's voice speaking in hushed tones.

Curiosity got the better of Nicole. She peered around and caught sight of Kennedy's glowing, warm ivory skin. Not even the night's darkness and the hedges she stood behind could dim it. She was leaning against the house, her phone pressed to her ear. "I want this over with as fast as you do. How soon can we meet?"

Kennedy's eyes snapped to Nicole. A flash of irritation crossed her face before she composed herself. "I'll see you then," she replied before ending the call and facing Nicole with a forced smile.

"Leaving so soon?" Nicole asked, taking a sip of her champagne.

Kennedy shook her head, placing her phone in her pocket. "I would appreciate you not eavesdropping on me. You of all people, should know the value of privacy."

Kennedy equating herself to a former con artist made Nicole suspicious more than the tail end of her phone call did. But she played it off, not wanting to tip her off. "I apologize. It was an accident. I didn't know you were out here and I wanted some air."

"Well, you got it. Now you can go back inside."

"Have I done something to upset you? Like recently, I mean. Because I thought we were past me trying to steal from your father. It's been nearly a year."

"I've made peace with your crimes because I love Maya, but I will never be past you taking advantage of my father. And roping Maya into it."

"If it weren't for my con, you and Maya would have never met.

Much less fallen in love. Don't I deserve a little credit?"

Kennedy's jaw tightened. "You may have introduced us, but everything else has been a battle against you. You've been nothing but an obstacle in our way. If anyone deserves credit for anything, it should be me. For convincing Maya, there was more for her out of life than becoming another you."

"Careful dear, the pool cover isn't on." Nicole glanced at it, then back at her. "It would be a shame if you fell in. As I recall, you don't do well in the water and Maya's too busy to come running to fish you out of it this time."

"You should take your own advice, Nikki. A fall at your age could be cosmic. The amount of blood on the tiles… Well, it would be a pain to get clean and your salary might not cover it."

Nicole's hand twitched with the urge to slap Kennedy's smug face, but she resisted. This was Maya's night, and she wouldn't let her relationship with Kennedy ruin it.

Didn't mean she couldn't threaten her. "Word to the wise. If it ever came down to it, Maya would choose me over you any day."

"Keep telling yourself that. If her play was any sign of the truth, she will always resent you for turning her into a criminal. Instilling in her the fear of getting caught. Making her live a lie her entire life. As much as you try to pretend to be a loving mother now, Maya sees right through it. The things you've done will always plague your relationship, no matter how hard you try to salvage what's left of it. "

"And you know what the worst part is, Nikki?" Kennedy asked, not bothering to pause. "Maya doesn't need you anymore. She's stronger than you ever thought she could be. She's outgrown you in every way possible. One day she's going to realize that and you'll be nothing but a distant memory. So go ahead, keep up your charade of being the perfect mom. Deep down, Maya knows who you are. And she knows she deserves better."

Nicole was silent, the words hitting their mark. When she went to speak, the sound of the patio door opening cut her off. "There you two are," Eric said.

"Here we are," Nicole confirmed. Brushing off Kennedy's words, she plastered on a smile for Eric. "Having a friendly chat."

He raised an eyebrow, noticing the tension in the air but choosing not to comment on it. "You two are holding the party up. Maya's waiting to give a toast."

Nicole trailed behind Kennedy as she led the way inside. If she learned anything from their encounter, it was that they needed space. Lots of it. Eric shut the door behind them, sealing them in with the rest of the guests. Chatter and laughter filled the living room, but Kennedy's eyes stayed fixed on Maya. She approached her and pulled her close, leaving a light kiss on her cheek.

Maya's joy radiated as she raised her champagne glass. "To Victoria, Derek, Talia, Jamie, Alice, and our crew, who helped me bring The Hustler's Heir to life. Thank you. None of this would have been possible without you. You started out as colleagues but soon became friends, and I wouldn't have it any other way."

There was a round of applause, breaking only to allow Maya to finish. "Bringing this play to the stage took 10 months' worth of energy, effort, fears, frustrations, and doubts. Never for a second did I quit, though. That's because of this amazing woman by my side. She has pushed me to want more for myself, cheered me on, and will be by my side no matter what the future holds. Kennedy, thank you for showing up for me in a way no one else has ever done before. I can't wait to return the favor."

The applause was louder now and the cheers deafening. Kennedy smiled, her pride visible. Nicole couldn't help but wonder if a part of her was smiling because she had won this battle in their war.

Before she could think too much about it, the applause died down and Maya spoke again. "My last thank you goes out to my mom. Our road to getting here hasn't been easy, but I'm grateful for how far we've come. And how far we still have to go. You are the person who has influenced me the most. The story of my life isn't complete without you. So thank you for so much, but most of all, thank you for getting me here."

Nicole joined the crowd in applause. It was a bittersweet moment for her. The daughter she had hurt and used was thanking her. She knew she didn't deserve it, but she took it anyway.

Raising her glass, Nicole proclaimed, "To Maya. My greatest accomplishment."

The words echoed around the room as everyone joined in on the toast. During the celebratory moment, Nicole made a promise to herself. She would do everything in her power to be the mother Maya deserved. Gwendolyn, the mother from the play? She was a thing of the past. Pure fiction from Maya's mind, banished to the pages of her play. Their story had to be rewritten for the better. Nicole wouldn't stop until it was.

# 3

# The Investigator Job

Spencer may have only been a PI for a measly year, but he picked up many tricks of the trade as a kid from his old man. It was how they bonded. Stakeouts, blending in, and knowing when to keep your mouth shut were a few of the skills his father taught him. But the most valuable lesson he learned was how to recognize a guilty man. And the one sitting across from him screamed it.

Mr. Curtis Johnson waltzed into Spencer's office, seeking his help about his unfaithful wife. At first glance, he seemed like an ordinary client. Desperate for answers and willing to pay top dollar. But as Mr. Johnson rambled on about his suspicions, Spencer knew something was off. Sure, money was tight, and he needed this case, but something about Mr. Johnson didn't sit right with him.

It could've been his twitch or the way he couldn't look Spencer in the eye for too long. Either way, it was clear to Spencer Mr. Johnson's story was smoke and mirrors. And he had no problem calling him out on it.

"So," Mr. Johnson concluded. "You think you can take me on?"

"No."

The man looked confused. "I don't understand. Do you have too many cases?"

"You would be my first since I performed a background check on a catfish two months ago."

"Then what's the problem?"

"Mr. Johnson, your wife isn't cheating."

"And you know this how?"

"Because I have a strong feeling, the only cheater in the relationship is you."

The man's face grew pale. "I — How—"

"For starters, you're not wearing your wedding band. You could claim you left it at home, but I doubt a man who is that distrustful of his own wife would be the type to take it off. And the tan line is very faint, as if you haven't worn it in months. Probably around the time your affair began."

Mr. Johnson gawked at him.

"I wouldn't be happy if I were your wife. Not only are you the one having an affair, but you have the gall to accuse her of having one? Look, I don't know if you're looking for something to ensure she doesn't take you for all you're worth. Or maybe you like wasting people's time. Either way, you won't be using me or my father's agency to do your dirty work. Leave the way you came in."

"The only one losing here is you. You're going to run this agency out of business by refusing to take cases like mine."

Spencer didn't bat an eye. "Get out before I call your wife and help her build a case against you."

The man glared at him, but didn't dare to challenge Spencer further. He gathered his briefcase and stormed out. As the front door slammed shut, Yara hurried into his office. "What did you do?!"

"Mr. Johnson will not be a client of ours."

"It was a simple infidelity case. How on earth did you manage to not only turn him down, but make sure he never comes back?"

Spencer understood Yara's frustration. The phones weren't ringing off the hook. They needed money to sustain the business, not to mention themselves. But he would never work with a guilty client. A lot of lines got crossed in this industry, keeping a moral code was important to him. It was what separated his father's agency from the sleazy ones.

"He was guilty, Yara."

"He could've been an arsonist for all I cared. As long as he could afford to pay us, you should have taken it." She threw herself into the chair across from his desk, her body deflating.

Yara was a junior in college who found the secretary listing on LinkedIn. She took the position because of how close it was to her campus, thinking it would be easy money to pay for books and supplies. She couldn't have known she would be boarding a sinking ship.

"Yara, I'm sorry. Clients will come."

"With how often you turn them away, we'll need a miracle to find one that'll stick."

As if on cue, the bell attached to the front door rang. "Anyone here? The sign on the window said you were open."

Yara bounced up and walked out to meet the male voice. A few seconds later, he appeared in the doorway. The man was older, late 40s or early 50s, Spencer guessed. Fair skin, salt pepper hair, aquamarine collar shirt, jeans, white slides, and sunglasses.

"Afternoon. How can we help you, sir?"

"Is there a private investigator I can speak to?"

"That would be me. Spencer Shaw, the owner," he forced himself to add despite how wrong it still felt to say. He offered his hand, which the man shook firmly. Yara closed the door behind them as they settled down in their seats.

"I'm sorry for walking in without an appointment. I'm not from around here. Your agency was the first one I spotted on my drive and I thought it seemed like a sign I should come in."

"First time in Philadelphia?"

"No, I was here last year on business. This year I'm here for something personal."

The man looked like he wanted to say more, but for whatever reason, was hesitating. Spencer gave him the go ahead. "I'm guessing it has something to do with why you're looking for a PI?"

"Yeah." He nodded, taking his sunglasses off. "Five years ago, I made the biggest mistake of my life. In a moment of weakness, I cheated on my wife with her nineteen-year-old daughter."

Spencer couldn't stop himself from cringing. What was it about his father's business that attracted the scum of the earth? He had qualms working with a cheater, but someone who would cheat with a kid was on a whole other level.

The man noticed his reaction and rushed to defend himself. "I know what you're thinking. Believe me, I have already said it to myself. But it must be worth something that I came out and admitted it instead of hiding it from you, right?"

Spencer supposed he had a point. He didn't see himself taking him on, but Yara would throw a fit if he threw him out without letting him present his case. "Go on."

"As you can imagine, my wife wanted a divorce. She got it plus a hefty settlement. Because of the infidelity clause in our prenup, I couldn't argue the price. After it was official, she left the city. That was the last time I heard from her. Until last year, when she contacted me on Facebook."

"Was she looking for more money?"

"No. She invited me to her wedding shower. Against my better judgment, I was in town and took her up on it. I was the one who screwed her over. It was the least I could do."

Something didn't pass the smell test. "Did anything seem... off to you?"

"Call me gullible, but no. Not until I spotted her now 23-year-old daughter there. The last I had heard was they weren't in communication anymore because of our situation."

"Affair," Spencer corrected. "Continue."

"Anyway, that set off alarm bells. I confronted her. We got into a spat and I got thrown out. The day after, I couldn't get it out of my mind. I rethought everything about my interactions with my ex-wife. I remembered the woman I married wasn't forgiving. In hindsight, it was weird she invited me to her wedding shower. Unless she wanted to rub it in my face. But coupled with her daughter there too, I knew something was up. I contacted her again and asked to meet."

"How did that go?"

"Not how I expected. Starting with it wasn't her who I had been in contact with. It was her fiancé's daughter who was looking for dirt on her."

"Why?"

"She suspected she was a gold-digger after her father's money. By swapping stories, we found out her suspicions were right."

"She was a gold-digger?"

"More than that. She was a con artist."

Spencer was beginning to feel his interest pique. "Don't leave me hanging now."

The man lightly smiled. "Turns out, me sleeping with her daughter was a trap. She and her daughter set me up to violate the infidelity clause in our prenup. She got her daughter to seduce me, then caught us in the act. All the proof she needed to take me to court. They did the same thing to her husband before me and the one after me."

"So, she's been orchestrating these elaborate cons to trap her husbands?"

"Exactly. Then she uses it as leverage in the divorce settlements to walk away with a fortune."

"That's diabolical." And genius. It was a plan that required meticulous planning and cunning execution. If what the man told Spencer was true, it was one of the most twisted schemes he ever heard of. It would also be the biggest case he would have worked on.

"You said you found out about this last year? Why have you been sitting on it?"

"Her fiancé's daughter said she was going to take care of it. Record proof of them admitting it and send them to jail. I trusted her word and looked online every week for news of their arrest. It never came."

"Have you been in contact with the daughter since?"

"She didn't return my calls or texts for months. Then finally she answered and said she was letting it go and suggested I do the same." He scoffed, like that was an option. "Forgive and forget may work for her, but not for me. I want justice. I'm hoping you can help me get it."

"What exactly is justice for you?"

"I don't care about the money I lost. It wasn't enough to hurt me. I want them sent to prison where they belong. I don't care how much you want to charge me. Like I said, money isn't an issue. I just want them out of the picture."

The man was no saint. Even if he was set up, he wasn't forced into getting involved with a woman young enough to be his daughter. With that said, the con artists were no better. By the sound of it, they weren't Robin Hoods. They weren't stealing from the rich to give to the poor. They stole to make themselves richer.

Spencer's code normally wouldn't have let him overlook the man's misdeeds, but his choices were limited. He needed a case, an income to sustain the agency and support him and Nessa. He couldn't be choosy over the client. Not when they were actual victims. Flawed or not. The best Spencer could hope for was he was helping the lesser of two evils. God, he hoped that was the case.

Spencer offered him his hand. "You've come to the right place, Mr. —"

"Mr. Harrison was my father and a Beatle. So call me William," he added as he took Spencer's hand.

"Well, William, it looks like you've found yourself a private investigator."

# 4

# Once More For Old Times' Sake

Nicole sat in a downtown restaurant waiting for Maya and, to a lesser extent, Kennedy to arrive. They were having a celebratory brunch for Maya. The Hustler's Heir was a success in its opening, by whatever metrics small community plays were measured by. And Nicole wanted to shower her daughter with food and praise. She could have done without Kennedy tagging along, but beggars couldn't be choosers.

To her delight, Maya walked through the door without her worse half attached to her. "Sorry for keeping you. Traffic held me up."

"Is it holding Kennedy up?" Nicole scanned the room, hoping not to spot Kennedy's familiar figure outside.

Maya slid into the seat across from her mother. "Last we spoke, she said she had to make a stop, but she'll be on her way."

"Don't take this the wrong way, but I'm glad we get a moment alone. Feels like you're always with Kennedy or your theater friends. It's nice for me to get you to myself."

"You got me to yourself for 23 years. Sure you aren't sick of me yet?"

Nicole reached across the table and took Maya's waiting hand. "No chance of that ever happening."

The question of whether Maya was sick of her mother died on Nicole's tongue. Swallowed down by a long sip of her water and the realization she might not want to know the answer.

Their waitress dropped off two menus and took their orders before disappearing. When she was out of sight, Nicole asked, too curious for her own good, "Where did you say Kennedy was again?"

"I didn't say because I don't know."

"You didn't ask?"

"No, mom. I don't need to know where my partner is 24/7."

"I don't know how you do it. The con artist in me can not comprehend how you can trust people so easily."

"Maybe that's why you were so successful. You were always looking for the angle, always questioning motives."

Nicole's mouth pulled upward at the memory of her thrilling past life. "You know me too well, always trying to stay one step ahead. But I hope you don't think that way about Kennedy. She's been good to you, hasn't she?"

"Of course. We just don't need to keep tabs on each other all the time. It's called trust. You should look into it before you get into a relationship of your own."

Nicole hid her snort behind her napkin. Maya knew as well as anyone Nicole didn't do relationships. Not since her marriage to Maya's father had Nicole been in a real one. Real defined as not using a man for his money.

Her con had been effective, but an unfulfilling one. There was no actual connection, only the one forged by lies. Though she'd given the con up at the same time Maya did, Nicole wasn't as far removed from it as her daughter was.

In a year and a half, Maya got a job, made friends, fell in love. In the same span of time, Nicole transformed her cover of a party planner into an actual business. It was a real accomplishment, one she was proud of. But it was sobering to see her 24-year-old daughter have it all while she was still at the beginning.

Nicole couldn't pinpoint why Maya had achieved so much when she hadn't. It could've been her age. She was in the prime of her life. Maybe it was because she was a better person. That might have had something to do with it.

Whatever the reason, Nicole didn't resent her daughter's success. In fact, she felt relieved. All she ever wanted for Maya was a better life than the one she'd been given. Running cons, marrying men she didn't love, living a dishonest life. It was the best Nicole could do to ensure Maya would never have to worry about her next meal or if the place she rested her head was safe.

Now, she didn't have to.

"Very funny, Maya. You know I'm happy to live without the headache of a relationship. I'm more than content focusing on my career and you," Nicole said before taking another sip of her water.

"You've been focused on your career and me for 23 years. Don't you think you've earned yourself a bit of fun?"

Nicole shook her head. It wasn't a subject she wanted to delve into. She deflected, saying, "I have fun. Seeing you succeed is fun for me."

"Mom, I don't want you to have to live your life through me because you've forgotten how to live your own."

Maya didn't say it with frustration or anger, but with concern that tugged at her mom's usually icy heart. Nicole didn't know how to tell her she was fine. More than fine. She was living a normal life, and she didn't have the weight of her past looming over her for the first time in years. "Don't worry about me. I have never needed a man to make me happy. That's not going to start now."

The look Maya gave Nicole unlocked a memory from Maya's childhood. Before knowing what Nicole did for a living, Maya had begged Nicole to find a prince charming so she wouldn't be lonely. Nicole assured Maya her only prince charming was her, but it wasn't enough for her.

It didn't seem like it would be enough for Maya now. She had become so... normal, and Nicole didn't understand it. She snapped out of the con artist's way of living and thinking so fast; it made her mom's head spin.

Their conversation slowed when their meals arrived. When they sat in silence, it was a comfortable one. Nicole was glad for it. It was nice to not have to speak, just exist in the same space with her.

She finished her last piece of waffle when a notification appeared on her phone. Maya's tardiness had delayed their brunch, and now it was time for Nicole to head to her office. She loved her job, but right now, she hated it for taking her away from her daughter.

After placing a few bills down to cover their meals, she got up. "I hate to leave, but I need to go into the office and do some prep work before my client meeting on Monday."

"Can't push it till tomorrow?"

"I'll be spending the entire weekend prepping for it. Better to get an early start now."

Maya swallowed her bite and nodded. "Sorry for running late. We'll have to do this again. One on one time, I mean."

"I know you're busy with the play and Kennedy. Don't feel forced to make time for me."

"I don't," Maya assured. "Our relationship isn't conventional, but you are the only constant person in my life. I don't take that for granted. You're always going to be a priority for me. I don't want you to feel that you're not."

Nicole was touched. Her daughter somehow knew the exact words she needed to hear. "You're a priority for me too. Let's make sure we schedule another brunch soon, okay? Next Saturday?"

"Sounds perfect. I'll be on time."

Nicole, unable to resist one last glance at her daughter, saw her still waiting patiently for Kennedy. She spotted the devil herself sitting in her parked car as she walked out.

Kennedy, on a call, only noticed Nicole when she tapped on the passenger side window. Her head jerked, her body relaxing a little when she saw it was Nicole. Rolling her eyes and the window, she asked, "What?"

"You've kept my daughter waiting for 45 minutes and counting. Don't keep her waiting a second longer."

"Do you ever get tired of acting like an overprotective father? I get you had to be both for Maya when she was a kid, but she isn't one anymore. You can cut the act and treat her like the adult she is."

"It's not an act. I care about my daughter's happiness."

"She is happy. With me. I don't see why you insist on wasting your energy fighting it. If you really cared about her, you would accept our relationship and move on."

She swung her door open and brushed past Nicole. Only coming to a halt when Nicole asked, "What was more important than joining us for brunch?"

Kennedy turned back with a grin, the glint in her eyes telling. Nicole recognized the look. It was the same one she and Maya had every time they pulled off a con. "Wouldn't you like to know," she said, bringing Nicole out of it. "I'm late. I have to go."

Nicole let her, but she wasn't letting this issue go. Between her phone calls and being secretive to Maya, Kennedy had some explaining to do.

Nicole's days of running cons were over. She planned to keep it that way, but if Kennedy was starting up one of her own, Maya needed to know.

That's what Nicole told herself as she blew off work and parked her car a short distance from the restaurant. She wasn't spotted by Maya and Kennedy when they left in their separate cars a half hour later. If Maya knew what Nicole was about to do, all the progress they'd made would be ruined.

The realization scared Nicole. The alternative scared her more. If Kennedy was up to no good, Maya would know the kind of heartbreak Nicole experienced with her first ex-husband. She wouldn't let that happen to her.

If Nicole could save her daughter from the pain that would come with the truth, she would. Even if that meant crossing a line and doing the one thing she promised herself, she would never do again. A con.

# 5

# A Storybook Start

If you had told Spencer Shaw three years ago he would devote his Sunday to work, he would have assumed it was like jury duty. Mandatory and painful. And yet, here he was, actually enjoying the work.

It was a refreshing change from the background checks and cheating spouse cases. This new case had him intrigued and on edge. It was unlike anything he had encountered before.

Sitting next to him on the floor of his office was none other than his own client. William arrived moments earlier with a thick manila envelope tucked under his arm.

"These are all the documents I have from my marriage and divorce to Nicole." William pulled out the stack of papers and spread them out on the floor between them.

Spencer picked up two, examining their marriage license and their divorce papers. "You have the standard documentation of your marriage and divorce with Nicole. The marriage license listing her as 'Nicole Wright', the prenuptial agreement, and the final divorce decree."

"That's right. But as you can see, there's nothing that points to this being anything other than a typical divorce case. Nicole was smart. She covered her tracks well."

Flipping through, Spencer noted the lack of financial irregularities and suspicious activity. "Hmm, yeah, I don't see any obvious red flags in these documents. No signs of fraud or money laundering we could use as evidence."

"You see, that's the problem. To everyone else, it looks like I was the one who cheated and Nicole got a lucky break in the divorce settlement. But I know the truth. She orchestrated the whole thing, so I look like the bad guy. While she escapes with a shitload of money, everyone's sympathy, and the moral high ground."

Spencer drummed his fingers on the folder, his brow furrowed in thought. "And since Nicole changes her last name with each mark, there's no obvious paper trail linking her to a pattern of criminal behavior."

"Exactly. That's why I couldn't take this to the police. I would've sounded like a hateful and paranoid ex with an axe to grind. You have to dig deep, Spencer. I know what Nicole is capable of, but proving it is going to be the real challenge."

Nodding, Spencer began organizing the documents. "Alright, well, these materials provide a good starting point. I'll start trying to cross-reference the details, to see if I can uncover any connections to her other victims. But you're right - establishing a pattern of her cons is going to be the key to building a solid case."

"What else can I do to be of help?"

"Did you bring your laptop and phone?"

"Never leave home without them." He went to retrieve the devices from his satchel.

"I know it was years ago, but go through your social media or articles and see if you can find anything where Nicole's full name is mentioned. Before she changed her last name to yours."

"It's like a light bulb went off on top of your head. What are you thinking?"

"If we can find proof of Nicole consistently changing her identity with her victims, then it becomes a lot harder for her to dispute her connection to the scam. If she was posing as someone else during the relationship, she would have a hard time denying she was a fraud. No woman changes their maiden name and legal identity with every new relationship they're in. It's suspicious to say the least. Especially if we can link her to the identities of other victims and confirm the same scam happened to them. We have her cornered."

"Damn, I should have hired you years ago. Would have saved me a lot of heartache."

"I wasn't doing this years ago. My dad was."

"Well, if your dad was as good at this as he taught you to be, then I would have hired him."

Spencer didn't think he was all that good at it. In fact, if his dad had seen the current state of the agency, he'd be ashamed of him. He raised him to be the successor to a business built from the ground up. Spencer was supposed to carry the torch forward, not extinguish it.

"Hey," he said, snapping back into the case. "You told me you learned about her con from her latest victim's daughter. She must've told her father about what Nicole was doing. Do you think he would talk to us?"

William shook his head. "Kennedy, Eric's daughter, and Maya, Nicole's daughter, are together. Hence why she was so quick to forgive and forget. I assume Eric feels the same way. He didn't press charges and Maya stays in his Philadelphia home with his daughter."

Stunned didn't begin to capture Spencer's reaction. Kennedy knew the truth about Maya and Nicole, knew their scam, and how they plotted to do it to her father. And she still chose to be with the woman who tried to con her?

"That's... wow."

"Yep. I know. She thinks Maya is a changed person. How could anyone be so naïve, I will never know."

"It's not naivety. It's hope. She's hopeful the new life they've built together will keep her from relapsing. People hold on to hope when they're happy."

Spencer didn't think it was possible for someone like Maya to flip a switch and go from a thief to an upstanding citizen. All for love. He believed people could change, but almost only for the worst. He couldn't understand Kennedy's choice, but he understood her hope. It was the same hope he used to have for his sister. Hoping she would change and be better. As they say, it's the hope that kills you.

"So Eric won't help us build a case, but knowing Nicole's daughter is in Philadelphia is good. Likely means Nicole is close by," Spencer said, pushing the conversation forward. "We'll need to find proof of her identity changes and her former victims' contact information. We need to see if they would be onboard helping build a case against her."

"What about this?" William handed over his laptop. It wasn't a social media post or an article, but a photo of a wedding invitation. Join Us for The Wedding Celebration of Nicole Alyssa Wright and William Allen Harrison. June 15, 2019.

"This is good, but we'll still need to track down the other names. We can't use this without any concrete proof it was her. Do you have photos of her from when you were together?"

"She claimed she hated having her pictures taken. And she hated social media, so she didn't want photos of her posted online. I'm sure that's what she told all her marks to get out of having her likeness plastered online."

"But you must have something. A bride doesn't go that long without being photographed."

"You don't think I checked already? Nicole deleted everything that could lead to her being traced to her wrongdoings."

"Well, the good news is, she can't erase the internet. So even if she erased pictures of herself, there's still a chance we can find something on her."

Both men gathered their laptops and perched them open as they delved into researching any clues about Nicole.

"So I take it you've done this before?" Spencer asked, his fingers typing at lightning speed on his keyboard. "Did anything pop up on her?"

"No. Not a damn thing."

"You said you attended her last wedding shower. Do you remember the last name she was using then?"

William racked his brain. "Thomas… Thompson… T—"

"Taylor?"

"That sounds right. How did you know?"

Spencer turned his laptop around. A webpage entitled Taylor For You Party Planning Services filled the screen. The page listed the owner of the company, Nicole Taylor. Though of course, there was no photo. But there was a location. Headquarters based in Philadelphia, PA.

"That's got to be her. She threw charity galas and parties in my name while we were together to keep herself busy." William slammed his laptop shut, his eyes full of anger and hurt. "That bitch. I can't believe her. After everything she put me through, she has the nerve to use her victims' money to fund her own company. All this time I've been paying my bills, saving for retirement, and she's been living it up without a care in the world."

Spencer frowned, watching his client. "Hey, take a deep breath, okay? Finding this means we are on track to get her."

"We still don't have an image of her or a way of contacting her other exes."

"We don't need her image. It would help, yes, but it's not a requirement. And if we can't get to her other victims, we have to get them to come to us. Would you be willing to pay for ad space in some major cities' newspapers?"

"Yes, anything. Anything to get the justice I deserve."

"Great. We'll take the information you gave me and create an ad. We'll list her aliases, her physical description, the details of her con. Then we'll publish it in as many cities as you want. Family, friends, coworkers of her victims, will see it. They'll recognize the details and want to contact us to find out if it's true their loved one was scammed by her. If we're lucky, we'll be contacted by her victims themselves."

"That's genius. I can't believe I haven't thought of it before."

"It's only the first step, and there's always a chance no one reaches out." It wasn't the normal response a private investigator would give to his client. But Spencer didn't want to get William's hopes up if his idea didn't pan out.

To his credit, William wasn't deterred by Spencer's realism. "I have faith. You should too. You're better at this than you give yourself credit for."

"Yeah, we'll see."

William glanced at the clock, his brows shooting up as it approached noon. He stood, stretching. "I didn't realize how long we've been here. I scheduled a meeting earlier I can't miss. We can regroup tomorrow. In the meantime, I'll start making the arrangements to buy the ad space."

Spencer put his laptop on his desk and rose to meet William. "Good, but William, I need to know you won't go to Nicole's office. We can't make contact with her right now. If she sees you, she might suspect you're looking into her."

Normally, Spencer would never forbid a client from doing anything, but this was a special case. William wasn't the normal client. By his own admission, he wasn't innocent in what happened to him. Until Spencer got to know and trust him better, he had to keep his guard up.

William didn't seem offended. More amused. "Don't worry. I'll leave the sleuthing to you. If you don't mind me asking, this is a big case for you, right? I mean, I've been here twice and there aren't other clients you're working with."

Spencer nodded, because he wasn't a liar. William didn't look concerned like Spencer expected, rather accepting of the admission. "Then I guess we both have something on the line with this case. Good to know it's not only me."

Spencer's eyes fell on the wallpaper of his computer screen. A photo of him and Nessa at the amusement park last year, sitting on a bench. The photo taken in between them stuffing their faces with corn-dogs and funnel cake. It served as a reminder of why he was doing this.

"We both have something we value on the line. I hope that means we can be honest with each other throughout this. Can you promise me you'll do your part?"

William returned his smile. "Only if you promise to do yours."

"I wouldn't have taken the case if I wasn't going to. So I'm holding you to your promise."

"And I'll hold you to yours."

With a handshake, their deal was sealed.

# 6

# The Color of Her Money

The time spent away from conning made Nicole forget how boring stakeouts were. She avoided them as much as she could when conning was her full-time job. Spending her Saturday following Kennedy around reminded her why. Her daughter's girlfriend was doing nothing to prove her suspicions right. It was making Nicole feel uneasy.

There were two possible outcomes. 1) Kennedy wasn't doing anything wrong and Nicole was wasting her time. 2) Kennedy was up to something and she was hiding it well. For Maya's sake, Nicole hoped it was the former, but she couldn't risk it being the latter.

And so the stakeout continued into the next day, pushing her actual work back. After getting up early, Nicole trailed Kennedy from Eric's house to a coffee shop. There she completed freelance work. She then went to the Arden, Maya's place of work, for lunch.

The fact Nicole's first full day of being a con artist in a year was boring didn't bother her. It was never the destination, rather the journey that gave her the rush. She learned early on there was no such thing as an exciting con.

They all required the same skills: patience, attention to detail, and the ability to improvise. Spying on Kennedy's and Maya's lunch date was no different. At least, it didn't require the use of the last two skills. All Nicole had to do was sit and watch.

After an hour, Kennedy returned to her car, but Nicole clocked the route she was taking was not her usual one. At every red light, she looked at her phone and around at her surroundings. It was as if she was confirming she was on the right track. When the drive ended, Kennedy came to a stop in front of a bank and took a backpack with her inside.

When she returned, her backpack was noticeably fuller. It was not a question of what was inside. The question was, who was it for and why?

Nicole didn't have to wait long for the answer. She followed Kennedy to a nearby restaurant and watched her as she sat out on the open patio. A pair of sunglasses now donned her eyes. Whoever she was meeting had not yet arrived, giving Nicole a chance to study her.

A black bomber jacket over a plain white tee, a backpack full of cash, tinted black sunglasses. A look Joe Goldberg would approve of. An attire for a covert mission. One involving a lot of money. Blackmail was Nicole's first thought. Kennedy was the daughter of a rich doctor. The granddaughter of even richer grandparents who left everything to her father. She was an easy target for someone who knew about the skeletons in her closet.

That was the thing, though. Kennedy was clean. Once upon a time, Nicole went looking for the woman's dirty laundry and came up empty-handed. She had expected to find something to use as leverage if she ever needed it. But there was nothing in Kennedy's closet that would tarnish her reputation. So what could anyone blackmail her for?

As Kennedy sat sipping a glass of wine, Nicole noticed a man approaching the table. He was hard to see from a distance, especially with his sunglasses and out-of-place baseball cap. It didn't help that Nicole couldn't eavesdrop from where she was. She got out of her car and headed inside.

"Ma'am, you have to be seated by one of our staff," the hostess stopped her.

"My daughter-in-law is already sitting with a friend. I want to surprise them," she explained, gesturing in the general direction of the table.

"Okay, well, they're sitting on our patio. Would you like me to take you to them?"

"No need, but thank you," Nicole replied, dismissing her with a smile before walking over.

The closest booth to them would allow her to have her back to them so she could observe them without them seeing her. As she approached the area, the man began to look more familiar. It wasn't until she was in earshot of them and heard the name "William" that she became sure.

William grinned, leaning back in his seat. "I can't believe it. The money I made over the course of a decade, you retrieved it in a few weeks."

"It's not like you gave me much of a choice."

"We both made choices. Yours happened to have more expensive consequences."

Nicole hadn't heard William's voice since her wedding shower to Eric. Where he crashed to accuse her and Maya of being gold-diggers. He disappeared without proof, leaving Nicole to believe she was safe. Now she knew she wasn't.

Her heart was racing, her blood boiling. William was the last person she expected Kennedy to be meeting with. She didn't have time to contemplate what their transaction meant; Kennedy was getting up to leave.

"You have what I owe you," she stated as she stood. "Now leave me alone."

"And if I don't?"

Kennedy was on the verge of responding when Nicole beat her to the punch. "Then you'll have me to deal with. And we both know how well that worked out for you last time."

William and Kennedy both turned to see Nicole standing there. For a moment, there was only silence as they tried to process the turn of events. William was the one who broke it. "The deal was I wouldn't go after your dear girlfriend if you got me the money Nicole stole from me. Why the hell would you tell her about this?"

"I didn't tell her," Kennedy shot back before turning to Nicole. "Why are you here? Did you follow me?"

"The next time you don't want to get caught keeping a secret, don't be so obvious."

William stood, more impatient than she had ever seen him before. "Keep your money, Kennedy. The deal is off. It's clear I can't trust you any more than I can trust Nicole."

"Oh, please." Nicole scoffed. "Like you were ever going to hold up your end of the deal. I'm willing to bet you were going to take her money and keep blackmailing her. Do I have that right, William?"

"You were always a piece of work, Nikki, and nothing's changed. It's about time someone knocked you down a peg, don't you think?"

His towering stature didn't scare Nicole. Little did. "You don't care about Kennedy's money. That's just a bonus. What you're after is revenge. For what I did to you."

It wasn't a surprise William still held resentment toward Nicole. He was the only one of her marks to find out the truth of her cons. To see half of his life's savings disappear and have no proof he was the one screwed over. Well, it would make anyone angry.

"For what you and your daughter did," he corrected.

The mention of Maya was like a knife through Nicole's armor. "Leave my daughter out of this."

"You made her a part of this when you made her an active participant in your criminal activities. It's your fault what happens next."

With the last word, William walked away. Nicole shook his threat off, facing Kennedy's death glare. "So, this is what you were hiding? You were paying William off to protect us?"

"I was protecting Maya. She shouldn't have to go down for your crimes."

"Something we can both agree on, but paying William off wasn't the way to go. Even if he took the money, there was no guarantee he wouldn't come back for more. He's not the type to forgive and forget."

"I was desperate and Maya is worth more to me than however much money he wants."

"That's what William was betting on. He would've bled you dry until there was not a cent left to your name."

"I wouldn't have cared because what's the alternative? Him going after Maya?"

"William has no proof of what we did to him. If he did, he would have turned us in to the police already. He's bluffing."

"And what if he's not, Nicole? What if he has more evidence than we know?"

The possibility of William having concrete proof of their cons was a reality she wasn't prepared to face. It should've scared her to think their facades could come crashing down at a moment's notice. It would've if Nicole was the type to cower in fear.

Empty threats didn't scare her. The product of being served them one too many times. In her bones, she could feel William was trying to intimidate her into making a move. To catch her slipping so he could pounce. She wouldn't give him the pleasure of seeing her blink first.

Nicole would not be responsible for bringing William back from the ladder she had kicked him down. It didn't mean she would ignore his warning. If William felt he had a shot at getting payback, he would do everything in his power to make it happen. He could try to get to her however he pleased. But like the men who came before him, he would meet the same fate.

"I haven't gone unscathed this long without covering my tracks," Nicole replied, no trace of worry in her voice. "William has nothing on us. He might sling accusations and threats, but without hard evidence, his bark is worse than his bite."

"I hope you're right. Otherwise, what happens next really will be your fault and you'll have no one to blame but yourself."

Nicole watched Kennedy take her backpack and leave the restaurant. She stood there, alone on the patio, the breeze making her shiver. At least, that's what she told herself was the reason why her skin was crawling.

## 7

# House of Games, House of Lies

From how he dressed and carried himself, Spencer knew William was a wealthy man. It didn't hit him *how* wealthy he was until he was the riding the elevator to William's penthouse apartment. It was in the fanciest building in Philadelphia. The doorman greeted him by name when he entered the lobby.

Inside the elevator, the spotless walls revealed Spencer was the only thing out of place with a juice stain on his shirt. "Fuck," he whispered at the grape juice he spilled that morning while getting Nessa ready. He thought he got it all out, but the elevator's lighting revealed it was still visible.

The doors opened in the midst of him tucking his shirt into his pants. Spencer stepped out and looked to his right, finding William sitting around the kitchen island. He walked over and met Spencer.

"You didn't have any trouble finding the place, did you?"

"No. Your directions were so clear I could have found the place by memorization," Spencer replied, shaking William's hand.

"Glad to hear it. How do you like the place?"

It was an airy room. Plenty of natural light poured into the center from an expansive window. The silk drapes did not stop the light from bathing the tile floor and everything else in white. The light blue of the walls reminded Spencer of the way Nessa colored the ocean. Brighter and cleaner than the real thing.

A grey modular sofa was propped feet away from a fireplace. A flat screen TV looked down at the cozy couch. The kitchen was tucked away, a wall blocking it from your initial view from the elevator. A round dining table sat behind it. Paintings by artists Spencer didn't know the names of hung on the walls.

He was sure the rest of the place reinforced how much of a pretty penny it was to buy. It was no surprise to see a wealthy client lived in a place like this. Seeing it just underscored how far apart the men were. Spencer's two-bedroom shoebox apartment was the farthest thing from this high-rise palace.

"It's great," he answered, hoping he sounded enthusiastic. "I don't think I could afford a closet this size, let alone an apartment."

"I love to hear that. It makes the news I have to report even better."

"Oh yeah? What news is that?"

"It's your lucky day, Spencer. The apartment is yours."

Spencer stared at him, not quite believing the words. He blinked a couple of times. "Excuse me?"

William chuckled, delighting in his confusion. "I said, the apartment is yours. You're going to need a place like this to help sell your cover."

"Did I miss a meeting or a phone call? When did I need to get a cover for this case? Or an apartment for that matter?"

"Yesterday, when I left your office. The reason I had to leave early was because I was signing the lease."

Spencer's mind was going a mile a minute. William didn't help by explaining the details as slow as possible. "Break this down faster for me."

"Okay. When we did the research on Nicole, I realized that to get the evidence we need, you have to go undercover. I mean, she has done this to several men without slipping up. We can't trust we'll somehow find something that no one else has before."

"What about the ad space in major cities' newspapers? You called the idea genius and had faith in it. Does that ring a bell?"

"I'm still interested in doing that. My accountant is figuring out the expenses now, but it would be wise for us to try other options. One of them being you going undercover and working your magic to get information."

"What information? If she's working as a party planner now and isn't running cons anymore—"

"Wait a minute, don't tell me you think that business of hers is real?" William looked at him hard, then scoffed. "You actually bought that? That business of hers is a front for her money laundering. She probably used the money she swindled to start the business and uses the business to clean the money. But she hasn't stopped, Spencer. No, no, no. She's running cons. It might not be the con she pulled on me since her daughter is out of the business, but she's scamming people. I know it."

"I can't go off a hunch. Not with something like this."

"I'm not asking you to. I'm asking you to go undercover and get proof. Hire her services, see how her business operates, look into her finances, prove she's the fraud we both know she is."

This was the last thing Spencer expected to come out of their meeting. They were on the right track with the newspaper ads. Why William wanted to divert from that to this without seeing its results first was a mystery.

"Going undercover is risky. She could catch wind of what we're doing. If the newspaper ads don't work, we can explore this route, but let's wait and see if our ads reach one of her other marks."

"And how long is that going to take? It would be one thing if time wasn't of the essence, but it is," William emphasized. "My life, my home, my career isn't here in Philadelphia. I'm putting my life on hold to go after Nicole. The quicker we can find concrete evidence that nails her, the sooner I can move on with my life. The quickest way to do that is to go straight to the source and catch her red-handed."

William wasn't wrong. Typically Spencer could get the information he needed to build a case in a week or two, but those cases weren't as complicated as this. The idea of going undercover was a logical one. It wasn't something he considered when taking on the case because in his year of running the agency, he never had to. This was unfamiliar territory for him, and as much as Spencer wanted to protest, he had no good reason to.

"It's a risk, but a calculated one," William continued. "Look at it this way. Nicole is a single mom. She raised Maya by herself. She knows what it's like to be a parent on her own, like what you're doing with your niece. That's how you gain her trust."

"I'm not interested in using Nessa."

"You don't have to, but having her as part of your story could add depth to your cover. It makes you more relatable, more human. Plus, it keeps Nessa close to you. She can stay with you in this apartment while you're working on the case. Tell her it's a work assignment. She won't suspect a thing."

Spencer hesitated, considering the implications of involving Nessa. She was his top priority. The reason he worked so hard to keep the agency open was so he could provide her with stability and security. But William was right. Using her as part of his cover story could give him an advantage in gaining Nicole's trust before he brought her down.

"I don't know. I've never done undercover work before. William, I could be out of my depth here. Are you sure I'm the right man for the job?"

The last thing Spencer wanted to do was lose the paycheck, but the job William was asking for was above his capabilities. He couldn't pretend it wasn't.

"Spencer, why do you think I hired you to be my PI on this?"

"You wanted the job done cheap?"

"Does money look like a concern of mine to you?" William laughed. "No, I chose you because I saw how badly you needed this. You needed a win and weren't stopping until you got one. Wanting to provide for your niece fuels you. You'll do whatever it takes to make sure she has the life she deserves. This job is the opportunity you've been waiting for, and I have every confidence in you to pull it off. You won't fail because if you did, you would be failing her. And that's unacceptable to you."

William's belief in him was comforting, but Spencer didn't share his confidence. He closed his eyes, trying to push away the doubts that were gnawing at him. His imposter syndrome told him he couldn't do this. But there was an even more terrifying thought that surpassed it. The thought of letting Nessa down.

With a deep breath, Spencer opened his eyes and met William's gaze. "Alright, I'll do it, but at a higher rate than we originally agreed to. You know, with the undercover work involved, the price goes up."

"You drive a hard bargain, Spencer. I respect that. You're taking on a lot for this, and you deserve fair compensation. I promise we will work out the details later. For now, let me fill you in on your cover story."

"You already crafted it?"

"Of course. I always come prepared. This is coming on short notice, so I kept everything simple. You, my friend, will play the role of a newly rich tech millionaire. Not too unlike myself. You will go by the name of Aiden Spencer. I choose Spencer as your last name, so you won't have to teach yourself to respond to Aiden."

"You have recently moved to Philadelphia with your niece. You're interested in using Nicole's party planning services, bringing you into contact with her. Nicole will keep things professional and refer to you as your last name. I've already set up your IDs, social media accounts, everything you need to sell this."

William went to his briefcase and grabbed them, then handed them over to Spencer. Spencer shook his head as he held the fake ID and fake social security number in his hand. "How did you get this stuff made on such short notice?"

He caught a guilty look crossed William's face. "I may have already had them made after our first meeting."

"So you knew we were going to go in this direction even before our second meeting? Why did you put me through all this trouble if you knew this was the plan all along?"

The older man's eyes dropped as he scratched the back of his neck. "I'm sorry, but I needed to show you how well she covers her and her daughters' tracks. You wouldn't have been so inclined to go undercover if you didn't think it was necessary. But you see it now, don't you?"

"Sure, I see it. Can you see how I don't like being lied to or manipulated with? We're supposed to be partners in this. I need to be able to trust you. My focus needs to be on catching the con artist in a lie, not my client."

"You're right. I apologize. You deserve better than that, and I'll do better going forward. No more secrets or surprises. That's a promise."

Spencer stared at William, searching for any trace of dishonesty, and found none. His expression was sincere. Spencer trusted he was genuine in his apology. "Okay. I'm choosing to believe you."

"I won't disappoint you, but what's important right now is coming up with a reason for you to seek out Nicole's services. Her business is relatively new. There has to be a reason you sought her out instead of a more reputable service."

A wealthy tech millionaire was a far cry from his actual self, but Spencer tried to get into the mindset. "Nessa's sixth birthday is in a month. She saw pictures of parties hosted under Nicole's branding and begged me to acquire her services."

"You think your niece can sell that lie?"

"She won't have to lie. I'll show her some photos of different parties that I know she'll like. Whichever one she likes best, I'll say it was done by Nicole and ask if she'd like a party hosted by her."

William's smile widened. "I like how you think, my friend. Nicole won't be able to resist the opportunity to plan a party for the city's newest heiress. Now, all that's left is for you to make an appointment."

They went over to the couch. While William dialed the number, Spencer wiped his sweaty palms on his pants. He was used to improvising. This was different. What William was asking of him required a level of acting that was outside his comfort zone.

The phone rang a few times before a male voice answered. "Good afternoon. This is Taylor For You Event Planning. How may I assist you today?"

Spencer cleared his throat, trying to sound natural in this unnatural situation. "Hello, this is Aiden Spencer. I would like to arrange a meeting with your boss."

As the details were finalized, Spencer exhaled the breath he'd been holding. For a second, he pretended things were normal. That he was normal. The second passed when it dawned on him the plan was now in motion, and there was no way to turn back.

# 8

# A Hustler At Heart

With William's return hanging over her head, Nicole wanted to keep things business as usual. She was already in the middle of planning a charity event for a client. She wasn't about to let William interfere with her plans to make a name for herself. If she continued as if things were normal, the issue with him would eventually fade.

His plans for revenge would subside when he realized there was no proof of her having a hand in his downfall. Or any other man's, for that matter. It wasn't as if he could pause his life indefinitely to find proof that didn't exist. And it definitely didn't exist. People could call Nicole many things, but sloppy wasn't one of them.

So she put William to the back of her mind when she arrived at her office. It was Thursday, and she had a meeting with a prospective client that required her full attention. She couldn't afford for William to ruin her reputation before she could even cement it.

"Good morning, boss lady," Reggie, Nicole's assistant, secretary, and only employee, greeted her. He stood from his modern curved workstation. One of the office's most expensive purchases. The first thing people saw when they entered her business should reflect the image she was after.

Reggie's station, a high-end, modern, black-topped piece of art, sat front and center. Equipped with its own spotlight and dedicated cooling unit. Nicole's own office desk didn't have its state-of-the-art features. She met with clients in the conference room, so they never saw her second hand desk and chair.

The entire front section of her office was an open floor plan. Navy blue carpeting stretched from the lobby to the back. A brown Italian leather couch sat near the door. Interior Design, Architectural Digest, and other design magazines stacked the sleek coffee table. The lone exception being The Wilder Way magazines. What could Nicole say? Something about hideous couture trends, advice from armchair psychologists, and fashion scandals kept her coming back for more.

She designed the front to welcome and impress people. The back of the office held the conference room, a small bathroom, and her office. Nothing in the back could compete with the front, but it got the job done.

"How many times have I asked you not to call me boss lady?"

"Not enough times for me to take you seriously."

Nicole rolled her eyes, but she wasn't annoyed. "Do you have the information for my meeting?"

"Right here." Reggie handed her the files. She handed them back.

"I already reviewed the digital copies. I asked because I need you to quiz me."

"On?"

"Him."

Back in her con artist days, Nicole would have Maya quiz her on their latest mark to ensure she didn't forget important details. It was a different industry, but the system still worked well in event planning. With Maya now busy with her own schedule, Nicole would need to turn to Reggie with these sorts of things now.

"Okay," he dragged out, shuffling the papers around. "What is the prospect's na-"

"Mr. Aiden Spencer. 30 years old. A tech genius who sold his fitness app for millions. Loves his sports. Favorite teams are the Knicks, the Rangers, the Giants."

"Ew, sounds like he's an aged up frat bro."

"With computer skills that have gotten him far. His now defunct Instagram showed him with a lot of women from his college days."

"So what, you're going to flirt with him until he signs on?"

"No," Nicole said firmly. "I'm going to point out he's a man—"

"I'm sure he already knows that."

"Who needs my womanly touch," Nicole said over Reggie's comment. "To plan a fantastic party for his five-year-old niece."

"How's your knowledge of kids' parties?"

"I've thrown my fair share." When Maya was younger, she made sure every one of her birthdays was memorable. She didn't want the absence of her father or lack of money to be felt. It got easier when Maya got older, but Nicole kept the same effort to this day. "I know what kids like, Reggie."

"You just need to know what this one kid likes. And to keep it professional with Mr. Spencer. Don't let your perception of him ruin your chances of landing him. If this goes well, we could be in a good spot moving forward."

"You're acting like we aren't already."

"It's true we're in a good spot for an up-and-coming business. But we aren't the first name people think of when they're looking to throw a party. Charm this millionaire and he might put in a good word for us with his other millionaire friends."

Reggie's advice was sound, as always. She had hired him for a reason. Treading carefully with Mr. Spencer was key. A balance of professionalism and charm would secure not only his business, but could open doors to a whole new clientele. "When he gets here, send him in. I'll be ready."

Nicole sat in the conference room, looking around at the small space. Compared to the conference rooms Mr. Spencer was used to, this one was modest. The size of the room wasn't grand like the lobby. The furniture was minimal with discounted swivel chairs and a table from Wayfair. A fake ficus and shelves from Family Dollar made up the rest of the room. The décor reflected her company's success. Or lack thereof.

Taylor For You Event Planning started from the money Nicole made from her cons. Yet Nicole didn't want to invest more of its money into it. It was there for safe keepings if times got tough, but she wanted to build the company on her own. Without her ex-husbands' money. They might have helped her lay the foundation, but she would make it successful on her own.

Nicole wondered if Mr. Spencer would be put off by her modest operation. Their website and Instagram were of photos of the parties and events they planned, not of their office. Mr. Spencer could walk in and be immediately turned off by them before Nicole even got to say a word.

What they lacked in money, they made up for in potential. If Nicole was going to get her company where she wanted, she would need more clients like Mr. Spencer. She would have to get him to see past their humble office space and recognize the talent and passion that fueled their business.

A knock on the door stopped her from thinking more negative thoughts. She collected herself before calling out, "Come in."

The door opened to reveal the man himself. Aiden Spencer was as handsome as his pictures suggested. His honey brown skin tone glowed and his hair was kept low in a natural look. His tailored tan suit emphasized his broad shoulders and trim waist.

The prescription glasses he wore made him look more studious than he probably was. He walked with the swagger of a man who was used to getting whatever he wanted. Nicole hoped his arrogance wouldn't affect their chances of scoring a deal.

She rose to greet him. "Mr. Spencer, it's a pleasure to meet you in person," Nicole said, extending her hand for a handshake.

He took it, flashing her a charming smile. "The pleasure is all mine."

"Please, have a seat."

"Thank you," he said, sitting across from her. He glanced around like he wasn't sure what to make of it.

"When you spoke to my assistant, you said you were interested in working with us for your niece's birthday party. May I ask what you're thinking of?"

"Well, I'm thinking about something big. Something that will amaze her. Something she has never seen before."

"What have her parents planned for her past parties?"

He shifted in his seat, a crack in his facade briefly appearing. "My sister used to hold her parties at Chuck E. Cheese with a princess themed cake. Now with her out of the picture and Nessa's dad never having been around, I want to do something extra special for her."

"I'm sorry to hear your sister isn't around."

He nodded. "Last year, I tried to lift her spirits by taking her to an amusement park, just the two of us. It didn't help the way I thought it would. I could see how sad she was her mom didn't bother to show. This year needs to be different. I want her to have fun and know she's loved and has a family that will always be there for her."

Nicole's reservations about Mr. Spencer were still there. Yet she believed the words he spoke about his niece. So many wealthy men she met in both her lines of work cared little about their families and showed it. It was a pleasant change to meet one who seemed to genuinely care. "We can do something special. You told my assistant that Nessa was turning six. Does she have the usual six-year-old girl's taste?"

"I mean, she's super artistic. She spends her free time either reading or drawing flowers on her sketchpad. Or on me." He pulled back his sleeve, revealing a colorful daisy drawn on his forearm. "This is from this morning. She has some imagination, so I want the party to be like a dream come true for her."

"And how do you envision that?"

"I have no idea," he admitted with a self-deprecating chuckle. "I'm clueless about stuff like this. That's where I was hoping you could help."

Nicole smiled, pleased to be working with someone who wanted a creative event. She didn't get many opportunities like that, so she was eager to put her own spin on it.

Mr. Spencer continued, "I want this to be the best birthday party she's ever had."

"I want that for her too. She's lucky to have an uncle like you."

"I'm blessed to have been gifted a niece like her. She's changed my life in more ways than I can count. She makes me want to be better."

"She sounds special."

"She is," he agreed with a fond smile. "Her party should reflect that."

"I understand, Mr. Spencer. This is my area of expertise. Leave it to me. I have a few ideas already forming in my head."

"I would love to hear them. Over lunch if you're free."

Nicole analyzed his tone. His expressions and body language revealed nothing. Normally, she would decline such an offer, not wanting the client to get the wrong idea, but he wasn't a normal client. Hell, he wasn't even officially a client. She still needed to convince him to hire her.

"It's almost noon," she stated, standing up. "How about we grab sandwiches from the deli next door and we can go over the details there?"

"That works."

They made the short trek in silence. Nicole was busy thinking about whether the meeting was going well. He was open when he didn't have to be about his family life, which was a good sign. But there were two things that worried her. One, he was withholding hiring her. Two, he moved things out of the office when they could've been drafting a contract right about now.

His excuse for being quiet on their walk? Nicole had no idea, and that bothered her. She read people well, even when they didn't want to be. The fact she couldn't tell if he was taking her to lunch to let her down gently or not was concerning. She dealt with closed off people before, but this was different. Mr. Spencer's next move could make or break this opportunity for her.

When they got to the front of the deli, he held the door open for her. The smell of fresh baked bread wafted through the air as they walked in. "Come here a lot?" he asked, breaking the silence.

"Sometimes. It's convenient, and I like their sandwiches."

"I used to have a go-to place in New York. Now that I'm in Philadelphia, I haven't found a new place."

"If you're not a fan of their selection, we can go somewhere else."

"No, no. I trust your taste."

Nicole smiled. She could work with that. She ordered a grilled turkey brie cranberry sandwich. Mr. Spencer followed her lead. He paid, waving off her attempts to pay him back. They sat in a booth by the window, the view of the street showing pedestrians and cars going about their day.

As they unwrapped their sandwiches, Nicole noticed how Mr. Spencer's eyes lit up at the first bite. It was an insignificant detail, but one that gave her hope. Maybe this lunch meeting wasn't a lost cause.

"So, about those ideas you mentioned earlier," he began, wiping his mouth with a napkin.

"Yes, well, I had a few. We can't decide on anything for certain until we see what your budget is, and I have to meet Nessa. But I had a few things in mind that would fit your parameters. By the looks of it, Nessa likes nature," she said, looking again at the drawing on his arm.

"One option would be to have a garden party. Picture this - a canopy of twinkling fairy lights hanging over rows of tables. Fresh-cut flowers scattered throughout. Tea sets fit for a princess. A face painting station where her friends can transform into butterflies and fairies. There can be a petting zoo with her favorites, within range. A dessert bar, filled with Nessa's favorite treats. And, of course, a piñata."

Nicole could have kept going, but she would've felt like she was rambling. She paused and checked how her prospective client was feeling about her idea. He was silent and not giving enough away for her liking.

"That doesn't sound all that different from the parties my sister threw for her. Just in a garden with actual mice instead of animatronics."

Nicole fought to keep a straight face. Her idea was a good one. Maybe too good. "Is this the kind of event that would impress Nessa? Or would she want something bigger?"

"She's not a materialistic kid. Unlike kids her age and even some adults, experiences are more important to her than extravagances my money can buy her." His tone was light, but Nicole sensed an edge to it. Like his comment was supposed to be a jab at someone. His sister, perhaps?

"So, maybe what would really make her happy is just a normal birthday party. Like, a sleepover with pizza, board games, and movies."

"If I wanted to give her that, do you think I would be sitting across from you right now?"

Her frustration mounted at his dismissive tone, but Nicole kept her cool. This was all part of the job, dealing with difficult clients who had their own vision. She had to step up her game. "What I'm gathering is you want her party to be extra special. Not in the sense of spending thousands on decorations or food or entertainment. But something truly special. Not because it's extravagant, but because it's meaningful to her."

"That's exactly what I want."

"In that case, I have one final idea. We transform a local venue into a gallery celebrating her love for art. We can set up different stations around the space for hands-on projects. One station will focus on painting. Nessa and her guests can try finger-painting or working with acrylics. Another area can explore clay sculpting. There could be a mixed media collage station. Easels will be available throughout. Professional local artists will be on hand to help her and her guests. It would be like wonderland for an aspiring artist like Nessa."

Nicole stopped to watch Mr. Spencer. He was taking in her proposal. She could see the gears working in his head. After a beat, he said, "How are you going to pull something like that off?"

"I have my connections like I'm sure you do."

He finished his sandwich and leaned back in his seat. "You may have stumbled onto something. What would you need from me?"

"Everything. I'll need a guest list. The budget. Your input at each stage. To be officially hired."

"Right." Mr. Spencer grinned and extended his hand. "We have a deal."

"Excellent. We can go back to the office and settle the details." She beamed, shaking his hand. "And I'll have to meet Nessa soon to make the party as personalized as possible."

"How about tomorrow? She's due for a skip day from school."

Relief flooded through Nicole. Making headway with him felt like a weight lifted from her shoulders. "Tomorrow it is, Mr. Spencer."

They stood, but he stopped her before she could make a move towards the exit. "My friends call me Spencer. Something tells me we'll be thick as thieves by the end of this. You can get a headstart by calling Spencer now."

Yet another thing she didn't do with clients, but she was willing to make an exception for him. "Spencer it is, then. Feel free to call me Nicole. Now, shall we return to the office and finalize the details?"

"Absolutely. Lead the way, Nicole."

# 9

# Love's The Trap

"William?" Spencer asked as the man's voice came through on the other line. He was in his office, an hour removed from his meeting with Nicole Taylor.

"Spencer, hi. Is everything okay?"

"Yeah, no, everything's fine. I figured you might want to hear how my first point of contact with Nicole went."

"Of course. I would love to hear the details."

"Well, I met with her at her office. She was as professional as they come. You would never know what a deceitful liar she is by looking at her."

Spencer could practically hear the grin in William's voice as he spoke. "Guess it's good to hear I didn't get scammed by a rookie."

A rookie Nicole was certainly not. "She was strictly business. We talked about Nessa's birthday. We discussed ideas for the party. The whole time, I couldn't figure her out. She has an impressive poker face."

Spencer went into the meeting with reservations, but it was clear by the end of it that Nicole was a skilled con artist. She could read people and adjust accordingly, a skill that was a necessary trait in her line of work. From the outside looking in, Nicole was a businesswoman looking to please clients and grow her brand. She was good enough to fool anyone. Anyone except him.

"So, what's next for you?"

"She wants to meet Nessa. To plan her party better, she needs to get to know her. I'm taking Nessa to her office tomorrow."

"Have you prepped her?" The concern in William's voice was evident. He was investing a lot of money and time into this. The last thing he wanted was for his plan to die on the shoulders of a five-year-old.

"Nessa will be fine. There's a minimal amount of lying on her part. She only needs to be her adorable self to sell the bit."

"Alright, Spencer. I trust your judgment. Just be careful. Nicole may seem harmless, but she's a master manipulator. Keep your guard up."

William's warning was considerate, but Spencer knew what he was getting into. Though this was his first undercover gig, he watched his father work enough of these cases to know the drill. The people he investigated didn't care who they hurt to get their way. Nicole wasn't any different from them.

The basic details of her con told Spencer everything he needed to know about her. Con artists operated by luring their victims in with charm and promises. Only to leave them broken and penniless once they were done sucking them dry. Nicole was no different. He had a sinking feeling in his gut as he thought about Nessa being around someone like that.

"I will, William. I'm immune to Nicole's charms. Trust me. I don't intend to let her beat us. We have a score to settle here, and I won't rest until we're even."

"That's what I like to hear, and I have something to tell you that you'll like to hear too. Our newspaper ads went live this morning in the greater California, New York, Chicago, Atlanta, Washington, and Boston areas."

"That was fast."

"You can thank my resources for that. I put your office number on the ad. That pretty secretary of yours is going to have her hands full sorting through the junk to find the gems."

That's when Spencer noticed the post-it note on his lampshade. In Yara's handwriting, it read, Went to lunch. Here are the ones you should follow up with. Expecting a pay raise if this keeps up.

"Yara left me some numbers she thinks have potential. I'll follow up with them and see if we have anything here."

"Sounds like a plan."

As they hung up, Spencer turned his attention to the messages on his desk. There were four numbers listed. Two didn't have any actual information, only claiming they did to obtain the reward William listed on the ad. The third one had the name, age, and a rough description of Nicole. He also stated the date and location where he last saw her, which was a year ago, in Seattle. The final one was the most interesting.

"Hi, I'm Lynn Martin. Nicole, the woman described in your Chicago newspaper ad, I think I catered her wedding two years ago."

Two years ago would be one year before Eric Hayes, Spencer calculated. It fit the timeline, so it was the best lead he had thus far. "Hello, Ms. Martin. This is Spencer Shaw from the agency featured in the ad. Would you mind telling me more about the woman you met?"

"No problem. I've catered a lot of weddings, but I remembered hers well because her husband hit on me during the reception. He was super wasted and hit on every woman on the catering staff. I remember a co-worker saying something to the bride. Nicole's reaction is what made me remember her. She laughed and said, 'That's him. Isn't he a character?'"

"Did she say anything else about him?"

"No, but she seemed annoyed and embarrassed by him, but not angry or upset by his actions. If what your ad is saying about her is true, then I understand why she acted like that."

Spencer did too. The guy played right into Nicole's hands. He set himself up to be the cheater Nicole portrayed him as when their marriage crashed and burned. "Do you remember his name?"

"I can't remember his first name, but his last name was Mitchell. The wedding was in Chicago, had a lot of out of towners coming in for it. Maybe they lived there?"

Spencer opened his laptop and typed in Mitchell Chicago. For good measure, he added Millionaires. Several pages came up, and a couple were for a Mark Mitchell, a local businessman.

A few articles popped up about his divorce and the details of it. No photos of Nicole, but there were mentions of her by the name of Nicole Hamilton. Also mention of a prenup and Nicole filing, citing reconcile differences. Same M.O. as her divorce from William.

"Lynn, you wouldn't have a way for me to contact Mitchell, would you?"

"I can give you the number to the catering company that worked the event. They might get you the information."

"Thank you. You've been very helpful." Spencer gave her William's email to send her PayPal information to, then dialed the number she gave him. Obtaining a client's number, especially one with money and power, was no straightforward task. But Spencer had enough practice to know how to handle these situations.

"Hello, my name is Spencer Shaw. I'm looking for contact information for a client who used your services two years ago. A wedding, to be precise. His name is Mark Mitchell."

"I'm sorry, but we don't give out personal information. Unless you have a warrant, you're going to have to contact him yourself."

"Listen, I'm not trying to stir up trouble, but Mark was a victim of a scam and I need to reach him to let him know."

"If you have a warrant, then I'll help you. Otherwise, you're wasting your time."

Before the operator could hang up, Spencer said, "Let's try a different approach, shall we? Let's talk hypotheticals. Say you were working a catering gig and the client, drunk, starts making an ass of himself. Worse, he hits on the female caterers. Maybe he gets handsy. Maybe one server says something to the company and they do nothing about it. Because at the end of the day, the client is the client. How his unacceptable behavior makes your caterers feel doesn't matter. What do you think would happen if that story got out? If everyone knew what your company was allowing at your events?"

The operator was quiet for a moment before responding. "Give me a second. I'll have the contact information sent to your email."

"I'll wait."

It took no time for the information to pop up in Spencer's email. The operator hung up once his inbox chimed. Spencer opened the email and saw the info, including a cell phone number and an address in Chicago. He dialed the number.

"Hello?"

"Is this Mark Mitchell?"

"Yes, this is he. Who am I speaking to?"

"I'm Spencer Shaw, a private investigator hired by a client, who claims to have been a victim of your wife's."

"What are you talking about?"

"Nicole Hamilton. Or Nicole Mitchell before your divorce."

"What do you mean your client claims he was a victim of hers?"

"I'll tell you the details of their relationship and subsequent divorce and you can tell me what you make of it. They had a quick, hot, passionate affair resulting in a marriage. Nicole pulls away from him not long after. Her daughter begins showing interest in him. An interest that culminates in them landing in bed where Nicole finds them. Sound familiar?"

Spencer didn't know how Mark would react, but he wouldn't have predicted with a sigh of what sounded like annoyance. "Listen, Mr. Shaw. Nicole and I had a whirlwind romance. We both made mistakes that caused our marriage to end. I don't want to dredge up ancient history."

"Do you understand what I'm telling you, Mr. Mitchell? Your ex-wife ran a scam on you. You weren't the only man she married and then allowed her daughter to seduce. My client had a similar experience with her. I have reason to believe there were others before him, and after you."

"I understand what you're telling me just fine. I'm not sure what you want me to do with it."

"My client is building a case against her. We want your help."

"Sorry, but no."

"What do you mean no?"

"Look, what Nicole got from our divorce wasn't enough to crumble me. I've stayed on course. My business is strong. I met and married my true love. We're expecting our first child. If I were to take part in your case, I would be making a public spectacle of myself. Nicole may be a scammer, but she didn't force me into bed with Maya. No matter what she did, that's a terrible look for me. I don't want my wife to know about it or for it to be out for my daughter to read one day. So no, Mr. Shaw, I won't be a part of this."

"But—"

"No buts. Don't call me again."

"Mark, wait. You can remain anonymous. Your name won't have to come up."

"I'm sorry, but my answer is still no. In some fucked up way, what

Nicole did sent me on a better path. I'm not looking to stray from it. Good luck, Mr. Shaw."

With that, the line went dead.

"Damn it," Spencer muttered to himself, tossing his phone onto the desk.

"You'll get him next time."

Spencer's eyes whipped up, finding his best friend Lawrence leaning against the doorway with his arms crossed.

"How long have you been standing there?"

"Long enough to hear you threaten to expose a guy's dirty laundry. People sneaking up on you sounds like it would be a bad thing for your line of work. Maybe it's time for a new prescription?"

Spencer took off his glasses and wiped them with his shirt before putting them back on. "My glasses are fine. I was distracted, is all."

"Clearly. Oh, Nessa, your uncle is off the phone," he called over his shoulder.

Nessa ran into the room. "Hey, Uncle Spence. Where did you go that you had to be dressed like that?"

"Like what?"

"So… formal."

"Work."

"But this is where you work," she said, looking around their… cozy office.

"It's a secret job."

"Oh, cool. Like a spy."

Spencer laughed and shook his head. "Enough about me. What did you guys get up to after Lawrence picked you up from school?"

"We went to the library for Drag Queen Story Time. It was fun, as always. Their readings are always more entertaining to listen to than my English teacher's."

"What about my readings? They're better, right?"

She paused to think, then replied, "What is it you're always telling me? Never lie, Ness."

"I'll make an exception this once."

She rolled her eyes. "Fine, yours are way better."

Spencer smiled, making her smile too. "How would you like to skip school tomorrow and hang out with me? We'll be going to meet with that party planner whose photos I showed you. She's going to discuss some ideas for your birthday party."

Her eyes widened. "I get to ditch school to plan my party? That's so cool, Uncle Spence! I can't wait!"

Spencer felt a warmth in his chest at seeing his niece this happy. It was such a good feeling he almost forgot to prepare Nessa for what was to come. "We're going to play a little game with the party planner."

"What kind of game?"

"Roleplaying. I'm going to pretend to be a tech millionaire, and you're going to pretend to be a little girl who has the best uncle in the world."

"Oh, is that all?" Nessa joked.

"Exactly, that's all. And I have a feeling you're going to be the best little girl in the world at playing that role."

"I'll do it as long as I get ice cream after."

"Consider it already done."

"Yay." She turned to high-five Lawrence.

"Ness, want to take a spin in Yara's chair?" he asked.

"Always."

"Don't go too fast and get dizzy," Spencer warned as she skipped back into the lobby.

Lawrence shut the door behind her. "That's a really nice thing you're doing for her."

"If it weren't for the job, I would've done something just for the two of us."

"Still. She's going to appreciate it even if it's for a case. You saw how happy she was hearing about it. That means a lot to her, especially after today."

"What do you mean?"

"When I picked her up, she was chatty, which I thought was a good sign. But when we were talking, she admitted something. This girl in her class has a birthday party coming up too. She handed out invitations to everyone but Nessa. She tried to put on a brave face, but I could tell she was upset about being left out."

Nessa had been attending Spring Ridge Elementary School since Spencer got custody of her. It was closer to his apartment. It rated better among parents than her old school. And didn't come with gossipy teachers and parents who knew about the situation with Melanie. Rayna, Spencer's mom, warned him that plucking Nessa out of a school where she already made friends could backfire on him. Spencer didn't listen, determined to give Nessa a fresh start.

He wanted the best for his niece and provided her with an excellent education in a place where no one knew about the drama in her home life. Adjusting to Spring Ridge proved more difficult for Nessa than he thought it would. The classes were further ahead than her old ones. She didn't have the same rapport with her teachers, and making friends was hard when everyone already formed their cliques.

Nessa never complained. They both knew it would take time and effort to get used to the new environment. She had been patient and kept her head held high during the transition. Hearing a classmate intentionally left her out didn't surprise Spencer, but it broke his heart.

"Thank you for telling me. I'll talk to her and her teacher." Spencer put his head in his hands, trying and failing not to get angry at himself. "Do you think I made a mistake pulling her from her old school? Putting what I wanted over what she wanted?"

Lawrence walked around his desk and sat on the edge. "Hey, don't do that. You didn't put your wants over hers. You did what you thought was best. And it's not a mistake, it just might take a little while longer for them to embrace her."

"It's been a year, Law. It feels like no progress has been made. I can't even blame this on me being oblivious. My mom said this might happen. I'm starting to feel like the biggest failure."

At his job and as a pseudo-father. He wouldn't dare say it aloud, because it would feel too real if he did. If his case went sideways, he would have no way to keep The Shaw Agency running. No money to keep a roof over his and Nessa's heads. He was one misstep away from dismantling the legacy his father left him and hurting a little girl who had already been hurt too many times in her short life.

"Spence, you're the furthest thing from a failure. You didn't ask to take over your dad's job or step in and raise your sister's kid. But you did them when you didn't have to. You could've walked away and passed the responsibilities onto someone else. You had every excuse and right to. But you didn't. You're here doing everything you can to keep the lights on. You're raising a wonderful, smart, compassionate young woman who is going to change the world one day. If you're a failure, what does that make the rest of us?"

Spencer leaned back in his chair and let Lawrence's words sink in without trying to fight them. "Thanks, man. I needed to hear that."

"You know what you really need?"

"No, but I'm sure you're going to tell me."

"You need a drink. Not one by yourself like a depressed person, but one with me. Come on, you know it's been a minute since we've hung out."

"You mean since we last had a drink?"

"Come on, Spence. I miss you."

"And I miss not having to work."

Lawrence laughed and patted Spencer's knee. "I'm sure you do. The last time you did anything for fun was for your birthday. That was four months ago."

"Meanwhile, that hasn't stopped you from having the time of your life without me."

"You got that right."

Since his breakup with his boyfriend, Lawrence had become more adventurous. While Spencer's life remained stagnant, Lawrence's life seemed to have blossomed. It was a different story when the two met in college. A meeting at a mixer led to casual sex that led to a lifelong friendship. A wild thing considering they were complete opposites.

Spencer was the party animal who prioritized having a good time over studying. While Lawrence was the studious bookworm who would only leave his dorm by his friends' shear force. Yet their differences didn't stop them from forming a bond destined to tether them to each other forever.

"We can do drinks soon. After I close this case. It'll be the perfect opportunity."

"That could be months from now. I need a wingman now. You know how it is when you're single."

"Actually, I don't," Spencer reminded him. Even before he gained custody of Nessa and got stuck with a job he didn't want, Spencer wasn't interested in dating. Casual hookups were about as much responsibility as he could handle.

"That's right. You still aren't interested in that. Just sex."

"Keep your voice down," Spencer scolded. He checked to make sure Nessa didn't have her ear pressed to the door.

"Oh, relax. Nessa isn't paying attention no way."

"She has ears, doesn't she?"

"Aww. You don't want her to know you're a manwhore."

"Was. If all I wanted was still sex, I would've hooked up with you again after things ended between you and Scott. From my memory, you were a pretty good lay."

"Just pretty good?"

"Okay, great then. And easy too."

"Some things never change." Lawrence grinned.

"Some things do. I'm not interested in casual sex or flings anymore. I don't have the energy for it."

"So if you're not interested in hook-ups or dating, does that mean you're going to be celibate the rest of your life?"

"If it means I can focus on taking care of my business and my family, yes."

"Wow," Lawrence replied like he couldn't believe what he was hearing. Spencer couldn't blame him. He almost couldn't believe it himself. The old Spencer would have never imagined uttering those words. Or that he would be responsible for caring for a five-year-old. The old him wrapped it up.

Life certainly handed him a curveball. Spencer accepted his priorities were different now, and he had to adapt. His focus was on ensuring Nessa's well-being and building a stable future for them. If giving up meaningless hookups helped in achieving that, then so be it.

"What if someone comes along who's worth breaking that rule for?" Lawrence asked, arching an eyebrow while he waited for his answer.

Spencer wasn't interested in entertaining the question. His best friend always had a penchant for romanticizing things. Spencer had no intention of playing his game.

When he didn't respond, Lawrence continued. "I'm not saying you need to go to a bar and pick up the first guy or girl you see. I get you're not that guy anymore. But if you met someone who made an impression on you, would you give dating a shot?"

"The answer is no, Law. Dating is a distraction I don't need. I have enough going on right now."

"Spence, I don't say this to be mean. But what you have is an agency that, despite your best efforts, may or may not go out of business. And a kid that may or may not have a mom who wants her back."

Spencer confided in Lawrence about Melanie's phone calls. He hoped not answering them would deter her from continuing to contact him, but she hadn't stopped. Messages where she apologized for leaving and expressing her desire to see Nessa. She wanted a chance to be a mom, and it wasn't something Spencer was ready to give her.

"I get why you're against Melanie being involved in your or Nessa's lives. You're being protective, but don't let that keep you from letting other people in."

"There's only one person I need in my life." Spencer looked at the photo frame of her sitting on his desk before looking up at Lawrence again. "And she's not going anywhere."

# 10

## In the Shade of Her Past

Changing meeting locations at the last minute wasn't the smartest move on Nicole's part when trying to endear herself to a new client. She was aware of that, but she had a feeling when Spencer saw the venue she was standing in that he would understand. She had taken him from a stuffy office to The Old Paint Factory, a venue that would fit their vision of Nessa's party.

Nicole was standing outside, waiting for Spencer to arrive, when her phone rang. "What the hell are you doing calling me? I'm at work. Whatever this is will have to wait until I'm done."

"Like you wouldn't just ignore my calls like you've been doing," Kennedy pointed out. "But I'll do you the favor of making this quick. I want to know what you're doing about William."

"Why? Has he contacted you again?"

"No, but he won't go away because you're ignoring him. Trying to blackmail me into paying him the money you and Maya stole from him was just the beginning. You didn't hear the conversations I had with him before that meeting. I thought paying him would get him to drop his vendetta, but since someone screwed that up…"

Nicole rolled her eyes. A second away from hanging up on the little brat. "He's determined to make you and Maya pay for conning him," she finished.

"I'm not afraid of William."

"Well, I am. I'm afraid he might take Maya away from me. You're her mother, doesn't that worry you?"

"What gives you the right to ask me that?" Nicole snapped. "You've been dating my daughter for a year. Now you think you have the right to question me about her well-being? You aren't Maya's parent. That's who I am. Who I've always been."

"Then why aren't you doing anything to protect her? William could send not only you, but her to jail. And you're going about your day like everything is normal. Ignoring the problem won't make it go away."

Nicole took a deep breath and tried to calm down. "I'm not going to worry myself over this when William has nothing on me or Maya. In fact, the only reason he knows the truth about us is because of what you told him. Don't you remember being the one who told him about our con? You're the reason we're in this mess."

"You think I don't feel guilty about that? In a moment of anger, I gave leverage to a man trying to destroy the woman I love. I know this is partly my fault. I own up to it. That's why I want to fix it."

Ah, so that's why she had been so willing to fork over a backpack full of her family's money when William came calling. Nicole should've known. "You don't get it. This isn't something that can be fixed. You tried money, and it didn't work."

"It would have if you hadn't followed me and scared him off."

"What was I supposed to do? Let him con you out of your fortune? You should be grateful. I saved your family fortune from being given to the devil."

"Saving me wasn't the reason you did it. You did it because no one else could possibly know better than you. You hated the idea of

William beating you and you interfered. If I wanted to give William the money, you should've just let me. He could be gone for good right now and Maya's future wouldn't be in jeopardy."

"Maya's future will be fine. You're worrying yourself sick over nothing. William will slither away like the snake he is in due time."

"Keep telling yourself that. In the meantime, I'll be the one actually trying to get rid of him."

Kennedy hung up, leaving Nicole alone with her thoughts. She was fuming, ready to throw her cell on the concrete. It wasn't enough that Kennedy was with her daughter and trying to poison her against her. Now she was trying to make Nicole question herself.

The sound of a car pulling up drew her out of her rage. Nicole took another deep breath and pushed her anger towards Kennedy to the back of her mind. She watched Spencer parked his Honda Fit. Nicole hid her surprise that a millionaire would drive something so humble. She expected a sports car, not an efficient hatchback.

Then again, his reason was likely the small child coming out from the backseat. Nessa had amber skin and wore a pink polka dot romper and pink Nikes. Her hair was braided into two floppy space buns, and her smile was the spitting image of Spencer's.

"Hi, Ms. Taylor," Nessa greeted, skipping toward her. She stopped inches away from her and extended her hand, very adult-like. "I'm Vanessa, but everyone calls me Nessa. Or sometimes Ness. Once or twice I've gotten Loch Ness Monster."

"Which one do you prefer?"

"Definitely Nessa."

"Nessa, it is then. It's nice to meet you," Nicole said, shaking her hand. "You can call me Nicole. How are you today?"

"Great! I get to skip school to tour places where my birthday party might be held. I'm turning six. What about you? Are you as old as my uncle?"

Nicole's eyes darted over to Spencer, who was busy getting a cup holder out of his car without spilling the drinks. He rushed over, trying to hush his niece. "Never ask a lady her age, Nessa." Spencer laughed to hide his embarrassment. "It'll be useful to you when you're older."

"I don't mind the question," Nicole replied. "I'm 42, much older than your uncle."

"You don't look that old."

Normally Nicole would take that as a compliment to avoid awkwardness, but Nessa was a young, impressionable girl. She wasn't about to reinforce society's harmful beauty standards to her. She smoothed her fawn colored skirt out and bent down to Nessa's eye level. "Don't believe everything you hear about your 30s, 40s, or even 50s. You won't turn into a fossil because of a few wrinkles. Age is just a number, and it's more about how you feel on the inside than how you look on the outside."

"So, when I'm your age, I'll be just as smart as you?"

"Oh, absolutely. And even smarter and wiser, I'm sure. Two qualities I'm confident you'll use to do amazing things in the world."

"Thanks, Ms. Nicole."

"You're welcome." Nicole straightened her posture, standing at her full height.

"Nessa, why don't you go wait by the door for us?" Spencer suggested.

He watched her go, making sure she was out of earshot. "Sorry about that. Nessa can be…"

"Curious?" Nicole offered.

"That's a good word for it."

Nicole smiled, her mind drifting back to her daughter. Maya used to ask so many questions about her father and her grandparents growing up. As she grew older, the questions became less frequent. "I've raised a curious child myself. Her name is Maya, and she was full of questions like that. She's 24 now and I consider myself lucky if I even get a phone call from her. So, I say enjoy Nessa's curiosity while it lasts. You never know when the questions will stop coming."

Spencer didn't respond, instead focusing on the rest of the near empty parking lot. Nicole berated herself internally for making him uncomfortable. She cleared her throat, trying to clear the awkwardness. "What do you have there?"

"Oh, right. I have a grande salted caramel cold brew. For you, a grande blonde flat white with three pumps of brown sugar."

Nicole took the drink, stunned. "You guessed my order?"

"As much as I want you to think I'm that cool, no. I asked your assistant, Reggie, how you took your coffee. Since we'll be working together, I wanted to know."

Nicole nodded, hiding her smile behind a sip. No client she worked with had gone out of their way to do that for her. If this was how their partnership was starting, Nicole had a feeling it would only get more rewarding.

"You know I may not think you're cool," she started, eliciting an audible snort from Spencer. "But can you settle for me thinking you're kind?"

Spencer looked down at his own coffee cup, sipping to avoid replying. A technique Nicole knew well. From her vantage point, she could see the tips of his ears turning red. "You tell me. You're the one who'll have to work with me."

"I think I can work with that. Makes it easier for me to bully you into approving my ideas," she said with a wink.

"As long as your ideas please Nessa. I have no problem being bullied into them."

"Speaking of Nessa, would you and her like the official tour?"

"Absolutely."

Inside, Nicole began with a brief history of the building. She detailed how the repurposed warehouse became a thriving event space it was today. As they walked through the spacious rooms with high ceilings and large windows, Nicole pointed out how the original soaring ceilings and giant skylights that once housed paint production had been preserved.

Nicole's eyes wandered around, imagining the party there. It was the perfect venue. A giant balloon arch with the number 6 printed on it greeting guests. A custom mural behind a sweetheart table for the birthday girl in the ballroom space. Each of the rooms set up to be a different artistic station for Nessa and her guests to explore.

"It would be perfect. There's plenty of space for the idea we discussed. Plus, the connection with art already makes it perfect for Nessa."

Spencer pursed his lips, his eyebrows raising at her comment. It was the same look he had when he shot down her first party idea. "But it doesn't matter what I think," Nicole backtracked. "It matters what Nessa thinks of it. Nessa, how do you feel about the space? You can be brutally honest. You won't hurt my feelings."

"Well, I like the ceilings. And the skylight. And the big windows. I like how big everything is! It makes me feel like a grown-up."

"I love hearing what you like about it. Could you tell me what you don't like? It would help me make this the best birthday party you've ever had."

Nessa looked up at Spencer, looking for his approval. He nodded, giving it to her. "My invite list is small. I don't have many friends or a lot of family. I don't think I'll have enough people to fill the space."

"Fuck," Nicole thought, but certainly did not say out loud. She spent hours researching and calling venues in town that could host a party of this magnitude. It never occurred to her these venues could make the guest of honor feel small, in the metaphorical sense. She knew the feeling Nessa was describing all too well.

At every school Nicole transferred to when she was sent to a new foster home, there were whispers about her. About her parents, their deaths, how she was a troubled orphan girl who everyone would be smart to stay away from. No matter what school she attended, the narrative was always the same. And it was lonely.

Nicole made a silent assurance that she would not let Nessa suffer the same fate. She was going to throw her the best damn party anyone could ever throw. Kids will be begging to be friends with her after seeing what kind of event she put together.

"Nessa, if you want, I have some smaller venues we can look at. But I want you to remember, you don't need a lot of people to fill this space. What matters is having the people who mean the most to you here with you to celebrate. Quality over quantity, always."

The corners of Spencer's mouth lifted up in the tiniest smile before it disappeared. "Nessa, would you like to see a smaller venue?"

She nodded. "Yes. If that's okay with you, Ms. Nicole."

"Oh, sweetheart, it's perfectly alright. Your birthday should be whatever you want it to be. It's your day. No one else's opinion matters."

Outside, Nessa skipped ahead of Nicole and Spencer until she was back in Spencer's car. Spencer turned to Nicole, lowering his voice. "You didn't have to do that."

"Do what?"

"Tell Nessa what she wanted to hear. I know you were probably counting on this booking."

"Your niece's happiness is more important than booking this place. I want her to have the best party. If this place is going to make her feel insecure, then it's not the place for her. There will be others that are a better fit. I have one in mind that we can go and look at now if you have the time."

Spencer nodded, seeming to agree with her answer. "That would be great."

"Can Ms. Nicole ride with us?" Nessa asked, poking her head out of the car window.

"That's a great idea, Nessa."

"That's very nice of you both to offer, but I drove here in my car."

"We could always drop you back off."

"That's really nice of you, but I wouldn't want to impose." Or break any more rules with a client. Especially one she had already broken enough rules for.

"You wouldn't be." Spencer covered his mouth so Nessa wouldn't read what he was about to say. "Honestly, you'll be doing me a favor. I'm terrible with directions. I could have a map tattooed on my body, and I'd still get lost."

"A real life Michael Scofield, you are not."

"Yeah. I have nothing on that Prison Break guy." Spencer looked up at her, his smirk widening. "Seriously, though, having you in the car with us would be an enormous help."

Nicole's eyes gazed over from his to Nessa's. Her big brown eyes grew round. "Please, Ms. Nicole?"

The little girl had won her over, pushing Nicole's boundaries further away.

"When you make such a compelling offer like that, I would have to be a monster to say no. I would be happy to join you guys."

## 11

## Con Meets Her Match

Spencer had to admit Nicole was great. Not as a party planner. Anyone else would have figured a girl as young as Nessa didn't have enough friends to fill a place like The Old Paint Factory. Not as a mother. From her own lips, she was an admitted failure.

But what she was great at, just like any con artist, was putting on a front. She could convince her marks she was whatever they needed her to be. That was her true talent.

She was a natural at making his kid feel comfortable. Spencer noticed by watching her in action. On the drive over, Nessa would ask her a question, and Nicole would answer it. Then she would follow up by asking Nessa how she felt, and validated her feelings. She was doing everything she could to sell she was a normal person who cared about her clients. Someone who cared about Nessa and her feelings.

Someone who could go from manipulating adults to connecting with a child was impressive. Spencer could give her that. Yet that only made him more wary of Nicole. He couldn't let his guard down around her, especially if Nessa took a liking to her.

"Is that the venue?" Nessa pointed out the window.

"That's right," Nicole answered. "Our next stop is to the New Horizon Community Center."

The moment Spencer turned off the engine, Nessa bolted out of the car and ran to the doors. "Wait for us," he shouted.

He opened his car door, then promptly opened Nicole's. He hated having to act nice to her, but William warned him the nicer he was, the easier it would be to gain her trust.

"Thank you, kind sir."

"Anytime, madam."

Nicole looked over her shoulder and grinned. "So this place is smaller in square feet than The Old Paint Factory, but you can still feel the creativity in its walls."

Spencer forced a smile and nodded politely as he followed her to the entrance of the community center. Spencer trailed behind Nicole as she led them in. He kept an close eye on Nicole and Nessa as they explored the space.

The place was definitely more modern than any community center he'd been to as a kid. It had a sleek, sophisticated look to it with its high ceilings, glass doors, and an elevator as clean as his penthouse's. While The Old Paint Factory had a rustic feel to it, the New Horizon Community Center had an upscale urban vibe.

"This place is so cool!" Nessa said.

"It's amazing. There's just so much space to work with. And you know what would go perfectly with this?"

"What?" Nessa asked, her eyes wide with excitement.

"An art studio," Nicole said, stopping at the door of said studio.

Spencer peered inside, his eyes wandering the room. It was huge and empty, save for easels and the stage where a model would stand. It was minimal, making it almost serene. A mural was painted on the back wall. It was a picture of a girl looking at the sky, her arms stretched out as if she was trying to reach up and catch the stars.

"This is amazing! Can I use the easel?"

"Go ahead. Test the space out."

Nessa went into the room and plopped down at an easel and picked up a pencil. Spencer and Nicole stood side-by-side, watching as she put pencil to the paper.

Nicole's voice broke the peace Spencer had watching Nessa do what she loved. "What do you think of it?"

"It's a very nice place."

"Your tone..." Nicole stretched out like she needed time to choose her next words carefully. "You say what would be a compliment like it's a bad thing."

"I'm not saying it's bad. I'm just... not sold. There's nothing wrong with the place. It's very nice, but not what I pictured for Nessa."

"Is it too materialistic?" she asked, recalling the use of the word in their first meeting.

He turned away from Nessa and stopped on her. "Renting out an entire state-of-the-art community center? Yeah, I'd say that's pretty materialistic."

"For who? You or her?" It was the second time she let her professional mask slip today. "Do you mind if I be truthful with you?"

This Spencer had to hear. "Please do."

"The reason I asked that question is that it looks to me you care more about appearances than Nessa does. You drive a Honda Fit, a modest choice for a millionaire. You shot down my more extravagant idea for Nessa's party because you wanted something more down to earth. Now you're talking about not being sold on this community center, a place most kids would kill to have a birthday party at. It's almost like you don't want her to have the things other kids her age would love to have. Why is that?"

Spencer stared blankly at her. Did she double as a therapist when she wasn't stealing money from unsuspecting men? Because she hit the nail on the head.

This party, the penthouse they were shacked up in. Even the Ralph Lauren suit Spencer was wearing. It was all temporary. They would vanish as fast as they appeared once this case was over. The luxuries they were being afforded were because of William, a figure in their lives that would be soon be gone.

He didn't want Nessa getting used to something he couldn't actually afford for her. It would be a cruel trick to play on a child to allow her to think this life could be hers. Only for it to be snatched away. It wasn't like he could tell that to Nicole, though.

"Because," he said, struggling to find the words.

"Because?"

Spencer exhaled, shaking his head. "Money is fleeting. Luxuries like this party can be gone in a flash. The last thing I want is for Nessa to believe these things will always be available to her, when we don't know if it will."

"And here I thought your reservations were rooted in vanity when you're just trying to protect Nessa. I'm sorry if my earlier line of questioning offended you."

"It didn't. I appreciated you lowering your mask, even if it was only for a second."

"My mask?"

"Yeah. You can't tell me you're always this buttoned up and reserved. The Nicole I've gotten to know has been very put together, but also very stiff. I can't help but think there's another side to you, one you keep hidden, that you show only when you need it."

Her eyes widened. For a moment, she appeared almost vulnerable before ridding herself of it. "You're quite perceptive, Spencer," she commented with a small smile. "There's more to me than meets the eye, just as there is to you, I'm sure."

Spencer returned her half-smile, feeling less forced now that he was getting her to come out of her shell. "You were right to call me out. You said it best earlier. This is Nessa's party. I shouldn't stand in the way of what she wants because I'm afraid."

"Right, but you're not wrong for wanting to protect her, either. You not wanting her to get hurt or be disappointed down the line is something any great father would worry themselves sick about. Don't be ashamed of that."

Nicole's words felt sincere, but feelings weren't facts. What was important was Nicole wanted Spencer to believe she was being sincere. She wanted him to have a high opinion of her. It told Spencer she didn't view him as a threat. Which meant he could gain her trust and have the upper hand when he needed it.

"Are you two coming in?" Nessa called, bringing them back to reality.

Spencer chuckled. "I guess that's our cue."

Nicole nodded, falling back into her professional demeanor. "Let's go join the birthday girl, shall we?"

Nessa showed off her sketch of a starry night. Like she was the girl in the mural, and she was committing the stars to memory. When she was done, Nicole took them to visit other rooms in the building. Rooms similar to the studio and some smaller. And one larger.

"This is the ballroom. The owner told me they use this space for many functions. A birthday party would be in line with stuff they've done before. It would be very easy to transform this floor into a dancefloor. Create a space for a DJ. After all the artistic activities and food, the party could end here with music and dance."

Spencer watched Nessa, half paying attention, as she spun around in the huge open space. Stopping herself right before she got too dizzy. The lights in the room reflected the sparkle in her eyes.

Spencer couldn't help but smile as he watched her take in the elaborate setup. He couldn't believe he was thinking it, but maybe Nicole was right. Maybe he had been too focused on protecting Nessa from disappointment. That he hadn't considered how much joy an experience like this could bring her in the present moment.

"What do you think of the place, Nessa?" Spencer asked.

"It's amazing," she gushed, twirling again. "It's the perfect size for how many people I want to come, and there are enough rooms to have the art stations like Ms. Nicole suggested."

Spencer turned to Nicole, who was standing quietly off to the side. He could tell she was biting back a smug look, as if to say, "See, I told you so."

"Well, Princess Nessa, your wish for the perfect party is my command. If this is what you want, then this is what you'll get."

"Yes, yes! I want it." She jumped up and down, making what was left of Spencer's reservations fade away entirely.

"Looks like you're sold, Spencer."

He shook his head. "You were right. It's perfect. Don't get a big head about it."

"The only one with a big head here is you," Nessa shot back.

Nicole covered her mouth, laughing at the burn. Spencer rolled his eyes. "You can be very sassy for someone so small, you know that?"

"I get it from you."

"Ooh, another burn," Nicole teased. "She's really besting you. Maybe now would be a good time to wave the white flag before she launches another one at you."

Spencer narrowed his eyes, turning his attention to her. "You're supposed to be helping me. Not teaming up with the enemy."

"As far as I'm concerned, my enemy is you."

Nicole had no idea how right she was. He was her enemy. Which made it all the more harder to see his niece leave his side to walk over to her and give her a high five.

Spencer wasn't annoyed with Nessa. She didn't know any better. He was annoyed that in two hours, Nicole had won her over so easily. His sweet and innocent niece was becoming another one of Nicole's marks. His only way of stopping it was to beat her at her own game.

Spencer held up his hands in mock surrender. "Alright. I'm done. You won this round."

And if it was up to him, it was the only round she would be winning.

## 12

# Where The Trouble Always Starts

It wasn't often Nicole took a day to sleep in, but her body had other plans for her. She didn't bother setting her alarm the night before. Making her more thankful when her body didn't instinctively wake itself up. What she wasn't thankful for was the loud knocking at her door which jolted her out of her soundless sleep.

Grabbing her silk robe from her dresser, she begrudgingly walked to the door. "Stop banging on the door before you wake the building," she warned before opening it.

"It's noon. Are your neighbors senior citizens?" Maya asked, standing in the hall.

The shock of seeing her daughter at her door almost caused Nicole to miss the flowers in her hand. "You got me flowers? Seems formal for an impromptu visit."

"Oh, this isn't from me. I saw them waiting at your door when I arrived. It's a good thing I did, or some nosy neighbor would have taken it."

"You could have texted me you were coming," Nicole sighed, taking the flowers from her.

"Where's the fun in that?" Maya pushed her way inside, looking around. "Mom, why does your apartment still look like you moved in yesterday as opposed to eight months ago?"

"I'm not home enough to decorate."

Maya gave her a knowing look. "I know lying is second nature to you, but we both know why your apartment looks the same."

Nicole didn't like where the conversation was going, so she busied herself with the bouquet. "Oh, look a card."

"Fine, deflect. I can make you so uncomfortable you'll regret changing the subject."

"And how are you going to do that?"

"By teasing you for having a secret admirer."

Nicole laughed at the suggestion. "Secret admirer? That's not what this is."

"You haven't read the card yet."

She shook her head. "It's not from a secret admirer, but I have a pretty good idea of who it is from."

"Then read it and find out if you're right."

"Why, aren't you being pushy today."

Maya sat on a barstool, making herself at home. "I could always read it if you don't want to."

"Pushy and funny today. To who do I owe the pleasure?" Nicole rolled her eyes at Maya's persistence, but opened the card to appease her.

*To Nicole,*

*I wanted to thank you again for your help in planning the birthday of Nessa's dreams. Her excitement at the venue was priceless. It's a moment I'll cherish forever, and it wouldn't have been possible if it weren't for you.*

*Our outing was meaningful for me too. It's not easy opening up about the challenges of parenthood, but I'm grateful for the wise words you offered me. You clearly have a caring soul beneath your professionalism.*

*I find myself thinking of our conversation and hoping all is well on your family front. If I could lend an ear or help in the future, don't hesitate to ask.*

*This is just the beginning of what I hope will be a rewarding partnership. Nessa is already asking when she can see you again! I look forward to our next meeting and to learning more about your vision.*

*Warm regards,*

*Spencer*

As she finished reading the elegant handwriting inside, Maya leaned over and tried to peek over her shoulder. "What does it say?"

Nicole turned around, blocking her view. "It's private."

"Come on, let me see."

"Oh, fine." She handed the card over and watched Maya's face as she read it.

She could see her expression shift, her brows furrowing together. "Mom, you little liar," she cried out. "You said this wasn't from a secret admirer, but it clearly is! This Spencer guy is into you."

Nicole snatched the card back. "He's not into me, Maya. He is a client who is grateful for the work I've done thus far for him."

"Nobody writes a thank-you card like that unless they're interested in more than your party planning skills."

Nicole shook her head. "No. I haven't done anything to give him the impression our relationship is anything but platonic."

"Yeah. Like that's ever stopped men from taking a hint. Why are you so against this? Even if I'm wrong, would it really be a bad thing for you to date?"

"No, but it would be a bad thing to date this particular man. He's a client—"

"He won't be forever," Maya interrupted.

Nicole ignored that tidbit. "Did I forget to mention he's 30? Six years older than you. I'm 42 years old. The last thing I need is to date a man I need to baby."

"I didn't get the sense he needed to be babied from that letter, but you've met him. What's he like?"

Nicole thought for a moment. "He's nice. A good father, though a bit overprotective. But also closed off and wary."

"Wow. He sounds like you, but with a penis."

Nicole motioned for Maya to zip it. "Spencer seems like a good man, with a normal amount of flaws, but we both know how looks can be deceiving. Whether he is as good of a person as he looks or not, I'm not interested in exploring our relationship beyond a professional capacity. Let's leave it at that."

It was true. Spencer wasn't a viable romantic interest. Nicole didn't see anyone as one. Not since Maya's father, Kyle. His leaving them broke the ability in Nicole to see romantic entanglements as anything but a means to an end. How could she manipulate someone into getting what she wanted from them? That was the question that rang through her head on a daily basis for years.

She got so good at conning because she never viewed her targets as actual people, rather a dollar sign. Relationships were the same way. Dating a mark, feigning intimacy, saying "I do" — it was all one and the same for Nicole. Tools in her arsenal helping her gain complete control over her victims' hearts. And with that control came the power to break them.

After years of sleeping next to the worst men the world had to offer, Nicole knew for certain she wouldn't ever be able to see romantic relationships like a normal person did. She had seen the atrocious behavior the sex she liked exhibited. It wasn't fair, but she could never see the good in their kind without thinking of a red flag.

A potential partner wouldn't be the only person in the relationship Nicole couldn't trust. How, after so long, could she enter one, a real one, without resorting back to playing it like it was a game? She couldn't. Not anymore.

She put the flowers down on the kitchen counter, ready to let them die along with Maya's hopes for her.

"Okay," Maya said. "I'm sorry for teasing you about this Spencer guy."

"It's alright. Now, are you hungry? I can fix you something." Nicole opened the refrigerator to find half a carton of eggs, four bottles of water, expired milk, a block of cheese, and some wilted vegetables. "On second thought, we should order."

"No, I'm good. I'll take water. Believe it or not, I didn't come by for you to feed me."

Nicole slid the water over to her. "So there is a reason for your drop-in. Can't say I'm surprised, but I'm also not complaining."

Maya visited Nicole at her apartment weekly when Nicole first moved in. Nicole had seen less and less of her in the ensuing months. She chalked it up to Maya being busy rehearsing for her play, but feared it was a sign of her daughter finally leaving her behind.

Maya didn't notice Nicole's apprehension, her mind clearly somewhere else. Nicole placed her hand over Maya's, stopping her from peeling the label off the water bottle. "Maya, what's going on? You seem distracted."

She sighed, putting the water down. "I don't know how else to say this, so I'm just going to come out with it. I'm 90% sure William came to my show last night."

Nicole felt the blood drain from her face. She was sure she was paler than the milk she had forgotten in the fridge. "90% is a lot better than 100. Are you sure it was him?"

"I didn't actually see him. The crew described someone matching his description, trying to come backstage after the show. Security said a man by the same description was hanging around the stage door during intermission. White, late 40s, salt pepper hair, 5'11. That matches how he looked the last time we saw him."

For Maya, that was nearly a year ago at Nicole and Eric's wedding shower. For Nicole, that was a week ago when she interrupted him blackmailing Kennedy. Nicole never told Maya about seeing him, and apparently neither did Kennedy. Nicole didn't know her reasoning, but her own was simple. She didn't want Maya to worry.

If Maya had known about William lurking around, it would've eaten her alive. There would've been no way Maya could've stayed focused on her show. But now she worried that keeping her in the dark had only made the situation worse.

"Get a photo of William and give it to the Arden's security," she ordered. "They need to know who he is."

"I know. Kennedy told me to do the same, and I'm going to. I just wanted to warn you first. If he was at my place of work, he could show up at yours or even here."

Nicole's heart raced at the suggestion. She spent years trying to keep their past from coming back to haunt them. Now her efforts were unraveling before her eyes.

Taking a deep breath, she met Maya's eyes. "Don't think like that. This is what William wants. He wants to make us tip toe through our lives, afraid he'll pop up and spook us. That's not happening. He's not the boogeyman. He's a 47-year-old tech bro who got his ego bruised by two women who outsmarted him. His pride got hurt, and he wants to come after us as some sort of penance. We're not going to let him. Okay?"

Maya nodded, but her eyes told a different story. She was terrified. Her mom grabbed her hands and rubbed them gently. "We've built a good thing going, you and I. You with your play. Me with my business. We can't let William take that from us. We're not going to live in fear of him. Got it?"

"You know you can't order my feelings to feel a certain way?"

"I know. What I'm asking is that you try. Fearing William is how he wins."

"And we can't have that," Maya replied in a passive tone.

"No, we certainly can't."

When Maya left, Nicole phoned the last person she wanted to. "Why did I have to find out from Maya that William came to her show last night? And not you?"

"Would you have picked up if you saw I was the one calling you?"

"Of course, not, but that's beside the point. If he has upgraded from blackmailing to stalking, there's no telling what he'll do next. We need to keep Maya safe."

Protecting Maya was the only common ground the two women shared. Nicole was at least grateful there was someone out there who cared for her daughter's well-being as much as she did. She would rather eat a raw onion than ever tell Kennedy that, though.

"So what's the plan?" she asked. "You have a plan, right?"

"Would I be calling if I didn't? Just tell me if you still have his number."

"Yeah. If he doesn't have me blocked."

"Arrange a meeting between him and I. Somewhere public, but out of the way."

"And then what?"

That was information she wouldn't be privy to. "I'll handle it from there. Just arrange the meeting and text me the details. Oh, and Kennedy?"

"Yeah?"

"Make sure William comes alone."

# 13

# The Ordinary Family

Returning to his childhood home always made Spencer nostalgic. His childhood wasn't perfect. His parents were often away, working to provide for him and Melanie. It made for a lonely existence, but Spencer knew he had it better than most and tried to not dwell on it. Coming back to the place where it took place made him long for the simpler days when his only worry was sneaking back in without waking his parents.

He let himself and Nessa in through the backdoor. "Mom, are you home?"

"In the kitchen!"

Nessa made a beeline for her, him trailing behind. Her eyes widened as she took in the chaos surrounding her grandmother. There were pots and bowls scattered across the countertops. She had flour in her hair and batter splattered on her apron.

"You've been back in town for less than a day and you're already baking?"

She turned her head back to them, her smile wide. "You're here early. If you had come at the time we talked about, I would have had a plate of fresh baked goods ready for you to take home. And fresh baked goods ready for my favorite grandchild to eat."

"I'm your only grandchild," Nessa said, rushing over to hug her waist.

She hugged her back. "Yeah, because your uncle likes playing the field so much. Now I only have you to spoil."

Spencer stopped himself from rolling his eyes. "Mom, I just walked into the house. Can I get comfortable before we get to the settling down talk?"

His mother was just teasing him, but it was incredibly frustrating for Spencer when she spoke about him like this. She didn't recognize the growth he'd undergone since taking over the agency and getting custody of Nessa. He wasn't the same party boy who spent every weekend night with someone new. Maybe if his mom spent more than a month or two at home, she would see that.

Rayna brushed off his annoyance, something she'd gotten used to since he was a teenager. "You're lucky, Nessa. Since you're my only grandbaby, I get to spend all my money on you."

"Does that mean…" Nessa trailed off, not wanting to jinx it.

"That I got you some presents? Yes! They're in my bedroom closet."

"Yes! Thanks, Grandma." She gave her another tight hug, then ran out of the kitchen, her backpack bouncing up and down with her clothes.

Spencer waited until she was gone to say, "Don't let her eat too many cookies. She'll be up all night."

"I've raised two kids, Spence. I'm more than capable of caring for one for two nights."

Rayna was in town for Nessa's birthday next month. After her husband, Neal's passing, and her 60th birthday, Rayna retired as an urban planner. She used their retirement fund to travel like they'd always planned. For the past two years, she had been all around the world. She dropped back into her home in Philly for holidays and birthdays, but otherwise was always on the move.

Spencer was happy she was getting to experience that. She worked hard her entire career and deserved to do what she wanted. There was a time where he thought his father's death would stop her from wanting that for herself. He was never more glad to be proven wrong.

The only downside to it was they went a lot of times without speaking. Depending on where Rayna was, they couldn't make a phone call or video chat work around their schedules and time zone differences. Yet that's what made her visits feel special.

"It's good to see you again, Mom." He bent down and gave her a kiss on the cheek.

"Good to see you too, honey. How's the agency?"

"Fine," he said, pulling out of her embrace.

"Is that true, or are you saying what I want to hear?"

"I'm working on a big case right now. Everything is more than fine." He didn't want to tell her more than that. Something told him she would find something wrong with him working with William or working undercover. He didn't want her poking holes in a case that would stabilize the business when it was over.

"Okay, that's good to hear. You know how much your father and grandfather loved that place. One of the first private detective agencies in Philadelphia to be run by a Black man. It's important that it stays afloat. It's what they would have wanted."

"Believe me, I know, mom. I'm doing everything I can to make sure it will." The last thing Spencer wanted was to disappoint his father and grandfather. He did it a lot while they were living, finding a way to do it in death was something he couldn't stomach.

"Tell me about your trip. How was Jamaica?"

"Hot," she chuckled. "But I loved it. The jerk chicken was divine. Nothing here compares to having the real thing over there. Their street musicians were so talented. Reggae isn't even normally my thing, but I found myself listening to it all the time. Oh, and their beaches were beautiful. You and Nessa would have loved it."

"I would love to take her on a trip once school is out, but I don't know if I could manage that right now. I would have to take time off from work—"

"Not unless you let me take her on a trip. Have ourselves a girls' trip."

"While I stay home and work?"

"Yeah, but we wouldn't keep you hanging. We'll send you postcards."

Spencer shook his head and chuckled softly. "I'm glad you're home, Mom."

"Me too. I didn't want to miss Nessa's birthday."

"Are you leaving again after?"

"I might stay a little longer."

"How much longer are we talking?"

She went back to stirring her batter, avoiding his eyes. Even when Spencer wasn't looking for signs of secret-keeping, he usually found it. "Mom, do I need to remind you I'm a PI and I know when you're hiding something?"

"You sound exactly like your father. It's eerie."

"Don't change the subject." He took the bowl away from her. "Is there something you want to tell me?"

"I talked to Melanie."

Spencer groaned. "Mom, you should have called me."

"If I had, you would've stopped me. I know she messed up. That she's messed up, but you need to talk to her. Despite her mistakes, she is still your sister."

"A mistake is leaving your passport at home when you have to catch a flight. Forgetting to put butter in your cake batter is a mistake. What's not a mistake is abandoning your child. That is a choice," Spencer hissed, his blood starting to boil at having to talk about her.

"I know you don't want to hear this, but she's sorry. She wants a chance to show that to you and Nessa."

"Is that what she told you? God, Mom, you're so gullible. She's always been able to pull a fast one on you. How do you think she was able to hide her alcoholism from you for so long? Or hide when she fell off the wagon again? Melanie won't change. The moment she gets clean, she'll find something else to replace her vice. Whether it's a man or another baby, she'll find something. Then, when they don't cure her desire for another drink, we'll be the ones left to deal with the mess. Again."

"That's where you're wrong. Melanie is clean. I know this for sure because she called me from a rehab facility. I talked to her sponsor. She's been in there for four months, getting the help she needs."

"She's been in rehab before. It never changed anything."

The first time Melanie went was when she was 18. She'd been drinking since she was 16, but their parents weren't home enough to notice. She'd always been the responsible one and Spencer, the wild child. They trusted her to do right. It's no wonder she wanted to blow off some steam by going to parties and drinking.

Spencer never snitched on her in those early years because he didn't see anything wrong with it. She drank no more than other teenagers. Or so he thought. He didn't know it would get so much worse. Or how much he would come to regret ever covering for her.

In her spring semester, a college party she was attending was busted. Melanie was one of the underage kids who got caught. Neal and Rayna didn't realize how out of control their daughter had become until they saw her in handcuffs. They sent her to rehab, the first of her now four stints. Spencer wanted to believe Melanie could get better, but they'd been down this road before. Each time ending in the same results.

"This is the first time Melanie has ever checked herself in on her own. A part of her recovery is making amends. That means making things right with you and Nessa."

"She had a chance to make things right. She blew it."

After Melanie left Nessa in Spencer's care and disappeared, he tried to get into contact with her. He left her dozens of messages. He only received a response after he contacted her friends. She called, telling him to stop harassing them. Their conversation was brief. Melanie claimed she was an unfit mother and Nessa would be better off with him, a man who never raised a living thing in his life.

Spencer thought there was one last thing he could do to get Melanie to come to her senses. He filed a Petition for Guardianship, thinking his sister would protest it. That was Melanie's chance to fix things, to show up and fight for her daughter.

But when the court date came, she was nowhere to be found. Spencer stood in the courtroom, clutching Nessa's hand, trying to keep her from crying. She was too young to understand what was happening. All she knew was her mother was absent again.

"As much anger as you have for your sister, she has just as much for herself. If not more," his mom said.

"I'm glad she does, so she understands why I don't want to speak to her or see her. And because I'm Nessa's father, she won't get access to her either."

"You aren't her father," Rayna replied, reprimanding her son like he was a kid again. "Nessa's father was Ronnie, one of your sister's many enablers, who didn't want her. You, my son, are that little girl's uncle and temporary guardian. Don't get that confused with being a parent. The only parent Nessa has is Melanie, and she wants to see her."

"How is it I'm the bad guy here? I didn't take Nessa away from Melanie."

"But you are keeping Nessa from her."

"Yeah, and I will continue to do so until I have some sort of guarantee she's sober and planning on staying that way."

Rayna yanked her bowl back from him and started stirring at a faster pace. "You know what I think? I think you've started to enjoy raising Nessa and you're afraid Melanie will take her from you if given the chance."

"So what if I am?" Spencer asked, not denying it.

"She's not your child. She has a mother who loves her, flawed as she may be. You can't just keep Nessa as your own if Melanie is healthy enough to take care of her."

"And if I do hand Nessa back over to her and Melanie messes up again, what happens then? I can't risk that. Not when it's Nessa's safety I'm risking."

"You know your sister would never do anything to hurt Nessa."

"Not on purpose, but accidents happen. Melanie can't be trusted. She's sick."

"That's not for you to decide." Rayna turned her back to him to pour the batter into a pan. "If you want a child to stake your claim over, have one of your own. Until then, you will talk to your sister and work out the details of when she can see Nessa."

"No."

Rayna slammed the bowl down on the tabletop, the leftover batter spilling out of it. "Spencer, you can't keep Nessa away from her mother forever. It's not fair to Melanie. It's not fair to Nessa. A real parent would see that."

Spencer gripped the counter closest to him. His grip was so tight he wouldn't have been surprised if it crumbled beneath his fingertips. "You don't get to tell me what a real parent is. Melanie was more of a mom to me than you were. And in the last year of Nessa's life, I have been the one who's been there for her. I've done everything for her. Where has Melanie been? Drinking until she hit rock bottom. I may not be her parent, but I'm more of one than her biological ones."

"When did you become so cruel?" Rayna chastised as Spencer neared the backdoor.

"Probably around the time you decided you liked your career more than your own children. Have fun baking, Mom. Try not to poison Nessa too much against me."

# 14

## Sweet Revenge of His

Public parks were never high on Nicole's list of places to hang out. The weather was never good. Insects flew everywhere. Too many families with loud children. Now she was going to use its many visitors to her advantage. It was Sunday, and she was meeting William in a neutral part of town while there was still daylight and people out.

Nicole sat on a bench, her knee bouncing up and down. The last time she could recall being this nervous was when she sat down to tell Kyle she was pregnant with Maya. She was 18 and on her own. She had gotten kicked out of her last home months prior. Pick-pocketing and stealing credit cards until she maxed them out allowed her to live in motels and eat semi-regularly.

She crashed frat parties to find marks. It was at one of those parties where she met Kyle. He caught her taking a girl's credit card out of her unattended purse. Instead of ratting her out, he ditched the party to take her to a diner to eat. Their unofficial first date.

Their courtship was spent living out of motels and finding ways to make a quick buck. He made her feel important and protected, the way he always kept her close. He was the first man she fell in love with and remained the only. How he reacted after she told him she was pregnant solidified that.

They were 18 and broke. Their relationship was only a few months old, and neither of their parents were in the picture. Nicole was sure he was going to leave her and she wouldn't have blamed him. Neither of them knew how to take care of another person. They barely knew how to take care of themselves.

But Nicole wanted the baby. It didn't matter if Kyle left her because of her decision. She was going to go through with it. Her 18 years of living were spent almost always alone. This baby. Her baby. It would never leave her. Never abandon her. She would never be alone again.

Kyle proved her wrong that day in the motel. He didn't leave or try to talk her into an abortion. He was as scared as she was, but he promised he would find a job to provide for them. A week later, they went to the courthouse and got married with rings from a pawnshop. Nicole thought she had found her forever person. Kyle would later prove her wrong again.

"I should really take a picture of this. Nicole Wright, or Taylor, or whatever the hell last name you're using these days, is about to beg. I never thought I would see the day." William chuckled as he sat down on the bench across from her.

"I wouldn't say I'm begging," Nicole corrected. "More like appealing."

"Either way, it's amusing. Unbecoming for you, yes, but amusing for me."

"Get the hell up," Nicole ordered. She went around to his side of the bench and motioned for him to stand.

When he finally did, he asked, "Now what?"

"Lift your shirt up."

He laughed. "Oh, doll, did you miss me? What would your new husband think of this?"

"Cut the shit, William. I want to see your chest and your sides."

"Fine, if it makes you happy."

He pulled his shirt up to his pecs. No wire. He turned, confirming it.

"Now, give me your phone."

"That's where I draw the line. You'll break it or throw it in the pond."

"Then show me you shutting it down."

William shook his head, but pulled the phone out of his pocket. He held down the button until it went into complete darkness. "There, now can we sit down?"

She nodded, going back to her side of the bench. "We both know what the other one wants. Let's find a way for us both to get it."

"I would love to know what you think I want, but make your demands first."

"How gentlemanly of you," she mocked. "Leave my daughter alone. That's not a demand or a request. That is a warning."

"Why? Did the little actress finally realize I was following her?"

"She knew. She's not stupid."

"I beg to differ because she thought she could run off and have a life of her own without repercussions. Looks like she inherited your one braincell."

"Well, I'm smart enough to know that you're the only thing standing between us and a prison sentence."

"You're damn right. So what are you willing to do to get me to back off?"

Nicole caught his eye. She wanted to see his face when she offered it. "I'll give you the evidence you need to have me arrested."

"What are you talking about?"

"After our near arrest last year, I figured something like this would happen again. Whether it was you or another old mark, so I created a fail-safe. It's a video of me confessing my crimes, including the ones I committed while you were my husband. It's saved on an untraceable drive, ready for me to deliver at a moment's notice."

"You're fucking with me. You would have to incriminate your daughter if you did what you're saying."

"True, but instead of making it sound like she was a willing participant, I tweaked it. Now it sounds like I forced her to do it. So if it ever reaches the police, I go down alone."

William eyed her warily. "Show me."

"No. That's not how this works. You assure me you won't continue stalking my daughter or try to implicate her in my crimes, then you'll have it."

"How am I supposed to assure you of that? For all you know, I could keep doing both things even after you're in prison."

"Why would you? You'll be getting what you want. Me in jail."

"I admit it, the image of you behind bars fills me with joy. But it's not what I want."

"What more do you want, William?"

"I want the satisfaction of knowing you lost everything. Your freedom, your fortune, your family, and your friends. You'll be left with nothing like you left me."

"All this because I took half of your life savings?"

"God," he let out a bitter laugh. "You don't even realize how much your stunt took from me. You think this is because of money? If you haven't noticed, I recuperated from the loss. What I didn't recuperate was my reputation and relationships. Because you talked to the wives of my friends, the news spread to my inner circle. Everyone knew I tried to sleep with my step-daughter. My name got dragged through the mud by people who didn't know me. The people who did wanted nothing to do with me. Friends and relatives dropped me like a bad habit. My own mom was so disgusted by me, she stopped speaking to me in the last years of her life."

"Am I supposed to feel sorry for you? I didn't force you into bed with my daughter."

"You set me up!" William exploded. He stopped himself, looking around. The few park goers either didn't notice or care about his outburst. He took a deep breath and continued. "You stopped being the woman I loved once we got married."

"You mean when I stopped sleeping with you."

"You want to go with that line of thought? Fine. You stopped having sex with me, then paraded your daughter around in those skimpy clothes. What was I supposed to do?"

"Not fuck her, you asshole!"

"Yeah, well, too late for that now. You know, it wasn't always like this. At the beginning of our relationship, we were a team. You were so strong-willed. I knew you were destined for more than that diner I discovered you in. I was glad to be a part of helping you reach your potential. We could have been great together. The money you stole from me? I would've given it to you. You wanted more? I would've robbed a bank for you. That's how deep by the balls you had me. I was a goner. Until you changed everything I loved about you and became this."

"I regret to inform you, William, but the woman you loved was a facade. A character I created designed for you. Everything you were attracted to, everything you fell in love with, was an act."

"Not everything." He leaned in closer, his breath warm on her ear. "You're as strong and cunning as I remembered. Only now you aren't hiding it under a layer of naivety. It would be a turn-on if I didn't know what a full-on bitch you were. It's really too bad. I would've much rather enjoyed screwing and ruling the world with you. Now I have to settle for ripping your world apart."

Nicole's eyes flashed over to his. "Whatever you're planning is going to backfire. If you continue to stalk me and my daughter, I will report you."

"To the police? Oh, that's a riot. The con artist is going to the cops. I'm scared," he mocked. "Get real, Nikki. You won't go to them because like me, you have no proof. You aren't the only one who can be meticulous. Accept that I'm here to stay. Not to put you behind bars, but to watch you and Maya suffer. I want you to spend the rest of your life looking over your shoulder. Thinking that every shadow you see, every whisper you hear, is me."

"Keep your fail-safe. It's useless to me." William stood from the bench, casting a large shadow over Nicole. "You once told me I would regret ever meeting you. Here's to returning the favor."

# 15

# Shattered Facade

"Thank you for taking me out. I needed it," Spencer told Lawrence as they sat down at a bar near Lawrence's home. After he told his friend about his fight with his mom, Lawrence suggested he take him up on his offer for drinks. With Nessa spending the weekend with her grandma, Spencer couldn't find a excuse why not. That's how he came to be nursing a club soda on Sunday night while Lawrence scouted for a hook-up.

"Repay me by finding me a half-decent looking man for me to go home with."

"Still in the rebound hook-up phase?"

"Still in the avoiding your problems phase?"

Spencer chuckled and took a sip of his drink. "Touché."

Lawrence patted his back. "In all seriousness, you're welcome. I know you're going through a lot right now. I'm here for you in any way you need me to be."

"I appreciate it." Spencer didn't want to talk about it anymore. He came out to get his mind off work and family drama, and he was going to do that. "That guy over there." He nodded in his direction.

Lawrence turned and groaned. "That's my neighbor, Ty. He's an asshole."

"He's kinda hot."

"He's not."

"Look at him objectively. He's not a terrible sight on the eyes."

"Fine. He's attractive. Doesn't change he annoys me."

Spencer grinned. "That can make it hotter."

"Ew. I hate when you say that."

"But it's true."

"How would you know? Anyone come to mind for you?"

"I always regret telling you stuff." Spencer had filled him in on his undercover case. What Lawrence took away from it differed from how Spencer viewed it.

"Are you trying to tell me this woman who has conned multiple men into marrying her isn't hot?"

Nicole was the first woman Spencer avoided looking at closely. Like Medusa. He didn't want to fall under her spell. He couldn't allow her looks to cloud his judgment like Nicole had done to her past victims.

His small glances at her made it easy to see how she had used them to reel men in. If you didn't want to wait until after sunrise or before sunset to see the golden hour glow, you didn't have to. You could find Nicole and have it whenever you wanted.

A smile designed to make it feel it was only for you. Her curves were barely contained, even in her modest knee-length skirts and dresses. Her sun-kissed skin that begged to be touched. They were all just a distraction to her victims. A way for them to miss the warning signs.

She had an innocent look to her that screamed, "trust me". Those brown eyes that could be seen as gold in certain lights could draw anyone in. Making you forget there was more to her than her looks. But that's exactly what she wanted. To be underestimated.

Spencer shook his head, but it didn't clear his thoughts. He still saw Nicole.

"Objectively, yes. Nicole is a beautiful woman, but she's evil."

"That can make it hotter," Lawrence said, using his friend's own words against him. "I'll do you a favor and let this go for now. I'm going to go test your theory if attraction born from hate is real."

Spencer watched Lawrence get up and go across the room to Ty. They chatted animatedly, occasionally laughing at something one of them said. He was happy for Lawrence, but the interaction made him remember how easy it used to be for him to go after what he wanted. Sometimes it was a girl, sometimes a guy. Nowadays, it was no one.

Spencer didn't miss the playboy he used to be, but he missed the freedom. The freedom to follow his impulses without a second thought. Every decision he made now was made with the reminder it wouldn't just affect him anymore.

The bell connected to the bar's entrance rang. Spencer's eyes glanced at the mirror above his head, pointed directly at the door. The glance was quick, but the sight made the hair on Spencer's arm stand up. He turned his head to get a better look and there she was — Nicole.

What was she doing here? Nicole lived across town like him. She was going to wonder the same thing when she spotted him.

Trying to sneak out through the back would get him stopped. Spencer stayed put, facing his head down. Only looking up slightly to watch her order a drink. She sat a few seats down from where he was.

"Can I get you another drink?" A man approached her and asked.

"I'm not the woman you're going to get drunk enough to sleep with you. Move along."

The man scoffed. "I was just trying to be nice to you, lady. Didn't have to be a bitch. A woman your age should be flattered."

"My age?"

"Yeah. I'm sure no one is lining up to get with you and if they are, they're after your money. Not your dry ass pussy."

"And the women lining up to get with you, are they blind and deaf? Because they couldn't possibly be with you for your looks or personality."

"Fuck you, old hag."

"You should take your own advice and fuck off."

"Listen here, you bitch—"

Spencer had heard enough. Nicole might have been a thief, but Spencer would never tolerate a woman being spoken to like that. Without second guessing himself, he made his way over to where she was sitting.

Nicole's eyes practically came out of her head at the sight of Spencer standing before her. And again when he brought his hand to the small of her back. "I'm sorry I'm late, babe. Parking was a nightmare."

"It's fine," she answered, looking back at him. "Did you find a space?"

"No, but I was able to drop the car off at the garage and walked the rest of the way."

"But I'm wearing heels. My feet are going to kill me."

Spencer leaned in closer, his voice soft and reassuring. "I'll carry you."

Nicole let out a surprised laugh. A real one, not forced.

He turned his attention to her harasser. "Is there a problem here?"

"I didn't realize she was with someone. My bad," he said, trying to save face. As he walked past Spencer, he muttered to him. "Good luck handling that bitch."

Spencer was about to tell him off, but Nicole placed her hand over his, stopping him. "Let it go," she requested. The lightness in her voice from a moment ago was gone.

He nodded. "I'm sorry if I overstepped, but I wasn't going to stand by and let him disrespect you like that."

"No, I appreciate it. Thank you. I'm the one sorry. Sorry you had to witness me not on my best behavior. It's been one of those kinds of days."

"Do you want to talk about it?" Spencer asked, curious about what could have made her unravel like this.

"Oh, no, no. We should maintain some level of professionalism."

"What if we didn't?"

"What?"

"Seems like we've already thrown it out the window. What if for tonight I was just a stranger at the bar who helped you out with an asshole and ordered you a drink, without expecting sex. Would that be okay?"

Nicole stared at him. He could see her calculating the risks in her head. "You won't hold anything I say or do against me?"

"No."

"You say that now, but..."

"No, Nicole, I swear. Tonight, whatever happens. This stays between us. It won't affect our working relationship in the slightest."

The gears in her head turned again until she relented. "Okay... I'd like that."

"What will it be?"

"Rum and coke, please."

He ordered and watched as she finished it without pausing. "Would you like another one?"

"It's not every day a millionaire offers to pay for my drinks, so yes."

After three more rounds, Nicole was no longer the stiff party planner he knew her as. She was a fun-loving woman who laughed easily and challenged him to pool. "I've never played before," he admitted as she grabbed a cue stick and chalked the tip.

"That's surprising. It's a great party trick and excuse to touch other people's bodies."

"So that's why you wanted to play. To get your hands all over me."

"Or maybe I wanted your hands all over me," she joked, whispering in his direction like they were in a library.

"Then I suggest you bend over," he told her, motioning to the table. "And show me how it's done."

"Ooh, that could be taken the wrong way," Nicole giggled, doing as he suggested.

She lined up her shot with precision. Her focus was unwavering as she sunk the striped ball into the corner pocket. She straightened up with a triumphant smile.

"Impressive. Looks like I'll have to step up my game if I want to keep up with you."

He took his turn, trying to mimic her concentration and finesse. The ball rolled across the felt and bumped against the striped one. Nicole watched as the ball teetered on the edge of the pocket before finally dropping in with a satisfying clack.

"Well, well, looks like you're not all talk after all."

"Beginner's luck."

"Beginner's luck, my ass. You've got skills, Spence. Don't sell yourself short." She grabbed their drinks, then sat on the edge of the pool table. The distance between them shrinking. "You know, I'm starting to think I misjudged you."

He wasn't aware he was being judged. "How is that?" he asked, taking his club soda from her.

"Like the rest of my clients, I did my research on you."

"So cyber-stalking?"

"More like professional due diligence. Anyway, I read you as an overgrown frat boy who liked his fair share of women."

"And men," he added. "I'm bi."

Nicole raised an eyebrow, smirking. "Well, well, Spencer. You continue to surprise me."

"Is it a good surprise?" he asked, not wanting to add homophobia to Nicole's list of crimes.

"I'm not one of those Karens who pulls a right to refuse service because of my clients' sexuality. If you ever see my office desk, there's a mini pride flag in my cup-holder. My pansexual daughter got it for me. I love it like I love her."

Her response was the bare minimal of human decency, but at least it showed there was something human about her. The alcohol was helping give him a glimpse of the real Nicole, whoever that may be. "I'm glad you're a safe space for your daughter."

"I try to be. I messed up with her in the past, so I'm trying to make up for it. How about you? Are your parents your safe space?"

"Uh… it's…"

"Complicated?"

"Yeah. Growing up, I was a disappointment to them for not living up to my full potential."

"Bet that changed when you became a millionaire."

"Sure did," Spencer replied, remembering to be his cover.

She took a sip of her drink, her eyes never leaving his. "I must admit, I find you more intriguing than I initially thought."

"What made me less two-dimensional to you?" He put his hands on either side of her, wanting to get a good read on what she said next.

"For starters, your ability to hold your own on the pool table." They shared a chuckle. "But beyond that, I see the way you are with Nessa. You're great with her. Do you want to have more kids?"

More kids. Not kids of his own, but more. Spencer loved Nicole's phrasing of the question. For a split second, it made him warm to her. "If I met the right person, sure. But if I'm destined to just be Nessa's dad, I'll be more than okay with that. I'm proud to be a father to her."

"You should be. You're a great father."

"My mother would disagree with you."

"That you're a great father?"

"That I'm even her father."

Nicole studied his face. For once, Spencer didn't try to mask what he was feeling. "My sister might want Nessa back and because I'm her guardian, not her biological parent, my mom thinks I should give her back."

His eyes dropped. He couldn't believe he was telling the woman he was investigating this. But what if this was what he needed to get close to her so he could nail her? Nicole's hand touched his, bringing his eyes back to hers. "I've been around a lot of adults who gifted themselves the title of being my parents. Not one of them loved me the way you love Nessa. That's what makes you her father. Not your blood or a piece of paper, but how much space you reserve for her in your heart. Situations may change, but your love for her won't. Neither will her love for you. No matter what happens, you will always be her father."

Spencer didn't know how to respond. He was close enough to her to know she wasn't lying. She was skilled, but not that skilled. In a moment of true authenticity, Nicole gave him words he hadn't even known he needed. His hand squeezed hers, not knowing what other gesture to do to show his thanks. They stared at each other, sharing something. Something he didn't have a word for.

"Are we interrupting?" Spencer turned to see Lawrence across from him with Ty, giving him "who the fuck is this" eyes.

"Not at all." He straightened his body, giving Nicole space. "Lawrence, this is Nicole. Nicole, this is my friend Lawrence and his friend Ty."

"It's nice to meet you."

"You too." Ty took a swig of his beer. "What brings you guys here tonight?"

"A need for a distraction," Nicole supplied. "Ty, do you play pool by any chance?"

"Yeah, but I'm rusty."

"I promise to take it easy on you."

While Ty and Nicole begun to play a round, Lawrence dragged Spencer closer to the bar. "Nicole? As in the con artist, Nicole?"

"One and the same."

"And you're flirting with her?"

"We weren't flirting."

"Bullshit, dude. You two were eye fucking the hell out of each other."

"My client encouraged this."

"Eye-fucking her?" Lawrence looked appalled.

"No. He wants me to get close to her so I can learn about her business. Find out what scam she's running currently and if her business is a decoy to hide the money she's stealing. It's the only way to take her down."

"Your client is an idiot for not seeing all the ways this could go wrong."

"Why are you jumping down my throat? I didn't do anything."

"Would you have if Ty and I didn't come across you guys?"

"No," Spencer insisted. Could he admit things got more personal than he was prepared for? Yes, but he didn't forget who Nicole really was. "Everything you saw was for show. And if you believed it, that means I'm doing one hell of a job."

Lawrence looked skeptical, but didn't push it. "Please, be careful."

"I'm not giving Nicole my credit card."

"No. I mean, don't lose yourself in this. You don't want to wake up and not know where your cover ends and you begin."

Lawrence left with Ty a quarter after 10. That's when Spencer and Nicole called it a night, too. They headed out together as rain scattered down the streets. They stayed on the sidewalk, huddled together under his olive Harrington jacket.

"This is what I get for not checking the weather report," Nicole huffed.

"Where are you parked? I could walk you to your car so you don't get drenched."

"In the parking garage. What about you?"

"I rode with Lawrence, but I'll call a ride-share."

"Or I could drop you off."

"No, it's okay. It's out of the way."

"I like long drives. Besides, it's the least I can do after you helped me."

"I wouldn't be the man my parents and sister raised if I didn't."

"That's a noble quality. Not many men have it."

"That's the second time tonight you've complimented me."

"Hang out with me a bit longer and I might feed you more." She moved out of their safe dry spot, walking backwards toward the parking garage. Not paying attention to her heel or it lodging itself in between the crack in the sidewalk. She stumbled backwards, her butt hitting the concrete. Instead of letting out a cry, she laughed.

"Are you okay?" Spencer asked, coming over and kneeling down to her, holding the jacket over her head.

"Yeah." She grinned while looking at her lap. "But the bruise on my ass is going to be nice and purple."

He closed his eyes, trying to not picture that image. "I should drive you. Something tells me you wouldn't fall on your ass if you were sober."

"Noble and smart. Good for you."

"You forgot one of my best qualities."

"Oh yeah? What's that?"

"Chivalry." Nicole gasped louder than the rain hitting the street as she felt him scoop her up in his arms. As if she weighed nothing, Spencer carried her bridal style down the rest of the sidewalk and into the parking garage. He had a smug grin on his face, enjoying catching her off guard again.

"I don't need to be carried. I'm more than capable of walking, Spencer."

"Really? Could've fooled me with that spill you took." She shoved his shoulder, not moving him in the least. "Besides, I promised to do this for you earlier."

"As a joke, not literally. Put me down."

"A promise is a promise. As you get to know me, you'll learn I like to keep mine."

Nicole wiggled in his arms, but he kept his hold on her. Spencer would not be held responsible for her falling on the concrete... again. He wouldn't put it past her to sue him for his fake millions.

"Okay, we're in the parking garage now. You can put me down and let me walk us to my car."

Spencer bit back a laugh. Shouldn't she be used to this? What with the six weddings? "The sooner you tell me which one of these cars is yours, the sooner I'll put you down."

She stopped struggling and looked at him, the alcohol in her system making her soft and pliant. "The silver Audi."

"Was that so hard?"

She rolled her eyes as she got her keys out of her purse. Spencer took them from her and pressed the button and unlocked the door. He settled her in the passenger seat, searching around for her seatbelt.

"What are you, a boys' scout?"

"Boy Scouts of America would have kicked me out for being bi, so no."

"Too bad. You would've been a great one."

Spencer avoided looking at her, finally finding the seatbelt. He pulled it around her and clicked it into place. He was a second away from moving, but her hand caught his. "Thank you."

Something about how she said it told him this wasn't a normal thank you. There was a weight to the two words, as if there was something deeper attached to it. Looking up and seeing Nicole's glassy eyes confirmed it. If Nicole wasn't a case, Spencer wouldn't have pulled on that string. But she was, and he had to.

"What are you thanking me for?"

He stayed bent down, so he was smaller than her, but her voice somehow managed to be the smallest thing between them. "I wasn't being nice when I offered to drive you earlier. It was self-motivated."

"Motivated by what?"

She stopped looking at him, changing her focus to the exit of the parking garage. He saw the rain still raging on through the reflection in her eyes. "I hate driving in this weather. Or being alone in it. My parents drove me to daycare in weather like this. They dropped me off, but never drove me anywhere again."

Shit.

Spencer wasn't prepared for her honesty and the heaviness of it. Her voice was still quiet, almost a whisper, like the words were coming out unwillingly. "I don't remember the day. I was too young to remember. Yet this feeling of panic comes over me whenever it rains. Spiders or snakes don't scare me, but rain does. It's silly, I know."

"No, it isn't. Do you want to hear an actual silly fear?"

"I'm sure it can't top mine."

"I'm afraid of leprechauns."

She turned back to look at him, surprised. "What?"

"My sister loves horror movies. When our parents were away, she would pop in one for us to watch. This was before I was old enough to know they were fictional. So I'm nine-years-old, watching Leprechaun: Back 2 tha Hood, thinking it's a documentary. It traumatized me for life."

Nicole's laugh was hidden behind her hand. "Is St. Patrick's Day a tough day for you?"

"Oh, yeah. I have to stay inside. Too scary to be out in the world."

She laughed harder. It relieved him to hear it. Making someone laugh never felt as good as it did then.

"You should have never trusted me with that secret. I could tell Nessa and she'll dress up as one for Halloween."

"Not with my money. She won't."

"I'll have to buy her the costume myself, then."

"You wouldn't," he said over her laughter. "You're an evil woman."

Spencer didn't say it with the same level of contempt he said it earlier with to Lawrence. There was a lightness, a playfulness to it that wasn't there three hours ago. It was two different situations, sure. But somewhere along the way, there had been a change and Spencer felt it.

Nicole dropped her hand, revealing that magnificent smile of hers. Her brown eyes staring at him with more emotion than they had all night. "Thank you for helping me with that creep from the bar. For not laughing when I wiped out on the concrete. But for most of all, thank you for waiting out the rain with me."

"How do you know that's what I was doing?"

"Because I'm a big believer in intuition. And mine tells me that's what you were doing."

Her intuition was right, but he hoped it wasn't good enough to scope out ulterior motives. Or else his investigation would be over before it started.

Spencer closed her door and got into the driver's seat. To their delight, the rain was clearing up. Good enough for Spencer to deem it safe to drive. Nicole gave him her address, and they drove back into town in the peace that only came after the rain.

They were at a red light when Nicole ended the quiet. "The thing about the silence is, it's supposed to be peaceful and comforting. For me, it forces me to rethink everything I've said and done in mortified fashion. Telling you, a client, about my parents, is going to be one of those things that haunts me for years."

"It shouldn't, Nicole. There's nothing embarrassing about it."

"It's not that it was embarrassing..." she trailed off.

It was that it was intimate. Spencer finished the sentence for her in his head. It was a glimpse into her inner workings, her fears, what drove her to become who she was. It was personal, and their relationship was supposed to be impersonal.

"It's just not how I am."

In the nature of the green light, Spencer kept going, pulling that string. This time with himself. "Would it make you feel better if I admitted something personal to you?"

"Something more personal than the leprechauns?"

"Yes. More personal than the leprechauns." He glanced at her with a smirk. "People treat me like the person I used to be, not who I currently am. You see, I used to be promiscuous."

Nicole looked at him and said in a false disbelieving tone, "No kidding."

"Yes, but I don't feel ashamed of it. It's part of who I was, but it's not who I am anymore. But people still look at me as the guy I was in my youth. They don't recognize how far I've come and how much more there is to me. My mom sees it even less."

"Why do you care? If your mom can't see the man you've become, why let it work you up?"

"Because I think she would be proud of me if she knew. And for once I would like to feel that she likes me. I know she loves me. She has to. I'm her son. But I don't think she likes me as a person. If we weren't connected by blood, I don't think she would give me a second glance on the street. She would want to have nothing to do with me."

Spencer felt Nicole's eyes on him even as he drove. She had a way of looking through him, seeing him. It was unnerving. Did she look at her marks like this? If so, he was beginning to understand how they fell under her spell.

Her hand fell onto his knee, giving him a squeeze. "If it helps, I see you. I see the man you are and what an amazing father you are. The people who don't, that's their loss."

Her hand lingered on him. It'd been two years since someone touched him there. The fact that the person touching him was a con woman he was investigating didn't stop his skin from growing warm under her touch.

"I'm pretty good at reading people, so don't take this lightly. You have a good heart, Spencer. I'd hate to see it get broken."

Nicole took her hand back, and the warmth he felt dissipated. It was replaced with something colder, heavier. Guilt.

It was nonsense. He was doing his job, cozying up to a professional liar. A thing she'd done for years to her own marks. It should've felt like winning, getting the con to open up and trust him. None the wiser to him or his plan. Yet, it didn't. It felt wrong. Like a line was being crossed. His line.

For being a private detective, Spencer had never felt this dirty before. When he got home, he would need a shower. Or three.

When they pulled onto her street 15 minutes later, Spencer turned off the engine and saw Nicole asleep against the window. Her purse sat by her shoes on the floorboard. Her phone sticking out.

For any PI, it was an easy grab, but Spencer was born with the curse of a conscience. So were his dad and his grandfather. It was what made their agency different and would make it run out of business. Mr. Johnson's words came back to Spencer then. He needed clients like him to make ends meet.

Clients that were dishonest, but could pay. He needed to do dishonest work to survive. That was the rationale for grabbing Nicole's phone and turning it on. The first place he went was to her Notes App. Surely, there would be files containing information on the people she conned.

Scrolling back months, he found files titled like E.H. and M.M. pop up. He clicked on them, but they required face ID. He put the phone in front of her face again, careful not to wake her. It unlocked. He repeated the process on each file he found and sent a copy of them to his email. When he finished, he deleted the emails from her end.

Spencer exhaled when he locked her phone and put it back in her purse. She remained asleep, unaware of the invasion of privacy committed against her by a man she believed had a good heart. "I'm sorry," he whispered as he watched her. He meant it.

# 16

# Navigating Tricky Waters

When Nicole fluttered her eyes open, the first thing that hit her was the pounding in her head. The second thing? She was in a bed, but it wasn't her own. Nor was the shirt she was wearing. The shirt she wore yesterday was now an undershirt, with a huge oversized tee thrown on top of it.

Her hand immediately went to her pants. She breathed a sigh of relief that they were still on. Fresh-smelling bedsheets caught her attention next as it covered her entire body. The room was lit by sunlight streaming in from a window, kept from completely sweeping over everything in its path by the blinds. The painted walls were an eggshell color. Art that looked to be bought firsthand from an art gallery hung on them.

A dresser beside the bed held no personal items or picture frames on top of it. Just a takeout coffee cup. She picked it up and read the ingredients, recognizing it as her order. She turned it around some more and saw a sticky note attached to it.

"It was only after you fell asleep in the car that I realized you never told me which apartment number was yours. I could've woken you, but I didn't want to. I wanted you to rest, so I brought you here. Had to leave for work, but make yourself at home. You'll find I left you some things for you to do exactly that. Like this coffee. Talk soon." — Spencer

Nicole wouldn't stay long enough to make herself at home. She opened the top drawer and found her purse inside. Her wallet and cellphone were still there. She checked her phone, and it was a little after 9:00 a.m.

Nicole needed to go home and change and be in the office. Yet she made no move to get up. She sat against the headboard, drinking her blonde flat white. Letting the coffee usher in the memories of last night. Meeting William, stopping at the nearest bar for a drink, an asshole barking at her, Spencer.

The way he touched her back, the way he talked to her, for her. Like he had a personal investment in her wellbeing. And what did she do in return? Embarrass herself. She groaned at her agreeing to pretend she wasn't Spencer's party planner and he, her client. Groaned again when she remembered asking him to buy her more drinks. Somewhere in there, challenging him to pool—

"No fucking way," Nicole gasped, covering her mouth as she remembered saying she wanted his hands on her. It was a joke! A reference to how men used it as an excuse to touch a woman they were flirting with. Did he know it was a joke? She didn't remember him laughing.

What she did recalled was him driving her car and her telling him about her parents. She never talked about her hatred of rain. Not even to Maya. She blamed the alcohol for getting that personal with a practical stranger. To say Nicole was mortified was a colossal understatement. She stared at the ceiling, remembering why she wasn't a fan of drinking. Alcohol lowered inhibitions and clouded judgement. She couldn't afford either at a time like this.

The decision to go off script came from William pulling the rug from out from under her. It wasn't smart to let him get into her head like this. It was exactly what he wanted. He was baiting her into making a mistake, to feed into whatever he was planning to get even with her.

The crazy thing was if William hadn't been a factor, Nicole would have remembered last night for being a good time. While, her interactions with Spencer were guaranteed to keep her up at night and not in a pleasant way. He had turned her miserable day around for the better. She hadn't laughed like that in a long time. And for that, she was grateful to him.

When Nicole finished her coffee, she made the bed and grabbed her purse. Her heels that were by the door, she grabbed and held them by the straps. As she closed the door behind her, she searched, not finding Spencer. He hadn't returned from work to check in on her. Nicole preferred it that way.

Her pride already took a hit. Him catching her sneaking out of his house like a one-night stand would have finished the job. Walking around the second floor of the penthouse, she found the bathroom. What was supposed to be a pit stop left Nicole in awe.

Yes, the bathroom was impressive with its double sinks and glass walk-in shower. Yet it was the bathtub that made her pause. It was a jacuzzi tub with jets and the whole bit. It was bigger than her queen sized bed. Even so, the luxe of it wasn't what amazed Nicole. It was that it was prepared for her that made her stop in her tracks.

A long bath tray laid across it. On it were candles, bubble bath, and a mug of peppermint tea. Perched in the middle were the latest editions of Interior Design, Architectural Digest, and The Wilder Way. Spencer must have seen the magazines in her office and bought the latest issues for her to read. The scene made her smile. And that was before she saw the postie sticking to the mirror.

"Robe is hanging behind the door. Clothes you can change into are in the guest room. May be a tad oversized, but you can pull it off."

Was she actually considering this? Staying in her client's home and using his tub? His clothes and his magazines? It was so far away from the boundaries she set with herself on how to interact with clients. And unlike last night, Nicole didn't have alcohol as an excuse to cross the line.

"It's just a bath," she said to herself. It didn't need to mean more than that. Spencer wasn't around to know if she used it or not. Plus, she needed it. She couldn't go into work smelling like she crawled out of a bar.

Nicole ran the water, settling down into the tub. The bruise on her backside wasn't too bad. The hot water eased the ache. She poured in the lavender and rose bubble bath. The smell of it was much better than the rum & coke still on her breath. The peppermint tea was strong, helping with that and soothing what was left of her hangover.

As she bathed, she couldn't help but enjoy the peace. The jets rejuvenated parts of her body from the stress of William and work. The latest Wilder Way issue was prime soap opera drama. And the best perk of all was she didn't owe Spencer anything.

She didn't have to reward him with sex. Or talk him up in local media interviews. Or tell him what a nice guy he was for doing this for her.

Nicole's intuition told her Spencer wasn't doing this to get something out of her like her ex-husbands. His generosity didn't have to mean anything more than that. It could have been that's all it was, a bath and magazines.

The guest bedroom had a similar note on the back of the door. "Hope you don't hate me for the clothes. If you do, hopefully the food downstairs will make up for it."

She could give Spencer this. He knew the way to a girl's heart. A bubble bath and breakfast. Eager to see what was downstairs, Nicole found the aforementioned clothes. A navy and white striped dress shirt, boxers, and a pair of fuzzy gray socks laid on the floor, having been kicked off the bed by her in her sleep.

She picked them up, debating whether to put them on. The cons were again destroying another boundary, and the intimacy of wearing a man's clothes. She never even wore her exes's clothes. The one article of male clothing she ever wore was her father, Terrance's leather jacket. She kept the rest of his and Amber's clothing in storage to preserve their scent as best she could.

The leather jacket resided in her closet at every motel or home she stayed in. It had kept her warm on nights where she had no heat or she needed the comfort and safety it provided her. Wearing Spencer's clothes wasn't the same, but it felt good. The shirt fell past her waist. The socks went up to her knees, warming her through the cold house.

In the kitchen, Nicole found another note. "Whatever you don't eat, take it home. Seriously, take it. My mom will get a spidey sense I wasted food and I would have disappointed her again. Do you want that on your conscience?"

Nicole smiled, putting the note with the others in her purse. On a bad day, she would want to remember this happened. To remind her that good days could exist in a world full of shitty ones.

In the fridge, there were three takeout bags from a place called Breakfast Boutique. She grabbed and unwrapped one container at a time. Inside the first were three buttermilk pancakes, scrambled eggs, and skillet potatoes. The second had French toast dusted with powdered sugar and strawberry compote and a side of hickory-smoked bacon. The last was a breakfast burrito made with sautéed onions, peppers, black beans, and avocado.

Nicole's mouth watered at the sight. She could tell Spencer put a lot of thought into what he was feeding her. It was a kind gesture, and one that could have easily backfired. He didn't know what she liked or if she had allergies. But he knocked it out of the park.

She sat there on a barstool at his kitchen island and took a big bite of the burrito, needing something savory. It was the perfect bite, followed by dozens of more. When she finished, she checked her phone and saw it was 10 a.m.. Time to go to her apartment, get dressed, and go to work. Nicole never expected to feel sad about leaving, but there was no denying that's how she felt walking out.

* * *

Neighbors passed Nicole on their way to work as she rushed up the stairs of her building. As she reached her floor, a figure by her door came into view. For a second, she worried it might be William, but the closer she approached them, she knew it wasn't him. It was, however, someone equally annoying.

"What are you wearing?" Kennedy gawked.

"Not interested in talking about it with you," Nicole said, irritated as she used her key to unlock the door.

Kennedy followed her in even without Nicole telling her she could. "Are you interested in talking to me about your meeting with William? I tried calling and texting to see how things went. You never responded."

"You wouldn't have wanted to talk to me yesterday. I was in a foul mood."

"Aren't you always?"

"It was worse than normal." She grabbed a simple black dress from her closet and closed the bathroom door behind her. If they were going to have this conversation, it would have to be while Nicole got ready for work.

"Let me guess, your plan to get William to end his crusade against you and Maya failed."

Nicole emerged from the bathroom, dressed. Without looking at Kennedy, she flipped her middle finger before searching for her mascara brush.

"So the plan backfired. What are we going to do now?"

"We aren't doing anything. You're going to do nothing and I'm going to handle this my way."

"Hello? You just did that, and it didn't work. I know you're a badass who thinks you have to handle everything by yourself, but you don't. We both want to protect Maya. Neither of us want to see her go to jail. We can work together on this."

Kennedy never sounded more like a child to Nicole than right then. She was 24 and in love. She would have done anything for Maya. It was an understanding, but stupid feeling. Nicole had been there with Kyle. Kennedy didn't see it, but Nicole was helping her. She was stopping her from doing something stupid for a relationship that wouldn't last.

She exited the bedroom and walked over to Kennedy, who was standing center of her living area. "Go ahead. Tell me your bright idea that will get William to back off. I'm all ears."

The younger woman maintained eye contact with Nicole, not backing down from the challenge she laid out. "You turn yourself into the police. Leave out or modify your retellings of your cons so Maya isn't implicated. William gets what he wants. Revenge on you for screwing him over and he hurts Maya by taking her mom away from her."

Kennedy must have thought Nicole would react in a rage at her suggestion, instead she smiled. "That was a great idea when I came up with it almost a year ago. Don't you think I offered that to William? He turned me down. He's more interested in seeing us suffer than seeing us do time."

"What exactly did he say to you?"

"That even if I turned myself in, he won't stop coming after Maya. He'll keep going after her, whether to implicate her in my crimes or make her live in fear." Repeating what William told her refueled Nicole's anger. She didn't care how he came after her, but Maya was a different story. She rather go to jail for murdering William than let him hurt her daughter.

"William can try to implicate Maya as much as he wants, but if you turn yourself in, it'll be your word against his. He doesn't have anything that proves Maya went through with the cons willingly. She was 18 when they started. You're one hell of a liar and manipulator, Nicole. You can easily spin a tale of you forcing your daughter into doing your bidding. Any good lawyer can dispel any accusations William could throw at her."

"I'm not willing to risk that. If I go to jail and William still goes after her, there will be no one on the outside to look out for Maya."

"What the hell do you call what I'm doing now?"

"You're her girlfriend. What you're doing is the bare minimum."

"Fuck you, Nicole."

"I'm serious, Kennedy. I have no clue if you're in this relationship for the long haul. If the police come knocking at Eric's door with a warrant for Maya's arrest, are you going to stand by her? Would you allow yourself and your family to be put through a criminal investigation for her? Or would you throw Maya to the wolves when the going gets tough?"

"I love your daughter. I'm in love with Maya. I want to build a future with her."

"Her father told me the same things in his wedding vows. Guess what? They didn't make him stay when things got rough, and they won't make you stay either."

"Would you stop this?" Kennedy pleaded. "Stop drawing undeserved parallels between me and your ex-husband. I'm not Kyle. Maya is not you. I won't leave her, no matter what gets thrown in our way. Now, I gave you a way to protect Maya. Is it perfect? No, but I don't see a better option. Turning yourself in to the police is our best course of action."

"Of course, you think that. You've been trying to get rid of me since I came into Eric's life. Admit it, you would love to see me have to go to jail. You'll pretend to comfort Maya while secretly celebrating inside."

"Oh my god, you're so damn full of yourself. I'm not out to get you. If I were, I would have gone through with sending you to jail myself a long time ago, but I know how much that would wreck Maya. And I care about her more than I hate you."

Nicole was taken aback. Hate was a strong word. "You hate me?"

"You're surprised? You tried to con my widowed father into giving you half of his life savings. So yes, Nicole, I hate you. I don't respect you. You're rude, manipulative, and selfish. It's a miracle that Maya turned out as well-adjusted as she is. It's even a bigger miracle that Maya cares for you. You used her for your cons to work. Let gross old men kiss and touch her for a payday. I don't care that Maya was of age and was up to do it. She was your child, and you put her in that position. You should've protected her."

Nicole was silenced by her own conscience. She did do that to Maya. The idea was Maya's, but the seed was sprouted by the environment Nicole raised her in. After Kyle left, Nicole resorted back to her pick-pocketing and credit card stealing ways. Only now with another mouth to feed. She needed bigger plays for money for them to survive.

Having men Nicole didn't like take her to bed so she could steal their cash and watches while they slept seemed like a good idea at the time. If it kept them with a roof over their heads, then it was a necessary evil. Keeping Maya away from that dark seedy underworld was crucial to Nicole. No taking these men back to their crappy one-bedroom apartment. No taking off to meet with a mark unless a neighbor could watch Maya.

But things slipped through. Marks knocking on her door, demanding their stuff back, calling Nicole every name in the book. Loud phone calls from marks who refused to believe Nicole scammed them. Men who scared them into moving.

It was all enough to make Nicole switch gears. Scams that didn't involve sex were cleaner, less complicated, and safer. When Maya was old enough, Nicole let her in on a small part of her world, allowing her daughter to come up with the plans and help her pull them off. A Girl Scout scam, a Big Sister, Little Sister scam, and more.

It shouldn't have surprised Nicole when Maya turned 18 that she wanted to stay around and help secure their futures with high risk, high reward cons. Nicole built a culture where the danger and risks from the cons gave off the same high of beating a tricky video game level. And because Maya grew up seeing the ways her mom let men use her for the sake of a payout, she was willing to do the same.

"You're right," Nicole muttered, barely reaching her own ears.

"What did you say?"

"You're right. I was an unfit mother to Maya. I should've protected her and shielded her from the horrors of the world. But I was a young woman alone with a kid to raise. I did what I thought I had to do, so that I wouldn't lose her. I thought because those men weren't taking advantage of her like they took advantage of me, that it was okay."

"Because she didn't sleep with them like I did, I thought the guilt would be easier to bear. When Maya was young, she had this twinkle in her eyes. It became like stars whenever we pulled off a con. Over time, the twinkle disappeared. I could tell the cons started not to be fun for her anymore, but she kept doing them for me. And I didn't want to stop because I knew one day I would be gone and there would be no one looking out for her. Money can't replace family or friends, but it could provide her with the safety and security I didn't always have. The most important thing to me was for her to be taken care of after I was gone. So I kept them going even when they were taking bits of her away from me."

"I knew one day she would resent me for it. I tricked myself into being okay with that. My parents left me with nothing but their clothes. No family, no money. I didn't want that to be the case for Maya. I rather she hated me in death than for me to have left her penniless, homeless, and alone."

"Do you still feel that way?"

Nicole put her hands over her head, as if she needed to quiet her thoughts. "No mother wants her daughter to hate her. It's the ultimate sign of failure. I thought failing Maya would be to leave her in the same position I was in as a child. I didn't realize there were other ways to fail as a parent."

She closed her eyes, wiping away her tears with the knuckles of her index fingers. Kennedy's neutral expression welcomed her when she opened them again. "No, I don't want Maya to hate me. Everything I've done, as misguided as it was, was done because I love her. And I wanted to spare her from the pain I experienced. It doesn't excuse me putting her in harm's way."

"Good, because it doesn't."

"I'm just glad I didn't break her. I thought I took things like her capacity to love and trust away, along with her twinkle. But after she met you, it all came back. You gave her back parts of herself after I'd stolen them. I might have resented you for that."

"Might have?"

"I'm giving you an apology." Nicole wiped her nose with the inside of her dress. "Don't push it."

Kennedy nodded for her to finish.

"I have a hard time trusting people. Every time I do, it bites me in the ass. I was critical of yours and Maya's relationship because I didn't want her to go through what I did. You're the first person I've seen her care about like this. That scares me. But despite my distrust of you, I do believe you have her best interests at heart. Something for a long time, I didn't. So thank you for helping her when I didn't."

Kennedy stared at her a long while before speaking. "Well, shit. If this is the new, less bitchy you, I kind of like it. Slowly, you could work yourself up from hatred to contempt."

Nicole chuckled before her face turned serious. "I'll do it."

"Do what?"

"Turn myself in to the police. If it's the only way we can find to protect Maya, then I'll do it. I don't want her to spend a part of her life behind bars because I was too stubborn and proud to sacrifice myself."

"Okay. Okay," Kennedy said, trying to process her words. "You know, when I said it earlier, I didn't think I would actually get you to agree with me."

"If it's the only way to save Maya, then it's the right move."

Kennedy nodded, but she didn't look convinced. "Let's say this is our contingency plan. If all else fails."

"Everything already has failed."

"Not necessarily," she began. "What we need is to change tactics. No more hoping William goes away or pleading with him. If he wants to scare you and Maya by digging into your skeletons, then we'll do the same with him. I'll have to ask my dad, but I'm sure I can convince him to pay someone to snoop into William's past. To find something he doesn't want out there and we can use it to get him to go away for good."

"Wow," Nicole said in a resigned voice. "You had that idea in your back pocket and you still wanted me to turn myself in? You really are an asshole."

"Takes one to know one."

Nicole could be pissed later. Kennedy's idea wasn't bad except for one thing. "What if he isn't hiding anything? I did research on him when I was casing if he would make for a good mark. I never found a whiff of him having a scandal."

"No offense, Nicole, but I think a high-priced PI can find more on him than you did. The current behavior he's displaying tells me he can't be squeaky clean. We just need to find that magic bullet and steer clear of him until we do."

Nicole wasn't completely on board with Kennedy taking the lead on this, but the girl looked like she couldn't dare be stopped. "Fine. We'll do it your way, but if this fails, I will haul myself down to the nearest police station the first chance I get."

"Please don't do that without approving it with me first," Kennedy asked as she approached the door to leave.

"Why? Do you want to do the honors yourself?"

Halfway out the door, she said, "You know, it would be my pleasure."

Nicole smiled because somehow this had been their most productive conversation.

# 17

## No Man of His Own

Betting Nicole wouldn't be interested in seeing him after their hangout, Spencer left for the office early. He knew she would be mortified to find herself in her client's guest bed and would need time to adjust. He'll check in with her later to clear the air, but he had to admit she wasn't the only one who needed time and space.

If Spencer had seen her after breaking into her phone, he wouldn't have been able to look her in the eye. It was ridiculous, considering Spencer had been lying to her this whole time about who he was, but it wasn't the lying that made him feel guilty. He could convince himself he was doing it for the greater good.

To take down a con artist, you had to act like one. Lying was a part of their job. Sometimes it was also the job of a private investigator. Where Spencer differed from the others in his field was, he had a moral compass and a strong sense of right and wrong.

Private detectives weren't known for those qualities, but the Shaw men built the agency on them. Spencer didn't want those principles to go away with him at the helm. He had kept that commitment until last night.

Breaking into Nicole's phone and accessing her private files violated her trust. She did that with the men she conned, but it was the first time Spencer crossed that moral line he cared so much about. He hated when Lawrence made good points, but he couldn't ignore when he was right. And last night, he was.

If Spencer kept sinking to Nicole's level to beat her, then he wouldn't like the person he would be at the end of the case. He never wanted to be like any of the other PIs in town. He didn't want that to change now. It was important not to cross another line like that again. Or it could destroy the agency's integrity his family had worked so hard to maintain.

The bell to the door dinged as William walked inside. "Hey," he greeted Spencer as he came into his office. "Where's that pretty secretary of yours?"

"Yara? She has classes on Mondays."

"That's good. That you're not hiding her away from me because of my history."

Spencer cringed. He did not like to remember his client landed in this situation in the first place because he tried to sleep with his 19-year-old stepdaughter. "I didn't think it needed to be said, but she's off limits."

"You don't have to worry. I stay away from women in that age bracket now."

"Music to my ears."

William sat in the chair across from him and asked, "What was so important you wanted to meet?"

"Don't ask me how, but I came into the files that Nicole kept on her marks, including yours."

"Really?" Spencer should have enjoyed the surprise in William's voice. To his ears, though, he sounded surprised at his capabilities and not at the rate he discovered them. He wrote it off as him reading too much into it.

"I printed and arranged them into separate folders. I haven't had the chance to read them in depth yet, but I thought you would want to know immediately."

"Thanks," he said, taking the top file on the stack off from Spencer's desk. He flipped through the first four pages before speaking again. "I appreciate you bringing this to me. Is one of these files on a new mark?"

"As far as I can tell, no. I had to go back months to get these. Her last mark was Eric Hayes."

"That's from a year ago," he muttered to himself. "Where are her files on the next guy she's after?"

"I don't know. Unless she's keeping her notes somewhere else, I'm of the belief she's not after a mark right now. Looks like she's really putting effort into making this cover of hers believable."

William didn't look pleased to hear that information. Spencer understood he wanted to gather proof to send Nicole to prison, but shouldn't he be happy to hear she wasn't playing another man like a fiddle? "I'm going to dig further into the files later. See if there's anything that might help your case."

William nodded, but his eyes were distant, like he was barely paying attention.

"Tell me what you're thinking. I have an inkling, but we're trying that honesty thing, remember?"

"I think the files might be too good to be true."

Spencer raised a brow. He did not like the sound of that. "You haven't even looked through them yet."

"I don't have to. I know how Nicole operates. She wouldn't leave such incriminating evidence lying around on her cloud. Nicole is too good at what she does to get caught that easily. These notes are probably decoys. You've already mentioned you couldn't find a file on a recent mark. That's a clear indication she's covering her tracks."

"Maybe she got cocky. She got away with this scam for years."

"Even if that's the case, Nicole has plausible deniability. She could say it's all made up and get a lawyer that could sell the story."

"Why can't you see this as the win that it is?"

"Because it's not one. Not really," William argued. "These files aren't enough evidence. Not when she can dispute them, say she was writing a novel or some shit. If you think this is good enough to send her away, then maybe you're not as good of a private investigator as I thought."

Spencer bit the inside of his cheek. William was a client. His only client. He was allowed to be a jackass when he was unhappy with the results he was getting. There was something else at play here, though. He was too quick to assume the worst. There was no reason to think Nicole wouldn't slip up or hadn't already.

"Okay. So you think we need harder evidence. What is that in your eyes?"

"Catch her scamming her next mark or proof her business is a money laundering front. There needs to be something she can't lie her way out of. It needs to be bulletproof. Something Nicole Taylor can't even shatter."

"How do you suggest we get that kind of proof?"

William smirked. "How do you feel about a surveillance operation?"

Spencer thought he had misheard him, but by the look on his face, he wasn't kidding. "Surveillance?"

"You watch her. Wait until she goes hunting for her next victim, then catch her in the act. Or wait until she leaves her office and you sneak in. You can go through her office computer and find her financial records."

"Are you serious?"

"You're a detective."

"Who's currently undercover posing as a millionaire for you, in case you forgot. I can't do a surveillance operation on Nicole. If she catches me, my cover is blown. And so is any of the trust I built with her."

"There's an easy fix for that. Don't get caught," William suggested, as though he wasn't asking Spencer to tail his ex-wife.

"No, no. I won't do that. We can get that type of proof without me blowing my cover or crossing a line."

"Crossing a line?" William gaped. "We're talking about a woman who has made a living on trapping men. That's her entire shtick. What line is that, exactly?"

"Nicole may not have a line, but I do. Surveilling her would cross it. You want concrete proof of her crimes? I will get it for you. I've already gotten close enough to her to get her phone. It's only a matter of time before I'm left alone with her office computer. Or get a hint that she's pulling a con on someone new."

William's eyes darkened. Spencer had a feeling this wasn't the answer he wanted. "Spencer, I respect your integrity and morals. They're one of the reasons I hired you. But I can't let Nicole get away with this again. If tailing her leads to us finding proof, I need to put her away, then so be it. You can't have it both ways. Either you're in or you're out."

"It's not a matter of in or out. You know where I stand. I'm in on this, but it has to be done my way. The right way."

"And the right way is tricking and deceiving Nicole? Wake up, Spencer. Everything we're doing is wrong. This whole goddamn situation is wrong. No one way is more wrong than the other, but one way is more effective."

Spencer shook his head. He could see the conversation was going nowhere. "We're done here."

"Yeah, I'll say," William said as he stood from his chair.

If he walked out that door with as many unspoken words as there were between them, Spencer knew he would regret it. "Look. I promise on my life that I will get this job done. All I'm asking for is a little faith."

William paused. With his back turned, his body relaxed. Spencer hoped it was because he had gotten through to him. "I'm trusting you, Spencer. You're the only person I trust right now. But don't expect me to have the same confidence as you do. There's a lot riding on this for me."

"I know. For me too."

At that, William nodded and left. Spencer watched him leave, the promise he made him still left on his tongue. Spencer waited until the door closed behind William before his shoulders slumped in defeat. He knew how far he was willing to go to bring justice for all those wronged by Nicole. The question was how far William would go for it. The fact Spencer didn't know the answer to that left a nervous pit in his stomach.

# 18

# Losing the Mask

While she spent her Monday at the office pretending not to have a hangover, Nicole planned for Tuesday to be different. She walked into her office with a cup of coffee, ready for a brand new day at work. For some, the possibility of going to jail would make them want to ditch going into work. Not for Nicole. Work was better than sitting at home wondering if a jail cell would be her next residence.

"Morning, boss lady," Reggie said with a warm smile.

On other days, Nicole might have pretended to be annoyed, but she reveled in hearing that greeting. She didn't know how many more times she would get to hear it. "Morning, Reg. Any messages?"

"Message in a form of flowers." Reggie nodded toward her office. "I already put them on your desk, and no. I didn't peek at the note, but share it with me when you've read it."

A large bouquet of white roses sat on her desk. Nicole was so used to flowers being delivered to her, she could have opened a flower shop like Lena Headley's character in *Imagine Me & You*. "Did the delivery boy tell you who these were from?"

"Sorry. He only gave me the name of the florist."

Nicole picked up the card, her stomach dropping as she read the note. "Debts eventually demand their due."

No sender named. No name was needed. It was William. His warning in his handwriting. He didn't even bother to try to disguise it. It wasn't the first threat Nicole had received from a mark. You didn't survive this long in this world without drawing them. What made this one different was how much it unnerved Nicole.

And that was before she noticed how the sunlight from her window disclosed faint markings on each of the petals. Nicole picked up the bouquet and walked to the window. She held the flowers up to the light and watched as letters slowly materialized, as if out of thin air. One by one, the labels revealed themselves.

"Gold-digger," "Bitch," "Liar," "Depraved," "Wretched," "Two-Faced," "Conniving," "Heartless," "Opportunist," "Vile," "Subhuman," "Irredeemable,"

Each petal on each of the twelve flowers had a word engraved on it. Each word was a reminder of all the things she's been called. All the things she was.

Nicole dropped the flowers into the trash and fell into her chair. She was no stranger to cruelty. In her former line of work, it came with the territory. It was a necessary evil to perform her job, but this was different. This was a direct attack against her. William wanted to rattle her, and it worked.

Words were one thing. His actions were another. He knew where she worked, knew where Maya performed. He wasn't playing fair. Nicole didn't want to play his game at all.

The worst part about his message was the reminder he wasn't going away. Her hopes for him to leave them alone relied on a private eye to find something they could use to blackmail him with. Nicole prayed this private eye was worth the money being spent on him because her and Maya's futures were in his hands.

She had never trusted someone with her future before. The feeling she had now told her why. She hated it, but would have to accept it. What other choice did she have?

Nicole's phone rang, bringing her out of her head. "Hello?"

"Nicole? Hey. It's Spencer," his strangely comforting voice said on the other end.

"Hi. What can I do for you?"

"Nothing. I wanted to check on you after yesterday. Kinda left you high and dry at my place. I apologize for that. I should've woken you, but you seemed like you could use the sleep."

"Oh, no, no. It's okay. You didn't have to. I was happy to get the extra rest. Thank you for being considerate and opening up your home to me. I'll have to return your clothes and robe the next time I see you."

"Did I ask for them back?"

Nicole smiled, biting her lip. "No, I suppose you didn't. But what am I going to do with a pair of boxers?"

Spencer chuckled, a deep, sexy sound that she hadn't realized he possessed. "Sleep in them. Make your boyfriend jealous, thinking you have someone on the side."

She swallowed a laugh as she leaned back against her headrest. "Is that your slick way of asking if I have a boyfriend?"

"Apparently, I'm not slick at all if you figured me out."

"The answer is no. I don't have a boyfriend. Not sure why that matters to you, but there you go."

"I was just curious."

"Curiosity satisfied, then." Nicole needed to find a way for them to get back on track before they derail further from it. "Uh — I'm sorry I fell asleep in the car and put you in an awkward situation. I never meant to put you in a position where you had to put me up in one of your guest rooms. Please tell me Nessa didn't see you have to carry me in?"

"No, no. She was spending the weekend at her grandmom's which let me have a night out in a bar. How much do you remember from that night?"

Nicole's cheeks heated at the question. "Um... I have a foggy memory of us playing pool, and me saying some very inappropriate jokes I would never otherwise say to a client sober."

"So what you're saying is I should get you drunk more?"

Nicole smiled at the joke, but it didn't reach her lips. She couldn't find it in herself to laugh. Her mind kept coming back to those petals, and the words etched into them.

"You still there, Nicole? To be clear, that was a joke."

"Yeah, I'm here. I'm sorry. For getting drunk and for embarrassing myself. You're my client and I want you to have respect for me and I feel like I have ruined any chance of you ever taking me serious again," she admitted.

"Hey, no, no. You don't need to apologize. I had a good time with you that night. It was fun to let loose and do something normal again. I haven't lost any respect for you, Nicole. Actually, I'm quite impressed. I was a little worried when you were drinking like a fish, but you're a pro."

A laugh escaped her then. "Thanks, Spencer. For the drinks and letting me confiding in you. No matter how inappropriate it was."

"I should be thanking you. You listened to me as I dumped my family troubles onto you. You gave advice I hadn't considered before."

"Oh, no. I am not the person you should take advice from. Or someone you should emulate."

"What do you mean? You have your own business that's up and running."

Nicole couldn't tell him there was a good chance she might be in jail and her business would be defunct as a result. Instead, she said,

"Work isn't everything. I have a relationship with my daughter that can at best be described as rocky. And she's building a life for herself that I fear one day I won't be a part of. Either by her choice or…" she trailed off, thinking back to those flowers. "…or my circumstances change."

"I'm sorry to hear that."

"Yeah, me too."

There was a pause. Nicole was waiting for him to ask more, but he didn't. "So… what are you doing today?"

"For Nessa's party? I have a meeting with a vendor tom-"

"No, I, uh, was wondering if you would be interested in taking an hour out of your day to spend with me and Nessa."

Spending a day with a precious five-year-old girl and a guy who inexplicably made her laugh sounded like a perfect distraction from her current situation. "Sure, but what would we be doing?"

"How do you feel about crashing a six-year-old's birthday party?"

\* \* \*

Nicole arrived at Spencer's house at 3 p.m.. The party wasn't scheduled to start until 4 p.m., but Nicole had the idea of them leaving early so they could buy a gift. If she was going to be a guest at a little girl's birthday party, she had to do it right. Even if the little girl was a bitch who hadn't invited Nessa. Killing them with kindness was never a method Nicole subscribed to, but it might just work in Nessa's case.

The elevator doors opened to Spencer's welcoming presence. "Hi. I'm—"

"Oh my God, is that Ms. Nicole?" Nessa shrieked as she ran out of the kitchen and met them. "I told Uncle Spence to get me when you got here!"

Nicole knelt to her level. "Hi Nessa. Are you excited about going to your friend's birthday party?"

"Cindy Green is not my friend. Friends don't leave other friends off their invite list."

When Spencer informed Nicole that Cindy invited everyone in her class to her birthday party, but Nessa, Nicole was furious. Spencer told her she wasn't alone. It was the reason they decided to crash the party.

"She did a bad thing, but don't worry. We'll buy her the greatest gift she's ever received and she'll be begging to be your friend."

"We're getting her a puppy?"

"No. Puppies are not gifts, but we will find her a gift she likes."

Nessa's mouth dropped. "Can we get her a pony?"

"Absolutely not," Spencer interjected. "Ms. Nicole and I will brainstorm while you go put on your socks and shoes."

Nessa ran up the stairs to her room. Spencer gave Nicole a knowing look. "Thanks for coming and joining this mess. I'll need someone to bring Nessa home when I'm arrested for trespassing."

There he was, doing it again. Doing the impossible. Coaxing a laugh out of Nicole. "You'll be fine. Worse comes to worst, you can flirt with Cindy's mom and get out of trouble."

"You say that like it's worked in your favor before."

"It has, but the key is to not get caught by their partner. Otherwise, you're in more trouble than you started in."

"I have a feeling I'll learn a lot about your past before our partnership is over."

"Don't be so sure. I don't like to rehash the past. I prefer to keep it in the rearview."

He nodded, considering her words. "Is there something you're running from?"

"Aren't we all?"

"I think we are, but not all of us have the skills to escape."

Nicole looked at him with a quirked brow. She didn't expect a response like that. "How are we on time?"

"We've got an hour before we need to head over. Any gifts you used to lure the popular girls into befriending you when you were a kid?"

"Nope. I wasn't popular growing up. I didn't make it a priority to learn how to befriend them."

"Why weren't you popular?"

"How do I word this that doesn't sound so pathetic?" Nicole pondered, then sighed. "Because I bounced from one foster home to another, I couldn't stay at a school long enough to make friends. On the flip side, I sure did garner a reputation. One that followed me from school to school. I was branded the troubled girl everyone should steer clear of. See, I told you. Pathetic."

"Yeah. You're right. Those kids were pathetic for choosing to believe those rumors about you instead of choosing to get to know you."

She shrugged. "Kids are mean. I think it's to prepare us for how mean adults are going to be."

"That sounds like a story."

"You really want to hear all my childhood traumas?"

"I want to hear what makes you, you."

Nicole stared at the ceiling as she remembered the story she spent her whole adult life avoiding. A story she had locked away so that no one could sneak a peek. Now she was ready to unlock it for someone to hear. There was a trusting and honest quality about Spencer. One that she wanted to embrace, not hide from.

"My senior year of high school, I tried to make friends with the popular kids. I thought, what the hell. It's my last year, and if I'm ever going to make friends, this is my last chance. I got assigned to be this popular guy's lab partner. All year, we worked together and built a good relationship. For our final project, I invited him to my house."

"You never did that before?"

"No. I changed houses and schools so often. I never felt comfortable asking or bringing someone over. But it was for a school assignment, so I did it. When he came over, we worked for a bit until his interests turned from science to sex."

"How old were you?"

"Seventeen. I wondered about it, but I wasn't seeking it out. Then and there in the moment, I didn't want to disappoint him. And I thought, if not him, then who? I didn't have any suitors knocking on my door, and I didn't think I ever would. So we had sex. It was okay. A little painful, but it could've been worse. Then it was."

"What happened?"

"My foster parents came home from Bible Study to find us in bed. They threw him out and berated me. Followed it up by throwing out my clothes. Ending it by slamming the door in my face. That's how I became homeless at seventeen."

Spencer's face fell. "Did you contact social services?"

"No. What was the point? I was turning 18 in a month and was going to be thrown out, anyway. It ended up being okay. The experience taught me to be strong."

"You shouldn't have had to be strong so young."

"Nessa shouldn't have to be either, but we aren't always dealt the hand we deserve."

"Is that why you accepted my offer to join us? You wanted to help her get a win?"

Nicole nodded. Nessa reminded her of herself. She didn't want to see her be hurt. "I'm going to help her win over her classmates if it's the last thing I do."

"How do we do that?"

"By winning over that brat, Cindy Green. Nessa will need the upper hand to win over the rest."

Spencer smiled. "And how are we going to win her over? I'm afraid puppies and ponies are out of my budget."

"Why don't we just give her money? Money gets their attention, and their parents' approval." Nessa hopped down the stairs, proud of her suggestion.

Nicole and Spencer shared a knowing look.

When Cindy unwrapped the large gift box and it revealed a check for $2,000 with the inscription, "This check is non-refundable. Happy birthday," the crowd went silent. Cindy stared at the check in astonishment and then at her mom, who was gawking.

"Mommy, can we get a puppy with this money?"

Her mom, Maggie, laughed nervously. "Let's wait and see what your father says first, honey."

"Oh, we're so getting a puppy," she whispered to her friend sitting next to her.

"Cindy, is there something you would like to say to Nessa and her uncle?"

"Yes!" She turned to face Nessa, who was sitting further down the table, a chair having to be added to accommodate her. "Thank you for the money. When I get my puppy, you can come over and play with it."

"That'll be awesome. I would love to. What would you name the puppy?"

"If it's a boy…"

As the chatter faded around her, Nicole's attention was solely on Nessa's radiant smile. It had been too long since she had taken joy in another person's happiness. Gently, she leaned into Spencer's side, their shoulders bumping as they stood, watching the children with the other parents. He reciprocated her nudge by bumping her hip with his own, his grin mirroring hers.

After they ate the pizza and cut the cake, Nicole went over to Nessa, using her chair to bend down and meet her gaze. "Are you enjoying the party?"

"I am. Crashing parties is fun. I'll have to do it again."

"I don't think you'll have to. After everyone sees your party, they'll never leave you out of anything again."

"Do you think they'll come to my party if I ask them?"

"Why don't you see for yourself?" Nicole pulled out the custom designed party invitations she got made for Nessa's party. They were printed on white cards, with pink and purple balloons adorning the borders, her name in gold glitter like the star she was. Nessa's eyes widened as she took one, tracing the details with her small fingers.

"These are so pretty," she whispered in awe.

"Why don't you go around and pass them out?"

She took them, then skipped around the party, handing out invitations to her classmates as each promised to attend. Nicole looked around for Spencer to see if he had the same stupid grin on his face that she had. When she found him, he was not grinning. Quite the opposite, in fact.

He was wearing a slight frown that the moms he was talking to either didn't notice or ignored as they talked his ear off about something. Nicole stood and went in for the rescue.

As she approached Spencer, she could feel the tension in his demeanor. His jaw clenched as he nodded along with the mothers' chatter. His eyes darted around as if looking for a way out. Nicole stepped beside him and placed a hand on his shoulder, as if to ask if he was all right. He looked down at her hand and gave a small shake of his head.

"Oh hi, Nicole. We were just discussing how noble we thought Spencer was for taking care of his niece while his sister is out of commission," the mom named Donna explained.

"It really is an amazing thing," said another mother named Susan. "We would love it if Spencer would join the PTA. It would be nice to have a man present at the meetings."

"Yeah. It would be nice," Kate interjected. "But if Spencer doesn't expect Nessa will be staying with him for much longer, it's probably best he passes the invitation along to his sister."

Nicole understood why Spencer was looking for a way out of this conversation. He was Nessa's guardian, but these women considered it to be a foregone conclusion his sister would get custody of her back. He must have felt hopeless hearing them discuss his place in Nessa's life as temporary.

As the three moms continued to prattle on, Spencer's discomfort radiated off him. While Nicole felt her own protective instincts kicking in. "Excuse me, ladies. I don't know if you know this, but it's considered disrespectful to make assumptions about someone's living situation."

The three mothers exchanged looks of surprise, taken aback by the comment.

Donna awkwardly cleared her throat. "Oh. We just assumed-"

"That's the problem right there. Assuming instead of asking for clarification. Spencer is doing an incredible job of taking care of Nessa. It's not for you to speculate on his or his sister's plans for Nessa's future."

Susan shifted uncomfortably. "We're sorry. We didn't mean to be disrespectful," she muttered. The other mothers echoed her.

"Thanks," Spencer accepted their apology. "For what it's worth, I would love to be a part of PTA. I'm sorry for not putting my hat in the ring earlier."

Nicole didn't move her hand from Spencer's shoulder, even after the mothers moved on to speak with the other parents. Once they were alone, Spencer sighed with relief. "Thanks for the save," he muttered, his tone still a little off.

"You saved me from a jerk in a bar. I saved you from a bunch of nosy moms. I guess that makes us even."

"No way. Those moms were much scarier than that guy at the bar."

Nicole smiled, having to agree. She dropped her hand from his shoulder and asked, "What was their deal, anyway?"

"I guess the only men who show up to these things are dads, not single guys in their thirties."

"What you're telling me is they find you irresistible," she teased. "You know what? I can see it. The good looks, the money, the nobleness, the prospect of you not being saddled with a kid forever. You're an attractive option."

"You think I'm an attractive option?"

Nicole blushed, her words catching up with her. She opened her mouth, ready to backtrack, but she couldn't deny what she said was true. "I just mean they would find you an attractive option."

"Uh-huh," he said with a sly smile.

Nicole rolled her eyes, not wanting to feed his ego. "You know what I meant."

"Sure I did."

Nicole ignored Spencer's gaze as it swept over her. She forced herself not to make eye contact, choosing to watch the party unfold in front of them. What she couldn't ignore was the burn of her fiery cheeks and the smile that remained plastered on her lips.

# 19

# The Truth Narrated by a Liar

It was dark outside by the time they arrived back at Spencer's penthouse. Nessa spent the ride raving about the party, her new friendships, and wishes for her own party. "Can my cake be an ice cream cake? I liked Cindy's cake, but it was a little dry."

"An ice cream cake sounds perfect. I'll make the arrangements for it," Nicole said, catching Nessa's gaze in the rearview mirror.

"And we can invite everyone from school?"

"Not everyone, Nessa, but yes, I'll invite the friends you want," Spencer conceded.

"Sweet!" She opened her car door and started running toward the doors of the building but made a sharp turn back to the adults as they exited the vehicle. "Ms. Nicole, can you come inside with us? I want to show you something."

"Um..." she looked at Spencer. He gave her a nod, not wanting to disappoint Nessa after the incredible day she had.

"What do you want to show her?"

"A surprise. It's a good surprise. I promise."

Nessa led the way to the penthouse. Inside their place, Nessa grabbed Nicole's hand and tugged her up to her room. Spencer couldn't quite fathom the direction today went. From calling Nicole to check in on her to inviting her to a six-year-old's birthday party, he couldn't have seen what a great time they would have.

Nessa had an incredible day, and Nicole was a large part of the reason for that. He was grateful to her for that, but reminded himself after every good deed she did today, she was still at her heart a con artist. He had no doubt she was going through the motions of a kind act to earn his trust. A small voice in his head said he didn't mind if it was all a ruse. He enjoyed their day together as much as Nessa did.

If he knew it was all a part of her act, there wasn't any way for him to get hurt. Unlike her marks, Spencer knew who the real Nicole was, what she was after. As long as he could differentiate between the real Nicole and the role she was playing, he would be fine.

Nicole came down the stairs with Nessa's sketchpad in her hands. Her eyes were on the drawings and not where she was going. Her foot caught on the last step, but she didn't tumble to the floor. Spencer was there in a nanosecond, having seen the spill before it could happen.

He caught her elbow and held her steady against his chest. "Whoa, you okay?"

"I promise I didn't sneak alcohol into a children's party. I swear I'm not drunk."

"So you just like falling when I'm around? Looking for me to carry you again?"

"Not as much as you seemed to be looking forward to carrying me."

"I was looking to be a gentleman that night."

She looked up at him, the ceiling light haloing around her eyes. "And now?"

Spencer was too close, so close he could see her breath catching. Smell the coconut oil in her hair, the light strawberry aroma of her perfume. He swallowed thickly. Knowing he should let go of her, but finding himself unable to do it.

"And now what?" he asked.

"Are you going to be a gentleman? Or ask me to repay the favor?"

"I'll never ask anything of you, Nicole." His tone was lower than he intended. The way Nicole was looking at him differed from the times she watched him before.

"Really? Cause I don't mind. Repaying the favor. Can't have you holding something over me." She leaned forward, and her hand rested on his chest.

The contact shot through him. Spencer swallowed again, the action difficult. "I'm not the kind of guy who uses a situation to his advantage."

"You're better than most men."

"Or maybe the men you've met just suck."

She chuckled. "Probably a little of both."

Spencer searched for signs on Nicole's face for wanting him to pull away. He came up empty. The truth was, he liked having her there, against his chest.

There he could feel her soft breaths against his lips. The rise and fall of her chest as her heart raced. He didn't want to analyze it, didn't want to think about the way his own body reacted to her touch. The way he felt more comfortable with her than he had with anyone he held this close to him before.

"Uncle Spence, look what I gave to Ms. Nicole," Nessa interrupted. Spencer dropped his arms to his side, stepping back from Nicole. Feeling a sudden gratefulness to his niece for her interruption.

"What did you give her?"

"Here." Nicole held the sketchpad open and showed him. Pages were dedicated to drawings of flowers, beaches, skylines, and more. Nessa kept her sketches closely guarded. She only showed Spencer ones that she deemed perfect. To see her showing Nicole them, imperfections and all, made Spencer realize how much Nessa had come to like and trust her.

"Wow. Nessa, these are amazing!"

"Your uncle is right. You have a talent for this."

"You're not just saying that, are you?" Nessa looked at Nicole skeptically.

"I'm not. You're a natural. Have you ever thought about pursuing this? Taking a drawing class?"

"I don't want my art judged."

"That's not a bad thing. Not all criticism is bad."

"No, but it feels bad."

Nicole took a deep breath. "You're right. Good criticism will help you better your skills. Bad criticism will try to hurt you. Your dad will try to shield it from you as best as he can, but there will be people who try to bring you down. But can I ask you something?"

"Sure."

"Do you love drawing?"

She nodded.

"Do you get enjoyment out of making art?"

"Yeah. I like turning a blank page into something beautiful."

"Then you should do what brings you joy and forget about the people who try to put you down. Some people will always rain on other people's parades because they see how happy they are. They're jealous they don't have that for themselves. Draw because you love it. It's a gift people envy you for having. Don't stop because you're scared of what those people may say about it. You put your art out there and you'll be braver than most. And you can be proud of yourself for that."

Spencer stood silently, letting her words sink in. Her words weren't a ruse. They were sincere. He could feel Nicole's passion. Feel she meant what she said. Besides talking about the rain, it was one of the first times she spoke and he knew she wasn't putting on an act.

"Okay," Nessa finally said. "I'll keep drawing. Thanks Ms. Nicole."

"You're welcome, sweetheart."

"Uncle Spence, can Ms. Nicole stay and read me a bedtime story?"

"Only if you change into your pajamas."

"Deal!"

When she was up the stairs, he turned to Nicole and said, "You don't actually have to do that. I'll tell her you had to go."

"Actually, I would like to read her one. If that's okay with you."

It was more than okay with him, which scared Spencer. "I don't mind at all."

* * *

Spencer stood in the doorway of Nessa's room as she finally gave out and fell asleep without protest. Nicole put the book back on her shelf and slowly inched herself out of the room. Spencer closed the door behind them. "You're really great with her," he said when they were downstairs again.

"You sound surprised."

"I didn't mean to. I just know—"

"I have a complicated relationship with my daughter so I couldn't possibly know how to talk to kids? Spencer, I'm aware. I get it. Trust me, I know I'm a shit mom. You don't have to worry about me filling Nessa's head with nonsense."

"Hey." He touched her elbow, stilling her long enough to look at him. "I'm sorry. I didn't mean anything by it."

"No. I snapped and I shouldn't have. Today, before you called, was a lot."

"Do you want to talk about it?"

She went quiet, then reached into her back pocket and pulled a card out. She handed it to him. Spencer took it, not understanding its significance until he read the words. "Debts eventually demand their due? What is this?"

Nicole sighed, making her way over to the couch. Spencer sat beside her, not wanting her too far away from him. "This note came with flowers to my office today. I'm being threatened by someone I screwed over in the past. This isn't his first threat, either. My daughter told me he tried to come backstage to one of her theater shows. I've been threatened by many men in the past, but this was the first one that actually got to me. I don't know how I can protect myself or my daughter from him. So I'm feeling more of a failure than usual."

For the first time since he'd met her, Spencer could hear the fear in Nicole's voice. Her tough as nails exterior was crumbling right before his eyes. As a con artist, he doubted she ever showed her vulnerable side to anyone for fear they might use it against her. Yet, here she was, showing him her soft underbelly.

Nicole trusted him. She wasn't scared of him. Knowing that should've filled Spencer with relief, but it made him sick. He was the last person she should trust. "Who is this guy?" he brought himself to ask.

"His name is William. William Harrison."

The pit in Spencer's stomach grew deeper. "Are you sure?"

"Yes. I confronted him about it, and he owed up to following my daughter. To wanting to make our lives a living hell. So far, he's living up to his promise."

The William she was describing was not the William he had come to know. It may have only been a few weeks, but the William Spencer knew was the one responsible for the penthouse they were currently sitting in. The suits in his closet were paid for by William. He was paying for the expenses of Nessa's party.

Sure, he was a flawed man. He made mistakes in his past, but everyone did. His anger directed at Nicole made sense, considering what she took from him. His pursuit of justice against her wasn't a bad thing unless he was taking things into his own hands.

Spencer was left with a choice in who he should trust. William, his client. Or Nicole, the con woman he was investigating. The answer seemed to be clear. "What did you do to him to warrant him coming after you?"

When Nicole lied, Spencer would know what she was doing. That the pain in her voice was a part of her act. A ploy to make him feel sorry for her. So when she looked him dead in the eyes and said, "I conned him out of thousands." Spencer couldn't believe it.

The lies he expected to hear weren't there. And for the first time since meeting her, Nicole was being 100% honest with him. He didn't know what to do or how to respond. "What?"

"It's true. I'm a con artist. Was," she corrected herself. "I used to run a scam with my daughter. We would pick out a millionaire and I would begin a relationship with him. By the next year, we were married, but I would gradually pull away from him. Sending him into the arms of my daughter. Him cheating broke our prenup, and I got a huge check, then we disappeared."

Spencer knew all the details. William had told them to him, but hearing it from Nicole in all its raw truth was another thing. "Why are you telling me this? I could turn you in to the police for all you know."

"You won't. Who else is going to plan Nessa's party?" She tried to smile, but it didn't reach her eyes.

"That's not funny, Nicole."

"I know, I'm sorry. I don't know why I told you, except I know I don't want to lie to you. Something about you makes me not want to lie. I've lied to everyone who has come into my life. I don't want to do the same to you."

He scanned her face. Not for signs she was telling the truth or lying, but for the woman who was sitting across from him. She was no longer the Nicole he met in her office weeks ago. This woman was scared.

That's why he didn't make a play to turn his phone on and record her confession. It's what he should have done. It was the evidence he needed to solve this case, but Spencer already crossed one line to try to end this case. He wouldn't cross another.

"I know what you're thinking. This is my karma. What I've had coming for stealing since I was a teenager. Maybe it is. I just wish he would leave my daughter out of this. It's my fault she was ever involved. I should have protected her, but I didn't. And now I can't protect her from him. If he wants to stalk her, there's nothing I can do to stop him."

"You could turn yourself in. Give him what he wants."

"Yeah. That's what I thought too, but when I offered, he said he would just keep doing it. He would still go after her even if I went to prison." A single tear rolled down to her chin. "William's not after justice. He's after revenge. He wants me to hurt as much as I hurt him. Going after my daughter," her voice cracked. "He knows how much she means to me. Going after her is how he gets to me."

Inexplicably and with little thought, Spencer reached out and wiped the tear off her face. His fingers trailed her cheek, the touch sending shivers down his spine. Nicole's gaze went up to meet his. Her brown eyes wide as they bore into his. Her bottom lip trembled as they stared at each other.

"Is this how you feel when someone talks about Nessa being taken away from you?" she asked, her voice barely a whisper.

"Yes."

"Then you must hurt all the time. How do you manage it?"

"I'm not sure how," he whispered, his thumb grazing her jaw. He swallowed hard. "By enjoying the time I do have with her. It's never promised we'll have another day."

Her eyes went down to his lips and back up. She released a low sigh and leaned back into the couch, further away from him. Her hand rested on top of his on his knee, her touch sending heat up his arm. Spencer left his other hand against her cheek, allowing her to nuzzle into his touch.

"Thank you."

"For what?"

"Not judging me when you have every right to. For not kicking me out when I admitted I was a thief. And for the last three days, you've done more for me than anyone I've ever known. You've been more generous to me than I deserve."

"You've done the same for me."

"Have I?"

"You have." He meant it.

They were silent. Neither knowing what to say next. What do you say to comfort the woman you're investigating for a client who's stalking her and her daughter? How could Spencer make the situation better?

He was the first to speak, his voice low. "I wish I could make this better for you. I want you to know, whatever happens, I'll do what I can to keep you safe. I got you."

She closed her eyes tight, laying her head against his shoulder. "There's nothing you or I can do."

"We'll see about that. No one is untouchable. Not even William Harrison."

"I hope not."

Spencer could sense her unease, her uncertainty, as she melted into him. Her head was against his shoulder as he hooked her legs over his lap. He never cradled another person before. Never interested in the closeness and intimacy of the act.

Holding Nicole, letting her derive what she needed from the act, made him change his mind. Something about the touch felt right. It shouldn't have. He was supposed to be sending her away to jail, but as she sighed in relief in his chest, Spencer couldn't imagine sending her anywhere.

As she snuggled further into him, he held her tighter, hoping the gesture would convey that his offer was more than just words. Spencer wouldn't let Nicole get hurt. Not when he had the means to prevent it.

## 20

## Breaking Old Patterns

Nicole awoke, disoriented and confused. Slowly, she opened her eyes and adjusted to the sight of Nessa in front of her, slyly smiling. "Do you mind waking my uncle? I have school," she said before going into the kitchen.

Nicole looked at her hand and saw she was still on the couch. She sat up and saw Spencer asleep under her. Her body draped over his, their legs tangled together. She remembered falling asleep, her head resting against his chest. The memory sent warmth through her body.

Underneath her, Spencer slept soundly, his face calm, his breath steady. Almost too peaceful to wake. That's when Nicole got the idea. She got out from under him, careful not to wake him. When she was free, she walked into the kitchen, where Nessa sat on a stool eating Frosted Flakes.

"How would you feel about me taking you to school?"

"Really? You would take me?"

"If you're okay with that, I would love to."

"Yes! Please!"

Nicole smiled. Spencer was there for her last night in a way no one had ever been before. The least she could do was let him sleep in. "Do you know your school's address?"

Nessa nodded. "It's in the car's navigation."

"Great." Nicole walked back into the living room and put on her pumps. She grabbed her purse and Spencer's keys. Worried he might wake up and think she stole Nessa and his car, she left a note. "Taking Nessa to school. See you soon. -N."

When they pulled up to Nessa's school, the kids were lining up in front of the building. The teachers monitoring them as they entered. When some of the kids from Cindy's party saw Nessa, they waved. "Nessa!" they greeted.

"Well, go on. Have fun with your friends."

"Thanks, Ms. Nicole."

"You did all the work by being your cool self."

"I mean more than just yesterday. My Uncle Spence needed a friend as much as I did. Thank you for being his."

"It's the easiest job I've ever had."

With that, Nessa got out of the car and greeted her friends. Nicole felt her heart swell. The love niece and uncle, father and daughter, had for each other was pure and beautiful. She was thankful she could see it and be a part of it.

She hoped to remain a witness to it, but she couldn't be sure. Spencer acted accepting of her past last night, but having time to think it over, he could change his mind. Even if he didn't, it was one thing for him to accept her past. It didn't mean he would want his niece hanging around her, a criminal.

As she pulled away, her phone rang. She answered it through the car's bluetooth. "Does this mean we're even again? I saved you from face planting on my stairs and you get my kid in school on time?"

"What can I say? I'm a saint."

"Clearly," Spencer remarked. She could hear the smile in his voice.

"I hope you're not mad that I took your car."

"Nah. Nessa likes spending time with you. I would never deny her that."

"So you won't keep her away from me?"

"Why would I do that?"

"You're still new to this parenting thing, huh? Let me fill you in on a basic rule. Keep your children away from criminals."

He laughed. "You're not a criminal, Nicole."

"I am."

"Okay, fine. You are, but I don't care."

"Why not?" She leaned into her seat, really wanting to hear his answer when she wasn't even sure what she wanted to hear him say.

A quiet moment passed between them before his voice came through again. "Everything in me is telling me not to trust you. That I should let you return my car, then kick you out of my life. I'm not going to do that and that may make me an idiot."

"So why aren't you kicking me to the curb?"

"Because the woman I want to kick out is the one who conned people without an iota of guilt. The woman who dragged her daughter into her scams. The liar, the schemer, the manipulator. The woman I want gone already is."

Nicole took a small, involuntary gulp. "And the other woman?"

"The version of you now? If she doesn't mind, I would like to keep her around."

"She doesn't mind. Not in the least," she replied, her voice the softest she's ever heard it.

"I'm glad."

"Me too."

Spencer took a deep inhale. "Nicole, I'm going against my instincts here, but I'm not going away. Not unless you ask me to. And if that makes me an idiot, at least I'll be a happy one."

His words had such an effect on her, her heart ached. It was so nice, the idea of someone trusting her. Not Hamilton. Or Mitchell. Or Wright. But, her. Nicole. Making it all the better was that it was him who was trusting her.

Aiden Spencer was a good man. As instinctively as a gut feeling or observant as a noticing a deep hidden red flag, Nicole knew he was. A person's goodness or lack thereof wasn't something anyone could hide. Spencer wore his on his sleeve.

No one person could be all good or bad, but they could be more of one or the other. The good in Spencer outweighed any of the bad in him. Nicole was sure of it. To have someone good believe there was good in you too was a feeling she hadn't experienced in a long time. As she sat there, trying to comprehend the weight of his words, Nicole felt something shift inside her.

It was like a door had opened, one she had thought was closed forever. It would be safer to close it and turn around, but knowing that wasn't enough to compel her not to step through it. "How can you be sure you're not making a mistake to trust me?"

"Because the mistake would be not trusting you. You wouldn't have confided in me last night if you weren't scared. I know I can help you. I'm not going anywhere until I do exactly that."

Her eyes blinked back the tears that had welled up. She didn't deserve the chance to get to know a guy like Spencer, but he was there anyway. "You'll never know how much that means to me."

The next words Nicole said to him were face to face. Spencer was standing outside his building, waiting for her to arrive with his car. She parked and stepped out. As he met her halfway, Nicole waved his keys at him.

"I think I found something that belongs to you."

Spencer smiled, taking and tucking them in his pocket. "Feel free to find them again if it gets you to come and talk to me."

Nicole couldn't promise that. Opening up to people was something she had long ago stopped doing and people stopped inviting her to. "We'll see."

"I mean it, Nicole. If you need anything, I'm here."

She heard those words before. From foster parents to partners. Always without meaning, she knew.

Nicole changed subjects, asking. "How was your sleep? As peaceful as it looked?"

"Yeah. I dreamed of a woman named Nicole."

"Oh, really? Was she a nightmare, or a dream come true?"

He leaned closer to her. "What do you think?"

Nicole's heart pounded in her chest at the closeness. The smell of his aftershave. The pink of his lips shimmering from his chapstick. The mint of his toothpaste. She could practically taste him, but played coy.

"If she's anything like me, she's gotten confused for both before."

"Let me clear up the confusion. She was the best dream I've had in a long time."

He was a step closer now. His gaze, the one she had gotten lost in before, locked onto hers, unwavering. They had a way of looking straight into her, of seeing her in a light no one else had in a long time. Nicole felt exposed yet covered, raw yet safe.

"Is that so?" she asked, her voice breathless.

"Mhm."

They had to stop. Nicole needed them to stop this. Her carefully constructed boundaries were collapsing around her anytime she was around Spencer. Not by Spencer knocking them down, but by Nicole tearing them down for him. If he got close enough, she feared there would be nothing left to separate them.

She had to stop it. "I'm sorry about using your couch last night."

Spencer blinked at the sharp turn she took. "It wasn't a problem. You can use it any time you want or the bed if it's more comfortable."

"Spencer," she said in a reproaching tone. "I'm working for you. I'm planning your niece's birthday. That's the extent of our relationship. Or what the extent should be."

"You're telling me to back off, but all I'm hearing is that you're telling yourself the same thing."

She opened her mouth to deny, but the sound of her ringing phone interrupted her. "Saved by the bell."

"Shut up."

He chuckled. "Call me. Whether it's professional or personal, call me. I'll pick up."

She watched him go, annoyed he was right. Annoyed that he wasn't letting her put up her walls again. Annoyed that she was enjoying him seeing all of her. The good and the flawed.

"Hello," she answered, directing her attention to her caller.

"Did you forget we have a meeting with the potential private investigator today?"

Nicole looked at the date on her phone and realized she had. "I'm sorry. I've had a busy couple of days."

"He's meeting us at my dad's in the next hour. Do you think you can make it or will I have to handle it on my own?" Kennedy didn't sound annoyed, but Nicole could tell her absence would bother her.

"I'll be there. See you soon."

\* \* \*

Since her last sleepover at Spencer, Nicole kept some fresh clothes in her car. So when she arrived at Eric's, she appeared as professional as she needed to look for the meeting. When she parked, the cars there were Kennedy's, Eric's and… Maya's. As she expected, her daughter was inside, waiting on the living room couch with Kennedy.

"Maya, I didn't know you would be here."

"I thought it was about time we brought Maya into the fold," Kennedy offered.

"By fold, you mean—"

"She told me everything. From William trying to blackmail her to you deciding to meet with him. Seriously, mom, what were you thinking?"

Nicole didn't appreciate being scolded. There was a lot Maya could criticize her for that she would take lying down, but not this. "I was thinking the sooner I handled this, the better for you. The last thing you need to worry about is William dangling our pasts over you."

"Mom, I'm not a child. You don't need to handle things for me. We have always been a team, working together to solve whatever problem came our way. Have you forgotten that?"

"Of course not."

"Then why try to shield this from me?"

"Because you shouldn't have to focus your energy on this anymore," Nicole answered in one long string of words. "It's been almost a year since the last con. You're making something of yourself with your show. William has the power to take what you're building away from you because of me. I gave him that ammunition. It's my job to take it away."

"I get it. You feel guilty. You want to take William out of the equation to rid yourself of it, but you don't have to keep me in the dark," Maya reinforced. She didn't sound quite as annoyed as before. "You didn't cause this problem by yourself and you don't have to fix it by yourself either."

Nicole nodded, understanding Maya's frustration. She wouldn't have liked the situation either if the roles were reversed. "I'm sorry. I thought I was looking out for you, but I see now I was taking your agency away. That wasn't my intention. You've just made incredible strives to distance yourself from our pasts. The last thing I wanted was to drag you back into it and have you get your hands dirty."

"These hands?" She waved them in a jazz hands motion. "Do they look dirty to you?"

"No, but when was the last time you had a manicure, sweetheart?"

Maya gasped, grabbing a pillow to throw at her mother. Nicole laughed as she caught it, not noticing Eric walking into the living room.

"I see we're getting along much better now," he said.

"Eric," Nicole greeted. "Thank you so much for paying for the PI. You didn't have to considering our history."

"You know me. I choose to remember the good of our relationship, no matter how fake it was. And everyone in this room loves Maya and won't let anything happen to her, or you by extension."

Nicole caught a lucky break choosing to scam Eric Hayes. She couldn't have foreseen any of the others being as forgiving or generous as Eric had been to her and Maya. "I will repay you for this."

"Be there on their wedding day instead of prison and we'll call it even."

"Dad!" Kennedy exclaimed.

"Oh, I forgot how touchy you two are on wedding talk." He did not forget, but the blushes on Maya and Kennedy's faces were well worth their daughters' embarrassment.

The doorbell rung, cutting the teasing short. Eric opened the door and in walked their potential savior, Thomas Fisher. Nicole had never met a private eye before, but assumed they more or less resembled Thomas. With his leather jacket, faded denim jeans, and slicked back hair. He looked like the kind of guy you would hire to find out if your spouse was cheating, and he found the proof to back it up.

"Good afternoon, Mr. Hayes," he said, shaking Eric's hand before shaking Nicole's, Kennedy's, and Maya's.

They led him over to the dining room table and expanded on the details explained to him over the phone. "We're interested in getting this man out of our lives permanently. Within legal means, of course. No hit mans," Nicole added at the end of the summary, driving their point home. "Do you think you could help us?"

"I can find skeletons in anyone's closet. And rich middle-aged white men have enough of them to fill Narnia. I'm confident I can find something that would get him off your backs, but I need to know how you want to do this."

Maya leaned in, listening harder. "What do you mean?"

"The approach I take is up to you and what you're comfortable with. Looking into his background, monitoring, surveillance—"

Nicole heard enough. "Whatever you need to do to find a weakness to exploit. Do it."

"Absolutely," Maya agreed. "Whatever it takes."

Eric nodded. "I'll cover the costs."

"We can all pitch in," Kennedy offered. "Since this is affecting our entire family."

Nicole smiled to herself. She couldn't have predicted that when plotting to steal the Hayes family' fortune, that today, they would consider her and her daughter family. It was a gift, better than any money could have gotten her.

"Okay, let's do this," Thomas said.

With a sigh, Nicole reached into her pocket. "I have the thing to get you started."

She slid the note across the table. Thomas's eyes took a moment to grasp the unsettling nature of William's words. "Debts eventually demand their due," he read aloud. "He sent this to you?"

Nicole nodded. "Yesterday, to my office, via a flower delivery boy."

"Oh mom, I'm so sorry." Maya put a hand on her shoulder, easing the tension in Nicole as best she could.

"I'm fine. What matters is that you," she directed at Thomas, her voice firm and clear. "Get this done."

Handing over control to another person was against every one of Nicole's core beliefs. But so was confiding and letting someone in like she had with Spencer. So far, that move hadn't bitten her in the ass. She had to trust this one wouldn't either.

# 21

# Maverick Gone Rogue

Spencer couldn't remember the last time he was this angry at someone. Even when Melanie ditched town, Spencer felt a sense of gratefulness toward her. She didn't take her daughter with her as she began another alcohol-driven downward spiral. At her sickest, Melanie would still do everything in her power to protect her daughter.

He couldn't say the same for his client. William Harrison was no better than the lowlifes his father chased down his entire career. Spencer should have never agreed to work with him. He should have turned him away. His desperation for money allowed him to team up with a man on a warpath. It blinded him from the truth of William's motives. He never wanted justice. He wanted revenge.

William had used Spencer as a pawn in his game, and now Spencer was ready to free himself from his strings. For good.

"Spencer, you told me to let you know when Mr. Harrison arrived. Well, he's here," Yara informed him, not yet let in on the developing situation.

"Let him in." Spencer came around his desk, sitting on the edge. His head bowed, not sure how he was going to confront William without letting his emotions get the best of him. And he had no time to figure it out.

A second after Yara left his office, William entered in her place. Spencer hadn't told William what the meeting was pertaining to, so he was clueless regarding what was about to unfold.

"Hey man," William started, sitting in the seat mere inches away from Spencer's bouncing knee. "I know we didn't leave things in a great place the last time we met, but I'm hoping we can move past that. We have to do what we can to close this case."

Spencer wouldn't waste time entertaining this moron for another second. "You're nothing but a liar."

William blinked, looking surprised at Spencer's tone. "Huh?"

"You heard me. You're a fucking liar. A moronic little boy stuck in a middle-aged man's body who gets his kicks by playing God with people's lives."

"Look, Spencer, I'm not sure where this is coming from—"

"You know exactly what this is about. Your vendetta against Nicole Taylor."

"Vendetta?"

"Are you going to pretend you haven't been going after Nicole and her daughter on your own? That you haven't been following them or sending them threatening messages?"

"No, of course not. How could you even think that? Where are you getting this from?" William was playing the confused card. Spencer didn't believe for one second he didn't know what he was talking about. He had been played once by William. He wouldn't be played again.

"You're lying."

"I'm not. What are you talking—" He stopped himself, a realization dawning over him. "Nicole. She tried to spin a story about me to you, didn't she? I should've seen this coming. That's right up her alley. What I'm really surprised about is how easily she got you to believe her. Spencer, do you remember who we're dealing with here? A manipulative con woman who has stolen a total of millions. And you think she's a trustworthy source?"

"It doesn't matter who she is or what she's done. When she told me the things you did, I saw how scared she was. There was genuine fear in her eyes. Not something she could've faked. You threatened her daughter. You sent her flowers with a note warning her that debts were coming due. She's terrified, and you're the one behind that."

William stood, shaking his head. "She's the one lying to you, Spencer. She's spinning a story to get you to sympathize with her. To make herself look like a victim when we know she's nothing of the sort."

"She gave me the note with the threat."

"She could have sent it to herself. Or here's a novel idea. Another person she conned found out about her and sent the message to her. Nicole has made a lot of enemies in her day. I'm sure some of them are angry enough at her to send her a note like that."

"She told me she met with you and that you admitted to wanting to ruin her life. Not going after justice or sending her to jail, but to make her life hell. Explain yourself out of that one," he demanded.

"I never met with her."

"Come on, William!"

"I'm telling you the truth," his voice raised, matching Spencer's. "Do I have to pull teeth to get you to believe me? Why are you taking Nicole's word over mine, knowing her history? Have you fallen for her or something?"

Spencer closed his eyes, shaking his head as he blew air from his nose. "Don't be ridiculous."

"I don't think I am. You have fallen for her. What happened? Did she bat her eyelashes at you, flash a smile, and you fell for it?"

"Fuck off, William. You know nothing."

"No, but I can see it clear as day. You are falling for her. You're so blinded by your feelings for her you can't see how she's manipulating you. I get it. She's beautiful, funny, charming. If anyone knows anything about that, it's me. But it's an act, Spencer. One she's very good at. And you're falling for it."

Spencer didn't appreciate how William was trying to turn this around on him. He was the one who had something to prove, not him. "You're wrong, William. I don't have feelings for Nicole."

"I hope that's true, but from where I'm standing, Nicole has her claws into you like she had in me and so many others. Look at what she's already done. Only took her a few days to get you to start questioning me when you were sent to investigate her. This is what she wanted to happen. To turn your focus off of her, and onto me."

"Nicole knows nothing about me being a private investigator. Or that you hired me."

"So what? She thinks you're a millionaire. She's peddling a story that she has a jilted ex to generate sympathy from you. It's a sob story to get you to feel sorry for her, to trust her. Because you do trust her now, don't you?"

"It's not like that. Nicole, by her own free will, admitted to me she used to be a con artist."

That wasn't what William expected to hear based on his expression. He didn't respond right away, thinking over his next words. "If that's the case, and she's truly being honest with you, then there's no way she didn't realize you're working for me. She must have found out about you and is trying to get ahead of things by doing damage control early."

"No. I've been careful. She couldn't have found out."

"Couldn't she?"

"She can't. She didn't. I'm telling you."

"You're not thinking clearly. If you were, you would have recorded her confession and gotten this case closed. Why didn't you?"

Because Spencer knew Nicole was telling the truth, that she was afraid for her safety. She knew there was a chance he could turn her in to the police and still didn't hesitate to tell him the truth. It was the realest she'd been with him, and Spencer wouldn't have her regret telling him. William wouldn't understand that. Just consider it proof that Spencer's feelings for her were interfering with his job.

"I was too busy trying to understand how my client that preaches about justice can be the same man who is threatening to ruin a woman's life. Is that what you think justice is? Causing someone else the same harm they caused you?"

William gripped the leather of the chair as it held the weight of his body against it. "If you think I'm capable of doing what Nicole told you, then you shouldn't be in charge of my case. Or taking my money, but let me ask you this. Are you willing to sacrifice the thousands of dollars I will pay you for closing this case off the word of a con artist?"

The answer to that was more complicated than William made it out to be, but the man wasn't done making his case. "Spencer, for years, Nicole has taken innocent people's money. Their trust, their dignity, and has gotten to walk away from the destruction to move on to her next target. Do you want to be the next victim she claims? Can you afford to be? The money I can offer you can keep your agency going. Money you'll need if you want to be a good father to Nessa. Don't let giving Nicole the benefit of the doubt screw with the money you need to raise your daughter."

As much as Spencer didn't want to admit it, William was right. He needed the money. Not just to keep his business running, but to be a good father to his niece. If he lost the job, not only would he lose out on the opportunity to save his agency, but the income that came from it.

"How about this?" William started, not giving Spencer a chance to make up his mind. "I have to go out of town on Friday for business. I'll be away for a week. Take the week to decide if you want to continue on this case. Really think about who you can trust. Me or Nicole. I hope the decision you make is the right choice for you, your family, and your future."

The men didn't exchange another word as William collected himself and left the office. For as many ways as the meeting could have turned out, Spencer hadn't seen the one that came to fruition coming. A part of him wanted to call William back and demand the truth from him, but a bigger part was too exhausted. He didn't have the strength to fight anymore.

He needed the break from the case, to step away and figure out the correct path forward. His future depended on it.

# 22

# The Art of Stealing Hearts

Cake tasting was just the thing Nicole needed to forget about her troubles. The company she was with also helped distract her from William too. She, Nessa, and Spencer were at New Horizon, trying out different cake flavors for Nessa's party. It was a matter of three weeks away. After the cake tasting, they'll meet the vendors set to be a part of the magical event.

Nicole finished her last of the sherbet cake sample and sighed. "It was delicious, but it was a little plain. Doesn't feel like a birthday cake to me."

Nessa licked the frosting off her fork, used on the cake in front of her. "What about this one? I think I could eat a sheet of it."

"Let's hope you don't," Spencer replied.

Nicole picked up a piece of the banana split cake and tried it. The sweetness of bananas, chocolate, and the crunch of the wafers exploded on her tongue. "This is it," she exclaimed, looking at Nessa. "I think your guests are going to love it. Good taste."

"Let me be the judge of that." Spencer motioned for Nicole to pass him the cake, but Nicole wouldn't risk dropping it.

She stabbed a bit of it with her fork and offered it to him. He opened his mouth, and she fed him the piece, the intimacy of the moment not lost on her. She'd done it at every one of her weddings. Not one of them felt as comfortable or natural as with Spencer.

His eyes widened. Nodding as he swallowed.

Nicole laughed. She took the fork out of his mouth and set it on the plate. "Was that a yes?"

"It tastes like heaven. Of course, it's a yes."

"Told you," Nessa said. "It's the best."

"Then it's settled. The banana split is the winner. Now that the hard part is done, time for the easy stuff."

Nicole scheduled for several artists to meet with Nessa and Spencer at the venue. Since the party would have art stations, Nicole thought having local artists who specialized in each station's theme would make it more special.

They met with the artist who would teach the kids how to make pottery, the two who would lead the drawing lessons, and the last who would instruct the children how to paint. All the artists were friendly and passionate about their craft. Nessa seemed excited to meet all of them, but most excited for the portrait drawing instructor, Emma, who showed her some tricks on how to draw people.

"All the people I draw are stick figures. How do you draw portraits?" she asked, her sketchbook open, ready to mirror whatever Emma did to her own.

"It takes lots and lots of practice. You can't expect yourself to become an expert overnight. In the beginning, you have to take small steps. Like when you learn how to ride a bike. You start slow, then the better you get, the faster you go. And if you mess up, that's okay. Because you know just by doing it, you're getting better. A good exercise would be to try drawing people in your life, it will give you practice. Then, once you're ready, you can draw the most important person in your life."

"So one day I'll be able to draw my mom?"

"If you work hard enough, then yeah, you can."

Emma begun drawing slowly so Nessa could follow along and learn. Their pencils were moving along on their notepads when Spencer and Nicole ducked out of the room. They meandered from room to room, settling inside one studio.

Nicole watched him closely, looking for signs of distress from Nessa mentioning her mom. He avoided her eyes, watching his shoes, his hands inside his pockets. "I'm sure the mention of her hurt," Nicole began. "But you can't let it."

"I would never want Nessa to stop loving her mom or forget about her. I want her to love with her whole little heart. I'm just afraid it'll get broken again and this time, it'll be my fault because I could've prevented it and didn't."

"Have you spoken to your sister?"

"No. She's left me more voice messages. The same stuff. She wants to see her and me, make things right. I want to believe her. I really do, but she's tried this before and failed. How many chances can you give someone before pulling the line and saying that's enough?"

Nicole gave him a small smile, understanding him more than he thought. "It's not the same thing, but Maya's father was a gambling addict. He was always after the next score, thinking the next one could set us up for life. I forgave him when he would blow through his paycheck or would leave me alone on nights to care for our daughter. Looking back, it gave me good practice for when he finally left us for good," she added with a hollow laugh. "The point is, I enabled him longer than I should have because I didn't want to see the truth of our situation. He never thought he was going to win the big one. Or get us set for life. It was an excuse for him to relive his youth that parenthood and marriage stole from him. He never intended on making it work with me. I was his mistake. And I'm still paying for it."

"So you think I shouldn't give her another chance because I'll regret it?"

"No. That's not what I'm saying. If I had a chance to redo things with Kyle, I wouldn't. I would still give Kyle a chance and live in delusional bliss for a few years longer than jumping ahead to the misery. At least then we got time to be a family, no matter how false it was."

"But is a couple of years of happiness worth the heartbreak that came afterward?"

"If I had pushed Kyle away in the beginning, he would have left me and Maya sooner. There's heartbreak regardless, Spencer, if you decide to keep Nessa from her mom. She's devastated at being kept away from her daughter. Nessa hurts from not having known her mom. And you agonize over your decision to keep two women you love apart. Yes, your sister could hurt Nessa if given the chance. Giving her an opportunity to make things right could open up a world of hurt, but it could also heal you from the misery you're already living in."

Spencer nodded, but Nicole had a feeling her advice didn't sit well with him, but she was happy she was honest with him. "And here I thought you were supposed to help me plan a kickass party. Not help me fix my life," he half-joked, bringing the mood up.

"I'm a woman of many talents."

"Okay, Iyanla," he said, grinning at her. Mentally, Nicole padded herself on the back for bringing that smile back to his face. She wanted him to never lose it.

"How is everything on your end? That guy hasn't sent you anymore threats, has he?"

Nicole's own smile dipped upon hearing about William. "Luckily, no, but he's always at the back of my mind now. It's hard to anticipate his next move when he moves with no rhyme or reason."

"Could he have ended his crusade?"

"I doubt it. He's probably in a cave, planning his next attack like an evil Batman."

"Batman is already pretty morally grey," Spencer corrected.

"But he's not a bad guy like William. Batman goes after criminals—"

"Like yourself?"

Nicole furrowed her eyebrows, her expression matching her state of mind. Where was this sudden defense of William coming from? "I thought you didn't care about that?"

"I don't. All I'm saying is it seems like this guy does. He might think he's doing the right thing, no matter how misguided he is. Every one paints themselves as the hero of their own story and casts someone else as the villain. You're William's villain. He's yours."

That didn't sit well with Nicole. William was a monster. His methods of payback against her far surpassed what she had done to him. Pretending to love him and tempting him into cheating was one thing. Stalking her daughter and sending her threatening notes was different.

"I gave you a hard dose of reality and now you're giving me some of your own? Is that what this is?"

"I don't agree with what he's done—"

"Then why are you defending him so hard? Do you think he's justified in doing this to me because I screwed him over first? I'll be the first one to tell you I'm far from a victim, but his actions are downright vile. He wants to ruin me, Spencer. If you're trying to get me to see him as a man and not a monster, then you're failing. Miserably."

Nicole turned on her heel, ready to forget this conversation ever happened. A tug at her hand brought her back. "Wait, I'm not defending him, okay? I'm sorry for giving you that impression."

"Then what were you doing?"

"I don't know," he sighed. He ran his hand over his fade, his face revealing how exhausted he was. "I guess I was looking for rationality in how someone could do something like this. But that's not fair to you and it's not what you need to hear right now. Nicole, I'm sorry. I'm on your side. I'm sorry for making you doubt that for even a second. You won't ever have to doubt that again."

Her eyes softened. She squeezed his hand, appreciating him realizing he hurt her and fixing it. That's all she could ask from somebody. "I'm sorry too, for jumping to conclusions. It's not easy for me to trust people. I'm always thinking of ways someone can screw me over. The result of being burned too many times."

"That's something I'll have to get used to. Not being one of those people."

Nicole couldn't stop her lips from forming a smile. "You're off to a good start."

"I want to be off to a better one. I want to do something for you. Something to give you some peace of mind."

"I'm listening."

"Have you thought about installing security cameras in your home and office?"

"I bought some before this William situation happened. I didn't bother to have them installed because I never thought I would need them."

"Do you still have the box?"

"Yeah, they're at my place. Why?"

"Let me install them for you."

"You know how to install security cameras?"

"Yeah. My father taught me everything I needed to know."

"You're serious?"

"Why not? If it'll prevent you from worrying all the time, I want to do it. I can even install some at your daughter's place."

"She stays with her girlfriend and her girlfriend's father. They have the security cameras covered."

"So that leaves just you." Spencer took a step closer, his voice low and smooth. "Let me help make sure you're safe."

Nicole swallowed the lump in her throat, her heartbeat picking up speed. A man hadn't had this kind of effect on her since Kyle. It had become a foreign feeling, not known to her since she was a teenager. Becoming reacquainted with it through Spencer both terrified her and excited her. She'd been alone long enough.

"Okay. I'll let you help me. When could you come by?"

"Nessa is spending the weekend at a sleepover at Cindy's. I can swing by your place around 3 p.m. tomorrow, then we can head by your office if that sounds good to you."

Nicole's mind was swimming. The idea of spending almost an entire Saturday alone with Spencer in her home made her dizzy with anticipation. "Perfect."

## 23

# Then the Fireworks Ignite

Nicole's apartment was everything Spencer imagined it would be. Like her office, it was sterile. Clean, pristine, and devoid of her personality. It was a replicate of the outer shell she presented herself as to the world. Cold, detached, unemotional.

Her home should have been her space. The one place she could be herself. Her apartment felt like an imposter. A stranger lived here, not her.

"Do you not decorate or something?"

"You sound like my daughter. When I moved in, I didn't expect to stay here long. I never expect to stay in one place long, so I avoid making them my own."

"I hope you make this one yours." A simple statement on the surface, but his words held a deeper meaning. He didn't just want her to stay here, he wanted her to stay in town. For as long as possible.

It was wrong to feel this way, but he couldn't stop himself. Every time he was with Nicole, he felt a pull toward her. It was something he'd never felt before. It was intense, and Spencer knew it wasn't one-sided. Every time things got too personal, Nicole would try to free herself from falling deeper into their connection.

The more they tried to fight it, the harder the current fought back.

"What are your plans once your business takes off?"

"I'm not sure," Nicole confessed, placing the box of cameras on the kitchen island. "I never went to school to be a business owner. Sometimes I feel out of my depth. A different kind of fraud than the one I already am."

"Then why do it?"

"I've watched Maya take a leap of faith with her play and I wanted to take one of my own and make her as proud as she has made me. If I fail, at least I won't look back on this and wonder what if. Does that make sense?"

"More than you know."

Nicole wouldn't know what he meant by that. Spencer only revealed one side of himself to her. His cover. A millionaire who lived in an overpriced penthouse, not the struggling paycheck to paycheck private eye. He hated keeping those authentic parts of himself from her, but it was necessary.

If she found out the truth, it would put a swift end to his job when he hadn't yet decided if he would finish it or not. Not to mention it would put an end to their developing connection. Another reason no relationship could happen between them.

Spencer was lying to Nicole about who he was and why he came into her life. It was the same thing Nicole had done in another life to her marks. If she discovered the truth about him, would she feel the same betrayal and anger they must have?

"So, where do you want the cameras installed?" Spencer asked, breaking the silence.

"Nothing too intrusive. A camera facing the outside of the door and one pointing to the living room."

"I can do that."

Spencer packed away his guilt and unpacked the cameras from Nicole's box. The idea of doing this was born from Spencer's guilty conscience, but giving Nicole some control back over her life was far from a bad thing. A selfish motive could still generate a stabilizing influence.

In the living room, Spencer stood on her step-stool and started working. Nicole sat on a barstool by her kitchen island, alternating between watching him and checking her emails. "Don't feel obligated to watch me. I know I'm not putting on a entertaining show here."

"Why do you say that?"

"I'm not exactly built to the gills, nor am I flexing what little muscles I do have by wearing a tank top or going shirtless. This is a pretty boring view compared to what you could be getting."

"I wouldn't say that."

Spencer glanced over his shoulder and caught her eye. "Really?"

"Really. I've never been the type to stand on my porch and offer the construction guys across the street lemonade just to get a peek at them. That has never done anything for me."

"Muscular men?"

"Men I don't know. Strangers. You could look like Denzel, but if I don't know you, I'm not giving you a second glance."

"Nicole, I think you may be—"

"Demisexual?" she asked, finishing his sentence. "My daughter told me the same thing. She explained it as not experiencing sexual attraction to someone unless you have an emotional connection to them first. It kinda just sounded like common sense to me, but whatever."

If Spencer could get Nicole to talk to Lawrence, he would give her a dissertation on asexuality. "So do you think you are demisexual?"

"How Maya described it? Yeah. I didn't enjoy sex until I met Kyle. I formed an emotional bond with him before we ever did anything, and it made me view sex differently."

Unless Spencer was missing someone, Kyle was the last guy Nicole had a real romantic relationship with. All her relationships since were fake on her part, a set-up for her con. Had she not been attracted to anyone in years?

"What made Kyle different for you?"

"It sounds so bare minimum now, but he paid attention to me. For a foster kid no one wanted to be friends with and no one wanted to parent. He didn't see me like the others did. He made me feel normal and seen. I wasn't the rebellious, pick-pocketing orphan. I was just Nicole, the wise-cracking ball-busting know-it-all, and he loved me for it. Until he didn't."

"That was his loss."

"You don't—"

"Don't what? Tell the truth? Because that's the truth. Anyone would be lucky to have you."

"Now you're really lying. Spencer, I was a con artist. No one would ever want to be with me if they knew about my past. I'm too flawed and difficult to have someone love me again, and that's nobody's fault but my own."

Spencer placed the drill down, his attention on her. "We all have our flaws. I'm a man with a lot of growing up left to do. My parents often put their careers before their kids. My sister likes to escape her problems by drinking, not caring how it affects the people who love her. You can't beat yourself up for your mistakes when everyone out there is making their own. None of us are perfect. We are human. And I'm sure someone will be happy with the real you, flaws and all."

She didn't look convinced. "Even if they get to know the real me, there's a good chance they won't stay."

"If someone is afraid to get close to you, because they think you're going to hurt them, they weren't ready for a relationship in the first place."

"Are you speaking from experience?"

"I wish I was. I've never had a real, meaningful relationship before. All the women and men I've been with were the same. We would hang out, fool around, and the moment anything got close to being serious, I would end it. Because I wasn't ready."

"Are you now?"

Spencer thought about Nessa and the commitment he was making to her. To not be an absentee uncle who dropped into her life when it was convenient. Instead, being an involved figure who was there to raise her and be there for her when she had no one else. It was the biggest commitment he had made to another person. It was also the greatest choice he ever made.

"For the right person?" he paused, making sure Nicole heard him loud and clear. "I'll make sure I'm ready."

She blinked slowly, her expression kept unreadable. She didn't say a word, her eyes speaking enough.

"But for the record, I'm not afraid of your flaws, or that you used to be a con artist. Or else I wouldn't be here. If it were me, I wouldn't care. I would love you just the same."

Her doorbell blared through their moment. Nicole picked her mouth up and went to the door. "Maya, what are you doing here?"

"I thought I would stop by and treat you to a dinner." The woman, who looked like a slightly younger version of Nicole, walked in. Her voice stopping when her eyes landed on Spencer. "Oh. I didn't realize you hired someone to install cameras for you."

"I didn't. Maya, this is Aiden Spencer. The client I'm working with that I told you about. He offered to do me this favor."

Spencer stepped off the step-stool and returned the woman's handshake. "Nice to put a face to the name. You've come up a lot in our conversations."

"Interesting. You know what else is interesting? My mom avoids talking about you whenever I bring your name up. Which is more often than you think. I have to pry information out of her and even then it's vague and surface level. I wonder why that is."

"She probably thinks I'm not worth mentioning."

"No, it's definitely not that." Maya smirked, shooting her mother a quick look. "Anyway, I'm sorry for interrupting. If I had known you were here, I would have avoided the premises. Not that I didn't want to meet you, I very much did. I just know my mom doesn't get a lot of time to enjoy another person's company."

Nicole elbowed her daughter's arm. "That's not true."

"Yes, it is. But I'm happy you're branching out. You need it."

The loudest blush appeared on Nicole's cheeks then. Spencer tried to avoid looking to lighten her embarrassment, but the blush made him smile. It was adorable to see this strong, often unaffected woman sport it. A reflection of how much power his presence had over her.

"If you're done embarrassing me, Maya, Spencer needs to finish."

"Alright. I'll get out of here. Raincheck on the dinner?"

"Of course."

Maya kissed her mom's cheek, then looked back at Spencer. "Who knows? Maybe you'll still be around to join us."

"I hope so."

Spencer watched Maya leave, the door closing behind her. Nicole started saying, "I'm sorry about her," before the sound of his drill took over again.

"Don't be. I like her."

"Hopefully not too much. She has a girlfriend," Nicole joked, but Spencer knew a warning when he heard one.

"Relax, Nicole. I don't date people younger than me."

"I didn't... I wasn't... Why?"

"Because there's plenty of women and men who are my age or older that are attractive and available. I'm not going to try to convince a young woman or man who's still figuring themselves out that a relationship with an adult is what's best for them."

Nicole glanced to the floor sparing a "Good to know," before sitting down and resumed typing on her laptop again.

She let him finish his work in peace. Occasionally, Spencer would feel her eyes on him. He would turn and catch her as she looked down again. He smirked to himself, wondering if she knew he was doing the same to her.

\* \* \*

After Spencer was done installing the cameras, he and Nicole ordered a pizza from a local joint. It was nothing fancy, but it was the best pizza and company he ever had. The conversation was pleasant, discussing their kids and their lives. Nicole seemed as invested in his family as Spencer was in hearing about her and Maya.

"Tell me. Do you miss the con artist life?" he asked, holding the car door open for her. Their next stop was to her office, where he would install another two cameras for her.

"I miss knowing I was good at something. I was a good con, and that felt good and rewarding. Until I saw how it made me not a good mother. So, no, I don't miss the lifestyle. I'm glad it's over. If I'm going to be a better person and mom, I needed to rid myself of it completely."

"I can respect that."

"Do you miss your life as a bachelor?"

Spencer snorted at the question. "No. I don't."

"Why not? Too demanding having to remember all their names?"

He bit his lip, glancing at her for a second before pulling onto the road. "I like where I am in my life now. I like who I surround myself with. I wouldn't trade where I am now for anything."

Nicole didn't respond. Spencer wondered if she understood he was referring to her. The woman who had taken over his mind since the day he met her. The woman he couldn't stop crossing lines with, no matter how hard he tried.

They didn't speak again until they arrived at her office just before 6 p.m.. Her assistant, Reggie, was off, so it was just them. "Where do you want me to install these?"

He held the cameras as she pointed to the lobby's ceiling. "There and outside the front door again."

"Got a step-stool?"

"Have a chair," she chuckled, bringing him a metal folding chair.

Spencer stepped on and started working. "I'll get this done faster if you aren't watching me."

"Are you saying I'm a distracting presence?"

"Very."

A shy smile took over her lips, like she took his comment exactly how Spencer wanted her to. "Alright. I'll give you your space. Call out if you need me."

Spencer focused on the camera. In all honesty, he wanted to delay the installations as much as he could. His heart didn't have the inclination to leave Nicole, while his head knew better. Spencer had been a PI long enough to know falling for a mark was a bad idea. If only his heart could have gotten that message.

It took an hour for him to finish. Afterwards, he wandered into the hallway between the conference room and Nicole's office. Both doors were open. In one was a crowded desk, an empty chair, and a desktop computer.

In the other room was the conference table. A body in one chair. Nicole, with her head laid back and her eyes closed. Not a witness to Spencer's contemplation.

The rooms offered two paths. One where Spencer could betray Nicole's trust by going through her computer until he found something to give to William. The other allowed him to keep his conscience and remain a friend to Nicole.

The first option was the easiest path. It would take no effort. Spencer could walk into the office, pull up a chair, and start clicking around. It would end the case, stabilize his agency, make it easier to give Nessa the things a good parent should provide.

But did it matter if Spencer got those things by not being a good person? What kind of example was he setting for Nessa if he took money from a man like William? He was dirty, and so was his money.

The Shaw men before him never would have been on William's payroll. When money wasn't coming in, they never lowered the standards they held for a client. The Shaws didn't work for just anyone. They helped those who deserved it. Spencer could hear his father's and grandfather's voices tell him William wasn't deserving.

Tossing away thousands in the name of morals didn't seem wise, but neither did tossing away the trust of a woman Spencer was already too attached to. He didn't want to become another name on the list of people who betrayed Nicole. He couldn't live with disappointing her, or himself.

Spencer's choice was made. It was a decision, decided with his heart instead of his head. A first time for everything.

He walked into the conference room and stood next to Nicole's chair. Her legs stretched out into the chair across from her. Her head tilted back and her eyes closed, a small smile resting on her face.

"You alright, Nicole?"

Her head rose, her eyes blinking rapidly. "Yeah. Just resting my eyes."

"You can rest them a minute longer. We don't have to leave yet."

He took her heels off the seat they were in and sat down, pulling them into his lap. Her eyes opened fully. "What are you doing?"

"What does it look like?"

"Like you're about to take off my heels."

"So let me."

Nicole's legs stiffened, and then relaxed. Spencer's hands slid up her calves, feeling the soft skin beneath his touch. How did he last this long in her orbit and resist touching her like this?

Simple black velvet pumps rested on her feet. He slid his hands down her ankles, his thumb brushing the inside. A breathy sound slipped from Nicole's lips. Spencer glanced up at her face, finding her eyes closed.

She took a small gulp. "Not to kink shame, but you don't have a foot fetish, do you?"

"No. I just like helping you."

Spencer undid the strap holding her shoe in place and pulled the heel off. He placed it on the ground and then switched to the other leg. She sighed when the shoes were both off, maybe thinking Spencer was done. He was just starting.

He pressed his thumbs into the ball of her foot, working the muscle. Her face melted at the touch. He could tell it had been a long time since she'd been taken care of like this. If ever.

"I caught a lucky break meeting you. You spent all afternoon working at my request, now you're doing this. What's next, a shoulder rub?"

"I could. If you want."

"This. What you're doing right now. It's good. Don't stop."

He pressed deeper into her skin, her foot rolling in his grip. The more Nicole relaxed, the harder she gripped his hands. She didn't want his touch to leave her. The feeling was mutual.

"You know, for most men, they only do foot rubs for their partners and after sex."

Spencer read in between the lines. Nicole was neither his girlfriend nor have they had sex. Each time he did something for her, she expected for him to ask for something in return. Would she believe him if he told her he just wanted her to be happy?

"I'm not like most men."

"I know you're not. You keep proving it to me. But you have your needs too, don't you?"

A quiet moan slipped past her lips, and Spencer's body reacted to it accordingly. He kept his face neutral, his hands still working at her feet. He needed a distraction. Something else to think about. Anything.

"They're not as important as yours."

"I beg to differ." Nicole's toes curled, her heels pressing into his lap. One foot rubbing back and forth against the bulge in his pants.

Spencer's eyes fluttered closed. He bit down on his lip. "Nicole," he warned.

"You can stop, if you want."

"Is that what you want?" he groaned, his cock straining against his zipper as she kept kneading him.

"It's not."

His fingers dug into her skin. Spencer could give Nicole what she needed while controlling himself. He kneaded the bottom of her foot, her breath hitching in response.

His hands focused on Nicole's feet while his eyes honed in on her features. Like her lips disappearing as she wetted them. Or the way her chest heaved as her breathing sped up. Every part of her called out to him, his body begging for him to answer.

Then came the panting, the small moans of pleasure. He imagined the sounds escaping her throat as she rode him. Her walls tightening around him as she reached her climax. Her wetness against his palm as he fingered her, her juices coating his fingers before he sucked her release off.

"Do you know what you're doing to me?"

"No idea what you're talking about." She didn't even try to hide the smirk.

He moved his hands up, settling on her lower leg, repeating his kneading from before. As expected, it produced the same moans and hitching of breath as his hands rose higher up her leg. She leaned forward, her eyes still shut as she rubbed her right shoulder.

Spencer knew what this was. Nicole was teasing him, seeing if he was going to make a move on her. It was an unspoken game they were playing, of which one would break first. The effect Nicole was having on him was unlike anything he experienced before, but he wouldn't give in that easily. She was a worthy opponent, but he could be too.

Lifting her leg to his mouth, Spencer dotted kisses from her ankle to her knee, right where her dress cut off. "Spencer," she breathed.

"You started it," he said, moving his lips along the edge of her dress, bunching it up in his hand.

Her foot slipped out of his hand, her body shifting toward him. He took the opening, leaning into her neck, kissing her soft skin. "Are you going to end this or am I going to have to?"

Finally, Nicole opened her eyes, meeting his. Without hesitation, she opened her mouth and panted. Slow intakes of air leaving her mouth as she watched him watch her. His restraint was weakening by the second, the bulge in his pants growing thicker.

Nicole didn't take her eyes off him. She didn't move either. She remained perfectly still, except for the rise and fall of her chest. At the edge of her lips were two crinkles. A closer look at them revealed they were a shadow of a smirk, a step away from the real thing. Her panting was all for fucking show.

He fell for her trap.

Spencer grabbed her waist, hitching her up onto the conference table. Her legs locked onto his hips. "You're driving me crazy with those sounds you're making. Worse yet, you knew they would."

"You're right. What I don't know is what you're going to do about it."

He pressed his forehead against hers, breathing in her air. Spencer wanted this more than he ever wanted something before, but he couldn't let himself have her. He couldn't. "I can't..."

Nicole searched for answers in his eyes. "You can't what? You can't kiss me? Is that it? Because if that's it, I won't tell if you don't," she teased, running her nose along his jawline.

"Nicole, I mean it. I can't..." He trailed off, not able to finish a sentence he didn't know how to end. What could he say? I can't kiss you because I'm lying to you? I can't touch you because I worked for a man who's out to get you? I can't take you looking at me like that without wanting to finish inside you. I can't... I can't... I can't.

Nicole's eyes dimmed, her face falling as her gaze dropped. "I get it." She unlocked her legs from his waist and gently pushed him back. She avoided meeting his eye. "It's okay. It would have been a mistake."

No, no, no, Spencer repeated in his head. The mistake would be to let Nicole go, to lose her before he ever had her. Spencer cupped her face, getting her to look at him. "You're right. This will be a mistake, but I've tried resisting this. Tried denying the undeniable. When all I've wanted was to tell you, I'm yours. Nicole, I'm yours."

He captured her lips. Tasting the strawberry lip balm he watched her reapply hours ago when she thought he wasn't looking. Nicole responded instantly, her arms wrapping around his neck and bringing him closer. She was a damn good kisser. There were a lot of things about Nicole Taylor that surprised him, but that wasn't one.

Their mouths moved against each other. The taste of Nicole's lips making him crave her more. Spencer slipped his tongue inside, eliciting a low, needy moan from her throat.

He kissed her with every bit of passion inside of him. The same passion that had him dreaming about her every night since that night at the bar. The passion that had him fighting not to have her every day since.

Nicole kissed him harder, her lips sucking on his, her hands sliding through his hair. His tongue slipped between her lips again, her mouth opening wider to let him in. He leaned them back until Nicole was pinned between him and the table.

Her hands ran up and down his body. His hands gripping her hips and pulling her closer. He broke their kiss, his mouth attacking her neck as he sucked her skin. "Spencer, you're going to give me a hickie," she panted.

"And?"

"I'm 42 years old. I haven't had a hickey since I was 18. How do I explain that?"

"I don't know, but it sounds like you're overdue," he replied, catching her collarbone with his teeth and nibbling.

She groaned in his ear. The sound traveled straight to his groin. He moved his kisses down to her chest, his lips sucking and biting her skin. The marks were proof that he was here, a reminder of what they shared tonight.

Nicole's long legs locked onto his backside again, pushing him closer to her body. And pushing her against his bulge. Before Spencer could become ashamed by how hard he already was, Nicole rocked her hips forward, pressing into him. The friction she was creating building a fire inside him. The need to be inside her was overwhelming.

"You're the evilest woman I've ever met," Spencer said, his breath hitching in his throat as she continued to move.

She chuckled, her head thrown back as she smiled. The sight would be forever ingrained in his mind. Her hair pushed up in the back, her skin a little flushed, her lips red and swollen. "You once called me a dream. What's changed?"

"You rubbing against me like that when you know I don't have a condom on me."

Her grin grew wider. "I guess I am evil because I like the idea of you cumming in your pants without me so much as touching you."

"Fuck you."

"You first."

He crashed his lips against hers again, their teeth knocking together. She was driving him insane. He could barely focus on kissing her, his brain was too busy registering the way she rubbed him, her thighs squeezing around him. The heat from her core was radiating through their clothes.

As much as Spencer loved the idea of her using him to get herself there, he needed some saying in the matter. She could use him to her own liking another night, when his head was clearer. Right now, all he wanted was to leave her completely undone from his tongue, driving deep into her until his name was the only thing left on her lips.

He broke free from the kiss, moving down Nicole's body, pushing her dress up and out of his way. "What do you think you're doing?" she asked, watching him as he slid his hand down her legs.

"Something that will leave you a shaking, incoherent mess."

"I don't... I haven't..."

"Been eaten out in a while?"

"If give or take 20 years is a while."

All the men she had gone to bed with in the name of her cons and not one of them offered to pleasure her? Spencer was starting to think they had the whole being scammed thing coming. His lips met her knee, leaving a wet line of kisses down her thigh. "Do I have your permission to remind you how good it can feel?"

Her gulp was audible. "You do."

Nicole lifted her hips up. Spencer hooked his thumbs under her panties and slid them down her legs, pocketing them for when they needed to be returned. His eyes never left her. Her arousal coated her sex, and Spencer felt himself get harder just from looking at her.

Now he was the one gulping. Spencer couldn't remember the last time he did this. That's how long it had been. What if he disappointed her? He built himself up as being a playboy in another life. But what if his skill set had rusted from being inactive?

Nicole placed her hand on his cheek. "What are you worried about?"

"It's been a while for me too. I don't want to disappoint you."

"You could never disappoint me. You just being here, wanting this as much as I do, is enough for me." She kissed his cheek, then laid back. "And if it helps, remember, I don't get wet like this for just anyone. You've already gotten me halfway there. All you have to do is finish the job."

A cocky grin spread across his lips. Spencer dipped his head and licked a path through her slit, ending his lick at her clit. Her sweet taste flooded his tongue while her moans flooded his ears, letting him know he was off to a good start.

He continued licking around the rim of her slit, circling it and then taking it into his mouth, swirling his tongue against it. His hand traveled down the inside of her thigh, his thumb stroking over one of her folds. Nicole squirmed under his touch, her chest heaving.

One kiss along the inside of her thigh, and she shivered. Spencer would have her riding his mouth for relief in no time. He moved back to her core, teasing the opening with his fingers and tongue. Her thighs squeezed around his head.

Nicole moaned, her hands gripping the edge of the table. "Disappointing me when you can fuck me with your tongue like that? Never."

"I aim to please."

"Please more."

Spencer obeyed, feeling his cock swell further when his finger slipped inside her wet cunt. He pumped his digit in and out, keeping his eyes locked on her. The view of Nicole was one he would never forget.

He reveled in the sight and the feel of her breasts rising and falling. Her eyelashes fluttering from each of his flicks. Her legs twitching under his touch, and her nails digging into the table.

When she saw the scratches again, would she think of him and what they did? The memory causing her pussy to take on the rhythm of a heartbeat. Eating away at her until she needed to excuse herself to take care of it?

That's what Spencer wanted. To give her the kind of pleasure that made her want more. That made her unable to walk, stand, sit without remembering him.

His cock was straining against his pants. He ignored the discomfort and continued pumping his finger in and out, adding another one when she was ready. Nicole's hips moved up and down with them. His mouth was still teasing her clit, his tongue circling and flicking.

He needed her to come so he could have more of her to taste. It was a craving he needed satisfied fast. "Goddamn. You're the best thing I've ever tasted."

"Did you expect anything less?" Nicole asked, but it was no question.

"I would be surprised if you weren't, to be honest."

"Good boy. Now, stop talking. Unless you're going to tell me to cum all over your tongue."

"Cum on my tongue, Nicole." He took all of her in his mouth, his tongue sweeping back and forth while he sucked on her clit like it was a popsicle waiting for the heat to melt it.

She gasped, either from his words or his mouth, or both. Spencer couldn't take his eyes off her. Not as the volume of her moans increased and her hands dug into his scalp as she fought to retain some control.

Nicole was growing as relentless as Spencer was, but she had just the trick to make them both go feral. She brought her legs around his head, her hips rocking against his mouth as she rode him. His finger and tongue continued their movements inside her. His mouth never stopping their attack on her clit.

Getting a show of Nicole riding him, her grinding her clit against his tongue, and her juices flooding his finger was more than enough for Spencer to almost cum in his pants like she wanted. Nicole was close too. Her grip was hard enough to bruise, her breathing erratic. All signs Spencer recognized well.

"Fuck! Open your mouth wide for me."

He did as he was told, his tongue darting in and out of her. He opened his mouth wider, his eyes closing as her fingers pulled his head closer to her. Nicole's walls clenched tight against his finger and tongue.

Spencer's hand moved up to hold Nicole's hips in place while his tongue kept her steady, letting her ride out her high. Every drop of her warm nectar hit his tongue. The first few drops he licked up.

The rest came out in a flood his tongue had to work to keep up with. But he did. Spencer didn't want to let one drop get away from him. Just as he didn't want to let Nicole get away from him.

When Spencer finished becoming acquainted with Nicole's taste, he kissed his way up her body. Not stopping until he found her lips. She kissed the taste of herself off of him, grinning. "I can take care of you the way you took care of me."

She nodded toward his crotch, which was pressing against her. Relief was calling for him, but Spencer couldn't answer it. "It's been a long time for me. If you wrap your mouth around my cock, I will lose control in a way that you will scare you off. As much as I would like to finish inside you, I can't. Not now."

He was afraid she would think he was pushing her away again, but her reaction was everything he needed it to be. "Nothing in your nature could scare me away. But I'll bid my time and wait to prove that to you."

Spencer wasn't a praying man, but he hoped to God that Nicole kept that promise.

## 24

# Night with The Red-Blooded Woman

When a man makes you cum from his mouth and fingers alone without asking for anything in return, you accept his offer to cook you dinner the next night. At least that was Nicole's line of thinking. And she had no qualms about it.

Taken on dates by millionaires was nothing new to her. Millionaires had wooed Nicole by trying to seal the deal with her. This was different. Spencer wasn't a mark. For the first time in years, he was someone she was interested in knowing. He wouldn't be the new leading man in her happily ever after. Women like her didn't have fairytale endings. Rather, Spencer could be a safe, judgment free place to go to when she needed it.

That, and a mind-blowing orgasm.

Another way Spencer differed from the men who wined and dined her before was he planned on doing it in his home. With his own cooking. Nicole liked an up-scaled restaurant as much as the next person. However, there was an intimacy to eating a meal specifically prepared for you that couldn't be beaten. Until Spencer, no man ever offered to do that for her.

Any man after Spencer would have a high bar to clear. That was the thing, though. Nicole wanted to believe there wouldn't be anyone that followed him. Partly because she wasn't sure she could do this again. The song and dance of becoming invested, building trust, and the inevitable breakup when things fell apart.

Spencer wasn't like the other men in her past, but that didn't mean the outcome wouldn't be the same. It could even be worse, because she wasn't playing a character around him. Nicole had simply been her authentic self and somehow won him over. But would it make him stay?

Nicole rode up to Spencer's penthouse, wearing a fitted off the shoulder burgundy dress that fell above her knees. The top portion and color choice were bold compared to her normal attire, but the night called for it. When the elevator doors opened, the smell of lobster filled her senses.

She walked past the living room and rounded the corner, watching Spencer by the stove for a moment without him knowing she was there. His navy button-down was rolled up on his elbows. The first two buttons were undone, and he had his Clark Kent glasses on. The sight had Nicole squeezing her thighs together.

"You look like you're having fun," she commented, entering the space.

His eyes flew to the voice, taking her in like she'd done to him. "Where have you been hiding that dress? I swear if you just bought that, we're going back to that store and buying it in all the colors they have available."

"This old thing? It was a gift."

"Now it's one for me."

Nicole couldn't stop smiling at him. "Thank you. You don't look too bad yourself."

"Oh this? This is my cleaning shirt. I only have it on because I didn't want it to get dirty when I was making our food."

"Can you keep it on? I like you in it. I mean, I like you in a lot of things, but this look is really doing it for me."

"Duly noted." He smiled, pulling her in for a quick kiss.

She kept him there, kissing him like she was desperate for him. Because she was. Nicole never wanted to admit to needing someone. It was beneath her. Which made it more sobering for her to realize she needed Spencer in a way she never needed someone before. And for the first time, she would proclaim it over and over again if he asked her to.

When it was time to come up for air, Spencer laid a kiss on Nicole's forehead. "I would kiss you all night if I could, but I made a meal I'm actually proud of. I would like to see you eat it. Plus, I think we need to have a conversation before this goes any further. Is that okay?"

Nicole agreed they needed to talk, but something about how Spencer said it made her worry. She hid it and said, "Yeah. That's more than okay. Do you need my help with anything? I know my way around the kitchen."

"Are you sure about that? Remember, I've seen your fridge."

"It's only bare because I don't make time to cook. Rest assured, I know how to."

"I believe you," he relented, pulling back a seat to the dining table. "That's why I want you to sit here and relax while I pour you a glass of wine and put the finishing touches together. I don't want you to do anything, but relax."

"Okay." She didn't put up a fight as he went to get her a drink. But there was only so much relaxing Nicole could do until she knew what Spencer wanted to talk about. Surely, it was about their relationship. What she wasn't sure about was how he felt about it. He came back with the wine and she sipped it, grateful to have something numb her nerves.

When dinner was cool enough to eat, Spencer brought the dishes over, along with the bottle of wine. A golden brown crusted lobster mac and cheese with four different layers of cheese and a grilled shrimp salad to top it all off. "What made you think to do this?" she asked, her mouth watering.

"I took one of the few meals I knew how to make, then I fancied it up. The first attempt ended with the crust burning."

"You're lucky Nessa wasn't here. She would never let you live that down."

"Don't I know it." He sat down across from her, looking as happy as she felt. "Anyway, I tried again and I have to say I think the result is much better, but I'll let you be the judge of that."

Nicole grabbed her fork and stabbed a piece, pulling the noodle, cheese, and lobster up to her. "You didn't have to go through all this trouble."

"It was no trouble. I enjoyed making this, knowing it might earn me a smile from you."

She brought the bite to her mouth, savoring the flavors as soon as they hit her taste buds. She resisted moaning, knowing how much that could rile Spencer up, but it was deserving of one. "It's amazing, Spence. You did an incredible job. Go ahead, dig in. I guarantee it will be the second best thing you've had in your mouth in the last 24 hours."

His head fell back as he laughed. "I guess I'll have to settle for second best, then."

Spencer took his own bite, smiling around the fork. Nicole had never seen him this content, this peaceful in the time they spent together. His worries extended to Nessa, to his sister, and to his mom. Tonight, there was no worry. Just the bliss he had rightly earned, and so had she.

They ate mostly in silent, trading back smiles when their eyes met. There hadn't been a time in Nicole's life where she had smiled this much. She wanted to grow used to it, whether Spencer was by her side or not. It was more likely to stay with him around, but she'll have to learn how to keep it even if he wasn't.

"You mentioned wanting to talk." Nicole brought the topic up after Spencer took their plates to the sink. He came back, pouring them their second glass before sitting again.

"Yeah. Fair to say yesterday didn't go how either of us had planned it."

"How do you feel about it?"

Spencer reached across the table and took Nicole's hand into his own. "It was the best night of my life." When he squeezed her hand, he squeezed out the worry flowing through her. And in a single word, he brought it back. "But—"

"Oh boy," she sighed.

"No wait, Nicole, listen. There's a lot going on in my life right now. With Nessa and my sister, and my… business. It's just a lot. I don't know how much I can devote myself to a full-blown relationship. I'm not saying we should stop this, but that we should slow things down."

"You want to be friends with benefits?"

"No. I'm not interested in doing an arrangement like that with you. I told you I'm done with the playboy stuff."

"Good, because I'm not a spring chicken, Spencer. I'm not interested in doing that stuff either."

"I'm not asking you to. I'm asking can we slow down what we're doing, not changing it."

The tension in Nicole eased, but she was still on high alert. "What would slow look like for us?"

"We see each other as much as we can. We call each other as much as possible. Not out of a sense of obligation, but because we both want to hear each other's voice. A weekly date night. That's what I can handle right now."

It wasn't the worst thing Nicole had ever heard. It was a reality check. Neither one of them planned on this happening or had their lives prepared for a relationship. Spencer had Nessa to consider, and William hadn't yet been eradicated.

If they were going to do this, they needed to do it smart and go into it knowing how much each other could offer. That was what Spencer was doing. It was smart. While also being infuriating. Nicole wanted to live in wonderland with him, not have their bubble burst like this.

"Everything you're saying makes sense. Not only for you, but for me too. I have my business to grow. I'm working on bettering my relationship with Maya. Going slow makes sense." Nicole wondered if Spencer could hear the disappointment in her voice. She tried to disguise it, but it wasn't her finest performance.

"There's a but, isn't there?"

"I wish there wasn't, but yeah. I don't want you to think I'm being selfish, or that I want more than you can give me, because that's not it. I guess I had different expectations for us. Nothing deep like living together or marriage, but bigger than what you described. Which is fine. You're figuring out your new normal, I respect that. I just wish this was the norm."

Spencer didn't say anything. Nicole began to think she had overstepped. She stood from the table, grabbing the bottle and her empty glass. "I'm sorry. You told me you haven't been in a meaningful romantic relationship before and here I am, coming into this with comically large expectations."

"Don't apologize."

"Too late."

"You're allowed to feel how you feel, Nicole."

"Then how come you don't look happy about it?"

Spencer rose from his chair, moving towards her. He grabbed the bottle and glass from her, placing them on the table behind her. "I'm not unhappy. I'm processing."

"Processing or debating? Wondering if you should even bother doing this?"

"Hey, no. Where's this coming from?"

"I don't know, okay? Maybe it's the wine. Or that you've had your mouth on me now, and I can't stop thinking about how good you make me feel. Or the fact that I don't want anyone else but you. Maybe it's all of that."

"I'm not debating. And you're not alone in those thoughts. I haven't stopped thinking about you. Your sounds, your taste, your touch. All of it is stuck in my head, and I've got nothing else up there but you. That's a problem, because I can't give you all that you want. I can't give you all of me, but I'm hoping that what I can give is enough for you for right now. And if you're patient with me, I can give you everything you deserve from a partner and more in due time."

It wasn't Nicole's ideal scenario, but it didn't need to be. "I'll take any of you I can get. I've waited my whole life for someone like you, Aiden Spencer. I can wait a little longer."

Spencer brought her into a hug, wrapping her up in his warm, safe embrace. "It won't be that long, I promise."

"Don't make promises you can't keep. I can wait. I will wait, because I want you."

He tipped her chin up to him and gave a sweet, but all too quick peck. "I have a meeting tomorrow or else…"

"I get it. Though one of these days you should probably tell me what exactly it is you do," she teased, getting him to blush.

"It's boring stuff. You know what isn't boring? Dishes."

"Subtle. Not."

Taking a cue, Nicole gave Spencer a hand and dried the dishes he washed. Why he was a millionaire without a dishwasher, she did not know, but decided not to ask. After they finished, he walked her to his elevator.

"Sure you don't want me to walk you to your car?"

"I'm sure. I don't need the temptation."

"What temptation?" Spencer asked as she pressed the elevator button down.

"You know... to drag you into the backseat of my car and, well... I'll let you finish putting that picture together."

"That... certainly would be the opposite of slow."

"Yeah. We wouldn't want to do anything fast, would we?"

The elevator dinged, and the doors opened. Spencer watched her step onto the elevator and pressed the button to the lobby. "Not yet, anyway. Soon, though. Hopefully soon."

Spencer spoke like he was a live wire. Nicole was willing to bet with a few words, he could be set off. "Right. Soon. In the meantime, I'll have to find a way to keep busy. A girl got to have her needs taken care of somehow."

The split second before the elevator doors could close, Nicole saw it. The change. It was written on Spencer's face, and spoke through his actions. He stuck his hand out, stopping the doors from closing. He stepped inside like a man possessed, crowding her until she was backed against the wall.

"Say that again."

"You heard me."

Spencer brought his hands down to her waist, lifting her up and holding her there. She wrapped her legs around his waist and her arms around his neck, waiting for what he was going to do. His lips hovered just above hers, the tips of their noses touched, and she could feel his warm breath.

"This isn't slow," she reminded him, her breath tickling his chin.

"The only slow I'm thinking about right now is how agonizingly slow I'm going to tease you with my cock."

Spencer's hips ground into her, giving her the friction she so badly wanted. "You're going to take your time with me, huh?"

"Punish and tease you like you love doing to me."

"I don't think you can do that."

"Why not?"

"Take a peek."

He followed her eyes to the end of her dress. Spencer slid the bottom part up, exposing her bare skin to him. His eyes widened when he realized she opted out of wearing a certain undergarment today. "Jesus, fuck. You came here like this?"

"Why waste underwear? I had a feeling you'd take them off, anyway."

"Nicole." Her name came out like a growl. He dropped the material and moved his hand up the inside of her thigh, not stopping until he felt the slickness between her folds. He drew his finger up and down her slit. "Is this what you did last night after I dropped you off? Did you think about me, touch yourself, and cum thinking of me?"

"Want a demonstration?" She didn't wait for him to answer. She knew it was yes.

She unwrapped her legs from around him, but kept his hand in between her thighs. "Two fingers," she directed, guiding his hand.

"That's it," she moaned as he pushed his digits into her. "You follow instructions so good."

Nicole moved her hips, matching his rhythmical pumping. She had already been wet enough for him to take. It was seeing him lose control. Hearing his dirty talk. Watching him be transfixed by her that left Nicole dripping.

When she sufficiently lubricated Spencer's fingers, Nicole took his hand out of her. She brought them to her mouth. She licked herself off of him. As she swirled her tongue around his fingers, she kept eye contact with him.

"That is how I did it, and how I'll keep doing it if you don't take me yourself."

Nicole was the one who was on the edge, but it was Spencer who looked ready to fall off of it. He leaned her into the elevator wall. She could feel the same hard press of him against her wetness. Except today he would satisfy the hunger they shared.

"I'm such a fucking idiot," he said, already out of breath. "I didn't think this would happen so soon. I didn't buy condoms—"

Nicole stopped him and pulled the packet out of her bra. "Don't you know by now that I have you covered? Always."

He took them, reading the brand. "How did you know?"

"Took a lucky guess."

Spencer kissed her hard, slipping his tongue past her lips in a quick caress, tasting the red wine that still clung to her. She responded with a soft moan that vibrated through his chest and into his throat. He deepened their kiss with slow, sweeping strokes of his tongue until she was gasping for air.

While she caught her breath, he found a spot under her earlobe that made her shudder. He nibbled it lightly before drawing it into his mouth. The swirl of his tongue around it made Nicole gasp. As eager as she had ever been, Nicole arched against him. Her hips thrusting upward as if she could actually get rid of the ache between them.

Spencer looked at her, smiling at her flushed cheeks. Her eyes were wide open, staring back up at him, searching, hungry for more. "What do you want, babe?" he whispered hoarsely. "Tell me what you need."

"This." Her hands moved down to his belt buckle, undoing it before sliding her hands underneath the waistband. Spencer groaned as she ran her hand over his cock and cupped his balls. "If that's okay?"

"If that's okay? It's more than okay. Take whatever you want from me, baby."

Hearing him call her that sent a chill down her spine. She sent one down his when she slid the rubber onto his shaft. Her hand trembled while putting it on, not from nerves but excitement from what came next.

Nicole lifted her dress up, giving him a show of her in her natural state. She guided his length to her center, pressing the tip against her.

"I'm yours, Spencer. Just as much as you're mine."

It was the second half of the vow Spencer had given her last night in her office. Hearing her repeat it was all the motivation he needed. His hands went under her, grabbing her ass and squeezing it.

He thrust his hips, burying himself deep inside her. Her legs wrapped around him as they rocked together. She bit the side of his neck and his fingers dug into her thighs as she ground against his erection.

"Babe, you're so tight," he grunted. "I might not last as long as you need."

"We've got time to work on your stamina." She kissed the spot just above his jawline. "Again, and again, and again."

The word died on her tongue when his thumb found her clit. Nicole threw her head back and Spencer used the opportunity to suck her skin. His thumb drew slow, teasing circles as he pumped into her. With each circle, Nicole grew tighter around him.

She wondered if he could see how hungry she was for him. Never to let her curiosity stop her, Nicole reached up and took his glasses off. She put them on, her vision blurring. "These things help you see how needy I am for you?"

"Among other things." He grinned, thrusting back into her.

"Just making sure you'll be able to see me in perfect quality when I'm riding you."

She could feel his pulse beat quicker inside of her. She started to take the glasses off, but Spencer slid them back into place. "Keep them on for now. I'm nearsighted. I can see you perfectly clear this close."

"You like pounding into me while I'm wearing your glasses? Does it make you feel like you own me? That I'm no one else's to touch, but yours? Is that it?"

Spencer's hips faltered. "You want to be owned by me, don't you? You want everyone to know who you belong to."

She bit her lip. "Fuck, you know I do."

Spencer's grip tightened. His eyes turned a shade darker. He pulled out and flipped her over. Her hard nipples pressed against the elevator's cold metal wall. She braced her hands on the railing as Spencer lined up against her ass.

"Tell me." Her body shivered as he whispered in her ear.

"I only want to be yours, Spencer. Only yours."

He sank into her, filling her to the hilt with one thrust. She cried out. His name tore from her lips. She could feel him twitch inside of her. Her back arched, and he began to thrust in and out.

"Mine." He kissed the side of her neck.

"Yours." She pushed against him, feeling him hit that spot deep within her.

"Prove it. Scream my name so my neighbors can hear who you belong to."

Her walls tightened. The thought of yelling his name for the entire floor to hear her orgasm made her pussy ache with anticipation. She turned her head, and he caught her lips. The kiss was messy, and hot, and desperate.

"Are you going to give me something to scream for?" she asked when their lips broke apart.

"Don't fucking pretend you're not close. I can feel you getting tighter around me."

"So are you." She rolled her hips back, her ass grinding against him.

His teeth caught the lobe of her ear. "Not until you come all over my cock."

"Then fuck me like I need you to."

Nicole felt his hand in her hair, twisting her head to the side and pressing her cheek against the wall. He pounded into her, their skin slapping together. His hand released her hair, sliding between her legs. He spread her open, and she whimpered.

"Is this what you want? Someone to claim you as theirs? For you to belong to someone so completely like this?"

"Not someone," she gasped. "You."

His finger dove between her folds, stroking her swollen clit. His cock hit a spot deep inside her and his thumb pressed down hard. Nicole shattered. She screamed his name as her climax stroke a note inside her that hadn't been played in years.

Nicole barely had time to catch her breath before Spencer's lips claimed hers. His fingers were digging into her skin. Their tongues tangled together, sharing something neither of them had the words for.

His lips trembled against hers before he tore them away. Nicole could feel his breath against the shell of her ear. She could sense he was about to say something when his breath hitched.

"Fuck! I don't deserve you." Spencer's last words before he was driven off the edge.

"You do," Nicole whispered so low she wasn't sure he heard it over his orgasm.

Spencer buried his face in the crook of her neck and moaned. He filled his condom all the way, disappointing Nicole. The first time she was envious of the damn rubber. But there would be other times. She would make sure of it.

She turned her body around, watching Spencer leave as he tied the condom. When he came back, she put his glasses back on him. "I think I unlocked a new kink for you."

"Everything about you is a kink for me."

Nicole's heart fluttered. "I need to ride you."

"Don't you mean want?"

"We're past want. Suit up and get on your back."

Spencer's grin widened. He picked a new condom from where she dropped them, tore it open, and rolled it on. The next second, they were on the floor.

Nicole had him pinned underneath her, her dress hiked up around her waist. Spencer's shirt was pulled out from his pants, the buttons on his shirt undone, and the bottom half of his pants were still on. It was a sexy sight.

Nicole ran her hands down his chest, down to his hips. "Are you enjoying letting me have control over you?"

"I wouldn't want it any other way."

"Good." She rolled her hips forward, his length brushing her sensitive bud. Spencer hissed, his hands grabbing onto her hips. He held on tightly, keeping her in place, but also allowing her to keep moving.

"Christ, Nicole! You're killing me here." His legs tightened around her hips. She pushed forward again.

"Oh god…" Spencer panted. He let his head fall back, resting it on the cool flooring. "Fuck me…"

Nicole smiled smugly. Her teeth glinted against the marble design and the elevator's reflection. She moved her hips, grinding against his pelvis, her body taking him deeper. "I already am. Haven't you noticed? Not sure what more I can do to make you feel me…"

Nicole's mouth said one thing, but her body did another. She rolled her hips. Her muscles tightened at the same time Spencer's breathing became shallow.

He gripped her hips tighter, trying to control the rhythm, but her strong legs kept her in place. He wasn't getting away from her, but neither was she. Not when the tip of his cock rubbed her G-spot over and over.

Nicole bit her lip to keep the screams that were building inside her contained. But Spencer saw through the façade. "Come on, babe," he groaned, "Let me hear those moans. You know how much I love to hear them."

He moved one hand from her hips and brought it up from her torso to her chest. He slid her top down low enough to grab her breast, massaging it. The pad of his thumb pressed against her nipple and rubbed in small circles, eliciting the moans he wanted to hear.

"God, you feel so good." He pushed himself into a sitting position, his arms wrapping around her. She could feel his breath hot on her neck. It made her skin tingle and her toes curl.

"I don't think I'll ever get tired of this. Or you," Nicole breathed before kissing him.

Spencer smiled into her skin. "Same."

His hand went between them, and Nicole felt his thumb against her clit. The pleasure shot through her like electricity, shocking her pulse. "Just like that. Take me just like that," she moaned as he rubbed her again.

Every nerve ending kindled in her body, ready for her implosion. It was almost too much. He was too good to be true. After all the lives Nicole ruined, she didn't think she would get rewarded with someone as pure, and loving as Spencer.

Spencer was a gift. A gift that chose her. She didn't know what she had done to deserve him, and she didn't care. She was done questioning why.

She gripped his shoulders, bucking against his cock. Responding in kind, he slammed into her, making her gasp. The heat in her core spread out to her limbs, threatening to burst her wide open.

"Come for me," he begged, sounding as needy as Nicole felt. "I can feel you. Come."

"Only if you come with me."

He gave her a smile that was too big to be called a smirk. "Whatever you want, baby."

The last word broke the dam. Nicole threw her head back and let out a primal scream, her muscles spasming as her orgasm hit her. In the last 24 hours, Spencer had given her more orgasms than any other guy she let inside her... ever.

"Jesus Christ, you're gorgeous." Spencer watched her ride her climax, her cunt gripping his cock like a vice. Nicole could feel his body tighten, his dick pulsating.

"Take yourself over the edge. Please, please. I want to see you give yourself to me."

Nicole never begged for her own pleasure. She didn't believe in it. Thought of it as a weakness, a vulnerability a partner could use to attack her. Spencer changed her perspective. He showed her how beautiful it was, how good it felt to ask for the things she needed. Right now, she needed to see this unbreakable man fall apart because of her.

"I'm there," Spencer panted. "I'm right there."

"Look at me, babe."

His head lifted from the crook of her neck. She caught his eyes, the same brown ones she lost herself in last night. Then the rest of the world faded away. He was no longer in his elevator, and neither was she. All that existed was him and her.

His arms circled her body, his fingers digging into her skin. She held onto him like he was a life preserver. His breathing quickened. His hips bucked. She felt him tense, and then release inside her. The warm flood filled the condom, warming Nicole's insides.

Spencer laid back, taking her with him. Her forehead rested on his chest. The only noise being their rapid breathing.

"I can't believe I get to check having sex in an elevator off my to-do list." His chest lifted with a laugh as he said it.

"You do not have a to-do list."

"Well, now I do."

Nicole couldn't help the smile forming. It was an infectious feeling. "What else would be on the list?"

"Oh, I don't know. Fucking the woman who owns me in every room of my penthouse? In her apartment. Her office again. In her car. A pool table. Everywhere."

"I can get on board with that."

Spencer tugged the zipper down Nicole's back and helped her step out of her dress. Her bra followed. It was the first time Spencer saw Nicole completely bare, and he reacted like she knew he would. His mouth watered, his fingers twitched, and his gaze went straight from her breasts to in between her thighs.

He enclosed her, going from one side to the other, and pressed kisses on her stretch marks. "You're a piece of art."

Her stretch marks were once imperfections her exes forced themselves to ignore when they fucked her. To have Spencer see and cherished them, like he cherished the rest of her body, made her heart clench.

"Which room would you like to hang me up in then?"

"The rarest art resides in my bedroom. And Nicole, you're the masterpiece among them."

Spencer picked her up and carried her to his bed. Where they made love with their mouths pressed together in a hungry kiss. Acting as one unit, they moved together, blazing the sheets until they left flames in their wake. There was nothing slow about how they moved.

It was fast, passionate, and consuming. They made a fire together with their desire and want. The more they made love, the more their desire burned and the faster it grew until their world became a blur.

When their bodies couldn't take anymore, they still couldn't tear themselves apart from each other. Having to touch something of the other, to know they were still there and weren't going anywhere. Nicole fell asleep, knowing this pull between them was insatiable, a force of nature neither one of them could ever fight.

# 25

# All That Money Can't Buy

Work was never so hard to leave for than it was when Spencer was with Nicole. If she didn't have obligations of her own to attend to, Spencer would have kept her in bed all day. She was the dream he imagined her being, plus more.

He was fooling himself when he thought he could take things slow with her. Nicole was like lightning in a bottle. Once you captured it, there was no giving it a chance to get away from you. You guard it close to your heart, or else risk losing it forever.

Spencer couldn't lose Nicole. He'd gone into the night not knowing what was going to happen, but he couldn't go on another day keeping her at a distance. He couldn't run the risk of her not waiting around for him.

Last night was meant to give a clear account of what Spencer could handle in his life right now. He was honest with Nicole, to a certain point. He did have a lot of his plate. The biggest being William.

Being around Nicole and hiding his connection to William was becoming an impossible feat. Pushing her away wouldn't solve the problem, but Spencer knew what would. Terminating his contract with William.

William was a man who held onto his grudges and would never let him go so easily. Spencer knew that now. Seeing the grudge he harbored against Nicole should have made him second guess getting into bed with him, but so much had changed since then.

Discovering Nicole wasn't the money-hungry femme fatale William led him to believe she was, changed everything. The heartless con woman he expected to find was guarded, self-reliant, and strong. The real person beneath the image William built of Nicole was a woman with a complicated, lonely life.

If the circumstances were different, Spencer would have completed the job. He would've taken William's money, and went on about his life a couple thousand dollars richer. But that would have required Spencer not to see Nicole for who she really was. He wouldn't have wished for that reality in the world.

It shamed Spencer that to get to this point, he was going to hurt the people he cared about. He didn't care about William's feelings, but his choice would affect Yara, his mom, Nessa, and Nicole. If they didn't get lucky and nab another high-paying case, Spencer couldn't justify keeping the agency's doors open.

Yara would be out of a job. His mom would lose yet another piece of her husband. Nessa would have two parents unable to provide for her. And Nicole? There would be nothing standing in the way of Spencer telling her the truth. That his first name wasn't Aiden, that he wasn't a millionaire, and he didn't hire her by chance. For them to have any hope of a future together, coming clean to Nicole was the only way forward.

"You have a look on your face."

Spencer looked up to his doorway to find Yara there, inspecting his appearance. "What are you doing here? Don't you have class?"

"Canceled. Professor's giving a lecture in another state. Thought I could earn a bonus coming in on my day off."

"I don't even have enough to pay you for your normal paycheck, let alone a bonus."

"Explains that grim look on your face." She came over and sat down in one of his chairs. "You're giving up on the case, aren't you?"

"How did—"

"I listened in on your meeting with Mr. Harrison last week. In my defense, it was hard not to. Your voices were loud, these walls are thin, and I left my headphones in my dorm."

"Yara, I'm sorry. I know you need the money."

"Yeah, I do, but there are job openings on my campus. And with your stellar recommendation, I shouldn't have a hard time getting one."

"I'm glad to hear it because I can't say the same for myself if this place goes under."

"I thought you told me you only took the agency over because your dad gave it to you? What did you want to do before that became an option?"

"To mooch off my parents."

Yara sighed. "I'm serious, Spence."

"I am too. I didn't have dreams of what I wanted to be. As a kid, I thought of jobs as this thing that took my parents away from me and preoccupied them when they were home. I didn't want that for myself. As much as I fought against running this agency, I don't know what I'm supposed to do if—" he stopped. Then corrected himself. "When I have to close the doors."

"Sounds like you're giving up."

"I didn't want to, but I have to be realistic here. I'm not my father or my grandfather. This wasn't my dream. It was theirs. I borrowed it for a little while, but I never made it my own. I think that's what pushed returning clients away. They could feel my passion for this line of work wasn't sustainable. I can do a good cosplay of my dad, but I'm not him. I don't want to take my work home with me or miss out on some of the greatest moments of my life because of my job."

Spencer laid his head back, facing away from Yara and up to the ceiling. "I took this job because my mom wanted me to. Disappointing her came so easy to me. I wanted to surprise her by actually doing something she wanted of me. It helped that by doing this, I was getting the chance to be closer to my dad right after I lost him. But above all, I did this to feel some sense that they were proud of me. I thought by sticking with this, I was showing them how far I've come."

"You don't think that anymore?"

He lowered his head, meeting her eyes again. "What I think is that I shouldn't be dictating my life based on what will make my parents proud of me. If I've really grown as much as I've said I have, I need to do what makes me happy. Even if it doesn't align with what they want from me."

Yara nodded, following his line of thought. "So, what makes you happy?"

"In a career?"

"In your life."

For his career, Spencer would need some time to figure that out. As for his life, he already knew for certain what did. "There's this little girl named Nessa. She's real short, but has this real big personality. Maybe you've met her?"

"She does sound familiar." Yara chuckled.

"And there's this woman." Spencer took a deep breath. "Her name is Nicole. It's new, but in the time I've known her, no one has ever felt as right for me as she does. That feels like it has to mean something."

"It does. So I say you should do whatever you have to do to hold on to them. Anything that makes your face light up like that is worth keeping. Everything else, you can figure it out later. But what do I know? I'm only a psychology major." Yara smiled, rising out of her seat.

"I will write you that recommendation if only to become your first client when you open your practice."

"I'll throw in a discount for you, and not just because I know you'll need it to afford me."

"Yara, please leave before I talk myself out of writing you that recommendation."

"Aye, aye boss. Catch up with ya later."

Yara's utmost confidence in herself aside, Spencer took her advice to heart. It gave him the courage to make the long overdue call. William didn't pick up. A good chance he was in a meeting, depending on what time zone he was in. But Spencer wouldn't wait to do this on his terms. He wanted this done now.

"William, it's me, Spencer. You gave me the week to decide if I could continue working on your case. Turns out, I didn't need a week. I've chosen to end our partnership. I can't in good faith pry into the life of a woman for you when you're a bigger criminal than she is. You think what you're doing to Nicole and her daughter is some kind of justice? It's not. It's torment, and only sick fucks like yourself get joy from inflicting that on others."

Spencer took a long sigh, calming himself. "So no, I will not be taking your dirty money. I'll have your suits returned in the same condition you gifted them to me in. Nessa and I will be out of your penthouse within the next two days. And I'll be refunding the money you paid Nicole for Nessa's party. I don't want any of your favors. The only thing I want from you is to leave Nicole and her family alone. If there's another threat made to her, I will know it was you and I'll be out of the country before they can even find your body. Let alone identify it. That's a promise. And I know those don't mean much to you, Mr. Harrison, but know this. I always make good on mine."

## 26

## There's No Going Back

Last night was one of the greatest nights of Nicole's life. Feeling as loved as she did with Spencer was something she didn't expect. Nicole couldn't put a name to what she and Spencer had yet, but she knew that if it ended here, she'd be okay. He'd given her some of the best memories she could have hoped for, and more.

But knowing she would be okay if their night together was a one-time thing didn't mean she didn't hope for more. Her body felt the lack of his absence from the moment she left his penthouse. His warmth, his scent, his touch were gone, and she was cold, empty. No one, not even Kyle, had gotten so ingrained in her bones like Spencer had.

It wasn't just a physical ache. It was an emotional one too. Being without Spencer felt as if she'd lost something special and irreplaceable. A lot of people had come and gone in her life. She would do anything for him to be the one who stayed.

Nicole spent her morning in the office, trying hard not to recall what they did on her conference table. She worked on finalizing a special surprise she had in store for Nessa. Her party was two weeks away, and Nicole wanted everything to go off without a hitch. The surprise would be the cherry on top of a perfect birthday.

As Nicole finished a phone call to a vendor, she got a call from Maya. A pit carved its way down her stomach. Something she never felt when Maya called. That was her first sign something was wrong.

"Hi, is everything okay?"

"I don't know. Thomas called and said he wanted to meet with us to discuss an update over the case."

"Already? We hired him less than a week ago."

"I know. That has to be a good thing, right? He wouldn't be calling us so soon with an update if he didn't find something."

That was Nicole's thought process too, but she didn't want to get her hopes up in case they were wrong. "When did he say he could meet?"

"In an hour. I gave him your address. I'm on my way to your apartment if you can meet us."

"Yeah. I can duck out of here early, especially if this is as important as we both think it is."

Never since the drive to the hospital when she gave birth to Maya was Nicole as worried as she was now. Thomas held the key to her future. His findings determined what their next steps were. Best-case scenario, he found something they could use to blackmail William into leaving them alone. Worst case, he found nothing, and they were down to their last option.

Nicole didn't fear going to jail. She feared missing out on Maya's life. 24 years wasn't long enough. Not for Nicole, and she hoped not for Maya.

She parked outside her building and spotted Maya in her car waiting. "Mom, Thomas is late," she said as Nicole approached her.

"It's been three minutes."

"I know, but I'm worried. What if something is wrong?"

"I'm sure everything's fine. I'm sorry for giving you the worry gene. Along with so many other things."

Maya unlocked her passenger side door and beckoned her mom to come in. She did, hugging her daughter. "Mom, please. I didn't call you here to have you apologize for the millionth time."

"I had to get one more in, in case everything goes to shit." She noticed the curious look Maya gave her then and sighed. "If Thomas called this meeting to tell us William's clean. I'm going to turn myself in to the police. I'll say I forced you to go along with the cons and that you were an unwilling accomplice. It's the only way to spare you and get rid of William's leverage over us."

"Absolutely not!"

"Maya, come on. You had to have known from the start this would be our last resort if the PI didn't come through."

"There has to be something else if this doesn't pan out."

"There isn't. I have looked. High and low, and this is it. I don't want it to be, but it is."

"Why do you keep doing this? Shutting me out, making these decisions without me? We're supposed to be in this together."

"We are, and I'm sorry if you don't feel that way, but I have to keep you safe. That's what my job as your mother is. I didn't do a good job of it for a long time, but that doesn't mean I can't start to now."

"You're using me as a justification for you doing this, and I won't allow it."

"You won't allow it?" Nicole asked incredulously. "I'm not asking for your permission."

"Do you hear yourself? You want me to give you my blessing to perjury yourself because you feel guilty for what kind of mom you used to be. I won't do it. I won't give you my blessing. You want to make things up to me? Stay here. Let's book a therapy session. Don't fall on your own sword to absolve yourself of your past sins. Nothing gets fixed by you doing that."

Nicole looked at her daughter, the woman who was becoming more like her by the day. She felt proud, and yet ashamed. "William wouldn't be coming after you anymore. That's what's fixed. I couldn't protect you from him and the other men like him once. This is my chance to do that. If you have to spend even a day in prison because of me, I will never forgive myself. You still have your future ahead of you and I want you to live it, even if I can't be a part of it."

"Don't say that to me. You promised me when I was a kid that nothing would ever happen to you. That I would never have to go through life without two parents like you did. Don't abandon your promise to me now. I still need you, Mom."

"Do you?" Shock flashed onto Maya's face, evaporating her growing tears. "I'm not being accusatory. I'm really asking because sometimes it feels like you don't. And I don't blame you if that's the case. I've put you in unimaginable situations that a mother never should have. I've done the worst to you and it's made you stronger than anyone your age should have to be. But it's also made you independent. So much so, I wonder how much you actually need me. Am I an anchor to you or dead weight you should have cut off a long time ago?"

Maya didn't hesitate. "There have been times in my life where I've considered you both. I can't tell you the number of times I wished you were a normal mom. Not this conniving con artist modeling me into her protégé. I wanted us to be normal, to have the typical mother-daughter relationship. Sometimes I wondered if I got away from you, I would get what I wanted. For me to be normal."

"You had the chance to leave when you turned 18. I saved enough money for you to go to college and live that life. Why didn't you?"

"I didn't want to leave you."

"I would have followed you," Nicole said, earning a smile out of Maya.

"I guess I worried that no matter how normal I tried to be. People would see through me and see me as a fraud. I was scared to have what I always wanted in fear of losing it."

Nicole understood how she felt. She felt it everyday running Taylor For You. "I'm sorry. You never would have had that fear if I didn't raise you to be different from everyone else."

"I made peace with it because I realized something. You were a normal mom in the ways that mattered. You comforted me when I was sad, scared, or lonely. You celebrated with me when I achieved a goal I was after. You held me and told me you still loved me when I told you I liked girls. I was angry the normalcy I longed for wasn't the one I got, but I never once question your love for me. Please, don't question mine for you."

"I don't. I question if I add any value to your life."

"You did a number on me. There's no sugar-coating that, but I know your heart, mom. It's the same heart that gave me mine. Everything you've done, misguided or not, has been to give me a better life than the one you had. Look around, you accomplished just that."

"No, honey, everything you've gotten you got on your own."

"With the tools you gave me. You focus so much on the bad, but you don't notice how much good you gave me too. I'm resilient, hardworking, and independent. I go after what I want because you taught me to. You didn't teach me by throwing me into the fire. Through it all, I could always come to you. You were my partner. Even though you aren't anymore, you're still my mom and I'll always need you. I want you in my life because I need you in it, not because I feel you have to be there. Don't doubt that again, please."

Nicole, teary-eyed, hugged her daughter. "Ugh. We need so much therapy."

Maya laughed. "My therapist would have a field day with you. Just about any therapist would."

"I bet," Nicole said, pulling away. "I have so much making up to do for you. Please don't think I don't know that because I do."

"You don't have to go to jail to make things right with me. It's not like you can braid my hair or paint my nails from all the way in there."

Nicole grinned. "You're the greatest thing I ever did, kid. I'll do whatever it takes to make sure there's no blemish on your shine. Yes, including going to jail if that's how the chips fall. I'm sorry if that hurts you, but I'm not leaving you alone. You're in safe hands with Kennedy and Eric."

"But they're not you."

"No one is, darling. Thank god," she chuckled, cupping Maya's cheek. She caught and wiped a tear before it fell further.

Maya pulled back and wiped her face with her sleeves. The sound of Thomas's car pulling behind them made them pull themselves together. "Let's see what Thomas has for us first before we jump to the worst possible scenario? Let's not lose hope."

"Alright," Nicole agreed, knowing how much Maya hated her saying goodbye.

Thomas knocked on Maya's window, and she rolled it down. "Excuse my tardiness, ladies. Didn't mean to keep you waiting. I have news of your interest. Let's go inside and talk."

Nicole let everyone into her apartment and gave them water bottles to hydrate with. "Are you planning on keeping us waiting any longer than you already have?" she questioned Thomas.

"No, of course not." Out of his satchel, he pulled out a file, but didn't give it to them. "You said I could do whatever I needed to find dirt on William. Naturally, I started following him the day after you hired me. He visited a couple of places, nothing out of the ordinary. Until around 2 p.m. when he visited The Shaw Agency."

Thomas took out the photos of William entering the business and passed it over to them. Nicole looked at it closely, searching for any familiarity. "I've never seen this building or heard of this place before."

"Neither have I," Maya added.

"He was in there about 20 minutes, and came back out, red in the face like he'd been in an argument. So I knew this wasn't a one-time visit. He had a connection to the place. Didn't take me long to find out that The Shaw Agency is of the private detective specialty."

Nicole's heart dropped. "William hired a private detective? To look into us?"

"We should've expected it. He has the money to afford one."

"Why hire a private detective when you're not after justice, but revenge? William said it to me himself. He doesn't care about us going to jail. He cares about making our lives hell."

"I had the same questions as you, so I dug deeper. William left on Friday on a business trip to New York. I couldn't follow him there, so I looked further into the agency. It's owned by a Neal Shaw, who is recently deceased. His son, Spencer Shaw, currently runs it. I haven't found anything on this man except for some local articles about his father's death. No criminal history, though the same can't be said about his sister. Underage drinking and trespassing were the two I found."

"Doesn't sound like anything major."

"Agreed, but with charges like that associated with the family, it makes their agency limited. People don't want to test them when it looks like they can't keep their own family in line. Makes you wonder why William sought their agency out instead of a more reputable one."

"You think he's having this guy do something under the table that a normal PI wouldn't do?" Nicole asked.

"Most likely."

"So, what do we do about it? Is there any way to find out what exactly this private investigator is doing for William?"

"I called the number listed on their website and posed as an interested client. His secretary answered. We had a conversation, and I asked when was the soonest I could be fit into Mr. Shaw's schedule for a meeting. I got an interesting response. She admitted he was working an in-depth case that demanded much of his time, but he could work around it to fit me in. It sounded to me he was working an undercover case."

Maya's breath hitched. "So William hired him to spy on us, but for what? To dig up enough dirt to get the cops to come after us?"

"Maybe. Or he wanted to have someone infiltrate your lives to play you both like fools, like you did to him."

Thomas said it with such finality. Not as if it was one possibility, but as if he knew it was the one. "You're holding back on us. Why?"

"I'm giving you all the information you need to prepare yourself."

"Prepare for what?"

Thomas gave Nicole the folder. "It's all there."

Nicole didn't want to open it, but she had no choice. She flipped through the contents, stopping at a page detailing William's purchases. "What am I looking at?"

"William's finances since he's been here in Philadelphia."

Maya went to Nicole's side and stole a peek over her shoulder. "See anything about him paying this Shaw guy?"

Nicole's eyes scanned the list of expenses. "No."

"What do you notice?" Thomas asked, patiently waiting for an answer.

She read it again. One discrepancy among the noise. "He's paying for an Airbnb and renting a penthouse suite. This place right here." She pointed the name out on the paper for Maya to see.

"It looks familiar to you, doesn't it?"

"What?" Maya sounded confused. "No. I—"

"Not you," Thomas clarified. "Her."

Nicole knew the address before she read the name. She should of. Considering she spent her Sunday night and other nights like it there over the last month. Her throat became sand-paper dry while staring at it. The truth staring right back at her.

"You do recognize it," Maya guessed. "Have you heard of it? Been there?"

Nicole couldn't talk, her mind was racing. It was trying to figure out how this could be possible. How the person she thought she knew for the past few weeks wasn't the real one. The man she thought was her friend, her lover, was an imposter.

Maya gave her the water bottle. Nicole took it and chugged it down. Thomas's eyes were watching her as if he expected something from her. "Are you okay?"

"No. I'm not." As showcased by her hand trembling as she put the cap back on the bottle.

"Maya, give us a minute."

"No, she can stay." Nicole didn't want Maya aware of her mistakes, but how could she not let her stay when she begged Nicole not to shut her out? She needed to hear this. More than Nicole needed to spare her from it.

"I've been to this address before. As a guest of my client, Aiden Spencer."

"That guy I met on Saturday? What does he have to do with this?"

"I think it's obvious what Thomas is implying."

Maya looked between her mom and the detective, reading in their expressions what their voices couldn't. "His name isn't Aiden Spencer. It's Spencer Shaw, isn't it?"

Nicole didn't speak. She didn't have to.

Thomas moved images he'd taken to the forefront of the file for them to see. Nicole couldn't bring herself to look, knowing what would be there if she did. Images of Spencer coming and going from the penthouse. Maybe even some of Nessa with him. Or even her.

"When I found the address, I staked out the place on Saturday. He left the building in the morning with a little girl who he dropped off at a friend's, then stopped by The Shaw Agency. I searched Neal Shaw's son within the articles written about him after his death. The details matched. He was 28 when his dad passed, making him 30 now. This man is the same age, looks alike to Neal, and has the same name. Spencer Shaw and Aiden Spencer are the same person, and he's working for William Harrison."

Nicole thought she was going to be sick. All this time, William had been playing her from the very beginning. He planted someone in her life to manipulate and deceive her, to give her a taste of her own medicine.

For the first time she could remember, Nicole had been outsmarted, outmatched, and outplayed. Worse yet, William won. His plan succeeded. He wanted Nicole to worry that every shadow and whisper was him, preparing to launch an attack against her. All this time, she was on the lookout for the wrong enemy.

Maya touched Nicole's shoulder, breaking her trance. "Mom, it's okay. You didn't know."

"I should've. I always taught you to be careful with who you trusted. I should've taken my own advice. I let in the wrong person. Who knows what he has on us or what he's going to do with it."

"Actually, I'm not sure that's something you need to worry about," Thomas interjected.

"Why do you say that?"

"If we are to believe his secretary, he's been working the long haul on this case. That means he hasn't gotten anything substantial on you yet or not anything to William's liking, at least."

"No, that can't be it. I…" She closed her eyes, not baring to see the look on Maya's face when she admitted it. "I told Spencer I used to be a con artist. I told him about the marriage con we ran on William and others."

"When was this?"

"A week ago."

"If he'd been recording you, you wouldn't be free right now. It's possible he's looking for proof."

Maya squeezed onto Nicole's thigh. "Is that why he offered to put up cameras in your apartment and office?"

"These are my cameras. He didn't buy them. Just installed them."

Thomas rubbed his eyes, sighing. "That doesn't mean he couldn't have tampered with them. Connected them to his own system to watch and listen in on you."

Nicole sunk deeper into the couch as the pit in her stomach grew into an endless black hole. "How could I be so naïve? Of course, Spencer wasn't a client interested in me or my services, but William's puppet. I don't know how I let myself believe he could want me when the signs were right in front of me the entire time."

"What signs?"

"Him wanting to know me outside of a professional setting. Meeting me at the same bar. Wanting to spend time with me after I told him the truth about who I was. What I saw as a good, forgiving man was really just one who knew how to play me!"

Nicole stood, rubbing the tension out of her forehead. "Now isn't the time to play the blame game," Thomas reminded them. "What happened can't be undone, but the plan hasn't changed. Leverage of our own against William will get him to back off."

"What about Spencer? Will he back off?"

"As long as he gets paid, I believe he will."

"Great, so we pay him off. Then what?" Nicole was fired up and nothing would get her to settle down. "We still have nothing to—"

Both noticed Nicole stopped mid-sentence. "What is it?" Maya questioned.

She was staring at the camera on her living room ceiling, a memory coming back to her. "Let me see William's finance sheet again."

Thomas picked it up and gave it over to her. "What did you just figure out?"

Scanning over the paper, Nicole found what she suspected. She dropped the paper on the coffee table and picked up her keys. "I have a hunch. Give me an hour to play it out."

"Mom, what are you doing?"

Nicole paused, turning the doorknob, looking over her shoulder at her daughter. "Getting our leverage."

\* \* \*

The nerves Nicole drove with earlier were gone, replaced by rage. It was her fault for believing in Spencer and opening herself up to him. She was foolish and naïve. Things she never allowed someone to make her before. Spencer and William would pay for that. All in good time.

Nicole entered the penthouse's lobby and waited for the elevators. She hadn't told Spencer she was coming. She wanted him off his game as much as possible. Like she had been in their entire relationship.

The elevator doors opened, and she stepped inside. The memories of their wild night inside of it were hard to push aside. She couldn't believe she let a stranger into her bed after a first date. She was no longer the con she once was, and she was going to have to accept that. Too long out of commission. She'd let herself become too vulnerable, too trusting. Nicole wouldn't let herself be played again.

Inside the penthouse, the light entered from the windows. The bright sunny afternoon contrasted with the darkness fueling Nicole forward. Her heels against the marble were the only sound at first. Then she heard him. His distant voice, coming from upstairs.

Spencer came from Nessa's bedroom, dressed in a t-shirt and slacks. His tie hanging loosely around his neck like he just came home from a meeting. "I didn't know you were stopping by," he said from the top of the stairs. There was a not yet broken-in box in his hands.

He was packing. Was he tipped off? If so, by who? He leaned the box on the railing and met her in the living room. "I'm glad you're here, though. I missed you today."

Nicole didn't go into the penthouse with a plan figured out. It was unlike her to fly at the seat of her pants, but everything she had done as of late was unlike her. What was one more thing?

The old her would have played along, not tipping Spencer off that something was wrong. Let him hug and kiss her as she tried not to cringe or gag. But the old her would've never been caught in a trap like this.

Nicole couldn't do it. She didn't have it in her to fake it with him any longer. So she didn't. "You'll get used to that feeling. Missing me, I mean. Because I won't be here tomorrow. No, I won't be here ever again. We're done, Spencer."

"What are you talking about?"

"Cut the bullshit. I know your name isn't Aiden. That you're not a millionaire tech genius, but a private detective who William hired to be his bitch. So how about you quit lying to me and let me do what I came here to do."

Spencer's shoulders dropped, and a deep breath left him. The first sign of guilt on his part. "Did William tell you?"

"Why would he have told me?"

"Because I quit. I ended our partnership today."

"How convenient. The day I find out the truth. I know I've given you the impression that I'm gullible, but believe me, I am not."

"I don't believe you're gullible."

"But you must think I'm a fool, because that's how you've played me. Tell me, did you and William have a great old big laugh when you told him you nailed me? Did he give you pointers? Did you compare notes?"

"It wasn't like that," Spencer insisted, gritting through his teeth. "He hired me to go undercover and gather proof of the crimes you've committed. That's it. I knew nothing about him threatening you, nor did I help him with his plans to come after you."

"Hard to believe that when you were going so hard for him. You defended him to me!"

"I was wrong to do that. William got into my head and made me consider for a moment that you could've been lying. Or that you made the note and story up."

"How could you believe him even for a second? You saw me! You saw how broken I was because of his actions, and you thought I made it up?" Nicole couldn't stop her voice from breaking at the end. To lose someone is hard. To discover you never really knew them after you bared your soul to them was another type of pain.

Spencer moved closer. His hand reached out to touch her. To comfort her, but she pushed him away. He had no right to offer her that. Not anymore.

"I had a momentary lapse in judgment, but it was just a moment. You're right. I saw your pain, and I believed it. I also saw William dealing with the pain of what you did to him when I first met him. That's what gave me a second thought about the truthfulness of your story. But, Nicole, after that one moment, I was yours."

"Don't ever repeat those words to me again. You were never mine. You came into my life to find evidence to put me in jail. You lied to me every second we spent together. I sympathized with you, trusted you, confided in you. If you wanted to take me down, you could've done that without sleeping with me. So tell me, what was the plan? Record a detailed confession from me? To make me tell you my deepest, darkest secrets as we laid in bed together?"

"I would never agree to sleep with a suspect to win a case. That was never a part of the plan. William believed you were money laundering and wanted me to gain access to your finances to prove it."

"Money laundering?" She scoffed, not believing her ears. "That's ridiculous."

"I figured that out the more I saw of your business. Then he wanted me to tail you and I got this bad feeling I was being used. You were right. William didn't hire me to send you to jail. That's what he told me. That's what I believed for a while, but when you told me about him threatening you, I put the pieces together. He was using me to get to you."

"You figured that out and still didn't quit until today?"

"You don't understand. I needed the money. I'm not the millionaire I've been pretending to be. My father's agency is on its last legs. It's the only source of income I have. William was promising me a lot of money to get the case done. I needed it to support Nessa."

"I know all about doing whatever you have to do to make sure your kid is taken care of. But you went too far. You should've fabricated the evidence William asked for. Get the money and end this charade. You didn't have to pretend to want me."

"You think I was pretending?" Spencer's eyes pleaded with hers. Begging her to listen, to hear him. But his words weren't the ones she wanted to hear. "Nicole, I fell for you during this. It was the last possible thing I've should have done because I needed William's money. I needed it to save my father's business and to create a safety net for Nessa. I didn't need to be paid off to fall for you. I did that for free."

"You expect me to believe that? Why would you want me? I'm a crook. You're a "good guy". The kind of man who takes in his niece, gives up his life to raise her and fight for his dad's legacy. I'm the anti-thesis of what you're supposed to want."

"You think I don't know that? That's what I've been telling myself this entire time, but you were undeniable. My feelings for you, that's real. That's why I quit after what transpired between us last night. It's why I have packing boxes upstairs, because I can't be a pawn in William's plan to destroy you anymore. I couldn't continue on like I had. Not when I was falling for you."

"If that's true, why didn't you tell me?"

"I was going to—"

"But held out because you knew you were in the wrong? That the foundation of our relationship was built on lies and manipulation. What a way to start a relationship, right?"

Nicole walked forward, her eyes looking around the wide room, searching. Spencer followed her as she scoped out the space. "I thought I was doing the right thing, taking on the case. Never did I expect I would feel anything but discontent for you. I was told you were a ruthless con woman who trapped her husbands into cheating on her. That you were a black widow. And it was a role you played well. So well, I believed it. But that's the thing. I stopped believing it at a certain point. Once I got to know you, I knew you weren't that woman anymore."

"I don't fault you for taking the case, Spencer. I've done worse things for money. It's the fact that you couldn't tell me. You couldn't let me know what was happening. If you had told me the truth the second I accused William of threatening me, we wouldn't be in this position. I told you the truth about who I was that night while you clung to your lies and let me believe you were in the dark about what was happening to me and my daughter. Then, as we got closer, you still didn't confess it to me."

"I know, and I'm sorry. More than you know."

She turned to face him. "I'm not a black widow. I've never killed anyone. I'm not out to kill William or any other man. I've only ever been trying to survive and take care of my child. I'm not saying that to absolve me. My cons hurt people, good and bad. It was a decision I made and one I will have to live with. You and William may not have planned for you to fall into bed with me, but you did. You hurt me the same way I hurt the men before you. That's the decision you will have to live with."

Spencer reached out for her. His fingers touching her shoulder. "Nicole, please. Let me make this right."

"The only way you could do that would be if you had a time machine."

"I fucked up. I regret how I went about this, but I don't regret us."

"There is no us. I don't know who you are, Spencer. I know what you have shown yourself to be, but the man behind the facade is a stranger to me. I won't have people in my life that I don't trust."

Nicole shrugged away from him. She moved toward the kitchen, not finding what she was looking for. Spencer was a step behind her.

"What are you doing?"

"Looking for something."

"Nicole," he pleaded.

"This isn't some movie where you can apologize, and I'll forgive and forget. I don't know what you expect from me. At least when I conned my marks, I left. I didn't expect their forgiveness."

"I didn't con you."

"You stole from me."

"I didn't take anything from you."

"No? What about my trust? My heart?"

"You gave those things freely."

"I didn't know who I was really giving it to."

"No one has ever known the real you," Spencer countered. "You've hidden yourself from everyone until me. Something about me made you open up. Not the millionaire cover, but something in my heart made you feel safe enough to show me the real Nicole. Who isn't a black widow or a con artist, but a woman trying to be better. I see the good in you, Nicole. Try to see the good in me."

"It's too late."

"It doesn't have to be. Let me prove to you that what we have is real. We can move past this."

"There is no moving past this. So stop, please. Just stop." Nicole pushed past him and went up the stairs. Spencer wasn't letting go as easily as she hoped he would, but she couldn't deal with focusing on him at the moment.

"Where are you going?"

"I'm looking for something."

"What?"

They stopped at his bedroom door, the scene of their late night romp. A room filled with love was now tainted by lies. "What are you looking for, Nicole? What can I give you so that you'll forgive me?"

"Spencer, shut up," she told him in a hushed voice.

She honed in on the ceiling above them. After their long night, Nicole stared at it for a long time before sleep welcomed her. There was nothing special about the ceiling. It was made of the same material as the guest bedroom and Nessa's room. With a fountain flush mounted light in the center. The transparent glass of the fixture revealed the lights above the fan.

Nicole spent hours staring at it, thinking about the man lying next to her. His arms wrapped around her, their legs tangled, their breaths in sync. The room was dark and her mind was in a daze. Now, in the harsh light of day, she noticed it. A glint of the sun reflecting off the glass, shining through the fan blades.

She pointed to the ceiling. "Can you turn the light on?"

Spencer's eyes followed hers, but he didn't ask questions. He turned it on, and bright light bathed the room. Nicole shielded her eyes, letting them adjust before moving toward the light. She kicked off her heels and stood on the bed; the frame wobbling underneath her.

Spencer moved from where he was standing and holding his hands out near her ankle. Not touching her, knowing better, but there if Nicole needed it. She wouldn't.

Nicole stretched her arms, her fingers inches away from the fixture. Standing on her tippy toes, she took off the glass light fixture. She dropped it onto the bed and reached up, her hand grasping the plastic. "Got it."

Nicole got off the bed, meeting Spencer on the ground. She held the small camera in her hand. Spencer stared agape at it. "Nicole, I swear on Nessa's life I didn't put that there. Or know it was there."

She believed him, but he could swim in the ocean of his guilt a while longer. "Get your laptop."

He rushed out of the room. She could hear his heavy footsteps as he ran down the stairs. She inspected the camera while she waited for him to come back. The brand was none other than Wison, owned and founded by William Harrison.

There were probably other cameras in the house, having watched Spencer and Nessa the whole time they've been living there. William had installed the same cameras in the home they shared, but Nicole consented to that. She and Maya were aware of them being there for "safety". They knew the cameras could prove helpful down the line for them.

Spencer and Nessa didn't approve of this. This wasn't done for their safety. Rather for William to spy on his good soldier.

Spencer returned, laptop in hand. Nicole set the camera down on the desk and opened the computer. She plugged the end of the device into the laptop and clicked a few keys. The screen was taken over with the view from the camera. She found its log and went back a couple of hours ago. Last night, to be exact.

With a click of the button, there she and Spencer were. Making love. Their naked bodies entangled. His mouth on hers, his hands on her body, and hers on his scalp. They didn't hold back, and it felt good in the moment, but watching it knowing everything she knew now made Nicole want to hurl.

"Nicole, I'm sorry."

"You didn't put it there."

"I'm still sorry."

Her eyes stayed on the screen. More than the intimacy of the act itself, it was the happiness on her face. She was laughing, moaning, kissing him back with the same enthusiasm as he was giving. That's what she had with him. A mutual adoration that was raw and pure. She would never have that with Spencer or another person again.

She unplugged the camera and them. "I'll be taking this with me."

"What are you going to do with it?"

"It's none of your concern anymore. From this moment forward, we're done. As friends and as anything more. Our only point of contact will be Nessa's party, which will continue as planned because I won't screw that little girl over because of you."

"Nicole, William was paying for—"

"I'll give you a refund to return to him. I'll handle the costs myself."

"You don't have to. I'll—"

"I'm not taking anything else from you, Spencer. I'll do the party for Nessa and once it's over, we'll call it. That'll be it for us. For good."

Spencer reached for her again, his fingers curling around her wrist, his skin burning hers. "I don't want to lose you, Nicole."

She looked up at him, making sure he heard her when she said, "I was never yours to lose." She walked away, and this time he let her.

## 27

# Light in the Aftermath

As a kid, when Spencer was having a bad day, the person he could talk to without judgment or jokes was Melanie. In the ensuing years, that would no longer be an option with Melanie's addiction slowly taking away the sister Spencer knew and loved. Times like now were when Spencer wished he could talk to her. The version of her from when they were kids, to listen to his troubles without passing judgment.

There was always Lawrence, but Spencer wasn't in the mood for his friend's loving, but passive aggressive "I told you so". Yara may have been training to be a therapist, but Spencer didn't want to unload any more of his problems on to her. As for Nessa, he would sooner bury himself alive than discuss any details of the situation with her.

That left one person.

Since their fight, Spencer kept conversations with his mom brief and vague. Fearing he would upset her more than he already had, Spencer didn't discuss the agency's shortcomings or Nicole. But as he sat across from her at her dining room table on a Thursday afternoon, Spencer came clean. About everything.

"Oh boy," Rayna sighed, leaning back into her chair after Spencer finished confiding in her. "How did you have the energy to live all this out? Because I'm exhausted just from hearing it."

"All of this has taken its toll on me. I'm not proud of the choices I've made. But, Mom, I really screwed things up this time. I don't know how to fix it or where to go from here."

"What makes you think I have the answers? I've never driven a company out of business, or let myself be used as someone's puppet, or driven away the person I loved."

"Woah, I never said I loved Nicole."

"You didn't have to. By coming to me and telling me about her, I know you do. You've never come to me about anyone you've dated. Let alone to ask for my advice to remedy the situation."

"Maybe I would've if you were around more."

There it was. The root of their issues. The boulder in the way of mother and son ever moving their relationship forward.

Rayna touched Spencer's hand with two fingers, not yet in the place for a larger gesture of comfort. "You know I love you, Spencer. And your sister. That's why I worked so hard. To make sure you two would have the opportunities that were never afforded to me. I made mistakes. Both your father and I missed signs of you two kids struggling. I regret that every day."

"Because you feel like if you caught Melanie's reliance on alcohol early, you could've prevented her addiction?"

"Yeah." Rayna nodded, her eyes turning sad and reflective. "No matter what the counselors tell us, I'll always think I could've done more by being more aware. I know you think that too."

"Mom, I don't."

"You do. That's why a part of you will always resent me and your father. If we would have been around more, we could have seen the warning signs in Melanie and got her help before that disease took her from you. It's okay that you feel that way. I resent myself for it too."

Seeing his mom carry as much guilt as she did over Melanie made Spencer want to argue back against her claims. He couldn't, though. She would've seen through the lie. "There's plenty of blame to go around. I was there. Every day, I saw her. I noticed the change in her, but I didn't tie it to her drinking. She took care of me so often I didn't want to have to turn around and snitch on her when she was letting off steam. I didn't want to betray her trust, but ended up betraying her anyway."

"You can't keep carrying this around on your shoulders, honey. You're not responsible for Melanie. None of this is your fault. It was our job as her parents to do right by her. Your job as her baby brother was to be her little brother. That was all you had to do, and you did. You were a great brother to her, Spencer. You still are."

"Really? I'm not a terrible brother for keeping Nessa away from her?" Touching on the topic that spearheaded their fight was a risky move, but if they were going to clear the air, Spencer needed to bring it up.

Rayna pulled her fingers back, but remained close across the table from him. "I'll admit, when you first told me you weren't giving Melanie a chance to speak to you or to Nessa, I was upset. I didn't understand how you could deny her something that could be so healing for her. It took me a little while to see it from your side. It is a big risk."

"A risk I don't want to take." Spencer got up and opened the refrigerator, needing the cool air to help calm him. "When Melanie is sober, she's great. I have a lot of wonderful memories of us together. She was the only one I could turn to growing up. That's why her leaving Nessa hurt so much. I want to be the safe space for Nessa the same way Melanie was to me."

"And you are, Spence. Nessa is so lucky to have you. You're doing an amazing job."

He closed the fridge, his back against it. "It's hard. Nothing I ever do for Nessa will make up for the loss of her mom. That's the one hole I can't fill, but I have the power to by connecting them again. I want to do that for her. I really do, but what if something happens? What if she falls off the wagon again and gets herself hurt? What if she hurts Nessa in someway? If something happens, it'll be my fault."

"Spencer, you're blaming yourself for something that hasn't happened yet."

"I can't help it. It's where my mind goes. Mom, I've been making a lot of mistakes lately. I don't want to make another."

Rayna got up and joined him. "Have you told Nessa that her mom wants to see her?"

"No. Why would I get her hopes up if I'm not interested in having them meet?"

"Sweetheart, you just got dumped because you hid the truth from your girlfriend. And here you are doing it to Nessa. That girl is your world. It's obvious how much she adores you. How is she going to feel when she learns you kept this from her? If the roles were reversed and Nessa was the one who had to tell you something big, would you be upset if she didn't tell you?"

It never crossed Spencer's mind that might be something Nessa would feel lied to about. He'd been too focused on his own feelings of betrayal. "You're right. She has a right to know. This is her life. She should have a say in this."

"And you already know what Nessa would want to do. She misses her mom. She's going to want to see her."

He couldn't dispute that, not after her sketches had gone from flowers to portraits. She was working her way up to sketch one of her mom. Spencer was Nessa's guardian, but controlling her life for her wasn't what a good guardian did. He could regulate and advise, but taking the decision away from her would forge a future of resentment between them. That was the last thing Spencer wanted.

"Have you gone and visited Melanie at her facility?"

"I have. Two weeks ago. She looked good and was in positive spirits. Your name came up a few times. She wondered if you would ever respond to her calls."

With a deep breath, Spencer did something he should've done a long time ago. Put Nessa first. "I'll do Melanie one better. I'll go and see her."

Rayna wrapped her arms around his shoulders and kissed his cheek. "I think that's the right decision. See her for yourself. Talk to her. Raise your concerns. Just get somewhere with her, and remember, she's still your sister. She loves you. You love her. That should never change."

"I hope it never does." Truly. His relationship with Melanie had become a roller-coaster with highs and lows, but never did Spencer stop loving and caring about her. He wondered if it was the same way for her.

"Well, we solved one of your problems," Rayna smiled, rubbing his shoulder.

"If only the other solutions were as easy to get to." Spencer rubbed his eyes, not having gotten much sleep since Nicole walked out on him. "Mom, I'm sorry about the agency. I really thought I could have done a better job with it than I did."

"I should be the one apologizing for that. You wanted to sell it from the start. I pushed you to honor your dad's wish of running it when we both knew that was his dream for you. Not your own."

"That's the thing, though. I don't have a dream for myself. I'm not artistic like Nessa or analytical like you. My major was in communication. The degree for people who have no idea what they want to do with their lives. I've graduated and am still no closer to knowing."

"You have time to figure that out."

"My business is crumbling and I'll be forced to move back here with Nessa if I don't find something else soon. I'm 30. All I have to show for it is failing my dad's last wish for me and chasing away the closest person I've ever come to loving. You and dad had your lives mostly figured out by this point? Why can't I do that?"

"Your 30 is not at all like my 30, and that's okay. 60 years ago, there were expectations placed on me by society, and I had to follow the path set out for me. Women didn't have many choices. They were expected to get married and start a family. Fortunately, times were changing when I turned 18. It was 1982 and women had more options more than ever. I chose a career in urban planning. I chose your father, chose to have a family with him, but not to have my family disrupt my career. Which we all know what became of that."

Her eyes again took on a reflective shine. "So no, your 30 is not like my 30. You don't have to have it all figured out right now. I don't regret my career, or marrying your dad, or having you or your sister. But if I had the time to focus on my career and then later on time for my family, I think it would have done us a world of good."

"Mom, I don't have the time to focus on one. Nessa is depending on me to provide for her."

"Okay. Then let's figure it out together. What do you like to do?"

Spencer laughed. Such a simple question, no easy answer. "That won't help."

"Humor me. What do you like?"

He shook his head, but answered. "I like… helping people. That was the easy part of being a PI. When I got clients, I liked solving their problems. It was when they asked me to do something unethical that I lost the joy of it."

"Okay, so you like to help people. What are your interests?"

"Nessa," he replied, without thinking. "She's my number one interest."

"Apart from her."

Spencer racked his brain. Then a laugh broke his silence. "I'm a freak—"

"Sex work is completely valid if—"

"No! Mom!" Spencer quickly interrupted her. "I was going to say I'm a freak because I enjoyed school. Things came easy for me there. I tested well. I enjoyed writing papers. I went to grad school just so I could stay in school."

Rayna smiled at her son. He returned her gaze, wishing he could read her mind. "What? What is it?"

"My baby boy is going to be a teacher."

"No—"

"Think about it. You loved the academics, but you enjoyed the social aspect of it too. You beamed when you went off to college because you got to surround yourself with other like-minded students. It would be like that again. Plus, you're great with kids. Imagine a classroom of Nessas wanting for you to impart your knowledge onto them. Don't tell me you wouldn't love that."

He couldn't. Her pitch excited him over the idea. "A teacher. Huh."

"Yes, a teacher. It's a stable job and one where you'll be helping the next generation. That sounds perfect for you."

"But I would have to go back to school and that costs money we don't have, nor can we spare. Then teachers don't get paid the money they should."

"Teacher assistant."

"What?"

"Become a teacher's assistant. That way you can get your feet wet in the field immediately and decide if you really want to do it. If you do, you can go back to school when you have the money. As far as the pay, you can't win them all."

"I'll consider it." Spencer would do a lot more than consider, but he didn't want to get his mom's hopes up if it didn't pan out. Regardless, he was happy to be getting somewhere. If only that could be applied to his romantic life. "I should've come sooner to you with my problems. I might still have Nicole if I did."

Rayna offered him a sad smile. "Like I said, hon, you can't win them all. There's no undo button you can press to fix things with Nicole. You hurt her. The best you can do for her is give her the space she needs. If it's meant to be, it'll happen."

"I don't like leaving things to chance."

"I know, but you're the one who screwed things up. What you want doesn't matter. It's your turn to listen to what she wants and respect it."

"Even if what she wants isn't me?"

Rayna squeezed his hand. "Especially then. You owe her that much."

That's where his mom was wrong. Spencer owed Nicole a hell of a lot more.

# 28

# Making Preparations

A lunch never held as much weight as the one Nicole sat in on now. "You better be here to tell me something good."

Thomas sat down across from her. The restaurant bustled around them with cackling plates and customers' chatter, but neither noticed nor cared. "Good is an understatement."

"Tell me more."

"My lawyer contact reviewed the footage. He believes we can get William charged with invasion of privacy, revenge porn, stalking, and harassment."

Nicole leaned forward, her eyes gleaming. "Are you sure?"

"I trust him, so you can trust me when I say this is the leverage you needed to get William to back off of you forever."

This should have been a moment that called for celebration, but Nicole wasn't ready to pop out the champagne yet. "If I press charges against him for this, he'll come back and hit me with charges for stealing from him."

"Your ex said he didn't give William any proof. And that he found no more cameras in the penthouse before he had to leave."

"That's what Spencer said, and his word isn't exactly the most trustworthy to me right now. William could've had a camera in the living room where I confessed my past to Spencer. We can't operate on the belief he doesn't have anything on me."

Thomas took a drink of his complimentary water, resetting. "The camera he used to record you was one of his models, right?"

"Yes, why?"

"Threaten him with a lawsuit. Not just against him, but his company too. You threatening to go public with charges related to him illegally recording you alone could tank Wison's stock and reputation. He, as the CEO, could get a big fine or lose his position. Hit him where it hurts. Make him choose between his petty need for revenge or his name, reputation, and fortune."

Nicole was used to shutting down ideas, but Thomas's wasn't bad. Flawed, but she didn't mind humoring him. "I don't hate it."

"But?"

"William could call my bluff. He could know I'm just using the threat of a lawsuit to get him to back off. He won't believe I'll actually go public with it."

"Nicole," Thomas sighed, leaning in, lowering his voice. "You conned him out of thousands. Along with five other millionaires. If anyone can trick William into believing they would do the unthinkable, it's you. I can't believe you haven't considered that."

Sweet talk for a good tip. Nicole recognized it all too well, but she smiled anyway. "I can't fool him again. He knows my game now."

"I wasn't suggesting that. All you need to do is make yourself believe the lie, then make him believe it too. This is your best bet, Nicole. Want William to go away without having to serve a jail sentence? This is how you do it."

Knowing when to accept a win was hard for Nicole. Harder this week with the massive two losses she took with learning the truth about Spencer and finding the recording. She wanted nothing more than to get the upper hand on William and walk away from this mess, no more hurt than she already was.

"Fine, I'll do it. I'll confront William with the video and threaten him with the lawsuit."

"Great. If you want to sell its legitimacy, there's one more thing you could do."

"And what is that?"

"Get Spencer to agree to participate."

She scoffed, not believing what he was telling her. "You have to be kidding."

"I'm not. If you go about this alone, William could fire back and threaten to go to the police with whatever proof he may have on you. But he doesn't have anything on Spencer. He committed no crimes during his investigation into you. If Spencer backs you up and says he'll join your lawsuit, William doesn't have anything to hold over his head. Worse case scenario, Spencer is the one who threatens the lawsuit. Unlike you, there are no skeletons in his closet that William can intimidate him with. He's innocent in this."

Innocent was not the word Nicole would use to describe Spencer Shaw. In the eyes of the justice system he was, but an innocent person did not spend weeks lying in the face of someone he claimed to care about. He was about as innocent as Nicole. Barely, if at all.

Thomas didn't see it that way. "Put your feelings for the guy aside. Him being in on this will help its believability to William. He was an employee of William's, who later found a hidden camera in a place William put him up in. I get it. He hurt you, but he's a victim in this as much as you are."

Nicole was tired of arguing. So she did the thing she had done a lot lately. Concede. "I'll talk to him. Get him to sign on."

"The bit of pain it's going to cause you asking him for help will be worth it. You're almost at the end of this, Nicole. Remember that."

Thomas got up and left. Nicole wasn't far behind him, paying for their drinks. On her way to her car, Maya called. "How did the meeting go?"

"Thomas and I worked out a plan. I'll threaten a lawsuit against William and his company for the recording. He thinks going after his livelihood will get him to drop his vendetta against us."

"That's great news. Why don't you sound happy about it?"

"Because," she drew out while she opened her door and settled into her seat. "He wants me to get Spencer involved. Thinks it will sell the credibility of my lie if I have him backing me up."

"Oh," Maya said flatly. "You're not going to want to hear this, but I think he's right. There's only so much you can do without your past getting drudged up. But if Spencer wanted to press charges, he could do it without the fear of something from his past hurting his case."

Nicole didn't want to admit she was right, but there was no denying it. "I'll talk to him. I just hate that I have to talk to him."

"You knew you would have to see him again."

"Yeah. At his niece's birthday party where we didn't have to interact at all. Not me having to ask him to do me a favor. That's the last thing I could ever want from him after he lied to me."

Maya didn't respond right away. In fact, she was quiet for so long Nicole started to think their lines must have disconnected. "What is it you're not telling me, but want to?" she asked when she saw her daughter was still on with her.

"I haven't wanted to say it the last four days because you've been going through a lot with Spencer and the revenge porn."

"Just say it, Maya. I can handle it."

"Oh boy, okay. You don't think you're being a little… just a tad hypocritical with Spencer?"

Suddenly Nicole was glad they were having this conversation over the phone, and she guessed Maya did too. "Hypocritical?"

"For years, we lied for a living. We lied to everyone. People who deserved it and people who didn't. I'm not saying what Spencer did was right. He should've come clean to you before beginning a romantic relationship with you, but I know from my own experiences that fessing up to someone isn't easy."

"Honey, please don't compare yourself to that man."

"How can I not? I fell for Kennedy while lying to her. I wasn't expecting to develop feelings for her while we tried to scam Eric, but when it happened, I didn't know what to do. I was betraying you and our livelihood by seeking something out with her. I was betraying her by hiding who I really was. I knew this, and I still didn't pull away from her. Instead, I got in deeper."

"Why?" Nicole asked her why when it first happened, but now she asked for a sense of clarity into Spencer's mindset.

"Because I knew if I didn't, I would be betraying myself too. As con artists, we never allowed anyone to get close to us. We were careful and guarded. That's what was expected of us, but with Kennedy, she was able to get to know the real me. And the real me wanted to get to know the real her. So I did. I betrayed you and what we held dear to us because I was afraid of losing a connection that I had never had with anyone before. I knew the consequences, but I decided I would be okay with them because for a brief moment I got to feel what it was like to love and be loved. And no, it wasn't perfect, but it was mine."

Maya took a breath. Her words were heavy, and Nicole let them wash over her. "Spencer was wrong for not telling you the truth. Just like I was wrong to hide the truth from Kennedy, but I see how happy we are now. A happiness we would have never experienced if she didn't give me a second chance. It's taken a lot of work and therapy to get here, but here is good. It's safe. It's home for me. I want that for you. I hate to think that you're so close to it, but a mistake will keep you from ever getting there."

Crying in a parking lot was a low Nicole had never achieved before. Not even when she was a single mom and couldn't find a quarter to get a shopping cart to bring home groceries for her hungry baby. Maya's words touched a nerve. Not the one that had her upset and angry at Spencer. It was the one that had her feeling sorry for herself and wanting to be alone.

"Maya, I love you, but I have to go. I'll call you later."

She didn't wait for her daughter's response before hanging up. Turns out Nicole was wrong after all. She couldn't handle it.

# 29

# At the End Lies the Truth

Spencer had been to a lot of places, but a rehabilitation facility in Michigan was a new one. He, Neal, and Rayna visited numerous in the Pennsylvania area since Melanie was 18, when it was clear her drinking went beyond a rebellious streak. Visiting one outside the state was new, but if it was getting Melanie the help she needed, Spencer welcomed it.

Rayna told him Melanie was doing well. She was working hard on her sobriety, and was excited to see him. He believed the former, but had a hard time believing the latter on his drive up. Spencer ignored her calls, gave her the silent treatment. Classic petulant behavior.

And if she felt like he was keeping her child away from her, Spencer couldn't picture how this meeting could go well. She was his sister. Someone he should've trusted more, but he put more faith into his fears than he did in her. Now as he sat on the lobby's couch, Spencer worried how that might cost him.

A shadow on the stairs made him look up. The golden shine her skin held was gone, dull as Spencer had ever seen it. The hair she always kept managed was simple in its frizzy braids. Her soulful brown eyes were wistful as she took in the sight of him. Something in it told

Spencer what deep down he always knew. Underneath Melanie's appearance and struggles, his sister was still there.

He got up in time to return Melanie's hug, holding her close to his chest. "I missed you, Mel."

"I missed you too, Spence." Melanie pulled back, inspecting him. "You look good. How's Nessa? Is she with you?"

"No. I'm sorry. I wanted to meet with you alone before I considered doing that."

Her disappointment wasn't hidden well, but she nodded like she understood. "I'm glad you came. I began to wonder if you ever would."

"I'm sorry."

"Here I thought I would be the one apologizing until my tongue was numb. At the rate you're going, you'll beat me to it."

The light tone to her voice surprised Spencer. He would've expected her to be angrier with him.

Melanie took his arm and walked them toward a side door. "Let's talk."

"I'd like that."

Not wanting Melanie to feel uncomfortable under his gaze, Spencer searched for something else to look at. It took him no time to find it. He noticed the facility's emerald grass field and how full it looked after the morning's bout of rain. Tall stone walls enclosed the expansive grounds around them on the deck. No other houses or buildings in sight. Just nature and its sounds, a bird chirping a song after the rainfall.

"The facility is nice. Getting this quietness and this view every day must be nice." Spencer hoped small talk would make her more comfortable.

"Yeah. It's something right out of Nessa's sketchpad."

"She's into sketching portraits at the moment."

"Really?" she asked, amazed at the ways Nessa had grown in her absence.

"Yeah. She's very talented. She does a lot of drawings on my arms." He rolled up his sleeve to show off a faded flower she drew on him before he left. "I don't know what flower this is."

"I do." Melanie held his arm, her eyes entranced by it. "It's a freesia. They're thought to represent friendship, trust, and thoughtfulness. Did she know you were coming here to see me?"

"Yes. I told her. I didn't want to hide it from her." A small smile took over his face. "She sent me here with a message for you. Smart kid."

"You have a lot to do with that, more than you know." Melanie looked at him, her eyes pleading. "How is she? Is she happy? Healthy?"

"As happy and healthy as can be. She's a little smaller than her age group, but the doctors assure me that'll change."

"Good. That's good. How is she in school?"

"Great. She's doing well academically and loves to read."

Melanie snorted. "She must get that from you."

They found a white bench by a windowsill to sit on. Their knees were close, but not touching. The little distance between them did little to stop Spencer from feeling her shaking.

"Nessa is really doing well."

"Is she... is she talking about me?"

"Sometimes." He didn't want to lie. "Less than she used to. I think she got used to receiving the same answer, so she stopped asking."

She nodded. "That makes sense. Thank you for being honest."

"It's the least I can do." Spencer placed a hand over hers. "How are you? Mom told me you were doing well."

"Yeah. It was a hard start. They always are, but I like the people here. Everyone is very supportive."

"That's good. Are you working through the steps? You've done those before."

"I have, but these are a little different. Instead of working on why

I started drinking, the focus is on staying sober. And what I have to lose if I don't."

"Lose?"

"Yeah. The counselors are encouraging me to look at the positive aspects of my life. The things I want to fight to stay in. I'm learning to see my sobriety as something I get to keep. Not a burden or a duty."

"That sounds healthy."

"It is." Melanie smiled. "I know it's a hard concept to grasp, but it's working for me."

"I'm glad." He squeezed her hand. She squeezed back. "Can I ask about the moment you decided you needed to come here? Every time before, we had to force you to check yourself in. What was different this time?"

She took a deep breath. "When I left Philly, I thought I was finally getting the freedom I always wanted. No younger brother I needed to play mom for. No parents to be the perfect daughter for. And no child I needed to be a role model for. Please don't judge me for saying that."

"I won't. I'm here to listen. Something I should've done a long time ago."

The sigh that Melanie released let go of the tension in her. "I won't lie. Being on the road was fun. I did what I wanted, went where I wanted, and saw what I wanted. I partied and drank with people who didn't judge or shame me for it. I could be myself, or who I thought I was, without anyone trying to hold me down."

Spencer stayed quiet, wanting her to say her piece without him interfering. "It was nice." Melanie looked ahead of her, not meeting his eyes. "Then, after a while, I couldn't ignore the truth anymore. The parties and the people got old. I wasn't having fun anymore. The freedom I thought I had was just another prison."

"My days were spent trying to fill a hole inside me. Nothing worked.

No matter what I did, the emptiness never went away. When it was your 30th birthday months back, I went out and got wasted. I mean it. I really outdid myself."

"Why?"

"Because I couldn't be there for you. No matter what our relationship was like, we never missed each other's birthdays. I didn't want to miss yours, but I lost the right to call or see you after what I did. I was feeling sorry for myself and tried to numb it. That's all I remember from that night. I blacked out. I woke up the next day alone in some motel room of a random girl I met. It scared the hell out of me."

Spencer felt the same fear and anger he always did when he heard about her drinking. But it wasn't directed at her, but at himself. "I should've done more."

"Hey, none of that," Melanie warned him. "This isn't your fault. If you're going to blame someone, blame me."

"No." Spencer shook his head. "I'll stop. It's just, I've always felt like I could've done more. Stopped you before things got this bad."

"You didn't do anything wrong. You were a kid. We both were. We didn't know this kind of pain existed."

"That's not true. You did, didn't you? That's why you went searching for relief in a bottle."

"I was in pain. I just didn't have the word for it back then. Mom and dad expected so much from me when we were growing up. Be a good sister, be a good student, a good daughter, a good role model. A good everything. They didn't mean for it to be, but it was so much pressure and I cracked under the weight of it. Drinking became a way to help me handle that pressure. When it was gone, so was the stress. But, the thing was, the stress was always there. Drinking only suppressed it, never solved it."

"When I was in that motel room, I had that moment addicts are always talking about. That moment where I knew things had to change because dad's gone. Mom's getting older. And I ruined things with you. I couldn't rely on you guys to save me anymore. Not when I'd pushed you away. You didn't know where I was. It's not like you could have looked for me. You didn't even know I needed to be searched for. I was alone and had no one to blame but myself. That scared me more than anything."

Spencer's heart broke. She looked so ashamed and broken. All he wanted to do was make it better.

"I checked myself into the hospital, the closest one I could find. Got myself sober, then found this place. It's taken a while, but I'm working through my feelings. I'm facing the pressure I always felt, but suppressed. I have to. In here, it's not a choice." She motioned toward the building they were standing on the outside of. "I'm getting better. Slowly, but surely. I understand your skepticism. We've been down this road before. What's different is I know what losing everything looks like. I never want to come close to living that reality again."

Spencer took her into his arms, kissing her head. "I'm proud of you, Mel. I'm sorry I wasn't here sooner."

"It's okay. We've both made our fair share of mistakes."

"I've been so selfish. I told myself I was afraid of letting you in because of how it might hurt Nessa if you left or fell off the wagon again. While that's true, I also kept you away because I didn't want to open myself up to being hurt by you again."

"That's not selfish. That's self-preservation."

"Not at the expense of your relationship with Nessa."

Melanie shook her head. "No. Not at all. I'm the one who abandoned my daughter. The sister you knew would never do something like that. I became a stranger to you and myself. The only thing I can do is try to be the best version of me, not only for her, but for me too."

"You will. I have no doubt about that. Nessa wants to see you. I won't deny you two that. Not anymore. If you're serious about your sobriety, then you have my full support. I'll contact my lawyers and we can discuss getting your parental rights to her back."

"Woah, pump the breaks, Spence. Did you think when I asked to see Nessa that I meant I wanted custody of her back?"

"You don't?"

"Spence, I'm not ready for that. I might never be. I love that little girl and I want to be involved in her life as much as you will allow me to be, but I can't be her mother."

"I don't understand. Why not?"

"Because I can't be the mother Nessa needs or deserves. I've got a lot of growing up to do. My therapist said I've never been my age. As a kid, I acted older than I was because I had to take care of you. Then I regressed in my 20s back into the teenager I never got to be. Now I'm 34 and it's time for me to live my life as the age I am."

She looked at him, seeing Spencer still wasn't quite getting it. "I'm learning to live with the pressure of being a human. It's scary and I'm being as brave as I can, but it's a lot on my plate. I can't handle the pressure of being a mom too. I know that sounds selfish, but I'm being honest with you about how much I can take. If I don't get to be a little selfish with my needs right now, I'll hit my limit and break again."

Spencer only had one word for her. "Okay."

Melanie was visibly surprised. "Okay? Really? You're not upset or disappointed?"

"No. It was my assumption. You know what's best for you better than anyone else. I would never force you to take on more than you can chew. You need to focus on your recovery. I'll focus on Nessa. And since we're being honest, I'm really happy you need me to. I love your little girl, Melanie. I think of her as my own, and I don't know if that's fair to you or Ronnie, but that's the truth. You can rest easy knowing she's with me. She will always be taken care of."

"Fuck Ronnie," she said, laughing, making Spencer cry for a different reason. She wiped away her little brother's tears like she used to when they were kids. "I couldn't pick anyone to be a better dad to Nessa than you. You've grown into the man that I always thought you could be. I know you never heard it from mom or dad, but I'm so proud of you. You have never been a disappointment to me because I always knew this person was inside of you. I'm glad you're sharing it with the world now because you're pretty amazing. And I'm so grateful for you, Spencer."

"I'm the grateful one. Grateful towards you for giving up your childhood so I could have one. Grateful to love and be loved by Nessa. She is the greatest thing to have ever come into my life."

"And into mine." Melanie sniffled, trying not to cry. "Thank you for looking out for her when I can't."

"Don't thank me. Just get better. So you can be a part of her life. She'd love that."

"She would?" Melanie's voice cracked asking.

"Yeah. You know how you said there was nothing but an empty hole in your heart? I think it's because you gave everything in it to her. She has so much love in her heart for everyone, but especially you. She loves you, Mel."

"I love her so much. You both mean the world to me. When I'm in here, thinking of you and her is what keeps me going."

Spencer held Melanie tighter, not sure how he could let her go again. "Her birthday is next Friday."

"I know. I have it marked on the calendar."

"If you're feeling up for it and your team here approves, I want you to come. Be the greatest birthday surprise she could ever ask for."

"I'd like that." Melanie looked up at him, smiling. "I love you, Spence."

"I love you, too, Mel."

It was Saturday afternoon when Spencer returned home. He spent his evening with Melanie away from the facility for dinner until he needed to bring her back. It was too late by then for the 10 hour drive, so he stayed the night in a hotel.

Nessa was with Rayna, and he didn't feel like being alone in their small apartment. The office was as quiet as it had ever been. No Yara typing her homework on her laptop, hoping for a distraction in a phone call. No Nessa running on its hardwood floors. Just the tickling of a distant clock and the creek of the floorboards under Spencer's footsteps.

As soon as they could find a seller, The Shaw Agency would be no more. Gone like the men who built it. It was a sobering thought, one Spencer needed. The agency was the last link to his dad and now he was ready to cut it. He was ready to start a new chapter.

With the lights turned off, Spencer settled at the head of the desk, watching the sunlight dance around his walls. The peace and quiet of the office, interrupted by the chime of the bells ringing.

"We're closed. Permanently," Spencer said right before looking up and seeing her. The woman he was so desperate to see. "Nicole?"

Nicole was as beautiful as ever in a slim-fit white and navy pinstripe dress. No red-rimmed eyes to show the toll the ending of their relationship might have had on her. Not that Spencer had expected them. She would never let him see her in a vulnerable state again. He lost that right.

He didn't know how long she had been standing there, but judging from the look on her face, long enough to hear him. "You're closing?" She had the decency not to look happy about it.

"There was no way to keep it going." Spencer got up from his seat, walking slowly around the desk towards her. "What are you doing here?"

"I have a plan to get William to stop coming after me and Maya. Your help… could be useful."

"I'll do anything. Name it."

"Call William and set up a meeting here tomorrow. Don't tell him I'll be there. He doesn't need to know."

Spencer wanted more details than that, but wouldn't push it. "That's it?"

"No. I need you to back up whatever I say to him. Follow my lead and don't act like it's your first time hearing it. Can you do that or not?"

"Of course."

She blew air through her nose, smirking, but there was no genuine joy behind it. "That's right. I forgot. You're a trained liar. I'm sure you'll do great."

"Nicole." He wanted her to be cruel. He wanted her to tell him what a scumbag he was. He didn't deserve any less.

"I'll be here at 10 o'clock sharp tomorrow night. Make sure everything goes according to plan and it'll be the last thing you'll ever have to do for me."

"Nicole, wait."

She didn't. She walked right out the door. Spencer didn't stop her. He wanted to chase after her, but his mom's words echoed in his ears. It wasn't about what he wanted. Nicole was the one who got to decide their fate, and Spencer would have to live with that decision.

# 30

# The Ultimate Gambit

Nicole stood by the front window, watching the clock. Listening out for any signs of the man who had made her life hell. Cars passed by, not one of them William's. Still, she kept watch. It was better than turning her head and paying attention to Spencer and whatever he was doing in his office.

In a few minutes, she would be stuck in a room with the two men she most wanted to drop dead. If this wasn't her only shot at getting the upper-hand on William, she would've left already. But this was it. If everything went according to plan, then this was the last time Nicole would have to deal with William and Spencer. That's what kept her pushing forward.

The end was near, and Nicole couldn't be happier.

"You sure you gave him the right time?" Nicole questioned loud enough for him to hear her, her eyes remaining locked out the window.

In the corner of her eye, she could still make out Spencer's frame. "Yes, I did. I know how important this is to you. I wouldn't make a mistake like that."

Nicole didn't have the energy to argue with him. Her heart and mind were too heavy with other matters. She was about to have her last stand off with William and was going to need to save all her strength for that.

"Nicole?"

"What?"

"What's your backup plan if this doesn't work?"

"This will work."

"What if it doesn't?" Spencer came to stand next to her, getting more into her line of vision than she wanted him to be. "Is that a possibility you've considered?"

Nicole was past confiding in Spencer. He didn't need to know more than he already did, so she shrugged, keeping her gaze trained out the window. Spencer stood closer than she preferred. She could feel his body heat and smell the scent of his cologne. She was trying her hardest not to become affected by his proximity, but her heart was pounding in her chest.

This wasn't how things were supposed to be between them. She should've hated him. Be disgusted by him. Yet she found herself feeling a longing ache for him that she never felt before. When Kyle left her, there was no deep pang of loss inside her. His leaving her wasn't hard because he left her a long time before. His body had simply caught up with the rest of him.

There was nothing there worth mourning. With Spencer, Nicole could feel herself grieving for their what-could-have-beens. The nights she dreamed of spending cuddled up next to him, wishing the world would stop existing, were gone. Their honest judgment-free conversations, her favorite thing about being with him, were a thing of the past.

Nicole so desperately wanted to live in a time and place where she could press herself into his chest. So he could hold her and whisper everything was going to be okay. She never needed comfort or reassurance from another person. Never felt the desire for it. Until him.

Nicole would never forgive herself for developing feelings for a private investigator. It didn't matter she didn't know. The damage was done, and her heart was left feeling the consequences of it.

Spencer touched her shoulder, the lightest and briefest touch she had ever felt from him. She didn't know what was worse. Her desire to lean into his hand. Or the fact she could tell the difference between his usual firm caresses and the tender touch he gave her now.

"I know you don't trust me. You don't want to have to be doing this with me by your side. I'm not going to pretend I didn't earn the way you're treating me now. But no matter what happens today, I want you to know that I'm always going to be in your corner. If this fails and we're left to find another way out, I'm with you. All the way. You're not alone."

Her voice cracked as she asked, "Why are you telling me this?"

"Because I don't want you to hurt further, Nicole. I can't undo the pain I've caused you, but I can try to limit the amount of it you feel in the future."

He let his hand fall, bringing it back to himself. Nicole had the urge to take it into her own, but she didn't act on it. She couldn't afford to make another false move. She remained still and silent, not knowing what else to say or how else to act.

Saving her from further conversation with him was William's arrival.

"He's here," Nicole notified Spencer, watching him park his car. "I'm going to go unlock the door."

"I'll do it. Element of surprise, remember? If he sees you, he'll know this is a trap."

"Yeah. You're right. Sorry." Her nerves were getting to her. No con felt as big as this. The stakes were high, and she was playing a game with a man who was determined to win at all costs.

"Don't be sorry. Be your best. William Harrison is no match for you."

"I know he isn't."

"Then prove it." Spencer pointed to his office. "Go."

She listened, leaving the door open a crack so she could hear them as they approach. "William, hi," Spencer's voice said from a distance.

Nicole stilled her shaking hands by holding onto Spencer's desk. Her palm hit the edge of his laptop, waking it up. The view on the screen was the paused video of their illegal sex tape. Something about seeing the thumbnail of the video William recorded without their consent subdued Nicole's anxiety. Anger took its place, and Nicole used the anger to steady her.

"After that voice message you left me, you could've left the refund and suits at the penthouse. We could've avoided seeing each other again."

Their footsteps were right outside the door. "I hear you, but if I did that, I wouldn't have gotten to see your reaction to this."

Spencer pushed open the door to reveal Nicole. She stood in front of his desk, looking every bit of the woman who had tricked William into trusting her five years ago. He stared between the two, a scowl on his face.

"Surprise, William."

His glare stayed fixed on her. "What is this, an ambush?"

"You would know all about ambushes. Wouldn't you, William?"

He crossed his arms over his chest. "You have a lot of nerve, Nicole. You really think you can intimidate me?"

Nicole was confident as she walked away from the desk and stopped in front of him. "Everything coming your way you've earned."

"Do you hear yourself? You're a con woman. You deceive people for a living. Are you really acting like you hold the higher ground?"

"When I conned people, I did it to their face. I didn't hide in the shadows while I let my henchman do my bidding for me."

William faced Spencer. "You aligned yourself with a woman who speaks of you like this?"

"She can speak of me however she wants. She's not wrong. You hired me to be your henchman. I was just the last to know."

Spencer's composure impressed Nicole. Him taking a step back and letting her lead this seemed to come easy for him. William was not as impressed by his response. "I can't believe you rather side with her. I would have paid any number you wanted to keep this place running. Now what are you going to do? Pray another multi-millionaire walks through the door and hires you?"

"No, I'm going to move on. Get a stable job and not rule my life based on money anymore. Unlike you, I'm not so obsessed with it."

"Obsessed with money?"

"You have to be," Nicole interjected, shifting William's focus back onto her. "Otherwise, why hold this grudge against me for stealing from you? You never loved me. You loved how I fulfilled your dream of having a gorgeous woman parade around for you like some trophy wife, but you never really loved me."

"Did you listen to any word I told you when we last met? You ruined my relationships with friends. Many of whom were industry contacts. Wison has lost out on a lot of deals because of you. Not to mention, you're responsible for my mother disowning me before her death."

"You say that, but I don't recall ruining anything. You forget I was there. I knew Annie. I knew your friends. Your relationships to them were already damaged before I got to them."

William's face reddened. "You don't know what you're talking about!"

"See. This is what I mean. You have such an ugly, violent reaction whenever you hear the truth. Your friends felt like they walked on eggshells every time they tried to advise you on a matter. And your mom, ugh, poor Annie. She tried her hardest to support you, but it wasn't enough. You blamed her for things that were out of her control. You made her feel bad for things she had no business feeling bad over. When it came out that you tried to sleep with your stepdaughter, it was just the final straw. They were looking for a reason to cut you out."

"No, no, no. Shut up."

"Why? Afraid of hearing the truth? I understand it can be quite bitter, but it's for your own good. Your inner circle hated you. They only stuck around because you were a tech wiz. When they found out you were a sexual deviant, they saw the writing on the wall. No matter how much of a genius you are, they found working with a man bound to be hit with a sex crime wasn't worth the risk."

William shook his head without stopping, avoiding looking Nicole in the eyes. "And with your mom? Well, after Annie found out, she couldn't deny it anymore. Money had either made you into a monster, or revealed you always were one. You may have been her son, but she saw you for what you really were. She wanted nothing more to do with you. If she were still here, she would know she made the right choice."

"You're a fucking bitch. A fucking lying whore," William spit out with venom. Empathizing his point by shoving his finger in Nicole's face.

Spencer slapped it away before Nicole got a chance to. He shoved William back by his shoulder, putting himself between the two. "I made you a promise if you went after her again, I would kill you. Call my bluff by taking another step toward her and I'll let you choose how I do it."

William stepped back, recognizing Spencer wasn't kidding. "This is what she does. She provokes. She taunts. If I'm a monster, it's because of her. She did this. Everything is because of her. She's evil."

"Call me whatever you want, but at least I don't hide behind a camera and a hired hand. You're pathetic, William."

"A camera?"

She lifted the laptop screen and pressed play on the video. The sounds of the love-making between her and Spencer filled the space, but it didn't phase Nicole. She focused on William's reaction. How it went from confusion, to disbelief, to settling on muted anger.

He took a deep inhale as he smirked. "I knew it. I knew I had it right when I said you were developing feelings for her."

"Are you seriously acting as if this is your first time seeing this? It was your camera hidden inside your penthouse."

"I'm not denying those things, but I didn't go out of my way of capturing that. If I was going to allow an employee of mine to stay in a place I was renting, you better damn believe I will have cameras around. I needed to ensure you weren't stealing or damaging the property. That's where this video came from. Not me trying to get back at you. Though I can't say I'm upset that I have proof that you're as much of a backstabber as she is."

"I owed you nothing, William."

"As I owed nothing to you when I put those cameras up. I'm glad we could reach a place of understanding there. I'll take my refund now. You can keep the suits. You'll need them on your job search."

Nicole almost laughed at how William thought he was in control here. It had been a long time since he felt this weak and small. It was time to remind him of his place. "You're not walking out of here. Not without agreeing to our conditions first."

"You think you have power over me? Nikki, I can dig up that recording of you admitting to Spencer that you're a con artist and have you in cuffs by tomorrow. If anyone has power over someone here, it's me over you."

"Wrong again." Nicole smiled snidely. "You can't use that video.

If there even is one. Pennsylvania's Wiretap Law makes it illegal to record private conversations where the individuals involved didn't give consent to be recorded. Did you give consent, Spencer?"

"No, Nicole, I did not. Did you?"

"Nope." She popped her lips. "Go to the police with that recording and you'll be implicating yourself. Which bodes well with our case against you."

William narrowed his eyes. "Your case?"

"Did I say against you? I meant you and Wison. You used your company's product to record revenge porn of your ex-wife and her new boyfriend. Obsessed much?"

"You're trying to prove I'm what, exactly? Still in love with you?"

Nicole took a seat on Spencer's desk, crossing her legs, and getting comfortable. "More like obsessed with me."

William's laugh bolted out of him. A laugh that would have made the Joker envious. "Good luck trying to prove that."

"I think I have a pretty strong case for myself. My attorney agreed. What with this not being the first time you've come after me."

"What are you talking about?" he asked, his low voice barely hiding the rage behind his words.

"Last year, you came to Philadelphia to crash my wedding shower to my ex-fiance. You got into a war of words with my daughter, scaring her enough to make her fall and sprain her ankle. I know you're getting up there in age, but surely you remember."

"I thought I was invited by you. I have screenshots of my conversation with you."

"You mean with the person who was impersonating me? No court is going to consider those screenshots proof. In fact, they will see the messages as proof you were still pining over a woman who left you years ago. Coupled with my guests' accounts of your erratic behavior and the scary language you used with my daughter, I think the judge will agree. The stalking and the revenge porn are just the cherry on top."

William was losing control fast. "You're crazy. Do you know how crazy you sound?"

"Do you know crazy it looks for you, a man who built his company and life in Sacramento, to drop everything to come to Philadelphia and stalk his ex-wife? Not once, but twice in two years."

"One incident from last year is not enough to say I've stalked you."

"You're right. Good thing I have more than one incident. Maya's coworkers can contest to you being the one asking to see her after her show last month. Lily Lane can also back up that you ordered flowers from them to…"

Nicole picked up William's order receipt from behind her. "To give to your wife. From the research Spencer has done on you, Will, you haven't remarried. So I have to assume you were referring to me. To a jury, it would look like you're trying to win me back. Or you're so delusional you somehow created a fantasy where we're still together. Either way, you're the one looking crazy."

"You think this little stunt of yours is going to make me forget how much of a fool you've made me look?"

"I say you're doing a good job of making a fool of yourself without my help."

He shook his head. "I'm done. You and Spencer deserve each other. I'm out."

William turned, and Spencer stepped in his way. "You're not going anywhere until we come to an agreement."

"What the hell do you want from me? Extort me of money?"

"No," Nicole said, standing. "I want your assurance that you will never come after me or my family again. You will not stalk us. You will not threaten us or blackmail anyone close to us. You will leave us alone or Spencer and I will move forward with our case. We'll sue you and your company. Take you for all that you're worth, get you replaced as Wison's CEO, and publicly wreck your image until it's in complete ruins. Is that what you want, William?"

He glared at her, and she glared right back. They had a stare off, the room thick with tension. Nicole knew the moment he gave up. His petty need for revenge wasn't worth his livelihood or public image. "You win. I'll leave you alone."

"Not just me, but my entire family. As well as Spencer's. We never want to see or hear from you again."

"Do you think I want to see either of your faces again? I'm not actually obsessed with you, Nicole. Maybe with getting back at you, but don't mistake that for love. I'm not in love with you. I hate you. Have ever since the day you left me and despised you the day I found out the truth."

"The feeling is mutual."

"I'll leave both of you and your families alone. You're not worth losing everything I've worked my life for. But while I get to move on from this with a clean slate, you two are stuck in the mess you created for yourselves. I never asked Spencer to fall in love with you, but I'm glad he did. I can imagine the moment you found out the truth about him being a liar. You must have felt something akin to how I felt the day I discovered you for the con you are."

"Did you feel betrayed and disgusted?" William asked, looking her right in the eyes. Nicole held his gaze, but wouldn't give him the satisfaction of an answer. He took her silence as a yes. "Good. The con got conned. I couldn't have written a better ending for you than that. Good riddance, Nicole."

William turned his back to her, snatching the envelope of cash out of Spencer's hands and left.

Nicole could feel Spencer's gaze on her, but she didn't face him. She had just bested her toughest opponent. It was a victory hard won. She should've basked in it. Glowed in it. Yet for someone familiar with what winning felt like, Nicole never felt more like a loser than when she left Spencer's office, too scared to look at him.

Too scared to say a word. Too scared to admit William might've been right.

# 31

# Forgive Me Tonight

"Is your back turned?" Nessa's small voice asked from behind the door to Rayna's living room where Spencer stood, in a tux, waiting for her.

"Yes, Nessa, my back is turned."

"Are your eyes closed?"

"Yes. They're closed. Now can I turn around, or are you not ready yet?"

"Hold on!" Another minute passed, the only sound being her and Rayna's muffled voices behind the door until Spencer heard the door crack open. "Okay, you can turn around."

Spencer turned slowly, giving her the chance to change her mind. When she didn't, he opened his eyes and his breath left him. Nessa stood in a lavender princess dress, the sleeves short, and the skirt billowing out. Her braided space buns were gone. Rayna transformed her hair into a cornrow ponytail with two-strand twists.

She was wearing the tiara Spencer had bought her, the pink jewel in the middle shining as bright as she did.

"Oh, my god." Spencer was speechless. "You look like a real princess."

"Feel like one too. Thanks, Uncle Spence, for the compliment and the party."

He didn't deserve her praise. He wasn't paying for the party and almost let his stubbornness get in the way of her vision of it. If it wasn't for Nicole, this party wouldn't be happening.

"Come here."

Spencer knelt, hugging her. He couldn't believe she was six. Where did time go? The day she was born could've been yesterday from how well he remembered it. He woke, hungover, to a voice message from his mom. She was fuming, having called him eight times to no answer.

When he finally did, she gave him the name of the hospital and he showed up, wearing sunglasses. They didn't hide his hangover or him from Rayna's wrath, but he showed up. Which was more than Ronnie could say.

While Melanie slept and his parents each took a turn ripping Ronnie a new one over the phone, Spencer held Nessa. With a banana bag IV in his arm, he hummed "All the Stars" to her and told her how much he loved her. Spencer didn't think his life would change all that much with becoming an uncle, but when those brown eyes and pudgy face met his, she instantly owned his heart.

Six tumultuous years later and Nessa had grown and developed into her own person. Their roles and what they meant to each other had changed. The one constant was how Nessa still owed every bit of Spencer's heart. He loved this kid, would give her the world if he could. Tonight he would have to settle for giving her back the one thing she'd been missing.

"Happy Birthday, Ness."

"Thanks."

Her voice was off. Spencer looked up at his mom. She didn't have a guess for why that was. "What's wrong?" he asked, pulling back to look at her.

"Nothing. I was just hoping mom could've come."

Neither he nor Rayna had let it spill that Melanie was coming. Currently, she was at Spencer's apartment, waiting for Rayna to pick her up. Spencer hated keeping it from Nessa, but the joy from the surprise when she saw her would be worth it.

"She wanted to, Ness, but she couldn't."

Nessa's small frown was enough to make Spencer second guess keeping this a secret.

"She wanted to. Really, really bad, but her rehab didn't think it would be a good idea. She's working really hard to come home so she can see you again regularly."

That made her nod, but her smile was still weak.

"But hey." Spencer lifted her chin, "I'll bet money they'll let her call you when we get home."

"Really?" The last time they talked was a year and a half ago.

"I'm positive."

"Okay, Uncle Spence." She smiled, a little brighter.

"Good. Now come on, you can't keep your guests waiting all night."

Spencer took her hand, giving his mom a look that he hoped she read as, 'tell me if I'm going to hell' because he felt like it.

Spencer was stunned when they arrived at the party. New Horizon looked even better than it did when Nicole originally showed it to them. Art donned every wall of the community center. Not just any art either. It was art customized for Nessa.

A sketch portrait of her smiling was the first sight guests saw when they walked in. Spencer recognized the artist as Emma, the artist Nessa, worked with the day of the cake tasting. After helping her practice, Emma sketched Nessa. The finished product was better than Spencer could have imagined it.

Following the music brought guests downstairs to the ballroom. The large space had been taken over by a dancefloor stage so the kids could dance to the DJ. Like promised, rooms in the center were open dedicated to a different art activity with a professional artist specific to the craft.

One room allowed the kids, with the help of a vendor, to paint different picturesque images. On the projector, the artist displayed images of ocean cliff-sides, zoo animals, superheroes, and more. He would go around the room, guiding and helping the young minds. Something Spencer could see himself doing and loving.

In another room, a pottery class was held. A vendor helped kids make clay mugs, plates, jewelry trays. A third and fourth room had canvas and easels set up, while Emma and another artist taught the basics of sketching.

Spencer and Nessa trek through the litter of kids and parents to get to the dining room. Set up like a rehearsal dinner, there was a table up front for the guest of honor and her guests. With smaller tables filling out the rest of the room.

Pink and purple cloth dressed the tables with matching flower centerpieces. Number six balloons were tied down to the floor. No chance of them getting loose. Between the dining room and hall was a face painting and photo booth. Kids could choose what they wanted to be painted as, then get their pictures taken.

In the opposite corner was where the avalanche of gifts Nessa was racking up stood. "This is amazing." Nessa smiled as she took everything in.

"It is." Spencer had to agree. He hadn't seen anything like it before. Nicole really pulled it off.

"There you are!"

Both Spencer and Nessa looked toward the voice, finding Nicole walking over to them. Spencer's heart sped up seeing her. She wore an olive green a-line knee-length chiffon dress. She easily could've been mistaken for a bridesmaid, but looked every bit as beautiful as a bride.

"Ms. Nicole!" Nessa met Nicole halfway and waited for her to bend down to hug her. Spencer saw Nicole's eyes close as she held Nessa tight for the last time. She wanted to be rid of Spencer, which unfortunately meant letting go of his little girl too.

"Hey, little one." Nicole kissed her cheek, her brown eyes blinking back at hers.

"Why do you look sad?"

"In all honesty, Nessa, it's been a hard two weeks for me. But nothing brought me more happiness than planning this party. I knew how much it meant to you. I wanted it to be the best."

"It is, Miss Nicole! I love it."

"That makes me so happy to hear." From the distance they were apart, Spencer could still make out that the stars in Nicole's eyes weren't the reflection of the above lights, but tears.

"Nicole," he called. It was the first time her gaze fell on him since she entered the room. "Can you keep an eye on Nessa for me for a second?"

She must've been questioning it, but didn't vocalize it. "Sure. Nessa, do you want to a tour of the kitchen and see the delicious food we're about to eat?"

The kid nodded her head and took Nicole's hand as they walked out of the room. It gave them time to hang out one-on-one like they both wanted and for Spencer to check in on the surprise. A text was waiting for him.

Melanie: Mom and I will be there in 10 minutes. Can't wait to see her. Thanks again for this.

Spencer smiled at the message. For all he had done wrong lately, he was glad to have gotten this one right. "Spence," a voice deeper than a kid's shouted towards him.

It was Lawrence with Yara by his side. "Where is the birthday girl?"

Lawrence questioned, looking around the room for her.

"You didn't forget her at home, did you?" Yara teased.

"She's with Nicole on a tour of the kitchen."

"Is she coming back soon? Cause we would like to give Nessa her gifts personally since we're special to her."

Yara nodded. "Exactly. I didn't buy this overpriced teddy bear from my campus gift store just for it to get lost in that mountain."

"She'll be back soon, guys, but I would recommend holding off on them. The best gift she's getting will be here in about five minutes."

Lawrence arched his eyebrow, then unfurled it. "Melanie is coming?"

"Oh," Yara added. She took Lawrence's gift wrapped present out of his hands. "The mountain suddenly doesn't look so bad anymore. I'll go and add Teddy and your gift to it."

Lawrence waited until she was away to ask, "How could you not give me a heads-up on that?"

"It came together at the last minute. Otherwise you would've been one of the first to know."

"Alright, alright. You're forgiven. I'm just glad everything worked out. She should be here for this."

"That's what I thought too. This wouldn't have been complete without her being a part of it."

Spencer looked down at his chiming phone again, then at Lawrence again. "My mom and Melanie are here."

Anxiety started to set in. "Relax," his friend advised him, seeing it take over his demeanor. "I'll go and get them while you get Nessa."

Spencer nodded, liking the sound of that. "Have them waiting in the courtyard. I want the moment to be Nessa's. No gossipy parents or overtly curious kids watching and commenting on it."

"I got you, man." Lawrence slapped his arm as he walked past him.

"Thank you." Spencer didn't know if Lawrence understood how

much his friendship meant to him, but he hoped he got to repay him for it one day.

After checking every room in the building what felt like a dozen times, Spencer found the kitchen. Catching Nessa and Nicole stealing cupcakes from the platter. "Nessa," he warned, walking in.

Nicole turned around and gave him a dirty look. "She's the birthday girl. She should get what she wants," she told him as she tried to defend their actions.

"I don't think the birthday girl wants a stomachache."

"I won't get a stomachache. My stomach is strong."

"Oh yeah." Spencer laughed. "I forgot, you have the stomach of a goat."

"A goat?" Nicole and Nessa both questioned him.

"Yes. I read they're supposed to have the strongest stomachs of all animals."

"Uncle Spence, stuff like this is why you're single."

Nicole snorted, covering her mouth when Spencer shot her a look. "Alright birthday girl, I'll let you have that one because it is your day and because it's time for you to get one of your gifts."

"Gift opening isn't supposed to happen until after they eat." Nicole eyed him warily.

"This one gift requires her to open it now."

That piqued Nessa's interest. She ate the rest of her cupcake in one bite. "I'm ready," she said with her mouth full.

"Drink something before you choke."

"I got it." Nicole gifted her with a strawberry milk carton.

She drank it long enough to seal Spencer's approval. Then he took Nessa's hand. "Close your eyes."

She did, and he led Nessa out of the kitchen. Spencer kept looking back to make sure Nessa hadn't opened them. She didn't, but each time he checked, it surprised him to see Nicole tailing them.

"Why are you following us?" he mouthed.

"We're on a schedule," she replied, pointing to the imaginary watch on her wrist.

She was right. They had a party to get back to. "5 minutes. That's all we need."

Nicole's face showed reluctance, but she didn't fight him on it. She stood a few feet away as Spencer stopped Nessa in front of the double doors leading into the courtyard. He opened the door.

"Don't peek," he whispered into her ear. He held onto her shoulders, guiding her to the middle of the garden where Melanie stood. Rayna and Lawrence stood aside, their faces beaming from a moment they knew this would be.

"Open your eyes," Spencer told her.

She did, her breath catching as she saw who was standing in front of her. "Mom?" Her eyes widened, looking between her and Spencer, who was bent down, closer to her height. "Is she real?"

"Yeah, sweetheart. She's real."

"But you told me—"

"I know. I lied."

"You say to never do that."

"There are exceptions. This was one of them."

Nessa looked at her again. Melanie was doing her best not to scare Nessa away by blubbering, but the tears were threatening to escape her.

"Go ahead, Nessa. Give her a hug."

His request gave her the permission to do the thing she'd been seeking for a year and a half. Spencer watched Nessa, in her ballet flats, run into Melanie's arms. His feet stayed planted where they were, knowing they needed this moment without interruption.

"You came!"

Melanie picked her up, holding her close to her heart. "I didn't want to miss another one of these. Going forward, I want to be here for every one of your birthdays, baby."

"What about when I'm sixty? You'll be pretty old by then."

Melanie laughed, wiping away her tears. "If I'm still here and you want me, I'll be there."

"I always want you, mommy."

"Me too, Nessa."

Spencer stood to his full height. Lawrence had his arm around Rayna's shoulder, while she sent Spencer air kisses. This moment wouldn't have been possible if he hadn't loosened the reins.

He could be protective of Nessa without being controlling. People she wanted could come into her life, and he didn't have to worry they'd disappoint her. Spencer couldn't take back the time Melanie missed or the pain that could've been avoided if he'd been less afraid, but he could be better. He planned on doing better.

"I really hate myself for interrupting this, but you all should probably get inside." Nicole's voice rang through his ears, breaking the spell. He turned and saw her standing by the door, the stars having formed constellations in her eyes. "The birthday girl has a party to attend."

## 32

## Foolish Love

While the guests ate from a hand crafted menu, Nicole holed herself up in the bathroom, crying in a stall. First crying in a parking lot, now this? It was like she was competing with herself for the most embarrassing place to have a breakdown in.

If Nicole from a year ago could see her now, she would make fun of her for getting in this deep with a guy and his child. So deep that seeing the child reunite with her mother left her reduced to tears. It shouldn't have affected her. Yet it did.

She had missed it. In the time where everything changed between her and Spencer, she missed the moment he decided to let Melanie in. She'd been a part of the journey in helping him see the situation in a different light, but she missed the end. The resolution.

The worst part of it was, Nicole wouldn't be a part of the next journey Spencer took. With his life, his career, his family. It wouldn't just be the resolution she missed out on, but everything.

It would be the same for him. Spencer would miss the next journeys Nicole would endeavor in the next stage of her life. He wouldn't be there to give her advice or offer her support. Their time in each other's lives was almost over. And when the party dwindled out, their respective paths wouldn't cross again.

The thought made her cry harder. How did she let someone become this important to her so soon? That the thought of them leaving her forever wrecked her?

The only thing that could quiet her was the door to the bathroom opening. Nicole covered her mouth and swallowing her sobs, not wanting anyone to hear her. Black flats paused outside her stall, but didn't attempt to open.

Nicole held her breath until the water began to run. She sighed, wiping the tears from her face, and left the stall. She washed her hands and patted her face with a cold water, hoping it would ease the puffiness.

The water temporarily blinded her vision, so she only heard the offer of a towel, but didn't see where it came from. "Thanks," she said, feeling the plush fabric enter her hands.

"I must say I have walked in on many women crying in a bathroom, but never at a kid's birthday party."

"I've always thought of myself as a trendsetter."

The woman chuckled momentarily, but shifted back to concern. "Are you okay?"

"I'm fine."

"I've heard that before, said it so many times too that I know when it's a lie. It's a gift." The woman touched Nicole's shoulder while her head was still bowed in the towel. "Come on. It's probably easier to talk to a stranger about it. Gives you a fresh perspective."

Nicole didn't share her logic, but the stranger was persistent. "Long story short, I found out this guy I was dating had been lying to me the entire time we've known each other. The lying I could get over because it started when he didn't know me. It's that he kept peddling the lies even after we grew close. He never even fessed up. I found out on my own."

Nicole said this all into her towel, her face feeling hot despite the cool water that just ran over it. She wasn't sure if the towel muffled her speech too much or not until the stranger replied, "He sounds like a tool. Why do you like him again?"

A laugh came out of Nicole. She dropped the towel and looked at the woman, still chuckling. The laugh got caught in her throat when her vision zeroed in on Melanie. Her face didn't register shock. Nicole was left to assume she knew nothing about her relationship with her brother.

"It's complicated."

"Complicated is my middle name."

Nicole didn't need her to elaborate. She knew she was being truthful. "He... he's the first guy to make me feel like I'm better than what I am. I was... not a good person for a long time. I've been finding my way out from being that person. It wasn't until I was with this guy that I felt like I'd actually made it out. Does that make sense?"

"Unfortunately."

The regret and sadness in Melanie's eyes was obvious. The last thing Nicole wanted was to trigger her. Melanie went into her clutch and pulled out some mascara and lipstick. "Keep talking while I fix the mess you made of your makeup."

Nicole looked into the mirror and gasped. A raccoon could've been her twin. Melanie sat her down on the sink. "So, do you only like this guy because of how he makes you feel? Because there are always other guys who could make you feel that way."

But there was only one Spencer. "No. I like him for the man he is. He's everything I didn't think existed. I've been around men who were nothing but red flags, but there wasn't one with him. He showed himself to me as thoughtful, selfless, and protective. He put me first. Something I never had with anyone before him."

"But?" Melanie pressed.

"I don't know if I can trust that was really him. What if the person I fell for was an illusion? What if who he really is, is someone completely different?"

She held her eyes wide open as Melanie applied the mascara. "Want to know what I think?"

"I'm at your mercy."

"You said you've been around men you knew were red flags and you were proven right. Yet you never saw or felt one when you were with this guy. Maybe you can't trust him, but you trust yourself, don't you? You have a good gut. Wouldn't it have felt the same knowing feeling about this guy if everything good about him was a lie?"

Nicole hadn't thought about it like that. Melanie smiled as she began applying the lipstick. "I got you there, didn't I?"

"Yeah, but he still lied to me and didn't come clean until I confronted him."

"So you're in love with a man who is just as flawed and fucked up as you are? Congratulations. Welcome to being a human."

Nicole's jaw dropped. "I didn't say I loved him."

"You're crying over him in a bathroom. Come on, don't be daft. Would you cry over just anyone in the bathroom?"

"No."

"There you go then." Melanie grinned, putting her makeup away. "Look, I don't know the guy, or you, for that matter. But if there's a chance he is the guy you fell for and he accepted you with your baggage, then try to do the same for him. Try to see him in the same light. Maybe the person he is, isn't the person you knew him as. He could be worse, or he could be better. It's a chance you have to be willing to take. If you're not, then maybe the relationship was never really worth it."

Melanie's words drummed in Nicole's head after she left the

bathroom. Could it be that simple? Give Spencer another chance to see if he would break her heart again? She wasn't interested in being made out as an idiot again. Would she look like one anyway if she let her pride keep her from a man she could've loved?

She stuffed the thought away when she returned to the party. Nessa had finished opening the last of her gifts. Which meant her surprise for the birthday girl was imminent.

"Ms. Nicole!" Nessa jogged over to her, ditching her friends. "You missed me opening my presents."

"Oh, sweetheart, I'm sorry, but you haven't seen mine yet."

"The party wasn't my gift from you?"

"Oh, no. I have a surprise gift for you if you're up for another one."

"I am! I am!"

Nicole's mood brighten under the girl's excitement. "Everyone," she said, catching their attention. "We'll be making our way to the ballroom to see Nessa's last gift."

The cast of children, parents, and Nessa's family followed Nicole downstairs. The ballroom was so spacious it didn't feel cramp as everyone filed into it. "Can someone cut the lights?" Nicole requested.

It took a second for darkness to splash over the room. There were muttering and questions, wondering what they were doing in the dark. When the show begun, it silenced everyone.

Lights of art danced onto the walls and ceilings of the room, but it wasn't the art of one of the instructors. No. It was Nessa's.

The day Nessa showed Nicole her drawings, Nicole asked if she could borrow her sketchpad for a few days. Nessa was more than happy to hand it over. After researching companies that created light art, Nicole sent the images off to the most reputable one. Now, they were the only light in the room, showing her creations for the world to see.

"What's happening?" Nessa's question wasn't a criticism, but an awestruck wonder.

"It's your art. Do you like it?" she asked, hoping she didn't overstep. Nessa's small hand fit into Nicole's palm. "It's beautiful."

Nicole smiled down at her. "Yeah, it is."

Her flowers, her skies, her scenery. Every piece was as unique as Nessa. Her drawings took on life in a way Nicole could see Nessa never envisioned before.

The light show of Nessa's art continued for another few minutes, ending with her signature proudly proclaiming them as hers. When the lights came back on, everyone's faces showed how taken aback they were by the display, including Nessa's. No one, not even her, had realized just how good at her craft she was.

"That was like I was an actual artist."

Nicole squeezed her hand. "That's because you are, sweetheart. You'll see your name in those lights again if that's what you want."

Nessa returned the warmth of the moment by hugging Nicole's waist. "Thank you."

She rubbed her back, believing it to be the last time. "You're welcome, Nessa."

"I love you, Ms. Nicole."

"I love you too, Nessa." Nicole closed her eyes tight, stopping them before they could produce tears. "You should go and see your family now, okay?"

When they broke apart, Nessa nodded, then ran to meet up with her mom and grandma. The lights remained dim in the room as the DJ encouraged the kids to make their way onto the dancefloor. It made it easy for Nicole to slip out without anyone noticing.

Or that's what she thought until she was walking through the courtyard, getting her keys out. "How come you're always running away?"

She turned around and found Spencer behind her. He was a vision to her in the soft lighting of the fading sun and the courtyard's fairy lights.

"Because I know when my time in a place is done." Ever since she was an unwanted kid to when she was an unwanted wife, Nicole was used to knowing when her time was done. It was a bitter pill to swallow, but one she could accept.

Spencer took a step closer to her, and she didn't tell him to stop. She wanted to see his next move because she didn't know what her own would be. "My mom gave me the advice to give you space even when that wasn't what I wanted. Because I'm the one who screwed up, so what I wanted didn't matter. Not as much as what you did."

"Smart woman," she complimented.

"I know. Except I think she may have gotten this wrong."

"Oh."

"Standing here, being here with you today, Nicole. I can't get this idea out of my head and tell me if I'm projecting. But I can't stop thinking that you want as much space as I do. Which is to say none at all."

Nicole's heart thumped against her chest. Her throat grew dry, making it hard to respond. Fearful of leading Spencer on and getting herself hurt again, she said nothing.

"Maybe you've forgiven me. Maybe you haven't, but I can't leave here until I know for certain we're over." Again, for the same fears, she stayed quiet. "Nicole, please. Talk to me. That was the one thing we were always good at."

"If we were so good at it, why didn't you tell me the truth about why you came into my life? You, more than anyone, should've known I would have understood."

"Because I'm an idiot, clearly."

"And you've given me a reason not to trust you. I know every way that trust can be built, manipulated, and destroyed. I know it because

I've experienced it. What I needed from you was not to break my faith in you. Trust is delicate. It gets broken by simple mistakes. I needed you not to make a mistake. If that's not fair, I'm sorry, but I've never needed anything from anyone before and I needed that from you."

A tear escaped down her face as she confessed these feelings to him. It felt as though she was ripping a wound open again.

"Tell me what I can do," Spencer begged. "Trust can be repaired. Tell me how I can repair it."

"I don't know. That's the one concept about trust I was never taught."

"Then let me learn it." He closed the gap between them. "I've been alone for a lot of my life, Nicole, but never more than when you walked out on me. Now that I know what life looks like with you by my side, I don't want to go through it without you."

"I don't know if I can go through it with you if I can't trust you."

Her eyes followed his up to his full height, down as his height lowered past hers. The sight of Spencer on his knees made the air leave Nicole's lungs. "Spencer, what are you doing?"

"I'm not proposing."

"Thank God. I'm glad you're not that much of an idiot. Because if you were proposing, I would've said no and really hurt your feelings."

Spencer bit his bottom lip, holding back a smile. "How do you expect to say things like that to me and not expect me to want you? How do you expect to say them, and not expect me to beg for your forgiveness?"

Nicole felt the urge to smile, but didn't. She wasn't going to make this easy for him. "Go on, then."

"What am I doing on the concrete? I'm showing you how serious I am. You've brought me to my knees, Nicole."

"No. You did that to yourself."

"Okay, you're right. And I'll keep doing this every day for the rest of my life, if I need to. Until I deserve you. I won't let myself off easy for hurting you. Not when you have to live with it. Forgiving myself before you even have would defeat the purpose of all this. I'm on my knees because I don't want to get up if you're not the one to tell me to. I don't want to stand if you're not the one I'm standing by. I don't want to walk unless you're the one I'm walking to. Nicole, you can dole out whatever punishment you deem fit for me. I'll take it without complaint. Anything except you walking away from me. That's the one punishment I can't bear to endure."

Spencer's eyes were red and wet, filled with so much emotion. Nicole was sure she would be crying to if she had any tears left inside of her. But she was out. Out of tears and out of words. This is what she wanted to hear, but how could she believe him? Spencer was a performer, just like her. How could she trust this was real?

Spencer reached for her hand, and she let him. "If you'll let me, I will show you who I am and prove to you that the person you fell for wasn't a lie. I will never make another mistake when it comes to your trust, not when the cost is losing you for good."

"Why are you doing this, Spencer? What's there for you to gain?"

"Nicole, there was a void in my heart that I didn't know existed until I met you. In a short time, you filled it. And just as fast, you ripped it away because I didn't earn it honestly. The way it felt when you took it, I'll never forget. The hole you left behind was the size of your heart and yours alone. Nothing can ever fill it. No other person, no other love, nothing."

Nicole's eyes looked up at the golden sky, not standing to let Spencer see the effect his words were having on her. He squeezed her hand. "Look at me. Please. Look at me."

Nicole didn't know what she would see when she did. She didn't know what she wanted to see. When her eyes found his, his solemn expression matched hers. "You want to put me through hell for destroying your image of me? That's your right. I've earned that.

But know this, I'm already in hell. I have been living there since you walked away from us. I'll stay there until you come back to me. And I'll go there again if I screw this up. Because, Nicole, you're it for me. Deep down, I think you know I'm it for you too."

"Stop," her voice broke. She dropped his hand, her eyes closed tight. "Just stop."

"Nicole—"

"No, you've had your chance to talk. You said a lot of pretty words. I'm sure the mirror you practiced them in front of was very impressed. Unfortunately for you, I'm not. You can give all the lovely speeches you want. At the end of the day, words are just that. Words. And as of two weeks ago, I lost all faith in yours."

Nicole turned on her heel and strode out of the courtyard, refusing to look back. She knew if she did, her resolve might crumble. She walked until she lost track of how long she'd been walking or where she was. Finding a brick wall, she stopped, leaning back against it.

Alone, she could cry. She could let her emotions overwhelm her and allow the tears to flow freely. Her shoulders shook, and her hands covered her mouth to keep the sounds from coming out.

This is the way Nicole had always dealt with heartbreak. When someone pushed her away, she didn't fight to make them stay. The shoe was never on the other foot. She never had someone fight for her after she tried to push them away. They decided she wasn't worth the trouble. Spencer hadn't.

Spencer was fighting for her. The fact he was willing to at all made Nicole want to hope. Nicole had lost hope in people before, but no one had ever given it back to her. No one until Spencer.

It was a dangerous thing. Hope. Unlike trust, it wasn't dependable. It didn't need to be built. It was a feeling. No sense or logic to it. It couldn't be faked or forced. You either had it or you don't.

To hope meant to risk. Risk losing your heart and your head. To sacrifice everything you knew about wrong and right. To risk the unknown and have no guarantee of a happy ending. But that was the thing. No matter what you risk losing, you'll never truly be lost until you lost hope.

It only took a minute for Nicole to realize she didn't want to lose hers.

She ran. Ran in the direction she thought she came and hoped it was the right one. Her legs felt weak, and her chest was heavy when she stopped in front of the community center. She had circled the building. The courtyard was in the back. She had no idea how long it took her to run around to the yard, but when she did, Spencer was still there.

Exactly where she left him. On his knees, his shoulders slouched, his face buried in his hands. The evening sky she left him in had since gone dark. Spencer said he wouldn't get up unless she told him to. He had kept his word.

"You know at that height, a leprechaun could sneak up behind you and kick your ass."

Spencer's head snapped up, looking around for her. He looked over his shoulder and his eyes finally landed on hers. His eyebrows furrowed together. His eyes were wet, his face in disbelief. He didn't get up, not letting himself believe what he was seeing was really happening. "Nicole?"

She nodded, wiping the dampness from under her eyes. "I saved a lot of money from over the years. Enough to hire a contract killer if you screw up again. I'm talking about having a guy in a leprechaun costume break into your home and cut off your fingers. Burn your—"

Spencer shot up from his knees, closing the distance between them. Her arms wrapped around his waist the second he was in front of her, her hands finding his back. The moment she touched him, Spencer was alive. His hands tangled in her hair, his lips pressing hard against hers.

His mouth was warm, his kiss desperate to mend what he broke. His arms wrapped around her back, holding her tightly against his chest. He held her like his life depended on it, and she clung to him like her life was slipping away. In many ways, it was.

Her old self never would have taken Spencer back. Her old self would have denied herself a chance at happiness to avoid looking like a fool again. The Nicole she was today wanted a future. A future that wasn't filled with regret.

She sighed into Spencer's mouth, relieved he felt the same. Tasted the same. For all the questions she might've still had, his kisses answered all of them. This was the man she fell for.

Nicole felt the tears rolling down Spencer's face. She pulled away from him, needing to see him. She cupped his face, using her thumbs to wipe the moisture away. "It wasn't long ago when you gave me a second chance. You could've held my past against me. Refused to see me for who I am today, but you didn't. I know better than most people how rare goodness is. In my gut, I can feel you're a good man, Spencer Shaw. Don't prove me wrong."

He ran his knuckles across her cheek, soothing her. "I won't. I promise I'm done lying. All I'll ever be is me."

"Good. Because I don't want Aiden Spencer. I want Spencer Shaw. He's the one I'm falling for."

"He's right here. Right here."

At once, with the fairy lights twinkling around them, they leaned in. Their hearts beating in perfect unison. The kiss, their first on equal footing and equal ground, was the best kiss Nicole had ever had. It was the kind that left you feeling breathless and warm.

A kiss that could seal your forever.

A first that felt like a last.

# Epilogue - One Year Later

The water rained down over Spencer's head and chest, his hands pressed against the tile. Guests would arrive in less than an hour for the party, but as Spencer felt Nicole enter into the space, they became the furthest thing from his mind. And when she pressed her breasts against his back, rubbing her hands over his chest, his mind went blank.

"People will start showing up soon," he reminded her. Although he had no leg to stand on with his hands betraying him, guiding her touch along his body.

"We have time," she assured, kissing the inside of his shoulder.

"Do we?"

"Well, that depends on you," she said, her hand traveling south.

"On me?"

She nodded, kissing her way to his neck. Her knuckles running over his hardness. "On how fast you can fill me with your cum."

"What if it's not that fast?"

"The longer our guests have to wait outside."

She stroked him until he was at his full length and ready to explode. Turning him to her, Nicole's hands pressed against his chest. Their eyes locked onto each other as he hitched one of her legs onto his hip, giving him the leverage he needed to slip into her.

Their decision to ditch condoms came after Nicole got an IUD, and their first round of tests came back that they were safe. After that, sex was no longer something they had to plan for or think about.

It was spontaneous. Spontaneous like a buying a pool table so Spencer could bend Nicole over it and have his way with her. As spontaneous as Nicole's decision to hop inside Spencer's shower and his need to be inside of her.

They had sex regularly over the past year, but Spencer still couldn't get enough of taking Nicole to bed. He could be surrounded by a thousand women who all looked and sounded just like her, and it wouldn't have mattered. They would all be lacking the one quality that made her perfect in his eyes: her imperfections.

There was no part of her Spencer would change. He loved her for her flaws, not in spite of them. Maybe because they were his flaws too.

"You take my cock so good," he breathed out, pushing into her harder. She whimpered when he reached a particularly sensitive spot in the center of her body. His hips rocked back and forth. She wrapped her arms tightly around his neck. Her hands clutched the back of his head as she met him halfway. "That's it, baby. Ride me. Take what you need."

He gripped at her hips as she bucked into him again. Her fingers ran through his fade as her hips pumped harder. Nicole bit her bottom lip to stifle another cry.

Spencer leaned forward as he licked and sucked on her nipples, teasing them until they hardened like pebbles under his teeth. Nicole threw her head back, releasing a deep moan. The water continued to fall onto their bodies, muffling their desperate sounds from leaving their sanctuary.

Her walls clenched tight around him, making him groan in pleasure as he thrust again and again. "Oh my God," he moaned. He lifted his head off her chest, staring down at her with a heated look in his eyes. "How I love watching you like this."

It was Spencer's favorite view of her. Nicole, not inside her head.

Not questioning herself as she let go of some of her control. Trusting him to know how to please her. The look of unbridled pleasure when he did. It was a gift he cherished and was determined to earn again and again.

Her fingers slid at the nape of his neck, tugging him closer. His hands moved from her hips, grabbing a handful of her ass as he guided her. This was a song and dance they knew well. With the next part being their favorite encore.

Nicole wrapped her legs around his waist, and he hoisted her up, pushing her against the tile. She kissed him hungrily, moaning into his mouth as her pussy throbbed. "Fuck me. Fuck yourself right there," she commanded, biting down on his bottom lip.

Spencer obliged her request, pounding himself inside of her. His fingers dug into her thighs as he took her harder. Their breaths mingled, growing heavy as their hearts beat as one.

Nicole arched her back and pressed herself closer to him until he groaned. He pulled away from her mouth to bury his nose against the side of her throat. Feeling it when she said, "God, I love you. Let me cum for you."

The words beckoned Spencer on. With a jerk, he drove himself deeper inside her, pushing Nicole higher up the tile. Her shower cap acting as a barrier between her hair and the wet hard surface. His hips met hers as she rode him with her eyes closed, lost in their moment of bliss.

A low rumble escaped his chest as his own release grew nearer. He kissed his way from her neck to her jaw. Stopping at her lips to grunt, "When you withhold like this, you think you're torturing me, and you are." She giggled, the sweet sound she only shared with him. "But you're not being very kind to yourself. Cum for me. I'm right there with you. Give yourself permission to cum for me. Show me how much you love it, Nicole."

Her name on his tongue was the last thing she heard before her orgasm washed over her. Nicole's body trembled as her mouth fell open. Her fingers dug into the back of his shoulders as she rode his hard length into her soul. "Fuck, Spence, that's so good."

That did him in. Her name fell from off his lips as he spilled into her, filling her with a warmth that he hoped she felt everywhere. Their bodies shuddered in unison, joined together by their shared euphoria.

Spencer held her afterward, breathing in her scent, savoring every inch of her body. "This will never get old. I won't ever get enough of you."

"It's only been a year, Spence. Tell me that when we hit 5."

"Oh, I plan to. Then again, when we hit 50."

Nicole laughed, kissing his neck. "Don't get ahead of yourself. We've got a long way to go, buddy."

"I know we do, but we'll make it. We love each other too much not to."

"You think we'll still be this obsessed with each other in the future?"

"No." He pressed his forehead to hers. "We'll be more. At least, I will."

"I will, too," she assured. "You don't have to doubt that."

Spencer couldn't take his eyes off the incredible woman that he still wasn't sure how he got to love him. This wasn't the right place or second to ask what he spent the entire year wanting to, but he couldn't hold it in any longer. "Marry me."

Nicole's eyebrows raised before she succumbed to a laugh, expecting him to join in. But Spencer wouldn't cover for himself. He was serious. When Nicole noticed, she stopped.

"Marry me," he repeated, confident this time.

She touched his face and met his eyes. "No."

"Why not?"

"Because I love you."

## EPILOGUE - ONE YEAR LATER

"You do realize those two things are connected?"

Nicole rolled her eyes, her smile returning. "You know what I mean."

"No, I don't. Explain it to me."

"I've been engaged seven times, got married to six. Out of the eight men, I only loved one of them. Marriage doesn't represent love or loyalty to me. Not when all of mine was built on power, control, and a game of which person had them."

"I get that. I do, but our marriage would be different. We'll be on equal ground."

"I know we would, but I like what we have. You've been more of a partner to me than any husband I've ever had. I don't want to mess with that."

Spencer nodded, not fighting her decision. Nicole still must have picked up on his disappointment. "Spencer, I once thought I would never fall in love. Then you came into my life and changed my mind. I'm not saying never to marriage. I'm saying if I do it again, I want to do it with my whole heart in love with the idea. I'm not going to do it to please you or because I feel like I have to."

She put her arms around his neck, pulling herself closer to him. "I understand if I'm asking too much from you. Having me as your girlfriend comes with built in sacrifices like kids. I get it if this is one sacrifice too many."

Spencer stopped her from continuing to spew nonsense by kissing her. Nicole responded fervently, her hands caressing his face. When they broke, he told her, "There's not a sacrifice in the world worth losing you over."

"Are you sure?"

"Marriage and kids would serve as welcome bonuses, but they're not essentials. Nicole Taylor, you're it for me. Anything that could drive you away isn't worth the risk."

Her eyes shined at him. "Ring or no ring. You're it for me too,

Spencer Shaw."

***

Nicole and Spencer's open-space living room was overtaken by their clans. They were there to celebrate Nessa's 7th birthday. A lot had changed in a year.

Spencer sold The Shaw Agency to a son of a former client of his father's. Apparently, Neal helped reunite father and son with the case he worked. Spencer had better offers, but history couldn't be beat and he took the man's offer.

The money, along with his part-time teaching assistant salary, was putting him through school. Spencer was working hard to earn the necessary requirements to have a classroom of his own one day. Nicole was proud of him for finding his dream and working to live it.

She did the same thing every day with Taylor For You Event Planning. The business had grown ever since Nessa's birthday party. Parents of her classmates wanted her to be responsible for their kids' parties and paid top-dollar to get it.

Another big change was Spencer and Nicole buying a place together. Their previous two-bedroom apartments turned into a one three bedroom. One for them, one for Nessa, and a guest room anytime Melanie, Maya, or any of their loved ones wanted to crash.

Nessa was still staying with Spencer, with no plans to change that arrangement in the works. Melanie received her one-year sober chip three months ago, but her sobriety was still a line she was balancing. It worked for all parties involved, that Nessa stayed with Spencer. With Nessa staying with Melanie at her apartment on the weekends.

"Do you need any help with that, darling?" Rayna asked Nicole as she lifted the sheet cake from the kitchen counter.

"I got it. You did enough by making it."

"My grandbaby says she wants a ding dong cake for her birthday, I'll bake it myself with no complaints."

Nicole understood Rayna meant that, as evidenced by her making Maya a red velvet cake for her birthday without prompt. Seeing her boyfriend's mother take a vested interest in her daughter was unexpected. But it felt good seeing the two bond. Maya always wanted a grandma, and Rayna liked having another grandchild to spoil. She never expected her to enter their lives when she was 24, but Rayna spoiled her anyway.

Nicole set the cake down on the table, liking how cozy this birthday felt compared to the last. With so many changes happening this year, Nessa opted for a quieter birthday just with her family. They were happy to oblige her.

"Alright." Spencer clapped, getting everyone to look at him. "Melanie will be here with Nessa at any minute. Put on the cones."

Everyone, including Nicole, groaned as Spencer handed out the cone-shaped party hats.

"Do we have to?" Lawrence asked. "I'll look ridiculous in this."

"I don't see a problem," Spencer replied, earning a gentle punch into his shoulder by his friend.

Nicole put hers on first, and Spencer rewarded her with a smile. "Follow Nicole's lead, everyone. Model yourselves after her."

"That has to be the first time someone has ever said that about her," Kennedy teased. Maya shushed her, but the jab was a big hit for everyone in the room. They all knew about Nicole's past.

It was out in the open. There was no one Nicole needed to hide it from. It was refreshing even after a year. Nicole wouldn't share her past with just anyone, but she was happy with the selective group of people who knew. They were becoming more and more like family each day.

Maya caught her mom's eye and smiled. This was the normalcy her daughter always wanted. Nicole was sorry it took this long to give it to her, but she was trying. They both were.

They started attending therapy sessions together almost a year ago. The sessions weren't easy. It was hard for Nicole to hear some of things shared in them, but not as hard as it must have been for Maya to say them. Part of her being a better mom was listening and taking accountability for the mistakes she'd made.

Nicole had a long way to go, but she was making strides. Maya and her relationship was as healthy as it had ever been. That was because they were finally being honest with each other, including themselves. They would never be the Gilmore Girls, but they were the Taylor Women, and that was better.

"Wait, was that a car door?" Maya asked, stopping the party like a record scratching.

They quieted and waited, then heard the second door shut. "See! Put the hats on," Spencer directed. This time, Rayna, Maya, Kennedy, and Lawrence listened.

They gathered near the front of the door with birthday blowouts in hand. When the door opened, Spencer held Nicole's waist, wearing the hats and big smiles.

"Surprise!" everyone shouted, their horns blaring.

Nessa jumped in shock, stepping back into Melanie's frame. "Mom, you said we were going to go to Chuck-E-Cheese."

"Baby, that was a little white lie."

"Keep lying to me every year for my birthday and I'm going to grow up with trust issues."

Melanie smiled, squeezing Nessa's shoulders with a hug. "We're sorry, honey. We thought you might enjoy this better. Did we think right?"

"Yes!" Nessa nodded confidently. "I didn't want to say it, but Chuck-E-Cheese would have been too baby-ish for me."

## EPILOGUE - ONE YEAR LATER

"Told you," Spencer gloated away from Melanie's line of hearing.

She rolled her eyes, having caught it. "Good to know. We won't have anymore of those. Okay, babe? Now, enjoy."

Nessa didn't hesitate, running into the room, her arms flailing. She stopped to hug her guests, but gave the biggest hug of all to Uncle Spencer. Nicole felt her heart swell.

The love he had for that little girl helped make her fall for him and what cemented her love for Spencer. The way he would read her stories every night and play tea parties with her. Or how he was her biggest cheerleader in the audience during her award ceremonies at school. His unconditional love for her. It was the same way he loved Nicole every day since he made his promise to her.

Spencer walked Nessa toward the dining table, hand in hand. Everyone met them at the table. As Melanie lit the candles and Nessa closed her eyes to make a wish. Nicole joined Spencer's side. He wrapped an arm around her waist, his beautiful smile growing brighter with her near.

Nicole couldn't take her eyes off of him, not when he was looking at her like she hung the moon. He squeezed her waist, leaning closer.

"You know my wish?" he asked, whispering into her ear.

She shook her head, but she could take a guess.

"It's the same one I make every day," he admitted, kissing her temple. "I wish for a future with you."

Nicole turned her head to catch his lips with hers. Marriage and kids may not have been in their cards, but she knew without a doubt they were building a life together. A home. One built on love. One Nicole knew would survive the test of time.

"Funny," she said, her smile matching his. "That's my wish too."

# A Bonus Chapter Awaits You

Subscribe to my newsletter to read a free bonus chapter detailing how Spencer and Nicole spend the rest of their one-year anniversary together. http://eepurl.com/h6Gg0r

## About the Author

No matter the genre or time, Dominique Davis writes affectionately about unapologetic out-of-the-box women and the people who love them. From a mother-daughter con artist duo to a revenge-driven college student, there's always something special about her characters, as she believes that all great stories should feature remarkable yet flawed female leads. Writing has been her passion since she could hold a pencil, and nowadays she divides her time between devouring books, fine-tuning manuscripts, and embracing her love for all things pop culture. You can learn more about her by checking out her website and following her on social media.

**You can connect with me on:**
- https://www.dominique-davis.com
- https://twitter.com/ddaviswrites
- https://www.instagram.com/ddaviswrites
- https://www.threads.net/@ddaviswrites
- https://www.tiktok.com/@ddaviswrites
- https://reamstories.com/ddavis

# Also by Dominique Davis

If you liked the romance and flawed leads making each other better, check out my other novels. If you liked the soap opera drama, check out my novellas.

**Falling For the Mark (Swindled in Love #1)**
Maya is the daughter of Nicole, a cunning grifter who has been deceiving people since she was a teenager. Together, they have perfected the art of scamming people out of their money without guilt.

Their most successful con sees Nicole duping affluent men into wedding her. But when the time is right, Maya lures the mark into her bed, getting them to break their prenuptial agreement. The duo then disappear with an impressive divorce settlement. Never to be heard from again. What should be another routine con soon turns out to be anything but.

Kennedy, the daughter of their new mark, is skeptical of the pair upon their arrival. She suspects they are after her father's money and she's determined to find proof of it. Matters are further complicated when Maya and Kennedy begin to develop feelings for each other. Though both have their reasons for why they shouldn't cross the line, their growing attraction is too strong to be denied.

But when the truth is revealed, both stand to lose more than they ever could have imagined

DOMINIQUE DAVIS
THE PRICE OF REVENGE

## The Price of Revenge

Whitney "Whit" Robinson and Sabrina Price have a deep and unbreakable bond forged through years of friendship. They've been through it all together, from first loves to family drama, and their bond seems destined to last beyond their college years.

But one fateful night changes everything. Whit is left reeling from the loss of her boyfriend, her once flawless reputation, and worst of all, her friendship with Sabrina. Wracked with grief, Whit devises a plan to get revenge against those who hurt her, including Sabrina.

Whit's plan is simple: she'll hurt Sabrina by befriending her estranged half-sister, Jordyn. But as Whit gets closer to Jordyn, she starts to question her motives and wonders if her quest for revenge is truly worth it. As Whit struggles to come to terms with her grief and anger, she finds herself facing a difficult choice. Will she be able to let go of her anger and heal, or will her quest for revenge cost her the one thing she never knew she wanted: love?

**A Wilder Welcome (The Wilder Way #1)**
https://reamstories.com/ddavis
Novella 1 in a Gossip Girl x Ugly Betty soap opera book series.

Fresh out of design school for the summer, Adaira Donovan lands her dream internship at iconic fashion house House of Wilder. Known for its exquisite designs and legendary legacy, the company is led by its pioneering female CEO Gillian Wilder and sits at the pinnacle of high fashion.

Working under notoriously demanding lead designer Blake Hartford, Adaira navigates the glamorous but treacherous world of haute couture. Making matters more complicated is the mysterious and increasingly viral fashion blogger Canarina Rossi. If Canarina has their way, the secrets spilled could unravel House of Wilder and shake the foundations of the industry.

When Adaira discovers she's becoming entangled in Canarina's web of intrigue, she realizes uncovering the truth could make or break her promising new career. Facing an uncertain future, Adaira must decide how far she'll go to protect House of Wilder's secrets - and her own.

**Losing It (Widowhood #1)**

https://reamstories.com/ddavis

Novella 1 in a Desperate Housewives x Sex and the City soap opera book series.

After tragic losses, four unique women seek solace in a grief support group. Free-spirited Marcy struggles to adjust after leaving her glamorous life. Reserved Florence hides pain behind proud familial duty. Driven surgeon Hayden refuses to acknowledge her own anguish. Young college student Gracie bears a secret that isolates her further.

Led by the empathetic Dr. Elena Cordero, the group provides an intimate space for the women to share their burdens. But these widows' paths to mourning differ as greatly as their personalities. As they reluctantly open up to one another, surprises lurk beneath the surface of each woman's sorrow.

Through shared understanding and challenges that test even the toughest among them, the widows must determine how to move forward - and whether finding themselves again is at all possible.

**Sparks Fly, Tempers Flare (Blooming #1)**

Novella 1 in a One Tree Hill x Friday Night Lights x All American teen drama/soap opera book series.

After her mother's death, 16-year-old Sloane Crawford reluctantly returns to her childhood home and the drama-filled small town she left behind. Moving in with her estranged father only reopens old wounds from his affair that destroyed her family.

Back at school, tensions flare as Sloane reconnects with old friends who resent her for abandoning them. Especially heated is her rocky relationship with her former best friend, Emory, the daughter of the woman her father betrayed them with.

As Sloane struggles to adapt to her new normal, long-held grudges threaten to boil over. To move forward, she'll have to confront the fractured bonds left in the ashes of her family's traumatic history. But finding forgiveness won't be easy in a place where the past refuses to stay buried.

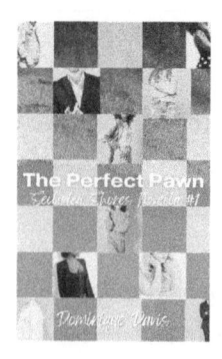

**The Perfect Pawn (Secluded Shores #1)**
https://reamstories.com/ddavis
Novella 1 in a The O.C. x Scandal teen drama/soap opera book series.

After months of surviving alone on the streets, 15-year-old Danica Herrera catches the eye of rising politician Pearce Maddox. Sensing an opportunity to improve his image, Pearce offers Danica a stable home in exchange for playing the dutiful foster daughter publicly in a move to boost his popularity during his mayoral campaign.

Though wary of being used as a political prop, Danica accepts Pearce's offer of a home in his lavish waterfront mansion, if it means finally finding stability. But adjusting to wealth and privilege after surviving on your own is no easy transition. Navigating elite private schools and high society parties, Danica struggles to feel she truly belongs in this glamorous new world.

While grateful for refuge, she wonders if this gilded cage is any better than facing an uncertain future alone. With her future now tied to Pearce's political ambitions, she's left to question how far she's willing to go to make things work or if she rather stand on her own even if it means giving up the only security she's ever known.

Milton Keynes UK
Ingram Content Group UK Ltd.
UKHW041052150824
446997UK00004B/134